READING ARCHITECTURE

Why write instead of draw when it comes to architecture? Why rely on literary pieces instead of architectural treatises and writings when it comes to the study of buildings and urban environments? Why rely on literary techniques and accounts instead of architectural practices and analysis when it comes to academic research and educational projects? Why trust authors and writers instead of sociologists or scientists when it comes to planning for the future of cities? This book builds on the existing interdisciplinary bibliography on architecture and literature, but prioritizes literature's capacity to talk about the lived experience of place and the premise that literary language can often express the inexpressible. It sheds light on the importance of a literary instead of a pictorial imagination for architects and it looks into four contemporary architectural subjects through a wide variety of literary works. Drawing on novels that engage cities from around the world, the book reveals aspects of urban space to which other means of architectural representation are blind. Whether through novels that employ historical buildings or sites interpreted through specific literary methods, it suggests a range of methodologies for contemporary architectural academic research. By exploring the power of narrative language in conveying the experience of lived space, it discusses its potential for architectural design and pedagogy. Questioning the massive architectural production of today's globalized capital-driven world, it turns to literature for ways to understand, resist or suggest alternative paths for architectural practice. Despite literature's fictional character, the essays of this volume reveal true dimensions of and for places beyond their historical, social and political reality; dimensions of utmost importance for architects, urban planners, historians and theoreticians nowadays.

Angeliki Sioli is assistant professor of architecture at Louisiana State University, USA and licensed architect in Greece. She obtained her professional diploma in architecture from the University of Thessaly, Greece, and was granted a post-professional master's in architectural theory and history by the National Technical University of Athens, Greece. She completed her PhD in history and theory of architecture at McGill University, Canada in 2015. Her research seeks connections between architecture and literature in the public realm of the early twentieth-century European city. It has been published in a number of edited books and journals, as well as presented at interdisciplinary conferences. She has worked as a professional architect and designer on projects ranging from residential and office buildings to the design of small-scale objects and books. She has also taught both undergraduate and graduate courses at McGill University in Canada and University Tec de Monterrey in Mexico.

Yoonchun Jung is originally from South Korea. He received his bachelor's degree in architecture from Hongik University, South Korea (2000), MArch from Cornell University, USA (2007) and PhD in architecture from McGill University, Canada (2015). His research interest focuses on various social, cultural and political phenomena in modern Asian architecture and cities. He taught at Cornell University from 2004 to 2006, The State University of New York at Buffalo from 2006 to 2008 and McGill University in 2010. From 2012 to 2013, he conducted PhD research in Korean architectural modernity at Kyoto University as a Japan Foundation fellow. He has won numerous awards and research grants, and his work has been published in many journals and edited collections. In the summer of 2015, he co-organized the Reading Architecture Symposium with Dr. Angeliki Sioli and Dr. Alberto Pérez-Gómez under the auspices of the Benaki Museum of Athens and the Hellenic Institute of Architecture. He is currently assistant professor at the Department of Architecture of Kwangwoon University in South Korea.

READING ARCHITECTURE

Literary Imagination and Architectural Experience

Edited by
Angeliki Sioli and
Yoonchun Jung

NEW YORK AND LONDON

First published 2018
by Routledge
711 Third Avenue, New York, NY 10017

and by Routledge
2 Park Square, Milton Park, Abingdon, Oxon, OX14 4RN

Routledge is an imprint of the Taylor & Francis Group, an informa business

© 2018 Taylor & Francis

The right of Angeliki Sioli and Yoonchun Jung to be identified as the authors of the editorial material, and of the authors for their individual chapters, has been asserted in accordance with sections 77 and 78 of the Copyright, Designs and Patents Act 1988.

All rights reserved. No part of this book may be reprinted or reproduced or utilised in any form or by any electronic, mechanical, or other means, now known or hereafter invented, including photocopying and recording, or in any information storage or retrieval system, without permission in writing from the publishers.

Trademark notice: Product or corporate names may be trademarks or registered trademarks, and are used only for identification and explanation without intent to infringe.

Library of Congress Cataloging-in-Publication Data
A catalog record for this book has been requested

ISBN: 978-1-138-22426-1 (hbk)
ISBN: 978-1-138-22427-8 (pbk)
ISBN: 978-1-315-40290-1 (ebk)

Typeset in Bembo and Stone Sans
by Florence Production Ltd, Stoodleigh, Devon, UK

Cover image: Painting by Jieh Kim, 2014. Courtesy of the artist.

CONTENTS

List of Illustrations ix
Notes on Contributors xii
Foreword by Alberto Pérez-Gómez xvii
Preface: On Reading Architecture by Elias Constantopoulos xix
Acknowledgments by Angeliki Sioli and Yoonchun Jung xxii

    Introduction: Reading Architecture: Literary Imagination
    and Architectural Experience 1
    Angeliki Sioli and Yoonchun Jung

Section 1: Readings on (Un)Familiar Places   7

1 Oran, the Capital of Boredom 9
   Christian Parreno

2 Discovering "Paris and its Folds, Paris and its Faces" 20
   Angeliki Sioli

3 Traces of Kristiania: A Topographical Reading of Knut
   Hamsun's *Hunger* 27
   Mathilde Simonsen Dahl

4 The Architecture of *Another Man's Room*: Unveiling Stories
   of Seoul's Apartments 38
   Yoonchun Jung

Section 2: Readings on Architectural Research — 47

5 Fabrics of Reality: Art and Architecture in László
   Krasznahorkai 49
   Mari Lending

6 How Places Speak: A Plea for Poetic Receptivity in
   Architectural Research 61
   Klaske Havik

7 W. G. Sebald's *Austerlitz*: Architecture as a Bridge
   between the Lost Past and the Present 72
   Rumiko Handa

8 Poetic Imagination and the Architecture of Poe 84
   Lisa Landrum

9 Montréal Mythologies: Narrating the City 93
   Panos Leventis

Section 3: Readings on Architectural Design and Pedagogy — 103

10 The Gesture of Drawing in Antoine de Saint-Exupéry's
    The Little Prince 105
    Jason Crow

11 Architecture Drawn Out of Bruno Schulz's Poetic Prose 114
    Anca Matyiku

12 Writing, Model Making and Inventing in Paul Scheerbart's
    The Perpetual Motion Machine 123
    Sevil Enginsoy Ekinci

13 Melvilla: An(other) Underline Reading 134
    Marc J. Neveu

14 Dreaming the City through Unicorn Skulls: Reading
    Murakami with Agamben 145
    Paul Holmquist

Section 4: Readings on Contemporary Architectural Reality and Practice   **155**

15 We Build Spaces with Words: Spatial Agency, Recognition, and Narrative   157
   Caroline Dionne

16 The Architectural Turn in Contemporary Literature   171
   David Spurr

17 "Like This and Also Like That": Tactics from the Tales of Nguyen Huy Thiep   182
   Lily Chi

18 Lost and Longing: The Sense of Space in E.M. Forster's "The Machine Stops"   194
   Susana Oliveira

Image Credits   *204*
Index   *206*

ILLUSTRATIONS

1.1 Oran from the fort of Santa Cruz, photograph by M. Lavina (Oran, 1930). Courtesy of Henri Lavina   12
1.2 Maison du Colon, postcard by unknown author (Oran, c. 1940). Courtesy of Musée de l'Histoire vivante   14
3.1 Map of Kristiania, 1 St. Olavsgate, 2 Abelhaugen, Palace Park, 3 Studenterlunden/Students Promenade, 4 Tivoli, 5 Stortinget/The Parliament, 6 Hammersborg, 7 Vaterland, 8 Stortorvet, Cathedral, Bazars, 9 Bogstad forest, 10 Akershus/Castle, Prlieutnt. Solem, *Kart over Kristiania*, 1881. Courtesy of Norwegian National Library   28
3.2 View to the castle from the Parliament across Studenterlunden, Axel Lindahl, *Det Kongelige Slot fra Stortingsbygningen*, Karl Johansgate (Oslo, Norway), 1870–80. Courtesy of Oslo Museum   34
4.1 Korea National Housing Corporation, Mapo Apartments, Seoul, South Korea, 1962. Courtesy of National Archives of Korea   39
4.2 One of the oldest apartment buildings in Seoul, Yeouido Sibum Apartments, Seoul, South Korea, 1971. Photo by the author   45
5.1 Ephemera and authorship I   55
6.1 The lake at Hvitträsk, Southern Finland. Photo by author   66
6.2 Herman Gesellius, Armas Lindgren, and Eliel Saarinen, Hvitträsk, Kirkonummi, Finland, 1902. Photo by author   67
6.3 Fireplace and seating room. Photo by author   67
6.4 Interior elements such as carpets were designed specifically for Hvitträsk. Photo by author   68
6.5 Interior staircase. Photo by author   69
6.6 Garden pavilion with view down the hill. Photo by author   70

6.7	Dining room. Photo by author	70
7.1	Liverpool Street Station, London. Photo by author	75
7.2	Royal Observatory, Greenwich, United Kingdom. Photo by author	78
7.3	Storefront on King Street, Nuremberg, Germany. Photo by author	81
9.1	Buckminster [Bucky] Fuller, United States Pavilion for the 1967 World's Fair. Île Sainte-Hélène, Montréal, Canada. Photo by author	95
9.2	Buckminster [Bucky] Fuller, United States Pavilion for the 1967 World's Fair. Île Sainte-Hélène, Montréal, Canada. Photo by author	101
12.1	Paul Scheerbart, *The Perpetual Motion Machine. The Story of an Invention* (Cambridge, MA: Wakefield Press, 2011), figure 2. Courtesy of Wakefield Press	125
12.2	Paul Scheerbart, *The Perpetual Motion Machine. The Story of an Invention* (Cambridge, MA: Wakefield Press, 2011), figure 26. Courtesy of Wakefield Press	127
13.1	Grade Level Plan, Douglas Darden, Melvilla, New York, 1989. Courtesy of Allison Collins, image used by permission from the Douglas Darden Estate	137
13.2	Longitudinal Section, Douglas Darden, Melvilla, New York, 1989. Courtesy of Allison Collins, image used by permission from the Douglas Darden Estate	137
13.3	Dis/continuous Genealogy, Douglas Darden, Melvilla, New York, 1989. Courtesy of Allison Collins, image used by permission from the Douglas Darden Estate	141
13.4	West Elevation, detail, Douglas Darden, Melvilla, New York, 1989. Courtesy of Allison Collins, image used by permission from the Douglas Darden Estate	143
14.1	Great Flight Cage, Richard Dimon and Daniel, Mann, Johnson & Mendenhall (DMJM), National Zoological Park, Washington D.C., USA, 1964. Photo by author	150
15.1	Metavilla, Patrick Bouchain and EXYZT, 10th International Venice Biennale, Italy, 2006. Courtesy of Cyrille Weiner	164
15.2	Metavilla, Patrick Bouchain and EXYZT, 10th International Venice Biennale, Italy, 2006. Courtesy of Cyrille Weiner	165
15.3	*Cabane de Chantier*, Patrick Bouchain, Loïc Julienne and François Delarozière, Calais, France, 2007. Courtesy of Construire	166
15.4	*Cabane de Chantier*, Patrick Bouchain, Loïc Julienne and François Delarozière, Calais, France, 2007. Courtesy of Construire	167
15.5	*Permanence architecturale*, Patrick Bouchain and Loïc Julienne, Tourcoing, France, 2013. Courtesy of Sebastien Jarry	168
15.6	Social Housing Rehabilitation and Transformation project, Sophie Ricard, Boulogne-sur-Mer, France, 2013. Courtesy of Construire	169

16.1	Emaar Properties Group and Atkins, The Address Downtown Dubai, Dubai, United Arab Emirates, 2008. Photo by David Waddington	174
16.2	Frank Gehry, Louis Vuitton Foundation, Paris, France, 2014. Photo by Yvette Doria	177
17.1	Nguyen Dinh Dang, Illustration for "The General Retires," pen on paper, 1990. Courtesy of the artist	183
17.2	Nguyen Dinh Dang, Illustration for "Fired Gold," pen on paper, 1990. Courtesy of the artist	185
17.3	Left: 6am, 69 Hang Trong Street. Right: 11am, 69 Hang Trong Street, Hanoi, 2013. Photos by author	190
17.4	Atelier Bow-Wow, Apartment Mountain Temple, Tokyo, documented by Atelier Bow-Wow for *Made in Tokyo* (Tokyo: Kajima Institute Publishing Co., Ltd, 2001). Courtesy Yoshiharu Tsukamoto	191
17.5	Gathering place of Filipino domestic workers on Sunday mornings, Foster and Partners, HSBC headquarter building, Hong Kong. Courtesy Winston Yeo	191
18.1	Carolina Moscoso, *Untitled*. Original AutoCAD drawing, 2016. Courtesy of the artist	196
18.2	Fátima Fernandes and Michele Cannatà, *Self Sustainable Modules*. Photomontage, 2003. Courtesy of the artists	200

NOTES ON CONTRIBUTORS

Lily Chi is associate professor of architectural design, theory and history at Cornell University, USA. She received her BArch in Canada and her MPhil and PhD in architectural history and theory at Cambridge and McGill Universities. Interested in the ways in which architecture construes and constructs temporality, Chi has written on filmic and literary spaces, on formulations of architectural "use," and on informality in contemporary urbanism. Vietnam is the subject of a number of recent projects, including a Graham Foundation supported study of tourism, city-building, and war in twentieth-century Saigon, and a Rotch Traveling Studio award for a graduate studio to Hanoi.

Elias Constantopoulos is the president of the Hellenic Institute of Architecture, professor at the Department of Architecture, University of Patras, Greece and practicing architect in Athens since 1985. He holds a diploma in architecture and a master of science from University College London. He has edited numerous books on architecture, design, philosophy, and culture like *The Significance of Philosophy in Architectural Education* (2012), *ON: The Modern and the Contemporary in European and Japanese Culture* (2006), *Contemporary Industrial Design in Greece* (1994) among others. His work and research has been presented in many international conferences and published in more than 100 articles.

Jason Crow is assistant professor of architecture at Louisiana State University and a licensed architect in Pennsylvania. He holds a BA in architecture from Clemson University and a MArch from Iowa State University. He earned a post-professional MArch from McGill University where he completed his PhD in the history and theory of architecture. His dissertation, *The Hierurgy of Stone in Suger's Restoration of Saint-Denis*, examines the twelfth-century understanding of stone architecture through the intertwined histories of theology, science, and craft. His research explores how technological changes impact the ontology of matter and the gesture of craft.

Mathilde Simonsen Dahl is a PhD candidate at the Institute of Form, Theory and History, in the Oslo School of Architecture and Design, Norway, where she also teaches theory courses. She has previously worked in the Architecture Museum in Oslo. She completed her archival-based master's thesis at OCCAS in 2012 on the Oslo Architects' Association anniversary 1956 exhibition, focusing on the public mediation of post-war Norwegian architectural culture. Her doctoral dissertation investigates the site-specific agency of full-scale transient structures and the debates on the urban transformation in the printed press, art, and literature in Kristiania/Oslo in the late nineteenth century.

Caroline Dionne is assistant professor in the History & Theory of Design Practice and Curatorial Studies at Parsons School of Design, The New School, USA. Her research interests sit at the intersection of architecture, literature, and language theories. Her current research is concerned with the concept of *usage*—of words and spaces—as a semantically productive component of spatial design in modern and contemporary practices. She was a research and teaching postdoctoral fellow at the Swiss Federal Institute of Technology Lausanne (EPFL) from 2011 to 2016, and a visiting scholar at the Canadian Centre for Architecture, Montreal, in 2014. She holds a PhD in the history and theory of architecture from McGill University.

Sevil Enginsoy Ekinci studied architecture and architectural history at Middle East Technical University, Ankara, Turkey (BArch and MA), and Cornell University, USA (PhD). Her research areas range from history of architectural books—with a particular interest in the intersections between architecture and literature—to architectural encounters across geographies in the fifteenth/sixteenth and nineteenth centuries. On these topics, she has presented papers and organized/chaired sessions at many international conferences, and published articles. Previously, she taught architectural history at the Department of Architecture/Graduate Program in Architectural History at METU. Presently, she is assistant professor of architectural history in the Department of Architecture at Kadir Has University, Istanbul.

Rumiko Handa is professor and interim associate dean of the University of Nebraska-Lincoln's College of Architecture, USA. Registered architect in Japan, she holds PhD, MS, and MArch from the University of Pennsylvania and BArch from the University of Tokyo. She received the American Institute of Architecture Students' 2001–2002 National Educator Honor Award. Her writings appeared in: *Interiors: Design, Architecture, Culture*; *Journal of the Society of Architectural Historians*; *Preservation Education & Research*; *Papers of the Bibliographical Society of America*; *Design Studies*, etc. She co-edited *Conjuring the Real: The Role of Architecture in Eighteenth- and Nineteenth-Century Fiction* (2011) and authored *Allure of the Incomplete, Imperfect, and Impermanent: Designing and Appreciating Architecture as Nature* (2015).

Contributors

Klaske Havik is associate professor of architecture, methods and analysis at TU Delft, Netherlands and visiting professor at TU Tampere, Finland. She studied architecture in Delft and Helsinki, and literary writing in Amsterdam. Havik teaches and develops master diploma studios as well as courses in experimental research and design techniques, focusing specifically on creative writing. Her book *Urban Literacy, Reading and Writing Architecture* (2014) proposes a literary approach to architecture. Havik is one of the initiators and contributors of the blog writing place.org, and of the international conference "Writingplace. Literary methods in Architectural Research and Design" (TU Delft, 2013). Klaske Havik writes regularly for architectural and literary magazines in The Netherlands and Nordic countries and is an editor of *OASE, Journal for Architecture*.

Paul Holmquist teaches architectural design and theory at the Azrieli School of Architecture and Urbanism at Carleton University with an emphasis on questions of politics and technology, and has also taught at McGill University, Canada and Kansas State University, USA. He recently completed his PhD at McGill University, in which he examined the correlation of Claude-Nicolas Ledoux's architectural theory with the moral and political philosophy of Jean-Jacques Rousseau. His essay "More Powerful than Love: Imagination and Language in the Oikéma of Claude-Nicolas Ledoux" appears in the volume *Chora 7: Intervals in the Philosophy of Architecture* (2016).

Yoonchun Jung is assistant professor at the Department of Architecture in Kwangwoon University in South Korea. He received his bachelor's degree in architecture from Hongik University, South Korea (2000), MArch from Cornell University, USA (2007) and PhD in architecture from McGill University, Canada (2015). His research interest focuses on various social, cultural, and political phenomena in modern Asian architecture and cities. He taught at Cornell University from 2004 to 2006, State University of New York at Buffalo from 2006 to 2008 and McGill University in 2010. From 2012 to 2013, he conducted PhD research in Korean architectural modernity at Kyoto University as a Japan Foundation fellow. He has won numerous awards and research grants, and his work has been published in many journals.

Lisa Landrum is associate professor and associate dean research in the Faculty of Architecture at the University of Manitoba in Winnipeg, Canada. She is a registered architect in New York State and Manitoba. She holds a BArch from Carleton University, and an MArchII and PhD in the history and theory of architecture from McGill University, Canada. Her research on dramatic agencies of architecture and architectural theory has been published in a number of journals and edited books, including *Architecture as a Performing Art* (2013), *Architecture and Justice* (2013), *Architecture's Appeal* (2015), *Economy and Architecture* (2015), *Chora 7* (2016), *Filming the City* (2016), and *Confabulations: Storytelling in Architecture* (2017).

Mari Lending is professor of architectural history at the Oslo School of Architecture and Design, and a senior researcher in the research projects *The Printed and the Built: Architecture and Public Debate in Modern Europe* and *Place and Displacement: Exhibiting Architecture*, run by OCCAS (the Oslo Center for Critical Architectural Studies). She is currently working on a book on nineteenth-century plaster cast collections, *Monuments in Flux: Plaster Casts as Mass Medium*. She recently published, with Mari Hvattum, *Modelling Time: The Permanent Collection, 1925–2014* (2014), drawing on the exhibition "Model as Ruin" at the House of Artists in Oslo, Norway.

Panos Leventis holds a BArch from the University of Southern California (USC), an MArch in Urban Design from University of California, Los Angeles, USA, and a PhD in the history and theory of architecture from McGill University, Canada. He is associate professor at the Hammons School of Architecture of Drury University in Springfield, Missouri. He has served as director of Drury's Study Abroad Centre in Volos and Aegina, Greece, and has also taught for USC in Milan and Como, for McGill in Montreal, and for the University of Cyprus in Nicosia. He is a licensed architect in Cyprus and Greece. His research engages the past, present, and future of cities.

Anca Matyiku is a PhD candidate in the history and theory of architecture at McGill University, Canada. Her research examines the interchange between fiction, storytelling, and architecture. It explores both how places participate to personal and collective stories, as well as how fiction and literary constructions inform the imaginative process of architectural design. Anca's work has been presented in architectural publications, conferences, and several exhibitions, including the Architecture Biennale in Venice. She holds a bachelor of architectural studies from the University of Waterloo and a MArch from the University of Manitoba, Canada.

Marc J. Neveu graduated with a professional degree in architecture after which he went on to complete a post-professional MArch and PhD at McGill University, Canada. While working on his dissertation Marc was awarded a Fulbright Fellowship for study in Venice and a Collection Research Grant at the Canadian Centre for Architecture. Neveu has taught history/theory and studio at universities in the United States and Canada. He has published on issues concerning architectural pedagogy in the Italian eighteenth-century as well as our contemporary context. Neveu is the current executive editor of the *Journal of Architectural Education*. In 2014 he was named chair of the School of Architecture at Woodbury University in Los Angeles.

Susana Oliveira teaches at the Faculty of Architecture, Universidade de Lisboa, Portugal, and is currently on postdoctoral leave with the project "Architectural Imagination in Literature" at CIAUD/GSAPP. She participated in conferences and museum projects and was co-organizer of the "1st International Conference in

Architecture & Fiction: *Once Upon a Place*" (2010) and edited the *Once Upon a Place* book (2013). Her PhD thesis *Lições das Sombras* was published by Gulbenkian (2012) with an FCT Publication Award. She is currently editing a book collection on architecture and literature, *Espécies de Espaços, at Abysmo*, and also works as a freelance illustrator having published over 20 children's books.

Christian Parreno is assistant professor of history and theory of architecture at Universidad San Francisco de Quito. He holds a PhD from the Oslo School of Architecture and Design, Norway, and a MA from the Histories and Theories Programme from the Architectural Association. In 2014 he was a visiting graduate researcher at the University of California, Los Angeles, USA and in 2011 a visiting PhD student at The Bartlett School of Architecture, University College London, UK.

Alberto Pérez-Gómez was born in Mexico City in 1949, where he studied architecture and practiced. He did postgraduate work at Cornell University, USA, and was awarded a MA and a PhD by the University of Essex, UK. He has taught at universities in Mexico, Houston, Syracuse, Toronto, and at London's Architectural Association. In 1983 he became director of Carleton University's School of Architecture. Since January 1987 he has occupied the Bronfman Chair of Architectural History at McGill University, Canada, where he founded the History and Theory Post-Professional (Master's and Doctoral) Programs. His most recent book *Attunement: In Search of Architectural Meaning* (2016) examines and contextualizes historically and philosophically the concepts of atmosphere and mood, arguing for the primacy of the linguistic imagination in architecture.

Angeliki Sioli is assistant professor of architecture at Louisiana State University, USA, and a licensed architect in Greece. She obtained her professional diploma in architecture from the University of Thessaly, Greece, and was granted a post-professional master's degree in architectural theory and history by the National Technical University of Athens, Greece. She completed her PhD in the history and theory of architecture at McGill University, Canada, in 2015. She has taught both undergraduate and graduate architectural courses at McGill University and Tec de Monterrey, Campus Puebla in Mexico. Her research on architecture, literature, and pedagogy has been published in a number of books and presented at interdisciplinary conferences.

David Spurr is emeritus professor of english and comparative literature at the University of Geneva, Switzerland. His most recent book, *Architecture and Modern Literature* (2012), was awarded the Scaglione Prize for Comparative Literary Studies by the Modern Language Association of America. He has published several other books and many essays on the relation between modern literature and the other arts. He currently holds a visiting appointment in architecture and literature at the University of Iceland.

FOREWORD

Alberto Pérez-Gómez

The field of architectural theory is rapidly changing. Long-held assumptions about formalistic aesthetics and its fixation with "object-buildings" are being questioned, while the crucial importance of embodied consciousness and the way the environment makes it possible, even contributing to long-term human evolution through emotional and cognitive meanings, is becoming scientific fact, corroborating the insight of earlier twentieth-century philosophical speculations in phenomenology.

The question then arises about what to do with this insight; how to convert it into strategies that enable the design of ethical and beautiful places. Human reality is fundamentally ambiguous: it is not dualistic like Descartes once thought, but unmasking this fallacy does not bring us closer to some scientific determinism. The fact that the physical, mostly urban environment matters immensely, that architectural meaning cannot be "created" through formal virtuosity alone, and that the best architecture gives us back as a gift the *places* that in many ways were already there, cannot be reduced to one more scientific methodology. It is in this juncture that reflections about literary language and architecture find their relevance.

Just before going to Athens to attend the conference which is the origin of this remarkable book, I had the pleasure of listening to an interview with the late Theo Angelopoulos, Greece's remarkable filmmaker. Perhaps the most important thing that Angelopoulos said in this interview from 2004 concerns his collaboration with the composer Eleni Karaindrou, who wrote the music for most of his films. When speaking about how he actually worked with her, he explained that she always asked him to tell her the story of the film just after he had shot it. *She never looked at the images*: she carefully recorded his stories instead, sometimes in fragments over many days, and then went home to work. She produced the remarkable scores, with all their poignant appropriateness, on the basis of the stories alone. Sometimes she came back to the director with sketches and options, but other times she produced just one finished, astonishing musical piece. Angelopoulos' own description for what she did is that she accomplished in music what he did in images, "she made a film in music"[1] he said, both emerging from the story.

This is a fascinating observation that speaks about the vividness of the literary imagination, the capacity of fiction to disclose reality—the emotional world as lived—capable of surpassing all other modalities of picturing. Philosophers in the hermeneutic tradition have recognized this fact, elaborating upon Aristotle's famous insight in his *Poetics* where he declared that fiction, expressing through metaphors that which is possible, is more philosophical than history, expressing merely what has happened. Indeed, this is particularly enlightening for the topics broached in this book, since what one usually admires in Angelopoulos' work, is the amazing visual imagination at play; and this is not unlike what is often admired in great works of architecture. Confessing to something that, in Angelopoulos' own words, any filmmaker is never happy to admit, he added that: "My films would not be what they are without the music."[2] This amazing enigma for a work that involves all the senses, such as cinema, with the literary imagination as generator, is one of the central questions this collection raises for architectural production, and a wonderful incentive to continue this line of enquiry: to understand and implement a literary imagination at the roots of an architecture capable of producing communicative atmospheres, both emotive and cognitive, for embodied human action, conveying its meanings in a multisensory way.

Notes

1 Theo Angelopoulos (Director), interview by Simon Gray in the DVD *The Weeping Meadow*, New Yorker Video, December 2006.
2 Ibid.

PREFACE

On Reading Architecture

Elias Constantopoulos

"Ceci tuera cela"
Victor Hugo, Notre-Dame de Paris, 1831

"This will kill that," says Frollo, the Hunchback of Notre-Dame; but actually we may say, "That has consumed this." The history of architecture from antiquity to today was always full of signs to be deciphered—be they the Pyramids, the Parthenon, Hagia Sophia, Chartres Cathedral, or the Jewish Museum—telling stories of man's relation to the world.

Even where there were no mythical subjects to be told and sculpted on stone, as in the abstractions of secular modernity, one could "read" architecture, thus gaining a privileged access into it. Rowe and Slutzky's "Transparency, Literal and Phenomenal" (1963), famously demonstrated such ways of perceiving and eventually "knowing"architecture, by learning how to read it. Peter Collins in his important treatise of 1965, *Changing Ideals in Modern Architecture 1750–1950*, writes on the linguistic analogy in functionalism:

> The analogy between architecture and language has been less popular in recent years than it was from the middle of the eighteenth century to the middle of the nineteenth century, probably because it lacks the scientific glamour possessed by analogies with living organisms and machines.[1]

However, in the second half of the nineteenth century, as semiology enters architectural discourse, and Saussure, Barthes, and Eco become household names in many architectural schools (as I recollect at the Bartlett in the seventies), various histories of architecture are also presented as "languages". Bruno Zevi's *The Modern Language Of Architecture* (1978), Charles Jencks's *The Language of Post-Modern Architecture* (1977), John Summerson's *The Classical Language of Architecture* (1966), all address the stylistic traits of particular *architectures*, according to their formal "syntax." So, not only "language," but also "syntax" come in vogue. From Peter Eisenman's differentiation between syntactics and semantics to Bill Hillier's analytical "space syntax" the organization of space borrows its terms from grammar.

Furthermore, in the wake of deconstruction, "text" itself becomes *à la mode*, in the newly established dialogue between architects and philosophers, such as Tschumi, Eisenman, and Derrida. Within this con[text], the French philosopher even writes an essay aptly entitled "Why Eisenman writes such good books" (1988). Thus, text, also related to "text-ile" and "text-ure," unexpectedly brings into proximity of the plot of a novel the weaving of a Semperian hut.

But this is also a new-found story retold. From Alberti's *De re aedificatoria* (1485), to Le Corbusier's *Vers une Architecture* (1923), Plato and Aristotle's presence has been looming heavy over architectural theory, as much as Heidegger's "Bauen, Denken, Wohnen" (1954), has been of recent, waiting for a nod to descend from its lofty cloud and raise the spirit of architecture, rescuing it from the chores of banality and consumerism. Wittgenstein, a philosopher-come-architect for his sister's house, famously noted once the difficulty presented in the practice of architecture as compared to philosophy. Recent architectural discourse displays an increased, wide ranging interest in philosophical approaches to space and place, as was for example evident in the University of Patras' international conference "The Significance of Philosophy in Architectural Education" (2009).

The architect, a builder who speaks *Latin* according to Adolf Loos, and the philosopher engage directly into a critical dialogue, as in Paul Valery's Socratic *Eupalinos ou l'architecte* (1921), in order to dissect the corpus of architecture, and reconnect it to the grand themes of human thought through the ages.

Two decades ago, in sensing the complex involvement and affinity of architecture to various other fields and disciplines, I guest-edited an issue of the review *Architecture in Greece*, entitled *Parallel Architectures*—in film, literature, photography, and advertising. Today, research in these and other related areas is widespread, if not commonplace among many scholars. The writings of important authors—the cellars of Edgar Allan Poe, the endless libraries of Jorge Luis Borges, the invisible cities of Italo Calvino, the language of space in Octavio Paz's poems—to mention the most well-known ones, often enter the curricula of architectural schools nowadays.

The essays in this book, however, propose that architecture is first and foremost a form of speech, rather than syntax or text. If, as they presume, orality is primary, analogous to our experience of living in buildings, then we have much to learn from literature about architecture and the cities in which we live. Even taking a stand against architecture may allow "reading" its essence. In his text "Why I didn't become an architect", the novelist Orhan Pamuk explains:

> I studied architecture at Istanbul Technical University for about three years, but I did not graduate to become an architect. I now think that this had to do with the ostentatious modernist dreams I set down on those blank sheets

... In those days, when people asked me why I had not become an architect, I would give the same answer in different words: "Because I didn't want to design apartments!" When I said apartments, I meant a way of life as well as a particular approach to architecture ...

So let's ask the question that I heard quite a lot twenty-five years ago and that I still ask myself from time to time: Why didn't I become an architect? Answer: because I thought the sheets of paper on which I was to pour my dreams were blank. But after twenty-five years of writing, I have come to understand that those pages are never blank.

I know very well now that when I sit down at my table, I am sitting with tradition and with those who refuse absolutely to bow to rules or to history ... Had I thought, at the age of twenty, that I could do the same with architecture, I might well have become an architect.[2]

Notes

1 Peter Collins, *Changing Ideals in Modern Architecture 1750–1950*, 2nd ed. (Montreal: McGill-Queens University Press, 1998), 173.
2 Orhan Pamuk, *Other Colors, Essays and a Story*, trans. Maureen Freely (New York: Alfred A. Knopf, 2007), 307.

ACKNOWLEDGMENTS

Angeliki Sioli and Yoonchun Jung

The book you are holding in your hands would have been impossible without the symposium that preceded its publication and from which, after many iterations and innumerable e-mails to contributors and editors, it emerged. It is with this thought in mind that we would like to address our acknowledgments.

Although initially reacting with some reluctance, warning us that the organization of a symposium is "too much work" and we "should avoid it at all costs," Alberto Pérez-Gómez's passionate disposition soon took over. We are deeply grateful for his sharing of experience and his gift of help in both important and trivial matters as we pursued our journey. Most importantly we would like to thank him for ensuring that our energy was spent no less on the social than on the academic side of the event. Given that a symposium is, in its original definition, a convivial party, we tried our best to live up to this expectation.

The scientific committee that agreed to help us with the selection of the participants consisted of the academics Caroline Dionne, Phoebe Giannisi, Klaske Havik, Mari Lending, Franco Pisani, and David Spurr (in alphabetic order). They all played a crucial role in giving the event its final shape, as well as providing for a most inspiring first day with their insightful and engaging short discussions. For all their passionate work and original contributions we owe them a heartfelt thank you. Our official responders Louise Pelletier, Panos Leventis, and Christos Kakalis graciously helped to heat up the conversations at the end of each session, demonstrating interesting connections between the presentations and posing critical questions. Twenty more participants eagerly shared their research, work and speculations on the questions raised by the symposium, helping to make this a thought-provoking event.

The symposium would have never found an appropriate venue if it weren't for the unconditional support of the Hellenic Institute of Architecture. President Elias Constantopoulos and Director Marianna Milioni helped us in a considerate and constant way since the very beginning; respecting the character of the event we wished to organize and helping us realize this wish. It is because of them that we could convene at and enjoy the beautiful premises of the Benaki Museum on Kanari Street, in downtown Athens. To the staff of the museum we extend whole-hearted thanks, as they took care of all the participants over the course of three intense days, in the most professional and polite way.

Web designer Stauros Siolis and his team at ArtLab gave our ideas a most aesthetic presence in the relatively boundary-free world of the internet (www.readingarchitecture.org), allowing a great number of academics and architects around the globe to submit their proposals. Korean painter Jieh Kim and Greek architect and photographer Nikos Kazeros provided enticing visuals for the website and the symposium's poster and program. Anca Matyiku with her overwhelming creativity designed tasteful name tags that encouraged encounter and conversation between the participants. Maria Vidali, our Athenian assistant, answered e-mails and made countless phone-calls always in her characteristically sweet, kind, and professional way. Dohan Kim offered as a gift high-factor sunscreen to protect the participants from the admittedly strong summer Greek sun (although the symposium was an indoors event). For dealing with all the last-minute, most unforeseeable practical difficulties, we owe our appreciation beyond words to the most dedicated assistant Giolanta Muthithra.

As the idea of a book started forming in our mind, Lawrence Bird edited and polished our book proposal with care, always asking critical questions as we prepared our submission to Routledge. There a team of kind, respectful and most patient editors replied to all our questions, understood all our difficulties and accommodated all our suggested changes to the original plan. Last, we would like to thank all the contributors in this volume who generously tolerated our suggestions and worked with them as they polished their essays and fine-tuned their arguments.

INTRODUCTION

Reading Architecture: Literary Imagination and Architectural Experience

Angeliki Sioli and Yoonchun Jung

The contributors to this volume, before their essays fell into place as the chapters of this book, first collaborated on the occasion of a small-scale symposium in Greece; an event organized by the History and Theory Program of McGill University's School of Architecture.[1] In June 2015 a group of approximately forty-five people gathered in hot and politically-charged downtown Athens, convinced that fiction might be the most promising path toward (grasping) reality. The objective was to discuss possibilities for the use of literature—novels, short stories and poems—in architectural design, research and practice, and to create a network of people determined to pursue their literary interests in the architectural world. The event undoubtedly echoed a number of related architectural conferences that had taken place in Europe in previous years,[2] but it differed from them in focusing exclusively on literary writing—that is, narratives produced by authors or poets—that could evoke/provoke an architect's literary imagination.

Our starting point was the advice Professor Aulis Blomstedt of Helsinki University of Technology used to give his students: for an architect, the capacity to imagine *situations of life* is a more important talent than the gift of imagining space.[3] We agreed that from the small scale of the domestic environment, to the level of the city, literature has systematically enabled us to imagine poetically-described and meticulously-captured *situations of life*; the very life that buildings, places and cities surround, enclose, and enable. We acknowledged that literature has moreover provoked architect's *literary imagination*, an imagination evoked by new meanings in the sphere of language, which as argued by philosopher Paul Ricoeur can lead to the productive creation of images that may be both new and culturally significant.[4] Given both the importance of image production for architecture and the vital connection of the field with life itself—our social, political, cultural or intimate personal life—the basic premises of the symposium became clear. The book you hold in your hands presents some of the many points touched upon during those hot days in Athens, but also how they continued developing and enriching the participants' research long after we had all dispersed along our diverse paths.

As a result, the essays collected in this volume explore the possibilities of literary imagination (in line with Ricoeur's hermeneutic phenomenology), study situations of life, focus on place-bound architectural experiences, and unpack aspects of lived space as captured in written fiction. They present readings of urban and domestic environments, research, pedagogy, and architectural practice through the lenses of literature and poetry. They look into novels, short stories, and poems with a particular urban and architectural focus, making space and buildings the main subject of their narrative. Through this approach they aim toward a qualitative, emotional and embodied understanding of the built world: a phenomenological apprehension much needed in today's formalistic and commerce-driven architectural reality.

As the conferences preceding *Reading Architecture* already reveal, the topic of architecture and literature is hardly new. A number of fascinating studies have already touched upon it across a range of disciplines. To focus on the most current bibliographical production: a great deal of writing in architecture since the late 1970s and early 1980s has described or provided scenarios supporting the use of fiction, narrative, and language in architectural design. This ranges from John Hejduk and his *Masques* to Bernard Tschumi and his exhibition catalog *A Space: A Thousand Words*. Another aspect of this field of interdisciplinary research focuses largely on architecture and the city, a topic with an extensive bibliography.[5] Moreover, many approaches to this subject shed light on formalistic analyses of architectural and narrative constructions, comparing methods employed by architects and novelists in world-creation.[6]

Acknowledging the already extensive interest in fiction and in representations of architecture in literature,[7] this book is interested in addressing questions that could profit from further examination in this interdisciplinary field, particularly inspired by the notions of literary imagination and situations of life. Some of these questions are: how can we do architectural research that defies strict historical boundaries and allows us to understand life lived in the architecture of the past? How can we use novels, and the literary imagination triggered by them, in design education? What understanding of city-life, essential if we are to build appropriately, can we obtain from the atmospheres and moods that novels can capture? How can participatory design be enriched by literary imagination?

Seeking to learn from allied arts, this collection focuses strictly on the output of authors and poets, leaving aside narratives or fictions created by architects themselves in relation to their projects. Moreover, it explores new literary sources: novels, short stories, and poems that have been studied only rarely in architectural research. Some of them are recently published and are just now becoming available to architectural research. Others were untranslated and unknown to English-speaking audiences until recently. Yet others are well-known works by renowned authors—Edgar Allan Poe, Albert Camus or Haruki Murakami—but have never been studied from an architectural point of view.

Although the reader can identify connections and underlying themes among many different essays, we propose a grouping of the essays in four distinct sections. The first section, "Readings on (Un)Familiar Places," opens the conversation, meticulously examining three novels and a short story. All are marked by a particular capacity to reveal the architectural context of the environments and times they portray, in ways that no conventional means of architectural representation and research can offer. On the one hand they allow a glimpse into otherwise intangible atmospheres and moods; on the other, they capture urban or architectural transformations over time, and the way its inhabitants respond to them through appropriating space. Four compelling twentieth-century metropolises become the focus of these inquiries. The authors Christian Parreno, Angeliki Sioli, Mathilde Simonsen Dahl and Yoonchun Jung focus respectively on the Algerian city of Oran and its atmosphere of boredom, Paris and its erotic nocturnal landscape, Kristiania—a city which no one leaves before it has set its mark upon him or her—and its transformation into today's Oslo, South Korea's capital Seoul and its homogenized, impersonal apartment buildings.

The second section of the book explores how literature and literary techniques can enable or inspire alternative modes of architectural research. Mari Lending's "Fabrics of Reality in Fiction" discusses the capacity of fiction to compete with, perhaps even overturn, the scholarly discourse that saturates our contemporary thinking on architecture and history. Klaske Havik develops a poetic way of writing as a mode of architectural investigation, demonstrating how the poet's receptive approach offers valuable insight for architectural researchers and for the engagement of lived experience in their work. Rumiko Handa looks at Sebald's *Austerlitz* and argues how a story that weaves imaginary events into the daily rituals around actual and familiar buildings allows us to examine architecture's psychological effects on its users. Lisa Landrum dives into the dense profusion and strange agency of eclectic objects in Poe's environments, and invites architectural researchers to consider their own imaginative involvement with multivalent settings of study—with a warning about the perils of unlimited imagination. The section closes with Panos Leventis' personal narrative on the city of Montreal; a writing which allows for the history of the city and its urban transformations to come to life and become tangible through our embodied engagement.

Following this conversation on architectural academic research, the third section explores possibilities that novels can open up for architectural pedagogy and design. Jason Crow examines the interconnection between the famous drawings of Saint-Exupéry's *Little Prince* and the story's narrative, arguing that drawing makes (living in) place possible only if constantly re-explained and re-appropriated through narrative. Anca Matyiku follows by arguing for a more radical position, one that sees literary language as an actual instrument for design. The poetic prose of Bruno Schulz—an author and trained architect himself—serves as a compelling example in support of her argument. Sevil Enginsoy Ekinci explores the potential of model-making, exploring the numerous fictitious models of Paul Scheerbart's imaginary machine as narrated in his relatively unknown *Perpetual Motion Machine: The Story of an Invention*. Studying the architectural work of American architect and educator Douglas Darden, Mark Neveu's chapter discusses how literature can become a guide for architectural making with cultural aspirations. The project of *Melvila*—a library, archive, and reading room based on Herman Melville's *Moby-Dick* and designed in detail by Douglas Darden—becomes the subject matter. Last, Paul Holmquist, through the example of a recently taught graduate seminar, demonstrates how Murakami's *Hardboiled Wonderland and The End of the World* can enable students to engage philosophical questions on the city as architectural concerns.

Continuing the conversation around architectural making through literature, the fourth section focuses on architectural questions that are particularly pressing for our contemporary globalized and capital-driven architectural reality. Caroline Dionne's essay starts this section with a philosophical approach, suggesting/testing how Ricoeur's thinking can constitute a theoretical basis for modalities of action and participation in current architectural practice. David Spur explores how the literary representation of architecture constitutes a mode of resistance to the excess of finance capital and the existential drift of contemporary western society. Lily Chi looks for resonances between literary tactics and those of urban design and suggests approaches to critical work in contemporary cities. Last, Susana Oliveira studies the fictional descriptions of futuristic technological spaces in E.M. Forster's *The Machine Stop*, and discusses how they can offer us a preview of architecture's future and possible shortcomings.

Working their way through the different essays, readers will realize that diverse geographical locations, a wide range of historical periods, multifarious situations of life, and distinct architectural and spatial representations—from the surreal to the futuristic, to those defying boundaries between fiction and reality—find themselves interrelated in the pages of this book. Our intention is that the cities examined, the methods suggested, the ideas presented and the criticism developed can allow the fictional world of literature to further affect the reality of architecture— a reality so heavily depended on the imagination of the architect. Although most phenomenological accounts of imagination have concentrated on its role as a form of vision, as a special or modified way of seeing the world,[8] with the hermeneutic turn in phenomenology for which Ricoeur argues, this privileging is significantly revised. Imagination is assessed as an indispensable agent in the creation of meaning in and through language, what Ricoeur calls "semantic innovation."[9] Replacing the visual model of the image with the linguistic, Ricoeur affirms the more poetic role of imagination—that is, its ability to say one thing in terms of another, or to say several things at the same time, thereby creating something new.[10] It is with this understanding of literary imagination in mind that this book looks into literature: a medium in which language thrives, and one determined to represent human reality in all its complexity as unavoidably bound by place. And it is with this same understanding that we hope our readers approach the volume's diverse contributions and perspectives, eliciting their own literary imagination to emerge.

Notes

1 The symposium was organized by Angeliki Sioli, Yoonchun Jung and Alberto Pérez-Gómez. The scientific committee consisted of (in alphabetical order) Caroline Dionne, Phoebe Giannisi, Klaske Havik, Mari Lending, Franco Pisani and David Spurr. It was partially sponsored by the Social Sciences and Humanities Research Council of Canada and took place under the auspices of the Hellenic Institute of Architecture. The current book is not a publication of proceedings.
2 Two important international conferences had preceded the event: "Writingplace. Conference on Literary Methods in Architectural Research and Design," organized by the School of Architecture at TU Delft (Delft, November 2013), and "1st International Conference on Architecture and Fiction: Once upon a place," organized by the Faculty of Architecture at the Technical University of Lisbon (Lisbon, October 2010). It is of course important to mention that conferences on the topic have been for a long time popular in the humanities. Among the most recent examples, we would like to mention the Northeast Modern Language Association (NEMLA) annual conference (Montreal, April 2010) which hosted a session dedicated to "Architecture and Literature," the conference "Intersections: Architecture and Poetry" (London, June 2011), organized by The Courtauld Institute of Art, the conference "Spatial Perspectives, Literature and Architecture, 1850–Present," organized by the Faculty of English Language and Literature of the University of Oxford (Oxford, June 2012), the conference "Descriptions of Architecture and Interiors in Literature," organized by the Institute of History of Art, University of Zurich (Zurich, October 2014) and the conference "Architecture and Literature: Inter-Arts Dialogue" organized by the Faculty of Social Sciences and Humanities, Universidade NOVA (Lisbon, December 2014).
3 As quoted in Juhani Pallasmaa, *The Thinking Hand, Existential and Embodied Wisdom in Architecture* (Chichester: Willey, 2009), 114.
4 Paul Paul Ricoeur, "The function of fiction in shaping reality," *Man and World* 12, no. 2 (1979): 127.
5 Among the most representative publications on the topic we would include those of David Spur, *Architecture and Modern Literature* (2012), Sarah Edwards and Charley Jonathan ed., *Writing the Modern City, Literature, architecture, modernity* (2012), Desmond Harding, *Writing the City: Urban Visions and Literary Modernism* (2002), Richard Lehan, *The City in Literature: An Intellectual and Cultural History* (1998), Burton Pike, *The Image of the City in Modern Literature* (1981), and Festa-McCormick, Diana, *The City as Catalyst: A Study of Ten Novels* (1979).
6 Some of the most characteristic publications on the topic are those by Joseph Frank, "Spatial Form in the Modern Novel" (1992), Maurice Blanchot, *The Space of Literature* (1982), Eve Ellen Frank, *Literary Architecture, Essays Towards a Tradition* (1979), and some essays in Susana Oliveira, ed., *Once Upon A Place, Architecture and Fiction* (2013).
7 Studies from an architectural perspective with overlapping interests with our book include: Klaske Havik, *Urban Literacy, Reading and Writing Architecture* (2014), Mari Lending, "Wandering among Models: Stendhal, Proust, Sebald" (2013), Rumiko Handa, *Conjuring the Real: The Role of Architecture in Eighteenth- and Nineteenth-Century Fiction* (2011), and Caroline Dionne, "Running Out of Place: Language and Architecture in Lewis Carroll," dissertation (2005).
8 Richard Kearney, "Paul Ricoeur and the Hermeneutic Imagination," in *The Narrative Path: The Later Works of Paul Ricoeur*, ed. T. Peter Kemp David Rasmussen (Cambridge, Mass.: MIT Press, 1989), 1.
9 Ibid.
10 Ibid., 2.

SECTION 1
Readings On (Un)Familiar Places

1
ORAN, THE CAPITAL OF BOREDOM

Christian Parreno

> Any country where I am not bored is a country that teaches me nothing.
> Albert Camus, *Death in the Soul*, 1937

In the writings by Albert Camus, boredom and modern architecture are encountered together. The built environment exudes the condition, contaminating everyday life. In a circular and self-referential manner, boredom is symptom and ailment. In *The Plague* (1947), Oran is portrayed as a restful city in the coast of Algeria, somnolent due to a specious modernity that had failed to install the accelerated rhythms of capitalist production.[1] The buildings are unattractive, with "no vegetation" and "no soul," composing "a town without inklings, that is to say, an entirely modern town."[2] The same lethargy foisted by the surroundings is imperative in *The Stranger* (1942). In a space characterized by monotony, Sunday afternoons offer respite when everyone goes to the cinema and the streets become deserted. With the exception of "the shopkeepers and the cats" who invariably remain in their customary places, everyone looks for distraction in settings dissimilar from those occupied during the rest of the week.[3] The regular pace of work and rest allies with the repetitive cycles of nature to perpetuate boredom—the sky "alone is king," always clear and blue, "intolerably dull."[4] In nature and the city, rhythmical sameness outlines a terrain of apparent stasis that defies mental stability. If every reality has multiple equivalents, then referential coordinates of existence disappear, rupturing protocols of social, moral, and ethical engagement. In *The Stranger*, a man is remorselessly and inexplicably killed by another who appears insanely bored. The criminal is deranged and dislocated, unemployed and unoccupied, escaping an empty house and feverish due to the implacable sun of North Africa.

Equally, in "The Minotaur, or the Stop in Oran" (1939), boredom is effect and cause of modern architecture. Enthused and informed by recurrent trips from Algiers to Oran during his university days,[5] Camus describes the city as "the capital of boredom," "besieged by innocence and beauty," surrounded by magnificent nature that architects decidedly ignore.[6] Its constructions, flat and taut, protectively turn their backs to the ocean. Rather than being a realm of latency, Oran is a realm of endless waiting where nothing happens and nothing is expected to occur. As a result, its inhabitants are simultaneously idle and restless. On the one hand, they are passive in their efforts to explore where they live. On the other, they are vigorous in adopting imported models of behavior, acting as if they were in the United States. In between the built environment and the practices of its occupants, the Minotaur reigns in a labyrinth of boredom—a state of ambiguity and ambivalence that exposes absurdity. For Camus, Oran is a space of pause and delay, which corroborates the suspicion that the world is unfathomable.[7]

Labyrinthine Boredom

Becoming evident midway through the essay, "The Minotaur" is written in first person. Its alternate title—"The Stop in Oran"—denotes that the omnipresent narrator is a visitor, forcibly or accidentally caught in the city, in a moment of rest in the journey to another destination. The foreign voice imposes critical distance, not only separating itself from the conditions of Oran and dissociating Oran from the rest of the world, but also creating a parenthesis for reflection. Within this enclosure, five sections tell an anticlimactic story.[8] "The Street", "The Desert of Oran", "Sports", "Monuments", and "Ariadne's Stone" diagnose and elliptically confirm boredom as the essence of the city. The condition is ubiquitous and porous, permitting the infiltration of parallel dimensions and temporalities through the many fissures of modernity. Like ghosts, Flaubert and his friends, protagonists of the novels by Gogol, temples from antiquity, the edifices of Florence and Athens, the twelve Apostles, and other characters meander amid the people of Oran, as luxuriant and convoluted figures that contrast with the scarcity and simplicity of the city:

> Atlas's task is easy; it is sufficient to choose one's hour. Then one realizes that for an hour, a month, a year, these shores can indulge in freedom. They welcome pell-mell, without even looking at them, the monk, the civil servant, or the conqueror. There are days when I expected to meet, in the streets of Oran, Descartes or Cesare Borgia.[9]

In "The Minotaur", boredom is a system of organization rather than a formal configuration, unceasingly informing the production of architecture and therefore characterizing Oran. Far from being subjective, the condition is the result of a process of historical layering, shaped by Spanish, Ottoman, and French invasions, but unsuccessful in creating identity. It holds Oran in limbo, a space devoid not only of past and future but also of permanent materiality. Similar to being in between locations, the city does not provide a stable here nor represents a significant there. Instead, it establishes a field of suspension that paradoxically depends on the particularities of its architecture but is detached from its physical attributes. Although unwanted at first, boredom turns incantatory and captivating, magnetically seducing the sensitive narrator who becomes intrigued with the possibilities of exploration, even rejoicing in them—"she bursts the unfortunate stage setting with which she is covered; she shrieks forth between all the houses and over all the roofs."[10] Nonetheless, Oran defers engagement and immersion by reductively appearing as a maze of solid fences.[11] The periphery is simple and clear, only to turn convoluted and confusing as the center approaches. In this domain—challenging the immaterial, inspirational, and vertical connotations of ennui—boredom signals to the material, ordinary, and horizontal, without possibility of sublimation:

> In the beginning you wander in the labyrinth, seeking the sea like the sign of Ariadne. But you turn round and round in pale and oppressive streets, and eventually the Minotaur devours the people of Oran: the Minotaur is boredom.[12]

The Dustiest City

Oran is the opposite of Paris or London, capitals of fabricated excitement, full of the revolutions of the past that have produced many expressions and left several residues. For Camus, the boisterous exhibition of historical data constitutes empty stimuli. Regardless of their elaborate architecture, the cities of Europe are no more than silent wastelands that promote introspection and aloofness—"the great value of such overpopulated islands is that in them the heart strips bare. Silence is no longer possible except in noisy cities."[13] In this respect, Oran is simultaneously similar and different. In the first instance, the Algerian city is also made of stone. But in the second, its architecture exposes its mineral tincture by being formally simple and lacking reverberations from previous eras. The edifices are incapable of suggesting more than their "heavy beauty," haphazardly scattered over a rocky landscape, like a matrix of alien appearance.[14] This "magnificent anarchy" is candidly arid, impossible to understand or redeem—as Santa Cruz, one of the three interconnected forts constructed in the sixteenth century, facing the bay,

> cut out of the rock, the mountains, the flat sea, the violent wind and the sun, the great cranes of the harbor, the trains, the hangars, the quays, and the huge ramps climbing up the city's rock, and in the city itself these diversions and this boredom.[15]

The "very ugly constructions" configure a "walled town that turns its back, that has been built up by turning back on itself like a snail."[16] Like the mollusk, Oran carries its architecture as an unchanging shelter. A contorted yellow wall protects the inhabitants from the persistence of nature, creating an indifferent dialogue between land and sea that produces too much despair as well as too much excitement. Since the people of Oran have forgotten how to live among the stones

FIGURE 1.1 Oran from the fort of Santa Cruz, photograph by M. Lavina (Oran, 1930).

Courtesy of Henri Lavina

of nature, they have taken refuge among the stones created by themselves, with a sensibility closer to the coarse ground than to the smooth sky, but with neither poetry nor spirituality since human development is outlawed and thus impossible to historicize. According to Camus, the opposition of the built environment to the natural surroundings is the merit of Oran, demarcating a sanctuary of boredom, protected "by an army in which every stone is a soldier."[17]

In the "dustiest of cities" where "the pebble is king," the slowness of pre-modern time becomes evident in the obstinate presence of dust.[18] The fine material covers and homogenizes the city, flying and resettling to subtly configure new surfaces. It moves if there is wind and its density changes if the weather varies—the streets become sandy in high temperatures and muddy when it rains. Furthermore, dust thickens the air. As Camus observes, the few trees in the city have turned into "petrified plants whose branches give off an acrid, dusty smell."[19] Unlike the grey pollution of the metropolis, the dust in Oran extends the ochre desert into the urban and architectural, instating untidiness, blurring the relation between figures, ground and sky, and mattifying and texturizing. The mineral coating "contributes to the dense and impassible universe in which the heart and mind are never distracted from themselves, nor from their sole object, which is man."[20]

Stone Monuments

Notwithstanding the dryness, the architecture of Oran is consistently extravagant, always with an "absurd look."[21] The entirety of the fabricated environment—from buildings to furniture and products for sale in shops—is vulgar and kitschy:

All the bad taste of Europe and the Orient has managed to converge in them. One finds, helter-skelter, marble greyhounds, ballerinas with swans, versions of Diana the huntress in green galalith, discus-throwers and reapers, everything that is used for birthday and wedding gifts, the whole race of painful figurines constantly called forth by a commercial and playful genie on our mantelpieces.[22]

As material culture, this merchandise is neither more attractive nor more repellent than any other found in other cities. Yet in Oran, these objects do not serve as capital since commercial transactions scarcely take place, becoming static adornments, incapable of initiating any ritual of exchange. Analogously, cafés, restaurants, stores, and even funeral establishments constitute centers of waiting, as locations where space has conquered time and so eliminated its passing. Even though their architectural arrangements have integrated international canons, they lack activity, abandoned to impassive dwellers whose lassitude prompts the question, "can one be moved by a city where nothing attracts the mind, where the very ugliness is anonymous, where the past is reduced to nothing? Emptiness, boredom, an indifferent sky, what are the charms of such places?"[23]

Drawing from the existing architecture of the Algerian city, Camus identifies three types of monuments—civic buildings, busts in public spaces, and infrastructure. The first category is exemplified by the Maison du Colon, built in 1902 on the former Karguentah farm that pioneered the plantation of tobacco.[24] Designed by the architect Wolf to accommodate all agricultural institutions, the triangular plan responds to the shape of the site, defined in the late nineteenth century by the rails of two intersecting car-trams.[25] In the top, a prominent frieze ties the volume, with an intermittent ribbon of colorful mosaics that depict not only the benefits of nature organized by human activity but also a fictional relationship of conviviality between local inhabitants and colonizers.[26] An inscription in the front reads "To the glory of the colonization work of France," updated in 1930 with the addition "Commemorating the centenary of Algeria."[27] In its narrowest side, two tall columns create the main entrance, crowned by a pyramidal pinnacle that resembles an extruded labyrinth, reminiscent of the Minotaur. To the ironic narrator, the "delicate building" exhibits the three main virtues of the people of Oran—"boldness in taste, love of violence, and a feeling for historical syntheses."[28] The syncretic style combines Egypt, Byzantium, and Munich to configure "a piece of pastry in the shape of a bowl upside down."[29]

The second type of monuments are the sculpted figures resting in squares. Contrasting with the Maison, the numerous "imperial marshals, ministers, and local benefactors" are faithful to their historical specificity.[30] Their static temporality quarantines them, materializing the boring rather than the heroic. Like irrelevant headstones, the solid tributes to the past do not succeed in establishing relations with the present, being instead territorial markers imposed by foreign civilizations. The exception to these unconvincing objects are two lions flanking the main door of the Place d'Armes. Crafted by the artist Cain in 1888, they are of low artistic

FIGURE 1.2 Maison du Colon, postcard by unknown author (Oran, c. 1940).
Courtesy of Musée de l'Histoire vivante

value—their faces are "hilarious snouts in the square of a mercantile province overseas."[31] However, cherished by the people of Oran, their representative force surpasses their material insignificance. The lions are repositories of memory, echoing the Arabic *Wahran* that means "two lions."[32] Like the stony dignitaries, the sculpted animals embody the will of the ephemeral to last, but unlike them, they are majestic and alive. The residents believe they become animated at midnight to parade around the building. In case of catastrophe, the lions would be saved and preserved—"they have the same chances as the ruins of Angkor."[33] The third kind of monuments are modern public works that structure the coast for ten kilometers. More than edifices and statues, they contribute to "transforming the most luminous of bays into a gigantic harbor."[34] This enterprise is not concerned with planning or progress. For the observer of "The Minotaur," the construction of infrastructure is an excuse of the locals to be in contact with stone and produce dust, the most genuine testament of the city. The exploitation and transformation of the nearby mines satisfy their disquiet and their need to act—"one must choose doing that or nothing."[35]

Despite the publicness, this architectural triad is timid and introverted. The collision of idiosyncratic temporalities causes rhythmical incompatibility, being self-indulgent, uninteresting, and too familiar, with components unable to resonate with each other or to extend their influence to spaces beyond their immediate surroundings. In Oran, municipal buildings, open areas, and roads are variations of the same condition of fracture, seclusion, and delay. Contrary to the suspense of the future, they operate within the limits of the present, inept in the task of evoking an alternate reality.

Without Ariadne nor Theseus

In the myth of the Minotaur, Ariadne falls in love with Theseus, the slayer of the half-bull creature who escapes the labyrinth with the help of a thread provided by the infatuated woman. Following Camus, if the Minotaur is boredom and the labyrinth is Oran, then evading the first requires staying within and then navigating out of the space of the second. Nevertheless, the inhabitants of the city are not willing to leave. They dwell in the labyrinth, immersed in the boredom inflicted by the Minotaur but unaware of their condition. Since Ariadne and Theseus are not present to strategize any rescue, apathy surfaces to instigate social anonymity—"the result is such that the only instructive circles remain those of poker-players, boxing enthusiasts, bowlers, and the local associations."[36]

In Oran, boredom is contagious, inhibiting thinking and feeling, evident in the public. Saturated with the condition, interpersonal relations promote a mode of alertness that lingers in the outside world.[37] The fixation with exteriority oppresses, impeding ontological movement and thus paralyzing the processes of interiority.[38] Stagnation favors boredom, and the boredom of Oran defies not only the Cartesian proposition of "I think, therefore I am" but also its equivalent "I feel, therefore I am."[39] To avoid internal confrontation, the residents turn their attention to other residents. This interest compels occupation, simply to pass time. For Camus, the adopted practices of the inhabitants of Oran are superfluous and directed to avoid monotony, framed by encouraging facades painted with advertisements that proclaim non-boringness—"sumptuous," "splendid," "extraordinary," "amazing," "staggering," and "tremendous" are common adjectives in billboards and signs.[40] Embodying these epithets, a parade of male youngsters get their shoes shined to display them to their female counterparts on the boulevard. With approximations to the aesthetics of American films, the "softhearted gangsters" dress up and strut:

> With wavy, oiled hair protruding from under a felt hat slanted over the left ear and peaked over the right eye, the neck encircled by a collar big enough to accommodate the straggling hair, the microscopic knot of the necktie kept in place by a regulation pin, with thigh-length coat and waist close to the hips, with light-colored and noticeably short trousers, with dazzlingly shiny triple-soled shoes, every evening those youths make the sidewalks ring with their metal-tipped shoes.[41]

Known as the "Clarques" for their imitation of "the bearing, forthrightness, and superiority of Mr Clark Gable," they are accompanied by "Marlenes."[42] Although the young women flaunt their make-up, also movie-inspired, their faces are emotionless, staring to the horizon. The facial ornamentations are consonant with the bright patina of the shoes of the male adolescents and the enticing colors of the posters that offer adventure and excitement. In all cases, by being flamboyant and thin, the pictorial coverings constitute excuses for facile sociability, distracting rather than engaging.

While the young circles of Oran extend their leisure activities from the city to the ocean—"at eleven a.m., coming down from the plateau, all that young flesh, lightly clothed in motley materials, breaks on the sand like a multicolored wave"—the working men gather around a boxing ring.[43] Although the closeness to the quadrangular stage unveils relations of social power, the surrounding space serves as a container of fraternity and naïve morality.[44] Having to decide which boxer to support requires involvement with others, surpassing the distance of the purely spectacular between actors and public and therefore providing a sense of shared purpose, with the possibility of emotional release.[45] Boxing attunes the spectators, mostly men of European descent, to a self-induced state of fascination that does not expose private vulnerabilities.[46] During the fight, the attendees compose an unfolding narrative that requires collaboration and concentration, anticipating bodily movements and speculating about strategies of attack, as if the result could be logically predicted.[47]

The event takes place in the Central Sporting Club, on the rue du Fondouk—"in the back of a sort of whitewashed garage, covered with corrugated iron and violently lighted."[48] Resonating with the Arabic *fondouk*, meaning "inn," the space provides a temporary shelter that induces expression.[49] On the one hand, the hermetic walls permit loudness, fusing songs by Tino Rossi with the chants of the crowd to produce a deafening and inchoate sound.[50] On the other, the enclosure creates an ambiance of sentimentality that transforms the occasion into an act of social memory, since one of the "young hopefuls" is from Oran and the other from Algiers.[51] Likened by the narrator to the rivalry between Pisa and Florence, the contestants become civic representatives of historical and political tension, re-enacting a 100-year-old conflict.[52] Furthermore, because witnessing the combat from the periphery of the arena does not provide sufficient catharsis, spontaneous fights occur among the public—"chairs are brandished, the police clear a path, excitement is at its height."[53] Yet gradually, after the climax of the first match, the second reinstalls sobriety, resynchronizing the audience with the ordinary tempo:

> The band of faithful is now no more than a group of black-and-white shadows disappearing into the night. For force and violence are solitary gods. They contribute nothing to memory. [. . .] These are rather difficult rites but ones that simplify everything. Good and evil, winner and loser. At Corinth two temples stood side by side, the temple of Violence and the temple of Necessity.[54]

In Oran, not being bored is an unusual condition, only achieved by those in the labyrinth who know how to find a space of exception. In between sparse moments of distraction, waiting emerges as the dominant disposition, perpetuating sameness by refusing creation and destruction as well as transcendence and transgression. Coherently, suggesting that their identity depends on absence rather than presence, the inhabitants defend boredom by remaining within the boundaries of the city, unwilling to realize that nothingness is as unfeasible as fullness—"like that friend of Flaubert who, on the point of death [. . .] exclaimed: 'Close the window; it's too beautiful.' They have closed the window, they have walled themselves in, they have cast out the landscape."[55]

Awaiting Oran

Although "The Minotaur" was written in 1939, it was not published until 1954, with an introductory note to dedicate the essay to Pierre Galindo, the alleged informant of the assassination narrated in *The Stranger*, and to briefly reconsider the portrayal of Oran.[56] Camus pledges that the city has changed since "all the imperfections have been (or will be) remedied."[57] At the onset of the Algerian war, the architecture of the city remained intact—"jealously respected"—satiating the space with boredom and thus propelling radical change, ending the period of waiting and entering a new reality independent from France.[58] Not supporting the separation but in favor of an increased political autonomy that envisioned communal wellbeing and cohabitation with the past, Camus liberates Oran from its distinctive lethargy. The transformed city is a site of possibility—beautiful, happy and truthful—no longer in need of taciturn writers but expecting lionizing tourists.[59]

Notes

1 According to Mandel, the failure of modernity in countries like Algeria is because "the mass population existed outside the realm of capitalist commodity production. The slow displacement of pre-capitalist relations of production led to the increasing immiseration of the indigenous population, which became willing to sell its labour-power at ever lower prices in order to be able to bear at least part of the ever more oppressive burden of ground-rent, usury and taxes." Ernest Mandel, *Late Capitalism* (London: Verso, 1978), 364.
2 Albert Camus, *The Plague*, trans. Stuart Gilbert (London: Penguin, 2001).
3 Albert Camus, *The Outsider*, trans. Joseph Laredo (London: Penguin, 1983), 26.
4 Ibid.
5 "They [Camus and friends] walked in the square near the cathedral and through the old Spanish town [of Oran] [. . .] they disliked the rich businessmen and were friendly with the small shopkeepers and the artisans." Patrick McCarthy, *Camus. A Critical Study of His Life and Work* (London: Hamish Hamilton, 1982), 36–37.
6 Albert Camus, "The Minotaur, or the Stop in Oran," in *The Myth of Sisyphus and Other Essays* (New York: Vintage Books, 1955), 130. Excerpts from *The Myth of Sisyphus* by Albert Camus (translated by Justin O'Brien, translation copyright (1955, copyright renewed 1983 by Penguin Random House LLC), are used by permission of Alfred A. Knopf, an imprint of the Knopf Doubleday Publishing Group, a division of Penguin Random House LLC. All rights reserved.
7 As explained in *The Myth of Sisyphus* (1942/1955).

8 McCarthy, *Camus*, 274. John Lambeth, "The Figure of the Labyrinth in 'Le Renégat' and 'La Pierre Qui Pousse,'" in *A Writer's Topography: Space and Place in the Life and Works of Albert Camus*, ed. Jason Herbeck and Vincent Grégoire (Leiden: Brill, 2015), 217.
9 Camus, "The Minotaur," 133.
10 Ibid., 121.
11 This resonates with the description of "The Labyrinth" (1936) by Bataille—"where what had suddenly come forward strangely loses its way." Georges Bataille, *Visions of Excess*, trans. Allan Stoekl, Carl Lovitt, and Donald Leslie (Minneapolis: University of Minnesota Press, 1985), 175.
12 Camus, "The Minotaur," 120.
13 Camus refers to Descartes—"Descartes, planning to meditate, chose his desert: the most mercantile city of his era." Ibid., 115–16, 119, 120.
14 Ibid., 121.
15 Ibid., 119.
16 Ibid., 120. In "Notes of a New Town" (1960), Lefebvre uses a similar analogy to describe "N," the city of pure boredom—"This community has shaped its shell, building and rebuilding it, modifying it again and again according to its needs. Look closely and within every house you will see the slow, mucoustrace of this animal which transforms the chalk in the soil around it into something delicate and structured: a family." Henri Lefebvre, *Introduction to Modernity* (London: Verso, 1995), 116.
17 Camus, "The Minotaur," 120.
18 Ibid., 130.
19 Ibid., 120.
20 Ibid., 121.
21 Ibid., 116.
22 Ibid.
23 Ibid., 121.
24 Jean-Jacques Jordi, "Juan Bastos," accessed on January 5, 2015, www.memoireafrique dunord.net/biog/biog11_Bastos.htm.
25 In the available digital records, only the last name Wolf appears as the architect of the building. Musée de l'Histoire vivante, "Maison Du Colon," accessed on January 5, 2015, www.museehistoirevivante.com/expovirtuelle/Algerie/ImgAlg/Chapitre3/Oran/pop MaisonDuColon20.htm.
26 Executed by Fernand Belmonte.
27 Musée de l'Histoire vivante, "Maison Du Colon."
28 Camus, "The Minotaur," 126. Philip Dine, "Shaping the Colonial Body," in *Algeria & France, 1800–2000: Identity, Memory, Nostalgia*, ed. Patricia Lorcin (Syracuse: Syracuse University Press, 2006), 41.
29 Camus, "The Minotaur," 126.
30 Ibid.
31 Ibid., 127.
32 In reference to the animals that lived in the area until its foundation in 902. "Histoire De La Ville D'oran," accessed on January 5, 2015, www.oran-dz.com/ville/histoire/.
33 Camus, "The Minotaur," 128.
34 Ibid.
35 Ibid., 129.
36 Ibid., 116.
37 McCarthy, *Camus*, 147.
38 As Heidegger explains in *The Fundamental Concepts of Metaphysics*, trans. William McNeill (Bloomington: Indiana University Press, 2001), 98. According to Morris, Camus must have been familiar with the philosophy of Heidegger. Christian Parreno, "Interview with Herbert Morris." October 8, 2014.
39 Camus, "The Minotaur," 147.
40 Ibid., 117.

41 Ibid., 118.
42 Ibid., 118, 120.
43 The first person of the essay surfaces in this moment—"a native having thrilled me with the firm promise that 'blood would flow,' I find myself that evening among the real enthusiasts." Ibid., 122, 130.
44 Dine, "Shaping the Colonial Body," 42.
45 The boxing presented by Camus is similar to the differentiation from wrestling posed by Barthes, almost two decades later. For the latter, "boxing is a Jansenist sport, based on a demonstration of excellence." Roland Barthes, *Mythologies* (London: Vintage Classics, 2000), 15.
46 Dine, "Shaping the Colonial Body," 41.
47 As Barthes points out—"the logical conclusion of the contest does not interest the wrestling-fan, while on the contrary a boxing-match always implies a science of the future." Barthes, *Mythologies*, 16.
48 Camus, "The Minotaur," 122.
49 At the time that Camus was writing, *fondouk* was "a derogatory term used by the pieds-noirs [people of European ancestry who lived in Algeria] to refer to a 'native' rabble." Dine, "Shaping the Colonial Body," 41.
50 Camus, "The Minotaur," 122.
51 Ibid.
52 Dine, "Shaping the Colonial Body," 42.
53 Camus, "The Minotaur," 124.
54 Ibid., 126.
55 Ibid., 129.
56 "When Camus was in Oran, one of his favourite companions was Pierre Galindo. Through him Camus learned of an incident on the beach at Bouisseville which took place in August 1939, when members of 'la bande Galindo' found themselves jostled by two Arabs and one of them was attacked with a knife." Douglas Johnson, "The First Man of France." *Prospect* (1996) www.prospectmagazine.co.uk/arts-and-books/thefirstmanoffrance.
57 Camus, "The Minotaur," 114. Camus visited Oran in 1942, after his departure from Algeria in 1940.
58 Ibid.
59 Ibid.

2

DISCOVERING "PARIS AND ITS FOLDS, PARIS AND ITS FACES"[1]

Angeliki Sioli

To the reader of Philippe Soupault's *Last Nights of Paris* (*Les Dernières nuits de Paris*, 1928) the title reveals already the place of the narrative's unfolding: the French capital. Moreover, it specifies when the events it ventures to present take place, the time of the narrative—the dark and mysterious night. As the author meticulously explains in the earliest pages of the story, it is that time when a hush descends over the city making its colors disappear; when our actions become hesitant and less decisive; and when the feeling that our decisions are less our own conscious choosing, but instead a reaction to the city's atmosphere and physical presence, is intensified.

Soupault, a founding member of the Surrealists,[2] is both the author of the book and narrator of the story. He specifically insists on calling the novel his "testimony,"[3] underlying the verisimilitude of the events he describes along with the fact that Paris is depicted without any fictional elaborations. Echoing the concepts of identity and chance already identified in Aragon's *Paris Peasant* (1924) and Breton's *Nadja* (1928),[4] he is in pursuit of a woman. Georgette, the obscure object of his desire, seems to possess a charm impossible to resist. She is a prostitute, a woman of the streets and the night, never returning home before the first crack of sunlight. Around her gravitate a number of petty criminals, professional vagabonds, and dark characters engaged in illegal activities: a gang. Soupault narrates how he spends his nights walking around the city in search of Georgette, or sometimes with Georgette, and how he interacts with the members of the gang at given moments.

The narrative is particularly compelling from an architectural perspective. During Soupault's nocturnal walks specific urban places, though familiar and encountered many times before, create new spatial experiences partaking of the city's prevalent emotional atmosphere. Metaphors in language, employed by the author to describe places and buildings, create architectural images that enrich our study of the city; they allow our emotional perception to inform our knowledge. This fact has an important bearing on our understanding of urban place because, as Nick Crossley argues in his study *The Social Body* (2001), emotions are not subjective entities sensed individually by each one of us; instead they are "out there in the world," and we partake of them.[5] Soupault's narrative in which "The rue de Medicis (. . .) is sad around ten-thirty at night,"[6] or as "she (. . .) reminded me (. . .) because of them the rue de Tournon was indiscreet,"[7] demonstrates this point.

As a result, during the winter of 1928 when the narrative of the *Last Nights of Paris* unfolds, Soupault is constantly affected and surprised by the way the city reveals itself in the cold winter darkness. To this end helps the fact that he already dwells in the city with the intentionality of being open to its mysteries: "I am not one of those who deny the truth of miracles and when I question myself, I am ready to affirm that it is upon them alone that I can count."[8] His peregrinations are wanderings for wonder, and as the scholar J.H. Matthews notes,

> deeply sensitive to the mystery around us, making each man's shadow revolve clockwise about him, Soupault expressed in his verses and prose a need to know more than our eyes can see and confidence that it is not beyond our capacities to do so.[9]

Under this light, the novel also discloses elements of Parisian urban space that remain unknown or untouched by the conventional architectural historiography.

Moreover, and as Rebecca Solnit in her work *Wanderlust, A History of Walking* (2000) notes, the Parisian night itself acquires for Soupault the status of a woman, while his love and sexual desire for Georgette are diffused into the city.[10] It is clear to the reader from the beginning that the urban space is described through the eyes of a man in love, through eyes full of desire. Writing on *Eros, the Bittersweet* (1986), Anne Carson argues that

> there is something uniquely convincing about the perceptions that occur to you when you are in love. They seem truer than other perceptions, and more truly your own, won from reality at personal cost. (. . .) Your powers of imagination connive at this vision, calling up possibilities from beyond the actual.[11]

Soupault himself will confirm that conviction almost at the very beginning of the narrative, in the most lyric way: "That night, as we were pursuing or, more exactly, tracking Georgette, I saw Paris for the first time. It was surely not the same city."[12] In this paper we too will see "Paris for the first time" following Soupault in two of the numerous walks he undertakes in the city: one in which he follows Georgette, and one in which he is searching for her, worried that she might have disappeared.

The Flashing Glacier; Following Georgette

Soupault's initial encounters with Georgette are not consummated with the physical fulfilment of his erotic desire. A distance is drawn between them, as other men seem to be after her as well. This distance is drawn even more sharply as, one of the first times he meets her, it is for the sake of another man. Soupault's friend Jacques, without knowledge of Soupault's sentiments toward Georgette, confesses he is in love with a woman, which Soupault only later realizes is Georgette herself. Before this realization, he has already suggested helping Jacques find her. This is how he ends up following Georgette with Jacques at his side. Instead of feeling jealous though, this distance between the two—along with the presence of a third person in the scene—amplifies his desire. This metaphorical space between Soupault and his beloved keeps his desire alive and further motivates the author to find ways to get closer to her. This is probably why, for the first time, Soupault imagines an appropriation of public space imbued with a similar attitude:

> The avenue de l'Opéra was no longer the stream that I had always followed, nor the highway that one usually pictures. It was a great shadow flashing like a glacier, which one must first conquer, and then embrace as one would a woman.[13]

A place of great familiarity, used casually many times in the past, is transfigured. The avenue is not understood either as a continuous flow of people that imposes a rhythm of walking—"the stream that I had always followed"[14]—or as a major circulation artery to be rapidly passed through in order to reach some destination, a means to an end—"the highway that one usually pictures." The public space paradoxically does not appear easily accessible to the walker, as it should according to a functionalistic understanding of circulation-spaces. This is a realization of particular importance to the city, even perverse in a sense, if one takes into consideration that the first architectural treatise to ever conceptualize public streets and roads purely as spaces of circulation—emphasizing issues of practicality and transportation—was written by the French architect Pierre Patte in the eighteenth century,[15] and dealt with the streets of the French capital itself, a work that actually prefigured Haussmann's urban interventions. The avenue de l'Opéra was constructed during that exact time, an important thoroughfare of the city's traffic scheme linking the Louvre with the Opera and providing better access to the wealthy neighborhoods being developed then in northwest Paris.[16] Diametrically opposed to this, Soupault's approach perceives the avenue as a place difficult to fully access, that requires the same trial and tenderness needed in the approach to a woman—"one must first conquer, and then embrace as one would a woman"—to establish a fully embodied relationship with it. A kind of respect for public space is aroused, in the same way that Soupault always respected Georgette despite her being a public woman: a prostitute.[17] Public space becomes personal and intimate, and despite its grandiose dimensions and impressive presence—"flashing like a glacier"—is experienced at the scale of the inhabitant's body; an experience bearing similarities with the bodily pleasure of an erotic encounter.

This quality of place emerging from the city's public spaces, as captured in the narrative, is definitely not of an intellectual order. It is not merely a "formal" question of proportional relationships (as would be for example the mathematical dimensions of the space of the avenue; its width, length or number of trees on each sidewalk)—or abstract aesthetic values. It rather originates in the erotic impulse itself, in Soupault's need to quench his physical thirst; "the existential condition to which humanity can only be reconciled within the realm of *poiesis* (the making of culture, i.e., art and architecture) and its metaphoric imagination," as Alberto Pérez-Gómez would argue.[18] As philisopher Jean-Luc Marion further explains

> in love I put myself on stage and implicate myself, because in loving I make a decision about myself like nowhere else. Each act of love is inscribed forever in me and outlines me definitively. I do not love by proxy, nor through a go-between, but in flesh, and this flesh is one only with me.[19]

Public space, as a woman, is appropriated and loved in flesh; it becomes an extension of Soupault's own body and negates any functionalistic or prosaic use.

The Whimsical Park; Looking For Georgette

Shortly before the narrative's end Georgette disappears. None of the members of the gang seem to have the slightest idea about her whereabouts, and they all conceive a plan to patrol the city in order to find her. Their aim is not only to walk through the areas where she usually plied her trade, but for each one of them to watch a certain section of Paris, covering in that way the whole city. Although totally unrelated to Georgette's usual itinerary, Soupault is assigned the area of Parc Monceau, an English garden built in the late eighteenth century in the north of Paris, particularly unique compared to the majority of the traditional French-style gardens that are found in the city. For Soupault, the foreign character of the area is immediately a strong indicator that a woman who is Paris herself would never choose the place to hide. His despair anticipates the darkness of his space-perception:

> All is gray in this park: the lake is of aluminum, the paths are sanded with dust, the trees covered with verdigris. (. . .)
> I walked about this whimsicality enclosed in a railing and grasped the shadows of hopes as they flitted by. (. . .) Georgette could not and would not have frequented these streets, this park, these boulevards, cold country of boredom.[20]

The original design of the park, conceived by the eighteenth-century painter and writer Louis Carrogis Carmontelle, could be argued to share some similarities with the premises of the Surrealists. Carmontelle's intention was to create a place where the visitor would encounter unexpected surprises. He didn't find it necessary to design gardens with the objective of achieving an agreeable form. Instead he thought it was necessary to preserve the charm that one encounters entering the garden, and to renew this charm with each step, so that the visitor in his soul will have the desire to revisit the garden every day.[21] Although the park was significantly altered over the years, and by 1928 was only half its original size and had lost many of its *follies*, elements of its original design intentions were still present. Nevertheless, Soupault doesn't seem to perceive the park in any unexpected or charmingly surprising way. Everything is delineated as dull and nondescript, colored in a hue of ashes—"all is grey in this park." The lake with its archaic colonnade is similarly described as light silvery metal—"aluminum." The dark and rigid spatial impression is further enriched by a feeling of aging: a sense that the place is old, rusty and disused—"the paths are sanded with dust, the trees covered with verdigris"— influenced most probably by the reconstructions of buildings from different eras interspersed in the park, like its Roman colonnade unfolding by the lake and the miniature Egyptian pyramid. And beyond these markers of time's passage, even the prostitutes in this park seem to maintain habits and employ techniques of a past era, as Soupault notices.

For the author the whole place seems to behave capriciously—"I walked about this whimsicality enclosed in a railing"—and he seems to feel his hope of finding Georgette slip away from him with every step. The experience of walking through this place for a few minutes has convinced him without question that Georgette would never have frequented this uninteresting and dull environment—"cold country of boredom."

Conclusion

Following Soupault on his peregrinations is almost like being in love with the city ourselves, assessing dimension and understanding proportion through a surrealist perspective that defines the term *straight horizontal* (a term one would imagine as emblematic of reason on a number of levels) as follows: "Straight horizontal: If a thread one meter long falls from a height of one meter straight on to a horizontal plane twisting *as it pleases* and creates a new image of the unit of length." [22]

The novel educates architects and urban planners on many different levels. On a first level, it informs us about elements that usually remain unnoticed and escape conventional historiography, though particularly relevant to our envisioning of the possible future of our designs. Territories of prostitution or illegal activities seem to define aspects of the city's nocturnal side, contrary to the visions of urban planning. The environs of the avenue de l'Opéra, for the construction of which a broad area of slums and poor neighborhoods with narrow and dangerous streets was demolished in the eighteenth century, still retain some of their original character, as the streets around it are still populated during the night by the city's prostitutes. The old habits of the city seem to take over with the setting of the sun. It is particularly interesting that only a few years before Soupault's story, two well-known and large *maisons de tolerance* actually opened their doors in the area, Hotel de Marigny in 1917 near the Garnier Opera building and Un Deux Deux in the mid-1920s, on 122 rue de Provence, behind the Opera.[23] These are instances of a deep resistance on the part of the city to the elimination, by planners and architects, of its most idiosyncratic and expressive places. The sadly diminished Parc Monceau is another such lost place. Expressing the sadness of the park, the novel also allows us to speculate how it has been appropriated; or what its status in people's consciousness back then might have been. Its many changes, which had significantly altered its original design, seem to have resulted in an atmosphere of misery and boredom, one that does not engage with the atmosphere of the city around it.

On a second level, through the sharing of imaginative linguistic metaphors the novel creates for us a necessary distance to see "Paris for the first time." In *The Rule of Metaphor* (1975), taking up Aristotle's definition of a good metaphor in the *Poetics*, Paul Ricoeur points that a good metaphor does not reveal the similarity between already similar ideas, but between semantic fields hitherto considered dissimilar.[24] He claims that imagination is precisely this power of metaphorically reconciling opposing meanings, forging an unprecedented semantic pertinence from an old semantic impertinence.[25] Avenue de l'Opéra's great shadow flashing like a glacier, or Parc Monceau's lake of aluminum, are only two of the metaphors encountered in the novels which forged, to use Ricoeur's vocabulary, an unprecedented semantic pertinence from architectural and urban images—thus enriching our very architectural imagination. They are metaphors that allow us to see architectural and urban elements as something unexpectedly different, producing for us new possible meanings and thus encouraging design decisions and architectural actions that can bring these meanings to life. The innovative power of linguistic imagination should not be seen as some "decorative excess of effusion or subjectivity," rather it is "the capacity of language to open up new worlds."[26] As Heidegger well points out, poetic speaking is not a conveying of pure interiority but a sharing of world. As a disclosure not of the speaker but of the being of the world, it is neither a subjective nor an objective phenomenon but both together, for word is prior to and encompasses both.[27] Reading Soupault's *Last Nights in Paris*, we partake of these possible shared worlds of public space. Through these metaphors we see our own field of study, the city, "for the first time." Literary writing creates for us a distance with the city that, like being in love, offers us a new and precious understanding.

Notes

1 Philippe Soupault, *Last Nights of Paris*, trans. William Carlos Williams (Cambridge, Mass.: Exact Change, 1992), 103.
2 Philippe Soupault (1897–1990) surrealist poet, novelist and journalist, co-wrote with André Breton the first self-proclaimed book of automatic writing, *Les Champs Magnétiques* (1919); a collaboration that coined the very term *surrealism*, as Breton explained in the First Surrealist Manifesto published in 1924. (A. Breton, "First Surrealist Manifesto," in *Surrealism*, ed. Patrick Waldberg (London: Thames and Hudson, 1965). Along with Breton and Luis Aragon, he was editor of the journal *Littérature* (1919–1923).
3 Soupault, *Last Nights of Paris*, 178. This assessment was also in line with the surrealist pursuit to overcome traditional literary forms: the novel was generally a genre not held in high esteem by the group.

4 Sylvie Cassayre, *La poétique de l' Espace et Imagination dans l'Ouvre de Philippe Soupault*, (Paris: Lettres Modernes, 1997), 14.
5 Nick Crossley discussing on Gilbert Ryle's *The Concept of Mind* (1949) and its contribution to a non-dualistic sociology. Nick Crossley, *The Social Body, Habit, Identity and Desire* (London; Thousand Oaks, CA: SAGE, 2001), 43.
6 Soupault, *Last Nights of Paris*, 3.
7 Ibid., 4.
8 Ibid., 37.
9 Pontus Hulten, ed., *The Surrealists Look at Art, Eluard, Aragon, Soupault, Breton, Tzara*, trans. Michael Palmer and Norma Coles (Venice; Calif.: Lapis Press, 1990), 81.
10 Rebecca Solnit, "Paris or Botanizing in the Asphalt," in *Wanderlust, A History of Walking* (New York, N.Y: Penguin Boks, 2000), 208–209.
11 Anne Carson, *Eros the Bittersweet, An Essay* (Princeton, N.J.: Princeton University Press, 1986), 36.
12 Soupault, *Last Nights of Paris*, 46.
13 Ibid.
14 Words and short sentences from the novel that are not followed by an endnote are always part of the more extensive excerpt that I have introduced previously.
15 Pierre Patte (1723–1814) was a student of Jacques-Francois Blondel. In his works *Mémoires sur les objets les plus importans de l'architecture* (1769) and *Mémoires qui intéressent particulièrement Paris* (1800) he proposed the construction of rectilinear long roads that would traverse through the old neighborhoods of the city.
16 Andrew Ayers, *The Architecture of Paris* (Stuttgart; London: Edition Axel Menges, 2004), 176. The construction of the avenue de l'Opéra led to the demolition of a poor district between the Louvre and the big Boulevards with numerous narrow streets, which were considered unhealthy and dangerous. (Ibid.).
17 Soupault actually admits that thanks to Georgette "who was no more than one of the hundred thousands, the Parisian night became a mysterious domain, a great and marvelous country, full of flowers, of birds, of glances and of stars, a hope launched into space." (Soupault, *Last Nights of Paris*, 45–46.)
18 Alberto Pérez-Gómez, *Polyphilo or the Dark Forest Revisited, An Erotic Epiphany of Architecture* (Cambridge, MA: MIT Press, 1994), xv.
19 Jean-Luc Marion, *The Erotic Phenomenon*, trans. Stephen E. Lewis (Chicago, Ill: The University of Chicago Press, 2007), 9.
20 Soupault, *Last Nights of Paris*, 161.
21 Dominique Jarrassé, *Grammaire des Jardin Pairisiens* (Paris: Parigramme, 2007), 77.
22 Marcel Duchamp, *The Writings of Marcel Duchamp*, ed., Michel Sanouillet and Elmer Peterson (New York, N.Y.: DaCapo Press, 2010), 33.
23 "Prostitution in France," Wikipedia, The Free Encyclopedia, accessed February 19, 2017, https://en.wikipedia.org/wiki/Prostitution_in_France
24 Ricoeur, Paul. *The Rule of Metaphor, Multi-disciplinary Studies of the Creation of Meaning in Language*, trans. Robert Czerny (Toronto: University of Toronto Press, 1981), 11.
25 Richard Kearney, "Paul Ricoeur and the Hermeneutic Imagination," in *The Narrative Path, The Later Works of Paul Ricoeur*, ed. T. Peter Kemp David Rasmussen (Cambridge, Mass.: MIT Press, 1989), 4.
26 Ibid., 5.
27 As quoted in Richard E. Palmer, *Hermeneutics, Interpretation Theory in Schleiermacher, Dilthey, Heidegger, and Gadamer* (Evanston, IL: Northwestern University Press, 1969), 139. Individual subjectivity is from the outset *intersubjectivity*, as a result of the communally shared, conventions, symbolic artifacts and cultural traditions in which an individual is already embedded. (Ibid.).

3

TRACES OF KRISTIANIA

A Topographical Reading of Knut Hamsun's *Hunger*

Mathilde Simonsen Dahl

In an early scene in Knut Hamsun's novel *Hunger* (1890) the nameless protagonist and restless wanderer sits on a bench at a peaceful, panoramic spot in Slottsparken (the Royal Palace Park) to write a piece for the newspaper *Morgenbladet* for a shilling and a meal. Below him lies Kristiania's one and only boulevard, a central space in the novel and in the city, Karl Johansgate. Adjacent is the Students' Promenade park, encircled by the University, the Parliament and the Tivoli garden.[1] In his solitude and agonized from hunger, he is unable to gather his thoughts. Recent impressions from his traverse across Karl Johansgate echo in his disintegrated mind.

> I couldn't sit down on a bench by myself or set foot anywhere without being attacked by small trivial incidents, miserable trifles that forced their way among my ideas and scattered my powers to the four winds. A dog streaking past, a yellow rose in a gentleman's buttonhole, could start my thoughts vibrating and occupy me for a long time.[2]

All at once a distinct clarinet tone reaches him from below. It is the two o'clock concert commencing the so-called promenade hour, gathering the bourgeoisie to stroll in the park. Born up by the wind, the affect of the clarinet tone—"I could think the clearest thoughts without restrain"—resonates in his mind and gives his thoughts "a fresh impetus."[3] He begins examining his shoes and the twitching motion at the beat of his pulse in his feet, a delicate, mysterious thrill spreads through his nerves. "When I looked at my shoes, it was as though I had met a good friend or got back a torn-off part of me: a feeling of recognition trembles through all my senses, tears spring to my eyes, and I perceive my shoes as a softly murmuring tune coming toward me."[4]

This scene emblematically captures how the psychological impact of hunger orchestrates an osmotic interrelation of the protagonist and his surroundings. By means of dissociation to and hypersensitive interception, the protagonist's desultory mind forms an optic by which the urban landscape renders visible. By hints and reflections, we sense bygone social routines and urban sceneries: The anti-heroes slippery subjectivity blending with images and sounds of the philandering in the Students promenade, documenting at the same time how the parks merged across the topography before the vegetation was cut and the Palace park was reduced to give space for a straighter curvature of the street below (1896), the Studenterlunden gave way for the National Theater (1899) and the Tivoli was demolished (1936). These observations prompt an embodied perception of the protagonist city in which

FIGURE 3.1 Map of Kristiania, 1 St. Olavsgate, 2 Abelhaugen, Palace Park, 3 Studenterlunden/Students Promenade, 4 Tivoli, 5 Stortinget/ The Parliament, 6 Hammersborg, 7 Vaterland, 8 Stortorvet, Cathedral, Bazars, 9 Bogstad forest, 10 Akershus/Castle, Prlieutnt. Solem, *Kart over Kristiania*, 1881.

Courtesy of Norwegian National Library

the narrative unfolds, from which the following questions raise: how can we trace this specific urban landscape through the ways it is reflected in the protagonist's hypersensitive mind? And in what ways may his restless walks throughout this urban topography unveil the historic spatiality in the Norwegian capital in rapid transformation?

> It was in those days when I wandered about hungry in Kristiania, that strange city which no one leaves before it has set its mark upon him . . .[5]

Hunger takes place in Kristiania between 1880–1890, at the time the fastest growing European city of its size before the stock market collapsed in 1899.[6] Only decades before, the only since 1814 Norwegian Capital still appeared as a small town within the Renaissance quadrature, as it had been laid out in 1624 by the Danish King Christian IV to be flanked by the mediaeval castle at a central ridge in the larger amphitheater-shaped valley.[7] Throughout the latter part of the nineteenth century, however, the urban territory expanded to include the working-class suburbs in connection to the industries along the river Akerselva and to the east. To the west, behind the Palace at the Bellevue hill, new residential areas for the bourgeoisie were built on the former city commons, still stretching upwards as open fields to the encircling forests. The lower plateau between the central ridge and the Palace was until 1862 flooded by Bisletbekken, a smaller river stream and sewage outlet, transformed from wild vegetation and swampy crop fields into a monumental panorama of a new civic society.[8] In the bay where the now piped Bisletbekken mouthed the fjord, the city's oldest slum and municipally regulated prostitution district Vika encircled the Tivoli garden. Later, this entire area was to be demolished as part of the twentieth-century dialectics of downtown reshaping and the municipal social housing projects in the upper hill outskirts.

During his aimless walks, the protagonist immerses himself into this topographically and socially layered landscape, before his departure out toward the fjord. "It had been going steadily downhill for me all along" the hero states in the opening before descending into the city.[9] In parallel, seasons shift from clear, warm autumn days to lethal, bitter cold winter. Hallucinating, desperate and furious he is lead through the streets, and a meteorologically portrayed landscape:

> The sun was warm by now, it was ten o clock and the traffic at Yongstorvet Square was in full swing. Where was I to go? (. . .) the sky flowed like a lovely ocean along the Lier mountain [. . .] Without knowing it, I was on my way home.[10]

Canonized as an urban, modernist novel, the ways in which the city takes on agency through the topographical and climatic framework as well as the metaphorical connotations of the spatial descriptions have been closely examined.[11] In these readings, the city has become intimately entangled with the persons the protagonist encounters. Thus the ways he continuously refuses or fails to establish relationships with them have been seen as an expression of how places "de-individualize," dissolve into nothing, letting the city become a dreamlike substance, a labyrinth in which the modern subject is imprisoned.[12] "Spatial proximity rather than plot is the main driver in the narrative," according to Tone Selboe, who asserts that the city represents a melodramatic backdrop oscillating between real and imaginary, to which the protagonist takes a distance in order to establish a sense of integrity and individuality.[13] In her reading, the protagonist's restless walks depict the streets as non-places against which the hero fights to liberate himself from.[14] Hamsun himself insisted in a letter to his friend and publisher Georg Brandes in Copenhagen that *Hunger* was not to be read as a novel. It was a "book" of "the sensitive human soul's delicate oscillations, the peculiar, strange life of the mind, the mysteries of the nerves in a starved body."[15] Commenting on Hamsun's reluctance to accept the novel as a genre for *Hunger*, Selboe—evoking a fundamental structuralist figure of thought—asserts that the protagonist's wandering detaches the places (*parole*) from the geographically traceable structure of the city (*langue*).[16] In dialogue with such perspectives, I propose to map the walks that unfold in order to reveal the factual city as mirrored in the protagonist's perception. The ways the urban spaces reflect and contrast in his fluctuating, nervous mind, unveil how the city's topographical characteristics play into the history of urban transformation. Thus, documenting his itineraries—traceable at times only through vague thematic and verbal hints—the history of the places is activated and questioned, distorted and reinvented.

Hammersborg—Vaterland

> From where I stood I had a view of a clothesline and an open field; in the distance was a forge, left over from a burned-down blacksmith's shop where some workers were busy cleaning up. I leaned forward with my elbows on the windowsill and gazed at the sky. [. . .] Autumn had arrived, that lovely cool time of the year when everything turns colour and dies. The streets had already begun to get noisy, tempting me to go out.[17]

The narrative commences indoors in his rented attic room. Sounds of the city seep through the walls, the wind makes long tears in the cut-outs of *Morgenbladet* papered on the wall.[18] The city invades the interior, it becomes exteriorized, Selboe observes.[19] It is only later into the novel that the siting of this room is given away, when the protagonist recognizes one of the shops on the street from the advertisements on the wall, and longs back to Hammerborg.[20] Leaving his room, he follows a street toward the cathedral.

> A strange mood, a feeling of cheerful nonchalance, had taken possession of me. I (. . .) caught a glance cast my way from a passing streetcar, and laid myself open to every trifle—all the little fortuitous things that crossed my path and disappeared.[21]

The mentioning of a streetcar indicates that he walks down Storgata, with Hammerborg above to the right, and to his left the lowest plateau Vaterland. His stroll draws out the subtle differences in the levels of the old city center at the ridge. The accentuated contrast between the open view in his room and the busy city below documents Hammerborg as a hill at the top of the central ridge, as it more palpably was before the area below was leveled out by the Government quarter development in the 1950s.

Central themes linked to the protagonist's physical survival are sited along the east slope of the central ridge: *Morgenbladet*'s editorial office was in Øvre Vollgate at the top. When he has nowhere else to go, he seeks sanctuary outside the cathedral at the middle, and food in the bazars (completed in the late 1850s), encircling the cathedral and built into the natural step in the landscape. Directly below the bazar, in the 1960s demolished Vaterland slum lays where Akerselva mouths the fjord; his whereabouts at the end of the novel.[22]

In what Kittang sees as a novel within the novel the plateau on the west side of the ridge is portrayed as the protagonist partly chases, partly dreams of the novel's main object of desire; a girl he names "with a nervous, gliding sound: Ylajali."[23] In the following sections I will look at how the features of this bygone rural field and wetland render visible in parallel with particular social rituals encapsulated in the topography along the direction of the water stream Bisletbekken, now weaved into the urban fabric.

Karl Johansgate

> Gradually I began to have an odd sensation of being far away, in some other place; I vaguely felt that it wasn't I who was walking there on the flagstones.

Walking down the Palace hill the hero passes two ladies. He brushes by the sleeve of one of them. Their eyes meet. Increasingly aroused by whom he names Ylajali, he chases her down the hill.[24] "All at once my thoughts, by a fanciful whim, take an odd direction—I'm seized by a strange desire to frighten this lady, to follow her and hurt her in some way."[25] With his back to Studenterlunden, he desperately seeks to draw her attention away from the shop windows at Karl Johansgate. "However estranged I was from myself at this moment, so completely at the mercy of invisible influences, nothing that was taking place around me escaped my perception."[26] He notices a big brown dog running past him "across the street, toward the Studenterlunden and down to the [Tivoli]."[27] The brief appearance of the dog becomes a vehicle for describing the view from Karl Johansgate toward the Tivoli through Studenterlunden below and between the until 1890 dense vegetation of trees and lilac bushes, marking a shift in direction perpendicular to the monumental axis. Strengthening the sense of this axis, however drawing in the opposite direction, Ylajali turns and leads him along Universitetsgaten, the old path of the river up to her home at St. Olavsplass number 2. Monumentally sited on a plateau above the lower field, this address is at a crossing point between St. Olav's street radiating from the palace, and Universitetsgaten. Universitetsgaten opens visual contact across Karl Johans street and Studenterlunden to the Tivoli entrance. As he stays outside, gazing up the façade, Ylajali appears in a window above. "We stand looking at each other straight in the face without moving; a minute goes by; thoughts dart back and forth between the window and the street."[28] Contact, almost intimacy, produced by distance as Selboe also observes allows the domestic and the urban space to merge, while overlooking the parade street.

As he walks down Universitetsgaten and reenters Karl Johansgate, his mood shifts to disgust and estrangement. "The sun was in the south, it was about twelve. The city was beginning to get on its feet; with strolling time approaching, bowing and laughing people were surging up and down Karl Johan Street."[29] The strolling hour marked the two hours when the bourgeoisie populated the class differentiated and socially coded parade street.[30] Women of honor were at other times not expected to be seen at the place, and female authors such as Camilla Collett wrote raging letters back to their home city from Paris of the liberty of the streets in the large metropolis. Hamsun's anti-hero however seeks the shadows cast by the University building to slip unseen away from some acquaintances who had taken position "to watch passers-by," and climbs the Palace hill to the bench in the park in a state of discontent and misery: "How lightly and merrily they bobbed their bright faces, dancing their way through life as though it were a ballroom!"[31] In this walk from plateau to plateau, the daily bourgeoisie routine "the strolling hour" is framed by the topography and by time of day, but contrasted by Ylajali's movements.

In a nocturnal scene Karl Johansgate is also crowded, and instead of hour of the day, the courting is disguised by the dark.

> The passion quivering in every movement of the passersby, the dim light of the street lamps, the tranquil, pregnant night. . . . people were strolling about everywhere, a jumble of quiet couples and noisy groups. The great moment had arrived, the mating hour when the secret traffic takes place and the jolly adventures begin. (. . .) The entire street was a swamp, with hot vapors rising from it.[32]

When characterizing the monumental Karl Johansgate as a swamp, the hero evokes a prism of urban histories pertaining to the site. Across the valley, the river Bisletbekken had been a popular place for youngsters to meet and walk under the willow trees and the swarming birdlife.[33] Before the city expanded to the west, this swampy crop field was still considered to be a long walk from the city's cramped insides. When palace architect Hans Ditlev Frantz Linstow in 1838 proposed a baroque plan with a parade street connecting the city and the Palace, he overrode the topography with a parade street with urban façades running on both sides in order to enclose the Palace in a "beautiful urban quarter."[34] This plan was however not realized. Instead Studenterlunden was kept as a wildly vegetated park, the

Parliament sited in 1866 in connection to the old city at the ridge top, facing the Palace.[35] Architect Heinrich Ernst Schirmer argued in the 1870s strongly for realizing Linstow's plan with the National Gallery in Studenterlunden, and characterized the promenade street as a swam; a disgrace as entrance to the Palace.[36] (According to Edvard Bull, in 1917 the stench from the Bisletbekken sewage still rose from below the ground at the middle of Karl Johansgate.[37]) In *Hunger* we sense reminiscences of the city's remolded agrarian land and wilderness, the monumental buildings still appearing as pavilions in the fields. The promenade is portrayed not by its potential architectural monumentality, but as a space of appearance orchestrated and regulated by the topography, set time of the day, light and dark.[38]

Tivoli, Vika

> It was the animal with all its peculiar awesomeness and peculiar wildness there was something special about. Those stealthy, noiseless steps in the dead of night, the soughing and eeriness of the forest, the screeching of a bird flying past, the wind, the smell of blood, the rumble from space—in short, the spirit of the wild in the wild beast . . .[39]

Being a scene for spectacles, the Tivoli garden in Kristiania developed from a park with small pavilions and cafés, into a larger leisure complex after the successful staging of a play of Jules Verne's *Around the World in 80 Days* in 1877. A so-called arcade building made since 1889 the entrance from Studenterlunden. The institutionalized shame and bourgeoisie double standard of the prostitution in this district was brought to light by the works of artists such as Christan Krogh and Hans Jæger in the 1880s and 90s, and not least increasing publications by female authors and essayists debating shedding light on the living conditions in the slum, leading to the end of the regulated prostitution in Vika in 1889.[40] The protagonist in *Hunger* however never sets foot in Tivoli. Rather he avoids it. In a nocturnal scene he walks across Karl Johansgate with Ylajali. Contrary to the customs, she has looked him up under the gas light in the dark. As they walk, she changes, Kittang finds, from a phantasmagoria character to a woman with desires and opinions of her own. (Later, she will invite him home, to her couch, and reject him.) "Over by [Tivoli] is a long row of bright colored lamps."[41] "Have you seen the menagerie?" he asks, "What is there to see?" she replies.[42] Aroused he agrees: "I wasn't interested in seeing animals in cages. These animals know that you are watching them; they feel those hundreds of curious eyes and are affected by them."[43] As if the coloured lamplight threatened to disclose his true misery, "that light, among so many people!" he confesses to her in the dark, empty street: "You shouldn't really be walking here with me, miss. I compromise you in the eyes of everybody."[44]

The menagerie, as Lewis Mumford states, was a direct expression of urban celebration of tamed nature.[45] The limits, however, of imposed order on nature is embodied, according to Richard Lehan in the character Dionysos, as beast and stranger, appears in many disguises "– among them the masked participant at the carnival or the masquerade, the mysterious stranger, and the man in the crowd."[46] As we shall see in the following scene, his mocking of the tamed beasts connect, from his springing associations, ties the civic institutions spatially across the open wilderness between them, as if unveiling the nature of untamed lusts in the park, masked by the urban monumentality.

At the Parliament, near the first lion, I suddenly remember, through a fresh association of ideas, a painter I knew, a young person I had once saved from getting slapped [at Tivoli].[47]

Tiered of spending the night on a bench by the cathedral and Brannvakten, the protagonist wanders up Karl Johansgate to the Parliament, where he halts.

Rather than following the boulevard, the stone lion at the Parliament entrance abruptly makes him recall a memory from Tivoli, visible at this point diagonally across the Studenterlunden. He heads to his friend the painter at his apartment in Tordenskioldsgate in Vika. This street follows the lowest stretch of Bisletbekken, before it enters the Pipervika bay. Yet, the painter rejects him, having "a little girl" visiting.[48] The hero finds himself back on the street and decides to sleep outdoors. "If only the ground hadn t been so damp!"[49] He turns, crosses Studenterlunden, catches a glimpse at the clock at the University building, passes the Palace, and walks "without a thought in his head" way beyond the city to the forest Bogstadskogen, the highest topographical level in the novel, and the profile

FIGURE 3.2 View to the castle from the Parliament across Studenterlunden, Axel Lindahl, *Det Kongelige Slot fra Stortingsbygningen*, Karl Johansgate (Oslo, Norway), 1870–80.

Courtesy of Oslo Museum

of the iconic far backdrop of the anxiety stricken figure in Edvard Munch's painting The Scream of 1893. This dismissal of the city to the forest stands in a binate relation to his final departure at the lowest point, the fjord. While spending the night in the forest in restless anxiety below the treetops and stars hearing "the owls of canaan hooting." At the end of the novel he finds himself stagnated in the Vaterland slum, living from the hand of a landlady forced to prostitution while her father and husband watch on. A sentence from his own writing echoes in his mind: ". . . so too, my own consciousness bids me," and he leaves the city.

Departure

> There was no end to my degradation. . . . I was sinking, sinking, everywhere I turned, sinking to my knees, to my middle, going down in infamy never to come up again, never![50]

The ever walking, nervous and hallucinating protagonist in Hunger portrays Kristiania through the optics of his shifting perceptions and moves, by foot and by thought. Its physical appearance, such as the contrast of the vast view from his attic room and the busy street are perhaps exaggerated in his hallucinatory mind, and descriptions such as "the street was a swamp" linger between metaphor and the tangible. As I have argued however, the novel portrays the city in a particular state when nature, agrarian land and urban fabric overlapped and the topography was about to be remolded, flattened out and veiled into the new urban built landscape. In the still small town-like city, the public spaces provide with no anonymity for the individual to seek shelter, instead they orchestrate a rhythm of shifting sceneries ordering individuals by gender, class and social position throughout the day. The starving, physically dissolved and psychologically shattered protagonist's movements and flux between the beastly, wild and (at least nearly) sensible, expose, ridicule and contest the city as a masquerade of bourgeoisie oppressive morals. His wanderings point out sites and unveil historical connections between them along a socially and temporal coded topography, concealed by coming regulation and redevelopment, that however the cityscape is still marked by.

Notes

1. The city was named Christiania after Danish King Christian IV in 1624, and renamed by its mediaeval name Oslo in 1924. Around the turn of the twentieth century, the official spelling was "Kristiania" with a K.
2. Knut Hamsun, *Hunger*, Trans. Sverre Lyngstad (Edinburgh: Rebel, 1996), 15.
3. Ibid., 15.
4. Ibid., 18.
5. Ibid., 1.
6. Jan Eivind Myhre, *Hovedstaden Christiania: Fra 1814 til 1900* (Oslo: Cappelen, 1990), 386.
7. Knut Hamsun wrote the novel from Chicago and Copenhagen in the 1880s, between his two visits in Kristiania in 1881 and 1889. For studies of autobiographical correlations

between the protagonist and Hamsun, see i.e. Lars Frode Larsen, *Den unge Hamsun (1859–1888)*, (Oslo: Schibsted, 1998) and Peter Sjølyst-Jackson, " Kristiania, that strange city : Location and Dislocation in Knut Hamsun's Hunger, in ed. Joan Fitzpatrick, *The Idea of the City: Early-Modern, Modern and Post-Modern Locations and Communities* (Newcastle: Cambridge Scholars, 2009), 45.
8 Bård Alsvik, "Lyden av Bisletbekken," *Tobias* 2+3 (2007), 60–5.
9 Hamsun, *Hunger*, 2.
10 Ibid., 65. The English translation erratically inserts a full break before the last sentence.
11 For an elaboration on how central themes is woven into the opening section, see Atle Kittang's classic *Luft, vind, ingenting: Hamsuns desillusjonsromanar frå Sult til Ringen sluttet"* (Oslo: Gyldendal, 1984). Tone Selboe emphasizes the topographical frame in regards of home and homelessness in Selboe, "Hungry and Alone: The Topography of Everyday Life in Knut Hamsun and August Strindberg." in ed. Lieven Ameel et al. *Literature and the Peripheral City* (Palgrave Macmillan), 2015.
12 Einar Eggen finds the protagonist's specifications of time and places along his walk paradoxical in regards of his confused state of mind, and questions the realism in the city descriptions. Einar Eggen, "Mennesket og tingene. Hamsuns Sult og den Nye Roman," in *Søkelys på Knut Hamsuns 90-årsdiktning* (Oslo: Universitetsforlaget, 1979). The reading of the city as a labyrinth in which the protagonist is imprisoned is further repeated by Katarzyna Tunkiel, "Om å vandre i Kristiania og Oslo. Byen i Knut Hamsuns' 'Sult' (1890) og Jan Kjærstads' 'Rand' (1990)," *Katedra Skandynawistyki UAM* (2010).
13 Selboe, "Hungry and Alone," 140.
14 Ibid., 133.
15 Translated by Mark Sandberg, "Writing on the Wall: The Language of Advertising in Knut Hamsun's Sult," in *Scandinavian Studies 3* 71 (fall 1999), 267. See also Harald Næss ed., *Knut Hamsuns brev 1879–1895* (Oslo: Gyldendal, 1994).
16 Selboe, "Byens betydning i *Sult*," in eds. E. Artntzen et al. *Hamsun i Tromsø II, Rapport fra den 2. internasjonale Hamsun-konferansen* (Tromsø: Hamsun-Selskapet, 1999), 150.
17 Hamsun, *Hunger*, 4.
18 For a study on the agencies of newspapers and advertisements in *Hunger*, see Sandberg, "Writing on the Wall," 265–92.
19 Selboe, "Hungry and Alone," 131.
20 Hamsun, *Hunger*, 120.
21 Ibid., 5.
22 The horse-driven tramcar through Storgata to Ringnes brewery at Grünerløkka was established in 1878. Knut Are Tvedt, *Oslo Byleksion*, (Oslo: Kunnskapsforlaget, 2000), 442–44. The central dates in the history of tramlines in Kristania from 1878 and 1899 reflects the period of large and rapid extension of the population in the city.
23 Lars Frode Larsen argues that Ylajali is modeled on Ida Charlotte Clementine Wedel-Jarlsberg (b. 1855), daughter of a count and whose cousin lived in the second floor apartment at St. Olavs street. Larsen, *Den unge Hamsun*, 221–23.
24 Hamsun, *Hunger*, 12.
25 Ibid., 12.
26 Ibid.
27 Ibid.
28 Ibid., 13.
29 Ibid., 15.
30 Kari Telste, "Karl Johans gate anno 1900. Kjønn, rom og moralske grenser," in *Tidsskrift for Samfunnsforskning 3* 43 (2002), 361–80.
31 Hamsun, *Hunger*, 15.
32 Ibid., 96.
33 Bård Alsvik, "Lyden av Bisletbekken" *Tobias* 2+3 (2007), 60–5.
34 Linstow, H. D. F., *Forslag Angaaende En Forbindelse Mellem Kongeboligen og Christiania Bye* (Christiania: Johan Dahl, 1838).

35 The debates on the Parliament's siting and architectural competition is documented in Mari Hvattum, ed. *Debatten om Stortingsbygningen 1836–1866* (Oslo: Pax, 2016). See also Mari Hvattum, *Heinrich Ernst Schirmer: Kosmopolittenes Arkitekt* (Oslo: Pax, 2014), 168–89.
36 Mari Hvattum, *Heinrich Ernst Schirmer*, 198.
37 Edvard Bull, "Kristiania som undervisningsgjenstand," *St. Hallvard* (1917).
38 Hannah Arendt, *The Human Condition* (Chicago: The University of Chicago, 1958), 199.
39 Ibid., 109
40 Jan Eivind Myhre, *Hovedstaden Christiania*, 401.
41 Ibid., 108.
42 Ibid., 109.
43 Ibid.
44 Ibid.
45 Lewis Mumford, *The City in History. Its Origins, Its Transformations, and Its Prospects* (Harmondsworth, Middlesex, England: Penguin Books, 1961), 381.
46 Richard Lehan, *The City in Literature: An Intellectual and Cultural History* (London: University of California Press, 1998), 20.
47 Hamsun, *Hunger*, 36.
48 Ibid., 37.
49 Ibid.
50 Ibid., 107.

4

THE ARCHITECTURE OF *ANOTHER MAN'S ROOM*

Unveiling Stories of Seoul's Apartments

Yoonchun Jung

> The apartments and studios that your siblings live in all look the same to me. It's confusing which house is whose. How can everything be exactly the same? How do they all live in identical spaces like that? I think it would be fine if they lived in different-looking houses. Wouldn't it be nice to have a shed and an attic? Wouldn't it be nice to live in a house where the children have places to hide? You used to hide in the attic, away from your brothers, who wanted to send you on all sorts of errands. Now even in the countryside apartment buildings that look the same have sprouted up. Have you gone up on the roof of our house recently? You can see all the high-rise apartments in town from there. When you were growing up, our village didn't even have a bus route. It has to be worse in this busy city if it's like that even in the country. I just wish they didn't all look the same. They all look so identical that I can't figure out where to go. I can't find your brothers' homes or your sister's studio. That's my problem. In my eyes, all the entrances and doors look the same, but everyone manages to find their way home, even in the middle of the night. Even children.[1]

Seoul's Apartments in Narratives

One of the best-known contemporary South Korean novelists, Kyung-Sook Shin, narrates her novel *Please Look after Mom* (2011) in the voice of her main protagonist, the missing mother visiting Seoul from the countryside for the first time in her life. Seoul's apartments have captured the attention of Korean writers, not to mention architects, urbanists, and even foreign researchers,[2] since they first sprang up in the early 1960s to combat the housing shortage of the post Korean War era.

It is not difficult to find descriptions of apartments in Seoul's urban settings in South Korean short stories, novellas, and novels, regardless of their significance to the development of the storylines.

The ways these apartments are portrayed vary. In some cases, as in the above quote from *Please Look after Mom*, the uniformity of Seoul's apartments is highlighted, and plays an important role in creating an atmosphere in which the story plays out; it is very plausible for the mother to get lost in a city where every apartment looks the same. In other cases, they are simply used as scenic backdrops without being related to the narrative. For example, in Kang Han's *The Vegetarian* (2015), the main protagonist gradually transforms into a vegetative state while residing in her apartment; however there is no substantial connection between her living in an apartment and becoming a tree.

The common literary characteristic of Seoul's apartments portrayed in such stories is that they represent the qualities of Seoulian situations of life—especially anonymity, loneliness, and marginalized living conditions. This is the reality of city dwellers "who have become 'misfits' by their failure to adjust to the ceaselessly—and rapidly—shifting architectural and urban conditions and who, sometimes, have been pushed to the perimeter of the city, literally and metaphorically."[3] In the case of Kyung-ran Jo's *I Live in Bongcheon-dong* (2013), the native city dwellers are gradually being driven away from their homes through the proliferation of apartment redevelopments in the urban slums of Seoul.[4]

As a modern precedent for narratives on Seoulian apartment-dwelling, Inho Choe's *Another Man's Room* (1971) falls into the same category. As one of his earlier

FIGURE 4.1 Korea National Housing Corporation, Mapo Apartments, Seoul, South Korea, 1962.

Courtesy of National Archives of Korea

works, it portrays "alienation resulting from life in rapidly industrializing urban society,"[5] culminating with the solution of "abnormal escapism."[6] However what is compelling about this short story is its emphasis on architecture. As the poetic narrative unearths the hidden stories of the protagonist's life through his embodied perception of his apartment, the reader understands that these memories are embedded in the architecture itself.[7] In the end, this unique work provides us with different readings of, and an alternative entry to, Seoul's most dominant housing typology: the apartment.

Another Man's Room

Another Man's Room (1971) was published in a South Korean quarterly magazine for literature, "*Munhak Kwa Chisong* [*Literature and Intelligence*]," in 1971. The story begins with an exhausted man returning back to his apartment from a long day's work and discovering that his wife has gone out for a short trip, leaving only a short note. Unexpectedly abandoned, he feels the emptiness and unfamiliarity of his apartment as he moves from one room to another. Before long he begins to "explore" the apartment himself, and soon finds traces of his wife's activities in her cosmetic products left opened and scattered on the makeup-chest. During this process, he imagines his wife's naked body by "investigating" her personal belongings.

After feeling a sudden searing heat from the brightness of the light in the living room, he decides to take a quick shower in the bathroom, where things suddenly start looking different from before. He feels someone else's presence behind him while examining his face in the bathroom mirror after the shower. As soon as he comes back to the living room, his naked body still wet, he senses the apartment beginning to transform spatially; this accelerates when the light is turned off. As time progresses, he even feels that the walls move and the physical gap between the space and his body gets narrower. In the end, the apartment becomes a living creature that approaches him, telling secret stories embedded within itself.

After being immersed in this strange atmosphere for a seemingly extended period of time, he suddenly feels that his legs have become immobilized. In no time, he finds himself unable to move even an inch as his whole body is solidified. After a couple of days, his wife returns back home from the trip; she observes no change in the apartment since she has left. She doesn't even recognize her husband who has been lying in the living room. Instead, she only notices a piece of furniture that seems unfamiliar to her. Without paying much attention to it, she leaves the apartment again, leaving her husband the same message as the last time.

A unique literary characteristic of the narrative of *Another Man's Room* is that it develops in relation to a series of stages in the protagonist's experience with the apartment's architecture. He approaches, investigates (and explores), is immersed into, and finally becomes part of the apartment. In this process, the protagonist's embodied perception is activated by the place, its mood, and atmosphere. This makes the architecture seem to come alive and allows it to speak of its untold [hi]stories through the narrative's poetic prose. In this way, *Another Man's Room* demonstrates that a phenomenological understanding of the apartment can help us detect nuanced conditions of the life present inside it, particularly Seoulian life.

The Architecture of *Another Man's Room*

Approaching the Apartment

The protagonist's first architectural experiences occur in the corridor of the apartment complex as he barely drags his exhausted body to his apartment unit. In the beginning, while depending primarily on his vision, he recognizes the emptiness of the corridor space: "he met nobody on the way; there was no one in the corridor either."[8] However, as he moves closer to his apartment unit his other senses gradually awaken. He smells boiling spinach, and understands that other tenants are preparing dinner on the other side of the wall. He fumbles to touch the bell that is designed, for security reasons, to be invisible from the corridor. Smoking while waiting for his wife to open the door for him, his sense of taste also comes alive: "it tasted acrid on his already burned tongue."[9] After hearing "no sound from inside"[10] for some time, the protagonist repeatedly presses the door bell, which only returns a "faint echo sound."[11] Then, he starts to imagine the situation behind the entrance door by reflecting on his previous experiences:

> He listened, lit the last cigarette he had left, but still there was no sound from inside. Again he reached his hand through the tiny metal box, felt the spring of the bell beneath his finger, and began to press in a way that showed that the delay was getting on his nerves. . . . But every time he pressed the bell, he heard a faint sound echoing far way on the other side. He concluded that his wife had been drinking alone and by now had fallen stark naked into a drunken sleep.[12]

Investigating and Exploring the Apartment

Upon entering into his empty apartment, the protagonist "stood there, not knowing what to do, like a man who has gone in to a strange place."[13] Before long, he starts to roam around the living room, feeling the high temperature of the air and the humidity, confined in an almost sealed space. Then, he moans like "an animal just caught in a cage."[14] Further awakened by the living room's fluorescent light, which "fluttered three or four times like an insect in a collector's jar before it finally came on,"[15] his eyes and ears carefully scan from living room to bedroom to check for any traces his wife might have left in the apartment. An undecipherable sound coming from the transistor radio, her clothes and worn stockings scattered about, and a container of cosmetics left untouched tell the story of the hurried atmosphere of the place that his wife left behind:

> He felt an intense loneliness. Naked as he was, he stalked around the living room, which was oppressively hot due to the lack of an outlet for the

steam-heated air, and he moaned like an animal just caught in a cage. The furniture seemed the same as a few days before; it was as if nothing had changed. There was a whirring from the transistor radio—his wife had left it on when she was going out. He turned it off. His wife's clothes were thrown in disarray all over the bedroom; holed stockings lying on the table, a container of rouge opened and left as it was.[16]

In the bathroom, dazzled by the brightness of the light, the protagonist's vision recognizes the space as "a sanitized butcher's shop,"[17] a place where vivisection is performed. In this atmosphere, he perceives things as living organisms: his wife's curled hair left in the bathtub look like worms, and the stopper in the water is like the back of a lurking crayfish. He even thinks that the water escaping through the drain makes a sound similar to that of smacking lips. Throughout, while looking at the shower, he imagines the metallic pipe as a tall creature challenging him to a competition in height. He sees the shower-head as alive and perceives it as the broken neck of an executed prisoner, casting a severe glance at him:

> Dragging his sore feet slowly behind him, he went into the bathroom. He put on the light, but the light was so bright the bathroom looked like a sanitized butcher's shop. The bath was still filled with dirty water where his wife had had a bath. There were a few strands of his wife's hair stuck on the rim of the tub, curled like live worms. He reached in and took out the stopper, which looked like the back of a crayfish hiding in dirty water. Whereupon a shiver ran through the tiny bath, the water ran out a furious pace, and in a little while, with a sound like smacking lips, the bath was empty except for the dirt sediment that remained here and there. . . . He stood there forlornly like a tall cockscomb and then went over to the shower, which was glaring at him. Every time he went toward the shower, he felt an urge to measure his height. The shower-head was broken, like the neck of a prisoner who had been executed, and it was staring at him very soberly.[18]

Into the Atmosphere (Becoming Part of the Apartment)

After being fully awakened by "the pleasant sensation of water flowing down his body, water gliding across his body like a young girl in dancing shoes,"[19] the protagonist comes back to the living room with "some fruit juice powder from the cool living-room sideboard"[20] and reclines his body on the sofa. As soon as he opens his eyes, after resting in darkness for some time, he experiences the atmosphere of the living room differently than before. His other senses gradually revive. He tastes the mix of fruit juice powder and cold water and listens to the monotonous music from the record player, which makes his heart more grounded.[21] Soon he feels "a tremendous power of sexual embrace,"[22] while imagining his wife's sexual organs. In this context, he feels that his body has melted into the gloomy atmosphere of the apartment, an atmosphere created by the dim lighting of the living room, and has become part of it, like a piece of furniture, an object:

The record player with its bad needle gives off static, but eventually it begins to spit out the music. He stretches out on the sofa and listens to the music. There are still a few things that haven't been straightened out yet, but he feels more settled. The subdued light of the shaded standard lamp fills the whole room gloomily. Seen from above, from the ceiling, he doesn't even look human. He is lying motionless. For this reason he appears lifeless, like a piece of furniture.[23]

The Apartment Narrates Its Own Stories

Lying on the sofa the protagonist begins to look at the furniture nearby. In contrast with the dusky atmosphere filling the space, the furniture seems to be alive; it emits a "brighter color and begins to give off light like leaves after rain."[24] At the same time, he also realizes that all the other household items, such as teaspoons, lamps, and tables, have started "pitching and tossing and rattling."[25] He even hears them making a barely audible sound. Whenever the fluorescent light of the living room is bright, they quickly return to their original places. However, as soon as he puts the switch down "rolling waves of darkness" approach every single item in the room and they start "whispering carefully at first, but finally giggling and laughing to their hearts' content."[26] Then, they realize that the man they are confronting is in a defenseless state, and their actions and voices suddenly become more violent and loud, and grow out of control as time progresses. By witnessing the spectacle before his eyes, he feels extremely helpless and finally gives in to the desire to jump into the new world they are contriving:

> In every dark corner within the room there is an audible whispering sound. Darkness and darkness conspiring together, discussing some treacherous plot. Friend, talk with us! In the right angle of every corner of the room one of them speaks out fearlessly. Sounds of the footsteps of millipedes crawling on the wall. Sounds of dressing-table mirror and clothes-closet mirror in transparent copulation. He opens his eyes wide in the darkness. The walls are rolling. He moves his body slowly. Sounds from between the two eyes of the wall socket for the electric iron. His ear makes contact at the narrow eyes of the socket, like an electrical accessory; his whole body begins to boil, like a high-class electric stove. Sparks spring to his body; his whole body feels replete with light. Listen well! The socket whispers. It was as if the voice were coming from a transistor earphone; it whispers in his ear alone. Tonight there will be a coup d'etat. Don't be afraid. He takes his ear from the socket. He bangs the light switch on again. The light comes on and everything that had been in commotion is stuck like paint to the wall, pretending to a disgraceful innocence.... But the articles he was peering into were not, properly speaking, ordinary articles. They were not already yesterday's articles.[27]

The Architecture of the [Hi]stories

The narrative ends with a scene in which the protagonist transforms into an actual piece of furniture. When he decides to escape the living room by moving "as soundlessly and stealthily as possible,"[28] he suddenly feels his legs get stiff; immobilized, he is unable to take a single step. He tries with all of his strength to drag himself over to the switch to turn it on, but the attempt ends in failure. In no time, he realizes that his whole body had become rigid and powerless, and it is impossible for him to control it, which is very strange. In the end, he feels "as if he were rising from the dead."[29]

After two days, his wife returns from her trip and senses that there is some sign of trespass. However, not finding any items missing from the apartment, her mind is put at rest. Instead, she discovers something that had been left lying there: a piece of furniture she once had cherished so much. For a couple of days, she takes care of it by cleaning and even caressing it. However, after getting tired of it, she finds that it is no use for her anymore. She puts it away in storage.

As this chapter demonstrates, Inho Choe's *Another Man's Room* is highly architectural; not in the sense of simply describing the spatial arrangement of the most dominant building typology in Seoul. Rather, with the help of poetic language, the story narrates, in Peter Zumthor's terms, "the atmospheric quality of [the apartment] by means of a feeling of [hi]stories" originated by the protagonist's direct interactions with the space. It challenges the contemporary understanding of Seoul's apartments.

As the quote from *Please Look after Mom* describes at the beginning of this chapter, architects and urban designers have criticized such apartments for their anonymous and inhuman qualities. The concern is that the only consideration in the design of these places has been maximizing economic and utilitarian value. The general understanding is that, never entering the realm of true architecture, these apartments remain simply products of the construction industry.

Whether you agree with that criticism or not, the apartment has become a major housing type in South Korea since its inception as a popular typology in the early 1960s. It has shaped the architectural and urban conditions of Seoul, as well as other South Korean cities. Apartments are still being built in large numbers, and there will be even more built in the future, as many of those constructed in the early years have reached their life expectancy.

What is crucial for architects to recognize, as Inho Choe does, is that an apartment is an ever-changing, living entity; it is a site of transformation, not in the sense of its form or style, but in its realization of the [hi]stories it can encompass. In this sense, the narrative of *Another Man's Room* teaches us an important lesson: how the protagonist's embodied perceptions of his surroundings and the articles of daily life they hold change day by day because, as he recognizes, "they were not already yesterday's articles."[30]

FIGURE 4.2 One of the oldest apartment buildings in Seoul, Yeouido, Sibum Apartments, Seoul, South Korea, 1971.

Photo by author

Notes

1 Kyung-Sook Shin, *Please Look after Mom: A Novel*, trans. Chi-Young Kim (New York: Alfred A. Knopf, 2011), 167–168.
2 As for foreign researchers, see Valerie Gelezeau, *Apateu gonghwaguk (Apartment Republic)*, trans. Hye Yeon Kil (Seoul: Humanitaseu, 2007). Francesco Sanin, Mvrdv (Rotterdam), et al., *Seoul Scenarios* (Seoul: Space, 2005).
3 Yoonchun Jung and Angeliki Sioli, "Modeling Narratives: Architecture of Desire in Contemporary Seoul," *Montreal Architectural Review*, Vol.3 (2016): 29. The original text reads "who have became 'misfits' by their failure to adjust to the ceaselessly-and rapidly-shifting urban lifestyle and who have been pushed to the perimeter of the city, literally and metaphorically."
4 This recent phenomenon in Seoul has given rise to another conversation on the problem of urban gentrification.
5 Bruce Fulton and Youngmin Kwon, ed., *Modern Korean Fiction: An Anthology* (New York, Columbia University Press, 2015), 181.
6 Lee Dong-ha argues that most of Inho Choe's works reflect some kind of "abnormal escapism." See Dong-ha Lee, "*Dopiwa geungjeong [Escapism and Affirmation]*," in *A Stranger's Room*, by Inho Choe (Seoul: Minumsa,1983), 415. The title of *Another Man's Room* is sometimes translated into *A Stranger's Room* depending on the translator. I prefer to use *Another Man's Room* for its subtlety of expressing the anonymity of the third person.
7 The inter-connected relationship between architecture and place-bound stories can be found even in works by Vitruvius. In his *The Ten Books on Architecture*, he tells us the

story of Caryatids, the female-shaped columns supporting the entablature on their heads as an eternal penance. The term "embodied perception" is borrowed from Alberto Pérez-Gómez, who has extensively written and lectured on the importance of phenomenological understandings in architecture.
8 Inho Choe, "Another Man's Room (T'ain ui pang)," trans. by Kevin O'Rourke, in *Modern Korean Fiction: An Anthology*, ed. Bruce Fulton and Youngmin Kwon (New York: Columbia University Press, 2015), 182.
9 Ibid., 182.
10 Ibid.
11 Ibid.
12 Ibid.
13 Ibid., 184.
14 Ibid.
15 Ibid.
16 Ibid., 185.
17 Ibid.
18 Ibid., 185–187.
19 Ibid., 187–188.
20 Ibid., 188.
21 This idea of music creating an architectural atmosphere touching human hearts in the domestic realm has a historical precedence in literature. See Jean-Francois de Bastide, Rodolphe El-Khoury, and Anthony Vidler, *The Little House: An Architectural Seduction* (New York: Princeton Architectural Press, 1996).
22 Ibid., 189.
23 Ibid., 188.
24 Ibid., 189–190
25 Ibid.
26 Ibid., 191.
27 Ibid., 190–191.
28 Ibid., 192.
29 Ibid.
30 Ibid., 191.

SECTION 2
Readings on Architectural Research

5
FABRICS OF REALITY

Art and Architecture in László Krasznahorkai

Mari Lending

I

In early May 2015 as I was heading for the architecture biennale in Venice, one of my PhD students gave me a book and insisted that I read it *en route*. The book came with specific instructions. She had marked two chapters and enclosed reproductions of the paintings that these two stories revolved around. The perfect present, as it were, still I was a little reluctant as I have very specific reading habits during traveling. Desperately trying to catch up on the news, the plowing through piles of unread newspapers starts on the airport train and continues at the gate and in the air. If there is a connecting flight I get more newspapers in transition, and should there be time left during a long flight I finally turn to the issues of the *New York Review of Books* that amass at home, with the final destination as the deadline for getting slightly updated on what is going on in the real world.

But of course I did as I was told. On the first flight from Oslo to Zurich I pulled up László Krasznahorkai's *Seiobo There Below*.[1] On the cover Susan Sontag and W.G. Sebald were praising this, to me, unknown Hungarian author and I felt confident this would not be a waste of time. Although the book was published after Sebald died in a car crash in 2001 and Sontag of cancer 3 years later it takes only a moment to discover that both the Sebald-Krasznahorkai and the Sontag-Krasznahorkai affinities are strong. For instance, Sontag's flip-flopping between a 1992 flea market in Manhattan and an auction in London in 1772 in the opening of *The Volcano Lover* ("Why enter? What do you expect to see? I'm seeing. I'm checking on what's in the world") soon springs to mind.[2] Sebald's play with historical facts, and the way he illustrated his fiction with archival photographs deeply resonates with the critical importance of images and empirical reality in Krasznahorkai's collection of stories.

On the Oslo-Zurich flight I immersed myself in "The Exiled Queen," equipped with the image I found folded in the book. On the Zurich-Venice flight I continued with "Christo Morto," armed with a postcard balancing on the folding table on the back of the seat in front of me. Yet, as this text deals with minute pictorial and forensic details and overall with conservation issues, I constantly had to pick up the postcard to have a closer look at the peaceful face of a dying Christ, his thorn crown, wounds, bleeding hands, closed eyes, the Greek letters on the backdrop, and the backdrop itself. Slowly I was realizing that I was making everybody around me uncomfortable. Should anybody possibly have watched me reading on the Oslo-Zurich flight, they might have seen an art historian studying a Renaissance palace interior and landscape. The manic consultation of the image of an image of the suffering Christ, apparently signified differently. Being caught in that very private act of reading, in public, I realized the obscenity of displaying religious artifacts, maybe even affection, in such a narrow, public space as an aircraft. In the Middle Ages, Barry Bergdoll observes, monasteries allowed members of the same community to read among people they knew and with whom they shared both values and the canon, while in the nineteenth century, the rapid distribution of printed texts brought world news to the private sphere. Henri Labrouste somehow combined the two when creating a public space for people of very diverse backgrounds, interests, and purposes. This is one of Labrouste's radical acts, says Bergdoll, optimizing the qualities of reading by architectural means: "The arrangement of readers in the *bibliothèque* Sainte Genevieve originally facilitated this sense of being alone in public."[3] Reading in these reading rooms that orbit the globe, among foreigners who might share neither canons nor backgrounds is a well-established practice. Apparently it was the preoccupation with the reproduction of Christ that caused awkwardness among my co-travelers, somehow breaking with the decorum of reading in private in public space.

Now, traveling with these two images, one apparently straightforwardly beautiful, the other more disturbing, did though make sense. The stories they belong to and the worlds they reflect is all about art and architecture traveling in space and time. Further, the ephemeral illustrations evoked a major issue in this collection of fiction. It has to do with what Roland Barthes famously coined *l'effet de réel*, and the reality hunger that has always been crucial to fiction. However, rather than idealizing aesthetic autonomy, this is a form of fiction that conflates historical realities and imagination by very particular means. The presence of specific art works, buildings, historical texts, and actual scholarship recharges the "referential illusion" that Barthes deemed obsolete in the 1960s.[4] The result is an intricate textual fabric that makes us think differently about artifacts of the past and their reception. Blending history and literature, media and images, real and invented characters and places, they expect as much of the reader as Barthes did at the time, in its presentation of layered spaces and layered times.

II

Upon his arrival in Pompeii in October 1811, Stendhal stated that he felt "transported back to antiquity," immediately "knowing more than a scholar."[5] The ruins and rubble induced a feeling of time travel that let the place come alive and reveal a feeling of history of a more profound sort than scholarly history could ever accomplish, he pondered. Reading Stendhal, we may feel catapulted in time and place as well, if perhaps to the early nineteenth century rather than to antiquity. More important is Stendhal's hinting at the capacity of fiction to compete, maybe even overtrump, the scholarly discourses that saturate our thinking about architecture, place, and history.

We were gathered in Athens to discuss ways of reading architecture in fiction in June 2015, in the very week of the bicentennial of the Battle of Waterloo. Stendhal, the novelist, presented one of the most sublime and perhaps realistic accounts of this battle in *La chartreuse de Parme*. Stendhal was not present at Waterloo, but as part of Napoleon's administration he knew what he was talking about when rendering the incomprehensible chaos of the battle, seen through the eyes of the Italian aristocrat Fabrice del Dongo. Fabrice, having turned against his habitus and nation, fighting for the ideals of the French republic, desperately longs to see the emperor first hand. At the moment when Napoleon, in the flesh, passes on his white horse, our hero however finds himself busy with the most mundane issues and misses the whole thing, while we, the readers, get to see straight into the surreal horrors of war. More architecturally, think only about one of the most memorable reviews of Dominique Perrault's Bibliothèque nationale de France at Austerlitz in Paris. It was authored by Sebald's fictitious architectural historian Austerlitz in the novel of the same name.[6] Fiction depicting historical reality makes the trajectory of "The Exiled Queen" and "Christo Morto."

A barometer placed above a piano in a bourgeoisie interior in a short story by Flaubert, is the most memorable object in Barthes' soon 50-year-old classic "The Reality Effect." In structuralist lingo, this barometer served to illuminate a certain kind of realism that had been codified in the nineteenth century novel, signifying "the direct collusion of a referent and a signifier whereby the signified is expelled from the sign."[7] Such apparently insignificant details—with which novelists furnished their novels to heighten their realistic atmosphere—were, according to Barthes, superfluous notations in regards of structure; a lavish, "narrative luxury."[8] In the concurrence of literary realism and nineteenth century "objective" historiography, these mechanisms were at work in both fields. While the novelist with descriptions of real people, objects, and events aimed at aesthetic verisimilitude and not least by the *ekphrasis*, with its capacity to evoke places, times, people and works of art; the historian employed similar techniques to present the realities of the past truthfully, to make the past alive and legible for the present. Both genres concern the relationship between the text and the world it attempts to signify.

The problem, according to Barthes, was the ways in which concrete reality —"insignificant gestures, transitory attitudes, insignificant objects, redundant words"—offered a "pure and simple 'representation' of the 'real'." In these *true-to-life* descriptions, the reality effect implied a resistance to meaning; in fact, it had become "a weapon against meaning."[9] Surely, this critique of certain codes of realism was itself part of a war on hegemonic concepts, such as myths (*doxa*), biographical authors, intentions, and originality, and is, accordingly, time-typical. Jacques Rancière has characterized it as an expression of "Modernist disdain for the useless object."[10]

Reading *Seiobo There Below*, it is striking how exactly what Barthes wanted to get away with, makes the core. When characterizing the city of Rouen as described in *Madame Bovary* as "a real referent if ever there was one," and "subjected to the tyrannical constraints of what we must call aesthetic verisimilitude," Barthes is close to capturing the essence of how Krasznahorkai describes urban space and architecture.[11] Whereas to Barthes, the futile details were detached from the structure, in Krasznahorkai they are integral; they are the stuff these stories are made of. The tyrannical constraint of aesthetic verisimilitude has become liberating and transgressive, and the result is an unusual, textually mediated experience of concrete reality. Perhaps a novel, perhaps not, this volume of stories present strong encounters with iconic monuments such as the Parthenon, the Ise temple, and the Alhambra by zooming in on issues of authorship, provenance, affiliation, ownership, value, historicity, and reception. The historian's preoccupation with events and documents of the past, and the novelist's anchoring of narratives in historical circumstances are tightly entangled. Addressing the significance of the insignificant, the reality effect balances on the boarders of scholarship and fiction, the historical and the imaginary.

Ambiguities are however no less present than the abundance of Barthesian reality effects—real objects, real buildings, real people, real places, real scholarship. Such destabilizing elements are at work also in the paratext. The epigraph reads: "Either it's night, or we don't need light.—Thelonious Monk—Thomas Pynchon." This apocryphal quote is placed directly opposite the colophon, the legal venue of any published book. On the exact same line as the epigraph a statement disrupts the usual masthead information: "PUBLISHER'S NOTE: The epigraph, which recasts a Thelonious Monk line once quoted by Thomas Pynchon, is a creation of the author." This little mannerism is a warning to the reader. A novelist has no constraints, and cannot be trusted, factually. Simultaneously, it places the book in a venerable tradition. Think again of Stendhal who introduced the chapters in *Red and Black* with real and invented epigraphs, attributing for instance the recollection "Absurd and touching memory: one's first appearance, at eighteenth, alone and unsupported, in a drawing-room. A glance from a woman was enough to terrify me!," to Immanuel Kant.[12] This kind of pseudo-pedantic annotation adds uncertainty to the text proper and throws the reader back and forth between trustfulness and doubt.

III

A similar play with paratext saturates the opening of the "Exiled Queen." A crossword in Italian downloaded from Quiz Biblici is followed by an advertisement from the website vashiskin.com and a company named Radical Damage, offering products to "rejuvenate the body and uplift the soul." In the real world, a search of vashiskin.com redirects to photographs of rejuvenated versions of Diane Keaton, Ellen DeGeneres, Demi Moore, Goldie Hawn, etc. A dark irony slowly emerges. Babylon-born Vashti was the first queen of Xerxes I/Ahasuerus, appearing in the opening of the Book of Esther in the Hebrew bible. Vashti is replaced by Esther, who—after 12 months of pampering with oils, perfumes, and diets in a royal spa in Susa, as elaborated in detail in the Holy scripture—is chosen by the king as his next queen during the Babylonian captivity. Her Jewishness is at the time still concealed. In Krasznahorkai, Vashti plays the lead, in a story that extensively draws on the Book of Esther in its portrayal of Achaemenid Persia, its multitude of residential and administrative capitals, the polychrome palace complexes with heavenly gardens in the cities of Susa, Persepolis, Pasargade, and Ecbatana, the extravagant outfits, the legendary banquets, and the massive drinking. Mad of love and apparently at all times drunk, the king orders the ravishingly beautiful Vashti to appear in court in front of his drinking fellows dressed only in a crown placed on her "magnificent, thick, golden-hued hair." Refusing, she signs her destiny. Her body and face disfigured from leprosy, certainly make the contemporary Vashti beauty products evoke darker horrors than the anxieties of Hollywood stars. Observing that the "theater of her ruin had commenced," Vashti's deterioration metonymically anticipates the future ruins of Persia.

These scenes revive for the inner eye of the reader a civilization with its cities and palaces; a geopolitical hot spot, many times destroyed through history. But Barthes' "referential illusion" increases in intensity when the drama unfolding at Susa flip-flops with scenes from another city and a different time. Quattrocento Florence is as evocatively laid out as Susa, with its biblical references and archeological associations. Here, a Jewish delegation shows up at the workshop of "Signor Alessandro di Mariano Filipepi, better known as Sandro Battigello," and eventually as Sandro Botticelli, to place an order for two *forzieri* or *cassoni*, a set of dowry chests for a daughter's wedding, that shall depict the entire life of Esther. While the lids and backs should be left unpainted, the one rectangular front should depict "Esther pleading for mercy before the king," the second "the portrayal of the gratitude of the Jewish people," and the four smaller parts "the main protagonists—Ahasuerus, Haman, Mordechai."[13] They wanted Botticelli but as he was busy traveling they reluctantly met with Filippo di Filippi Lippi, at the time an apprentice at Botticelli's workshop. In short fragments and long intricate sentences, in a prose characterized by the shunning of full stop, these Florentine parts unfold a Renaissance world of urban, political and social history, the art market and contemporary architecture, private histories and city scandals. At the workshop, the deal is concluded, the price and date for delivery set. In Krasznahorkai,

Filippino Lippi did the paintings, and had Lorenzo di Medici's architect Giuliana da Sangallo do the carpentry and Botticelli's brother Antonio the goldsmithing.

Yet, there is a third layer and a third time woven into this fabric of "insignificant details" of fact and fiction, that recounts the afterlife of these paintings, as they were turned into art works by being removed from their original setting and purpose. Broken into six pieces, they traveled through auction houses, collections, and museums in many cities, building complicated provenance. The real drama of "The Exiled Queen" is about authorship. "So little was known, still they didn't know anything," states the withdrawn narrator:

> this is not a question of the "wider public"—even though the term encompasses fewer and fewer people, this lack of knowledge going along side by side with erudition—but rather of the endless hordes of experts, who have sacrificed numerous works of scholarship to demonstrating that, of course, Sandro Botticelli painted the series of panels depicting Esther's story, as well as others demonstrating that Sandro Botticelli did not paint them; then to prove that perhaps he only painted the essential parts, and then not even that . . .

Such uncertainties a piece of fiction can readily fill in according to the author's wishes. Likewise, a novelist can flesh out historical figures with thoughts and mindsets and everyday realism as he or she pleases. Krasznahorkai portrays Xerxes's mother Parysatis as a mother-in-law from hell in great, imaginative detail when describing the backstage of Persian palace intrigues. He lets the child Filippino Lippi, who had "inherited in a truly astonishing fashion all of his father's genius," develop constant colds from accompanying his father while he was working on the frescos in the chilly cathedral in Spoleto in the 1460s, making his parents worried sick about his health. On his deathbed Fra Filippo Lippi has his son promise to always dress warmly, and "under no circumstances should he drink cold water while working." Such plausible details function as Flaubert's barometer. They bring historical figures alive in realistic atmospheres. That is nothing special. The remarkable thing is the way in which this piece of fiction—while catapulting the reader back and forth between Achaemenid Persia and Renaissance Florence—introduces scholarly debates on the attribution of the panels, by referring to a number of named academics. The art historian Patrizia Zambrano is "doubtlessly ranking among the greatest masters of saying absolutely nothing." Alfred Scharf's *Filippino Lippi* of 1935 "awkwardly and laboriously ponders over the date of creation for the panels, but—thankfully—nothing more." Yet, as surprising, even shocking, as it is to see named scholars critiqued in fiction, the reality effects run deeper. In "the terrifying and unknown machinations of chance and accident, these panels have actually been handed down to us," states the auctorial voice. It is at least not possible "to contradict the fact that they exist." The panels are factual and survived their transition from domestic objects to art, and are handed down across the

FIGURE 5.1 Ephemera and authorship I: "Esther Pleads for the Jews, ca. 1480." Louvre's website says with reference to the six panels: "Botticelli may have entrusted Filippino Lippi with most of their execution."
Photo by author

centuries. The print harvested from the internet that I was consulting in transition from Oslo to Zurich came without caption and the text does not name it directly.

Thus I did at the time not know that I was looking at the panel "Esther Pleads for the Jews," which is in the Louvre collection. What is doubtable, as both the author, that narrator and we, the readers, know, is that "everything that stands in the Book of Esther is so indemonstrable, so unlocalizable, so unidentifiable and confabulatory, that it simply cannot stand," that it "simply has *no foundations in reality*." Thus, the oscillation, for instance, between Xerxes I, Ahasuereus, Artaxerxes II, Artaxerxes Mnemon II, etc., emphasizes what we in fact do not know for certain. Historical and legendary, actual and factual, probable ancient, Renaissance, and modern scholarly reality insists, by the work of the reality effect, on a reality that can only take place in fiction, by pointing to the real.

IX

The story starring the postcard of Christ is in-depth Venetian. "Christo Morto" intensifies issues of authorship and provenance and further destabilizes fact and fiction by concrete denotations. The middle-aged narrator from eastern Europe, who biographically aligns with the author the way the narrator of *Austerlitz* resembles Sebald, has returned to Venice for a "visitation of which was more important to him than his entire mediocre, senseless, barren, and superfluous life." The labyrinthine quartier of San Polo arouses from the sound of the soles of the narrator's black leather Oxfords, and lets Venice spring from the stones of Venice in a dark version of the Venice that rises from the cobblestones at the Guermantes palace in Paris in a series of epiphanies at the end of Marcel Proust's *In Search of Lost Time*. Having spent the night at a pension at Calle del Pistor with an "elegant, useless entrance arch designed by Pietro Lombardi," he heads through narrow streets and deserted piazzas during siesta on an April day, described with architectural and topographical precision. Yet another "barometer" is introduced on this anxiety-inducing stroll, in an extensive stream of consciousness. For "no particular reason at all something came into his head, a newspaper article, as it happened, which had nothing to do with anything," namely that he the same morning read on the front page of the *Corriere della Sera* under the headline "HELL REALLY EXISTS," that Benedict XVI had in a recent public speech said that hell was not a "metaphor, an emblem, an abstraction," but existed in a "real, physical sense." In "Christo Morto" this is a hyper signifying insignificant detail, among many others.

Center stage resides the painting of Christ as depicted on the postcard I was studying on the Zurich-Venice flight. The dry, factual text on the back of the postcard hints at the drama at work: "Venezia: Scuola Grande di San Rocco," and then in five languages: "School of Bellini, Christ in devotion." Finally at the destination of the exhaustive excursion through San Polo, the reader is given the full building history with all architects involved in this "most exalted and perfect architectonic conception." The deadly drama is however one of restoration, chemical analysis, X-ray scanning, attribution, authorship, provenance, and a centuries-old debate on who in fact painted this Christ in devotion. The little canvas belongs among the Tintorettos in San Rocco. Yet, it has never found a fixed place in this architectural abundance of decorated walls, ceilings and floors. As the atheist pilgrim arrives at his destination—where he by accident had come across the painting a decade earlier and experienced the miracle of Christ in devotion fluttering his eyelids—the reader is catapulted into a *tour de force* of theories on the authorship of the painting across the centuries: Titian, Giorgione, Giovanni Bellini, and others, referencing scholars, books, curators, conservationists, and institutions. The last restoration that took place over several years is described in minute detail, and the solution to the mystery of whom in fact made the painting, reads as a thriller on conservation, historicity, and authenticity. Earlier restorations are termed "philistine and irresponsible," and the critique of a history of retouching, repainting, and the smearing of "the surface with some cheap junk, some kind of lacquer-like substance, which in the course of time had oxidized and yellowed, and with that, the fate of the picture was sealed, [. . .] because that for the most part ruined it, more precisely [. . .] they *falsified* the original effect of the painting," resonates with contemporary debates on authenticity in original works of art.[14] While reading, one might in fact become genre blind and believe that one is reading a (stylistically slightly unconventional) conservation dossier. Yet, one is suddenly brought back to reality—that is, to the fiction—as in the portrayal of the conservator Mr. Arlango, "a person of fairly disagreeable aspect, perhaps because of his physical deformity or perhaps because of something else, he was decidedly humorless, unfriendly, and taciturn," etc. Mr. Arlango might exist, he might not. Most probably, the author does not know him, the narrator-protagonist never met him or– within the frames of the fiction—was present when the restoration work took place. The "complex pomp and monumentality" of the Tintorettos "were not the real thing," the latter concludes when he for the second time stands in front of the painting. What does become very real, though, is the hallucinatory madness he experiences when re-exposed to the miracle of Christ's flickering eyes: "NOW THEY REALLY WERE ALMOST COMPLETELY OPEN." From this experience he dies.

Again, these details line up as a multitude of Barthes' barometer, the useless details: Lombardi's arched entrance, the description of Venetian buildings and architects, Benedict XVIs talk on hell, the scholarly debates on attribution of the 56 by 81 cm painting. And the processes of authentication debated in the text is not weakened by the fact that the story is set in Venice. The last decades, Barthes wrote in 1968, "the incessant need to authenticate the 'real'," had only increased by new techniques: "reportage, exhibitions of ancient objects (the success of the Tutankhamen show makes this quite clear), the tourism of monuments and historical sites."[15] By rehearsing the ancient distinction of mimesis and verisimilitude by juxtaposing innumerable actual facts with obvious fiction, Krasznahorkai makes us doubt it all, while similarly feeling that we got it all.

When I landed in Venice after having read "Christo Morto" I went straight to San Rocco rather than to the biennale previews as planned, and spent the day among the Tintorettos. I did not find the Christ in devotion. Communicating in poor Italian and in English, it appeared to me that nobody there had any idea what I was talking about, and that I was experiencing exactly the "absence of the signified," the very definition of the reality effect in Barthes' terms. But I do have the postcard that gives the image's provenance, which in its cheap ephemerality makes it probable that "Christo Morto" is not entirely made up.

X

If the dichotomy of fiction and nonfiction has been deconstructed in theory over decades and in literature across centuries, maybe millennia, it still lingers in debates on the media specificity of the novel. In the end it might mean little beyond the discourses of bureaucrats, the book industry and scholars, as we prepare our reading lists for students, dividing the recommended reading in awkward categories of primary and secondary texts, for instance "novels" and "theory." Dealing with such institutionalized taxonomies, we easily understand what Stendhal was thinking about when reporting from Pompeii, addressing the limitations of so-called scholarly prose. Yet, Stendhal was not evaluating the mimetical power of different genres. He was visiting the ruined city in the capacity of being a budding art critic and an established military bureaucrat, and he was talking about the place itself, and thrilled to finally seeing antiquity "face à face."[16] Still, this feeling of experiential immediacy appears slightly ironic. Stendhal's contemporary readership and even more his present-days readers, know that this is an imagined immediacy of an antiquity that has been destroyed, restored, reconstructed, and reinvented over and over through history. In fact, the massively and many times curated ruins of Pompeii makes the city and the place an extreme fiction, a complete mediation, making it hard to believe in immediacy at all. By now, Stendhal's testimony has become part of that mediation.

A few years after Stendhal visited Pompeii, Quatremère de Quincy—a renowned expert on Greek antiquity who had never set foot in Greece—traveled to London to see the first public display of the Elgin Marbles, and experienced a similar feeling of traveling in space and time. Exposed to the Parthenon fragments in a provisory gallery in the British Museum under construction in Bloomsbury in 1818, Quatremère felt that he was propelled back to the workshops of the makers of the Parthenon.[17] The dismembered bits and pieces of the temple became building elements and the gallery a construction site. Only fragments and the act of the imagination allows for a fundamental understanding of architecture and lost or otherwise inapproachable totalities: "One single fragment could show us both the makeup of a chef d'oeuvre and the ideals and style of the man who fashioned it."[18]

Stendhal and Quatremère's experiences of lost worlds and the possibility of grasping impossible totalities through fragments, by an act of the imagination, resembles the way the city of Susa is made manifest in "The Exiled Queen." In its pre-ruined reality, the story encompasses an architectural repository allowing glimpses into the history and historicity of the city. Likewise, in describing quattrocento Florence and contemporary Venice, Krasznahorkai is doing exactly "more than a scholar," catapulting us, the readers, into a vertigo-evoking time travel where the act of the imagination makes partly mundane, partly fantastical fragments transgress the sum of the bits. "The light of poetry is not only a direct but also a reflected light that while it shows us the object, throws a sparkling radiance on all around it," as William Hazlitt put it while Quatremère was admiring the Parthenon in London.[19]

Fiction helps us understand something about reality and history, and more particularly about architecture and art. Reading fiction obviously also represents a longing for the real, a desire that mirrors the ways in which fiction has always been longing for the real, in the innumerable screws of the old debate on changing conceptions of mimesis, and the mimetical power of literature. Prior to theorizing the reality effect, Barthes in a questionnaire in *Tel Quel*, presented a slightly different take on how literature might relate to the real, one that much resembles the way Krasznahorkai's objects of the past and their contemporary reception work. Literature is Orpheus returning from the underworld, he said, and "as long as literature walks ahead, aware that it is leading someone, the reality behind it which it is gradually leading out of the unnamed—that reality breathes, walks, lives, heads toward the light of a meaning."[20] The moment literature looks back at what it loves, all that is left "is a dead meaning." When writers "write ambiguously enough to suspend meaning," and when writing "troubles what exists," literature "does not permit us to walk, but it permits us to breathe."[21] In this interpretation of an ancient myth, literature leads, reality follows. That light of meaning, caused by the troubling of what exists, also hints to the fact that literature might change both reality and the perception of the past.

Notes

1 László Krasznahorkai, *Seiobo There Below* (2008), trans. Ottilie Mulzet (New York: New Direction Books, 2013).
2 Susan Sontag, The *Volcano Lover. A Romance* (1992), (London: Penguin Classic, 2009), 3.
3 Barry Bergdoll, "'The Public Square of the Modern Age': Architecture and the Rise of the Illustrated Press in the Nineteenth Century," in *The Printed and the Built. Architecture, Print Culture and Public Debate in the Nineteenth Century*, eds. Mari Hvattum and Anne Hultzsch (London: Bloomsbury, 2018), 31.
4 Roland Barthes, "The Reality Effect," (1968) in *The Rustle of Language*, trans. Richard Howard (Oxford: Blackwell, 1986), 148.
5 Stendhal, *Rome, Naples et Florence* II (1817), in *Œuvres complètes*, vol. 14 (Paris and Geneve: Slatkine Reprints, 1986), 2.
6 W.G. Sebald, *Austerlitz* (2001), trans. Anthea Bell (New York: The Modern Library, 2001), 275–290.
7 Barthes, "The Reality Effect," 147.
8 Ibid., 141.
9 Ibid., 146.
10 Jacques Rancière, "The Reality Effect and the Politics of Aesthetics," lecture at the Berlin Institute of Cultural Inquiry, September 21, 2009.
11 Barthes, "The Reality Effect," 144.
12 Stendhal, *The Red and the Black. A Chronicle of the Nineteenth Century*, trans. C.K. Scott Moncrieff (New York: Modern Library, 1926), epigraph to Chapter 2.
13 Among the most popular images on Florentine Renaissance marriage chests were "the submissive Griselda dressed and undressed by her lord and husband; humble Esther, who appeared before King Xerxes dressed in her finest robes; and the queen of Sheba rewarded with royal bounty for journeying far to hear the wisdom of Solomon." Julius Kirshner, "*Li Emergenti Bisogni Matrimoniali* in Renaissance Florence," in William J. Connell, *Society and Individual in Renaissance Florence* (Oakland: University of California Press, 2002), 94.
14 While heavy-handedly restored original works of art and architecture risk disappearing, "a well copied original may enhance its originality and continue to trigger new copies." Bruno Latour and Adam Lowe, "The Migration of the Aura, or How to Explore the Original through Its Facsimiles," in *Switching Codes: Thinking Through Digital Technology in the Humanities and the Arts*, eds. Thomas Barthscherer and Roderick Coover (Chicago: Chicago University Press, 2011), 278.
15 Barthes, "The Reality Effect," 146.
16 Stendhal, *Rome, Florence, Naples*, 3. "C'est un plaisir fort vif que de voir face à face cette antiquité sur laquelle on a lu tant de volumes," 3.
17 Quatremère de Quincy, "Letters to Canova," in *Letters to Miranda and Canova on the Abduction of Antiquities from Rome and Athens*, trans. Chris Miller and David Gilks (Los Angeles: Getty Publications, 2012), 137.

18 Quatremère de Quincy, *Le Jupiter olympien, ou l'Art de la sculpture antique* (Paris: Firmin Didot, 1814).
19 William Hazlitt, *Lectures on the English Poets* (London: Taylor and Hessey, 1818), 5–6.
20 Barthes, "Literature and Signification," (1963), in *Critical Essays*, trans Richard Howard (Evanston: Northwestern University Press, 1972), 268.
21 Ibid., 267.

6

HOW PLACES SPEAK

A Plea for Poetic Receptivity in Architectural Research

Klaske Havik

> The main thing is knowing how to see,
> To know how to see without thinking,
> To know how to see when you see,
> And not think when you see
> Or see when you think.
> But this (poor us carrying a clothed soul!),
> This takes deep study,
> A learning to unlearn[1]
>
> Fernando Pessoa, "The Keepers of Flocks XXIV"

The traditional tools of architectural research, often foregrounding rational and formal modes of thinking, fail to address the fundamental ambiguities of architecture, such as the intricate relationship between subject and object, crucial to understand and address architectural experience. A poetic way of writing as a mode of architectural investigation could help investigations into architectural themes such as sensory experience, atmosphere, and memory. Through a double reading, I will discuss how the receptive capacity of poets offers valuable insights for architectural researchers to engage lived experience in their work. This contribution reads and re-reads two different pieces of writing: I will discuss a quote by the Dutch poet Rutger Kopland which magnificently reveals the essence of the poetic gaze, and I will show how I used poetic writing in my own description of a particular architectural place in Finland called Hvitträsk: the house of three Finnish architects built in the early twentieth century.

Poetic Receptivity

As the above quoted lines of Fernando Pessoa clearly demonstrate, it is important for poets to learn to see without prejudice. Poetry often starts from the simplest daily observations, in which architectural features such as materials, shapes, colors, smells, shapes, light, and shadow, trigger associations and memories. It is the poet's capacity to meticulously observe such details, and to be receptive to sudden connections between such details and human emotion. Such a phenomenological gaze, stressing the importance of perception before reflection, is found in the works of poets rather than in contemporary architecture. The close and meticulous reading of architecture, carefully registering sensory perceptions, memories, and associations, have a clear parallel to poetic reading and writing. Reading Architecture requires the skill of observation, and with a sense of poetic receptivity. The Dutch poet and psychiatrist Rutger Kopland said that the poetic reading of places ". . . has not so much to do with subjectivity but rather with receptivity for what is different than expected. Maybe one could call it an absence of prejudice."[2]

Indeed poetic receptivity has to do with an openness to receive, to receive and take seriously seemingly simple information about reality through the senses, as well as through the filter of your own memory, imagination, and frame of reference. Echoing the words of the Dutch phenomenologist Van den Berg, Gaston Bachelard argues, in *the Poetics of Space*, that "poets are born phenomenologists, noting that things speak to them."[3]

Indeed, in phenomenological inquiries, we are interested in how things appear to us, how we perceive the world before reflecting upon this perception. Bachelard calls this "reception" of how things speak to us, the moment they evoke movement, emotion in us, the moment of the poetic image. The poetic gaze enables us to cherish moments of perception, and thereby enables us to think more deeply about the way people experience their environment. Like Bachelard, also Edward S. Casey sees topo-analysis as the connection between places and the images they evoke.[4] What then, are these images that places evoke, what is it that buildings "tell" us, how can we read their stories? Kopland states that words are not so much given to the poet, but as a poet, he notices moments of being emotionally moved by the world, and tries to find the words to express it. Likewise, Alberto Pérez-Gómez suggested that the poem speaks "primarily about the world, not about 'a subjective author'."[5] I propose to take seriously this idea of poetic receptivity in "topo-analysis,"[6] focusing on revealing the characteristics, associations, and fragments of atmosphere that constitute the very specificity of place through a poetic gaze.

A Site that Speaks: From It to I to It

The poetic gaze allows to address the complexity, the layered nature of architectural perception, simultaneously taking into account different aspects of architectural experience. I will discuss in more detail my reading of a place called Hvitträsk, a reading in which different layers of perception are present: the immediate encounter with the building's materiality and atmosphere, it's situation in the landscape, a sense of history both of its conception, and of its former use. Hvittråsk is the house that three Finnish architects—Herman Gesellius, Armas Lindgren, and Eliel Saarinen—built around 1900 for their shared office and for their families at a rough, uninhabited site west of Helsinki. The architects were the stars of their time, working at the turn of the twentieth century when Finland was seeking for it's own identity. Inspired, on the one hand, by Jugendstil tendencies elsewhere in Europe, and on the one hand by Finnish nature, especially as expressed in the national epos Kalevala, the architects and designers of the time gave Finland its own style, its own tone: dark granite, heaviness, and warmth, with motifs from Finnish nature: leaves, owls, and wolves. The style was named National Romantic and is manifest in important buildings in Helsinki such as the National Museum by Gesellius, Lindgren, and Saarinen, Helsinki's central railways station by Eliel Saarinen and the National Theater by Lars Sonck.[7]

My first encounter with Hvittråsk took place in the winter of 1998. Within the house, everything was warm and dark and heavy: brown, deep red, wood, carpets, heavy wooden cabinets, enormous wooden desks with rulers, dark baked tiles. But when, after visiting the house, I strayed from the path, through the woods and down the hill, it happened. I was in the whitest white, a place without boundaries. At the end of the path, it seemed that space, or at least its confinedness, disappeared. The lake was covered in snow, the most open white I had ever seen, there was no horizon, I could not see where the lake was and where the air was, there were no boundaries to the space. I ran on the lake, the snow dulled the sound of footsteps and I found myself in a circle, infinitely white, an endless sphere. I no longer knew how long I had stood on the lake, in the light and the silence. I turned around when the spots appeared before my eyes: first small and black, moving like little flies in my field of view, then red and yellow and blue, growing in size and like stripes.[8]

> *still, that this vastness is inhabited*
> *silent steps from the lake*
> *towards the fire*

In this first reading of the Hvittråsk project, it was the powerful relation between the house and its landscape environment that had struck me. Especially in winter, the dark, warm rooms, the heavy furniture, the carpets, the indoor spaces that invited the inhabitants to sit together and speak slowly in soft voices, counterbalanced the crisp cold, endless white. I realized that it was the endless white that Saarinen, Lindgren, and Gesellius had known, this was why they knew the Finnish soul and why they integrated warmth into their designs—the comfort of the house could only exist thanks to this endless, limitless white. The sudden impression of the vast whiteness revealed to me a certain knowledge about the site. Kopland stated: "This is what the scientist and the poet share, this ability to have an aesthetic experience, when the 'I' disappears for a moment in favour of the 'it'."[9]

Indeed, when I stood in the white immensity of the lake, *I* realized that *it* was the endless, limitless white that caused the architects to build as they did. And here, my personal impression of the vastness of that aesthetic image pointed to a more general realization, "received" through a poetic reading, through the very receptivity to the site. It is precisely this experience that is of great importance for topo-analysis and Reading Architecture: the discovery, or revelation is precisely that phenomenological moment when the highly personal experience gains a larger relevance, when subject and object merge, when, in the words of Bachelard, "the duality of subject and object is iridescent, shimmering, unceasingly active in its inversions."[10]

It is in this aspect that a poetic gaze should not be discarded as something vague, subjective, or internal. The same skill of making unexpected connections unites the poet and the scientist. As Kopland's argument shows, poetic writing as well as scientific discovery are both a form of precise and careful observation that reveals answers within the studied reality:

> As if you get an answer to an unposed question, as if you experience a connection of which you did not yet know it existed. And not only that: it is like, at the same time, reality could unveil more of its secrets, as if it has new connections already there for you. All you need to do is pull away the veil.[11]

The Poetic Moment and After: Time and Again

Indeed, the poetic moment that Bachelard and Kopland describe, the moment in which reality unveils certain knowledge to the receptive observer, when subject and object merge and when new connections are made, is a crucial moment in architectural investigations. In which way, however, can a researcher in architecture go forward from there? Kopland suggest that even though the aesthetic receptivity of the scientist and the poet are much alike, their modes of working differ:

> From the moment, however, they start to reconstruct their aesthetic experience, their ways part. Method literally means "the way along which one goes forward." The one comes up with new experiments within which he is able to unveil from reality new secrets; the other polishes the lens of language over and over until he sees what he suspected.[12]

After my first visit to Hvitträsk in 1998, when my knowledge about the background of the project was still limited, I returned several times, in different seasons and with different company. Meanwhile, I had gained more knowledge and experience of Finnish architecture and of the specific period of National Romantic that Saarinen, Gesellius, and Lindgren represented. I had visited several of their other buildings, knew more about their biographies and the position of the Hvitträsk episode in their lives, I knew from my own experience the particularities of the Finnish landscape and its seasonality. This knowledge may have colored my subsequent readings of the project. Despite what the idea of receptivity may suggest, this does not blur the perception. Seeing things as anew, as Kopland recommends, does not means that things have to be seen for the first time only. Poetic receptivity should remain an attitude that transpires through subsequent "readings" of architecture and that may add layers of perception and layers of meaning. For instance, I realized that these heavy rooms had been at one stage thin pencil sketches on transparent paper, sparks of imagination that did not yet materialize. There is an intriguing contrast between the fleeting, temporariness of sketches and the solidness of their realization. These sketches, capturing the light, the view from the hill, the delicacies of the site and the imagination of a sheltered family life in that still uninhabited landscape:

once pencil sketches,
ephemeral as the light
caressing the hill

At my visits to Hvitträsk, of course, I was a perceiving subject, but I was receptive to the way the object and even its former inhabitants "spoke." I noticed the craftsmanship, the hands which had drawn the details, which had shaped the floors and corners and tables—Hvitträsk was a true *Gesammtkunstwerk*: the collective design included not only the house itself but also the annexes and interior elements. Not only the spaces, but also all pieces of furniture, from chairs to children-beds, from desks to carpets, were designed specifically for the house. They seemed to transpire and idea of nestling, finding nooks and shelter, creating intimate places in the vastness of the land.

they had become
transformed by knives and paint
by running feet and touching hands
these trodden floors and creaking doors
these corners and uneven stairs and
rooms nestling between full-grown trees

With almost a century between the construction of the house and my visits, it was evident that the rooms were marked by use, by simply being lived in; they showed traces of life itself. Looking at the many details, the house seemed to be so full of memories and a sense of continuity as well became apparent. Did, in a distant way, the perceptions of the original dwellers resonate within my own? How did they smell the blossom of roses in the garden after rain, hear footsteps of children on the stairs? I could imagine the sounds as if time, the century in between my experience and theirs, had for a moment disappeared.

*between years and seasons
bathing in sunlight
floating on the lake-
the children's voices
the roses, the rain, the wood, it all
still smells the same.*

Indeed, while the poet and the scientist each follow their own paths after their poetic moment of revelation, I suggest that the researcher in the field of architecture, may benefit from architecture's mediating capacity, and follow both paths simultaneously. Indeed, architecture, as a discipline balancing between poetry and science, between the artistic, the technical and the social, may require a multi-faceted way of research into its field. Maintaining a sense of receptivity while diving deeper into historical and analytical knowledge around the object, may allow for a rich reading of architecture, combining the intuitive with the analytical, the historical with the descriptive. In this way, the reading of architecture becomes a rich and complex field of study, which reveals multiple dimensions of architecture. The outcomes of such investigations will include poetic texts, analysis of historical and contemporary plans and sketches, and precise and careful descriptions of site specific forms, shapes, details, colors, and materials, bound together by the careful, receptive reading of the lived experience that architecture has to offer.

FIGURE 6.1 The lake at Hvitträsk, Southern Finland.

FIGURE 6.2 Herman Gesellius, Armas Lindgren, and Eliel Saarinen, Hvitträsk, Kirkonummi, Finland, 1902.

FIGURE 6.3 Fireplace and seating room.

FIGURE 6.4 Interior elements such as carpets were designed specifically for Hvitträsk.

FIGURE 6.5 Interior staircase.

FIGURE 6.6 Garden pavilion with view down the hill.

FIGURE 6.7 Dining room.

All photos in this chapter by author

Hvitträsk[13]

still, that this vastness is inhabited
silent steps from the lake
towards the fire
once pencil sketches,
ephemeral as the light
caressing the hill
they had become
transformed by knives and paint
by running feet and touching hands

these trodden floors and creaking doors
these corners and uneven stairs and
rooms nestling between full-grown trees
between years and seasons
bathing in sunlight
floating on the lake-
the children's voices
the roses, the rain, the wood, it all
still smells the same

Notes

1 Fernando Pessoa/Alberto Caeiro, *The Collected Poems of Alberto Caeiro*, poem "The Keeper of Flocks XXIV" English translation Chris Daniels (Exeter: Shearsman Books, 2007), 15–72.
2 Rutger Kopland, *Het mechaniek van de ontroering*, [the Mechanics of Emotion] translation Klaske Havik (Amsterdam: Van Oorschot, 1995), 30.
3 Gaston Bachelard, *The Poetics of Space* (Boston, MA: Beacon Press, 1994), xxviii.
4 Philosopher Edward S. Casey argues that: "Less a method than an attitude, topo-analysis focuses on the placial properties of certain images." Edward S. Casey, *The Fate of Place— A Philosophical History* (Berkeley: University of California Press, 1997), 288.
5 Alberto Pérez-Gómez *Attunement. Architectural Meaning after the Crisis of Modern Science* (Cambridge, MA: MIT Press, 2016), 181.
6 Gaston Bachelard uses the term topo-analysis as a field of research, connecting the poetic imagination to the physical reality of place.
7 See for instance Egon Tempel, *New Finnish Architecture* (London: The Architectural Press, 1968), 15–17.
8 A version of this description appeared in Dutch in the literary magazine DW B. Maria Barnas and Klaske Havik, "Een huis van huizen, fragmenten van een correspondentie" (A house of houses, fragments of a correspondence), DW B, issue 3/2012.
9 Rutger Kopland, *Het mechaniek van de ontroering*, translation Klaske Havik (Amsterdam: Van Oorschot, 1995), 30.
10 Gaston Bachelard, *The Poetics of Space*, xix.
11 Rutger Kopland, *Het mechaniek van de ontroering*, 30. I have used this particular part of the quote of Kopland before in the chapter "Reading Places" of my book Klaske Havik, *Urban Literacy. Reading and Writing Architecture* (Rotterdam: Nai010 publishers, 2014), 68.
12 Rutger Kopland, *Het mechaniek van de ontroering*, 30.
13 Poem by the author.

7

W. G. SEBALD'S *AUSTERLITZ*

Architecture as a Bridge between the Lost Past and the Present

Rumiko Handa

Introduction

Architecture has a way of bringing the past to the present for us. It is an important asset, for the experience of the past constitutes a positive moment in our everyday conduct of life, allowing a contemplation on our existential meaning. It is an often-neglected aspect, as it lies outside of architecture's aesthetic, functional, or structural realms. Mechanisms at work in effectuating this feature can vary, among which the following are notable: A building may commemorate a particular event or individual by being a monument. A building may refer to the time of its origin by way of its style. I also have likened architecture to palimpsest, on the surface of which an old writing, once washed off, has resurfaced.[1] Not unlike palimpsest, a building may call back a once-forgotten past event by way of physical traces it carries. My focus here, however, is on the everyday architecture, which, without having deliberate designation (monument), requiring specialized knowledge (style), or carrying physical trace (palimpsest), nonetheless brings the past to the present for us.

Needless to say, I am not claiming that the presentation of the past happens anytime, to anyone, or with any piece of architecture. Nor am I here to find out under what circumstances it occurs. Instead, I am interested to see how architecture participates in people's experience of the past when it does so in their everyday life. My study is about experiential, rather than physical, qualities of architecture, although of course I certainly am interested in the physical attributes that contribute to the experience. And the study will benefit from exemplary experiences rather than actual ones of any kind, especially since the accounts of my own experiences would not have much credibility. For these reasons, I have chosen a piece of fiction for my study, with the expectation that by doing so I will take advantage of a literary author's acute sensitivity to the environment and keen ability to describe his reactions. The literary piece is *Austerlitz* (2001) by W. G. Sebald (1944–2001) in particular. In the story full of architectural descriptions, the physical environment works as a catalyst by which the eponymous protagonist regains the past he once lost and as a place in which he seeks his parents' past he himself has never experienced.

Ephemeral Past Event—Personal Recollection

Human actions are physical but ephemeral, and hence, they sometimes leave their material trace on the building but other times do not. London's Victoria and Albert Museum, for example, carries scars of a past event. On July 3, 1944, a flying bomb hit the other side of Exhibition Road, which runs along the Museum's western wall. The blast caused visible damages on the Portland stone, but not to the extent to threaten the building's structure or the museum's function. The Museum left them unrepaired, adding an inscription carved into the wall to explain their provenance. Some passers-by today notice the imperfections on the stone surfaces.

In comparison, London's Chinese New Year celebration leaves no physical trace on the buildings. Every year, a line of people winds through the streets of London's West End carrying a long dragon puppet on stilts. A lion puppet leads a procession, stopping at each door on the street to give blessings for good fortune and prosperity for the year. Others follow with drums, gongs, and cymbals, making loud noises to scare away evil and bad luck. Onlookers maneuver through the crowd, attempting to capture the dancing parade with cameras and eyeing store windows for the best roast duck. Children play with firecrackers, and street vendors test their luck selling zodiac charms, paper dragons, and toy drums as well as spring rolls, noodles, and steamed dumplings. But when these activities are over and the red hanging lanterns are taken down, the buildings return to their previous calm and quest state as if the festivities never took place there.

When the Chinese New Year celebration is recalled by those who revisit Chinatown, it is a case of memento, rather than palimpsest. To appreciate the nature of memento, Hans-Georg Gadamer's explanation is useful:

> Of all signs, the memento most seems to have a reality of its own. It refers to the past and so is effectively a sign, but it is also precious in itself since, as a bit of the past that has not disappeared, it keeps the past present for us. But it is clear that this characteristic is not grounded in the being of the object itself. A memento has value as a memento only for someone who already— i.e., still—recalls the past. Mementos lose their value when the past of which they remind one no longer has any meaning.[2]

Relying not on physical trace but on people's personal memory, Chinatown's reference to the Chinese New Year event fulfills Gadamer's definition by being "not grounded in the being of the object itself" but instead having value "only for someone who already . . . recalls the past." That is, strictly speaking, a memento's effect applies only to the person who personally experienced that specific past. (Although this statement may seem self-evident, I will need to come back to it later as we discuss the role of architecture in recalling the ephemeral past.) Beyond being useful, solid, or pleasing to the eye, the everyday architecture has a potential of being a memento, and as such, it is "a bit of the past that has not disappeared" and "keeps the past present for us."

W. G. Sebald, *Austerlitz*

In W.G. Sebald's *Austerlitz*, Dafydd Elias is brought up by a minister and his wife in a small rural Welsh town. With the minister committed to a mental asylum after his wife's death, Dafydd is told at the boarding school that he was adopted, and his real name is Jacques Austerlitz. Shortly after taking an early retirement in 1991 from a London institute of art history, Austerlitz is in Liverpool Street Station, where he has a vision of himself as a small child being met by his foster parents at the same spot. Hearing by chance about Kindertransport on the radio in a Bloomsbury bookstore, Austerlitz is convinced that he was one of the children brought on the program from Prague. Determined to find his lost past, he visits the city, and meets his old nanny, Věra Ryšanová, who had been his mother's neighbor and still lives in the same flat. Věra confirms that Austerlitz in fact left Prague on a train in 1939 at the age of four. From Prague, Austerlitz goes to Theresienstadt, the site of the ghetto to which his mother, Agátha Austerlitzová, was taken before being sent further east. Austerlitz then traces back his childhood journey from Prague to London. He takes a residence in Paris, having learned his father, Maximilian Aychenwald, lived there after escaping the Nazis. The story ends when Austerlitz decides to take himself to the site of the Gurs internment camp, to look further for the past of his father.

Austerlitz unarguably is a story of someone, who in his childhood was separated from his own parents during the persecution of Jewish people by the Nazis. And yet, at its core is a much more universal question of how the past figures in one's existential meaning of life. And throughout the book the physical environment works as a catalyst, as Austerlitz experiences the past.

Liverpool Street Station

The novel's section that features Liverpool Street Station demonstrates how Sebald incorporates a piece of architecture into his story. One "quiet Sunday morning" shortly before 1992, while the station was undergoing a renovation project, Austerlitz is sitting on a bench on "the particularly gloomy platform where the boat train from Harwich comes in."[3] He had repeatedly come to this station since long before the renovation began in the late 1980s, which he describes as "one of the darkest and most sinister places in London, a kind of entrance to the underworld, as it was often been described," "with its main concourse fifteen to twenty feet below street level."[4] From the bench he wanders off to find himself

W. G. Sebald's *Austerlitz* 75

FIGURE 7.1 Liverpool Street Station, London.
Photo by author

in a disused old ladies' waiting room. There he has a vision in which huge halls open up, with rows of pillars and colonnades leading far into the distance, with vaults and brickwork arches bearing on them many-storied structures, with flights of stone steps, wooden stairways and ladders, all leading the eye on and on. He wonders:

> whether it was a ruin or a building in the process of construction that I had entered. Both ideas were right in a way at the time, since the new station was literally rising from the ruins of the old Liverpool Street.[5]

And there and then, he sees in his mind's eye a minister and his wife, both middle-aged and dressed in the style of the thirties. He then sees the boy whom they had come to meet, sitting on a bench with the small rucksack.

What stirs Austerlitz's memory in the story, which entices the reader's imagination as well, is the station building, which Sebald describes in detail, without hiding the imperfections of the everyday architecture:

> The ballast between the tracks, the cracked sleepers, the brick walls with their stone bases, the cornices and panes of the tall windows, the wooden kiosks for the ticket inspectors, and the towering cast-iron columns with their palmate capitals were all covered in a greasy black layer formed, over the course of a century, by coke dust and soot, steam, sulfur, and diesel oil. Even on sunny days only a faint grayness, scarcely illuminated at all by the globes of the station lights, came through the glass roof over the main hall, and in this eternal dusk, which was full of a muffled babble of voices, a quiet scraping and trampling of feet, innumerable people passed in great tides, disembarking from the trains or boarding them, coming together, moving apart, and being held up at barriers and bottlenecks like water against a weir.[6]

Sebald describes Austerlitz at Liverpool Street Station as if the latter has encased him in a capsule within the environment, stimulated by the surrounding sights and sounds but without the pragmatic immediacy of, for example, the need to find his train before it leaves the station.

The Imaginary in the Real

Two literary strategies that Sebald applied in *Austerlitz* are of significance both in terms of the piece's literary success and to the present study. From the literary point of view, these strategies help succeed in bringing together two sets of two spheres each: Setting fictional events in actual buildings allows the imaginary to merge with the real; and the use of the first person singular, "I," to multiple personalities without separating their speeches by quotation marks takes the personal to the collective. From the point of view of the present study, what these literary strategies accomplish demonstrate the important nature of the experience when architectural pieces bring the past to the present for us: the experience is unavoidably ethereal and at the same time forcefully grounded, and it is at once acutely personal and assuredly shared. In other words, when we contemplate in a building on the past that took place there, we experience both the sense of identity, as "the past is what makes the person," and that of solidarity, with our contemporaries as well as predecessors, no matter if they are our blood relation or only connected to us by being human. I do not know whether Sebald himself intended his work to demonstrate this aspect of architecture; however, with or without his intention, Sebald's narrative, which undoubtedly is fueled by his acute sensitivity to the environment and keen ability to describe his reactions, provides us with important material for the study of architecture.

When it comes to placing a fiction in real buildings and succeeding in sharing with the reader the world of historical past, a parallel can be drawn to the literary strategies of the nineteenth-century author Sir Walter Scott, the champion author of historical fiction. For example, in *Kenilworth: A Romance*, the story takes place in real buildings—Kenilworth Castle in Warwickshire and Cumner Place near Oxford. Not only are Scott's buildings real, but their descriptions also are factual and attentively given, about their forms, details, materials, and even histories. And Scott's characters—Queen Elizabeth, Robert Dudley, the Queen's favorite at court, Amy Robsart, Dudley's wife, and others—are historical although their actions in the story are historically accurate only to a small extent. Visitors rushed to the castle to experience the story in place, among whom were Charles Dickens (1838), Queen Victoria (1858), and Henry James (1870s). Eelco Runia characterizes the parallel between the two authors as the "translation of time into space," in which a physical place "is not just a scenic backdrop, but the dense, laden, and multifarious presence of what had happened" in the past, and is where "the whole of history is stored . . . that can be 'visited' on the plane of the present."[7] Runia has articulated this aspect of the space of the present standing in for the time of the past by the notion of "presence," that is, the past (time) is present (alive) in the present (space), and has characterized it as metonymy. Literally meaning change of name, metonymy is often considered as a figure of speech in which the name of an attribute or adjunct is substituted for that of the thing meant, e.g., scepter for authority. Comparing metonymy with metaphor, Runia emphasizes the notion of presence in the former:

> Whereas metaphor is instrumental in the "transfer of meaning," metonymy brings about a "transfer of presence." A metonymy is a "presence in absence" not just in the sense that it presents something that isn't there, but also in the sense that in the absence (or at least the radical inconspicuousness) that is there, the thing that isn't there is still present.[8]

Unlike Scott's, Sebald's key characters are not well-known historical figures; however, they come very close. The narrator, born in Germany and residing in England, is remarkably like Sebald himself. As to Austerlitz, a number of Sebald reviewers looked for a model in real life, in vain. Austerlitz's place of employment, "a London institute of art history," undoubtedly refers to the Courtauld Institute, part of the University of London system, not only because of the Institute's location and specialization but also from the reference to a book supposedly written by a colleague of Austerlitz's. The book, which is about the author's search for his grandfather, a Jew whose family escaped the persecution because of his premature

FIGURE 7.2 "... I was surprised by the simple beauty of the wooden flooring, made of planks of different widths, and by the unusually tall windows, each divided into a hundred and twenty-two lead-framed square glass panes, ..." (2011, 315). Royal Observatory, Greenwich, United Kingdom.

Photo by author

death, is *Heshel's Kingdom,* although Sebald does not refer to it by the title, and its author, Dan Jacobson, whom Sebald explicitly names, is a Professor Emeritus in English at University College London.[9] Since University College London also belongs to the University of London system, it is natural to assume Courtault as the model, and it is understandable if critics and readers looked for a model of Austerlitz at the Institute.

Many buildings in the story, in addition to Liverpool Street Station mentioned above, are familiar to the general reader. The Great Eastern Hotel next door to Liverpool Street Station is the site of repeated meetings between the narrator and Austerlitz, where the latter recounts his experiences to the former. In the Royal Observatory in Greenwich, Austerlitz questions the notion of the passage of time.[10]

In Palace Hotel at Marienbad, in 1972, long before him knowing his past, Austerlitz has an unexplainable sense of unease, which makes him turn away from the present and especially from Marie de Verneuil, the only human being with whom Austerlitz has ever been able to build an intimate relationship. And later, Austerlitz learns from Věra that it is a place where his parents took him on a vacation the year before he was to be placed in the Kindertransport program.[11] In Estates Theatre in Prague, sitting in a seat in the auditorium, Austerlitz remembers having seen "a sky-blue shoe embroidered with silver sequins" behind the stage curtain, through the space between the stage floor and the hem of the curtain, which Věra later tells him his mother wore.[12] And in Gare Austerlitz in Paris, while Austerlitz has a premonition that he was coming closer to his father, he also has a vision of his father leaving Paris from this station, leaning out of the window as the train moved away.[13] Not so familiar but actual nonetheless are the ghetto at Theresienstadt and the camp at Gurs. Austerlitz's house in London and his apartment in Paris as well as the building in which Agátha had her flat and Věra still does in Prague, are identified by addresses that actually exist in reality, although these residential buildings are not publicly accessible.

The Personal to the Collective

The second strategy concerns the use of the first person singular. The book is written as various pieces of the past recounted by the book's narrator. The narrator strikes up a conversation with Austerlitz in the waiting hall of Antwerp Central Station in 1967, and since then repeatedly meets him, in varied intervals of a day to 30 years, sometimes by chance and other times by the protagonist's invitation. In these meetings the narrator hears Austerlitz' stories, which sometimes are Austerlitz's own personal experiences recounted by himself, sometimes are Austerlitz's experiences that he had forgotten but Věra told him, and other times are Věra's experiences she recounted to Austerlitz. Sebald the author has assigned "I" equally to all these three persons when their experiences are told. As a result, "I" can be any of the three individuals. The "I" in many cases is immediately followed by "said Austerlitz," specifying the person who is recollecting the past, but the "I" narration sometimes goes on a number of sentences before another insertion specifies the subject. Furthermore, especially when Věra's narrative is being recounted, "I" can be Austerlitz, as in the former of the following quotations, and can be Věra herself, as in the latter:

> But I was particularly anxious, *Věra told me, said Austerlitz*, not to miss the moment when Moravec put down his needle and thread, his big scissors and the other tools of his trade, cleared the baize-covered table, spread a double sheet of newspaper on it, and laid out on this sheet blackened with print the supper he must have been looking forward to for some time, a supper which varied according to the season and might be curd cheese with chives, a long radish, a few tomatoes with onions, a smoked herring or boiled potatoes.[14]
>
> And I remember, *Věra told me, said Austerlitz*, that it was Aunt Otýlie who taught you to count at the age of three and a half, using a row of small, shiny black malachite buttons sewn to an elbow-length velvet glove which you particularly liked—jedna, dva, třii, counted Věra, and I, said Austerlitz, went on counting—čtyři, pět, šest, sedm—feeling like someone taking uncertain steps out on to the ice.[15]

Characterized by James Wood as the "repetitive attribution" borrowed from Thomas Bernhard, the strategy succeeds in blurring the distinction between biography and autobiography and allowing the memento, which by definition "has value as a memento only for someone who already—i.e., still—recalls the past," to leave its confines and to enter the spheres of the narrator and, furthermore, that of the reader.[16] This strategy gives rise to interchangeability between the narrator and the protagonist, and encourages the reader's empathy toward the characters. Walter Scott applied a similar strategy. In *Kenilworth: A Romance* mentioned above, Scott the author/narrator oscillated between the "tale-teller" or a contemporary witness to the sixteenth-century events, and the nineteenth-century antiquarian who historicized them, and succeeded in telling an intriguing story of ambition and love surrounding Queen Elizabeth.[17]

Flight from the Memento

Setting the imaginary in the factual and shifting the personal into the collective, Sebald has demonstrated how everyday architecture goes beyond being a memento. As discussed earlier with an example of Chinese New Year celebrations, when the past is recalled in a piece of architecture by a person who directly experienced it there, the building is working as a memento. In *Austerlitz*, the experience of the past in an architectural setting is released from the bounds of a single individual to the shared horizon. What Sebald's writing demonstrates furthermore, by succeeding in moving the reader, is the desire that exists in human nature to make common

FIGURE 7.3 "In any case, said Austerlitz, I felt more panic-stricken with every passing minutes, . . . I had to stop under the red sandstone arch of a window displaying the pages of the local Nuremberg newspaper, . . ." (2011, 141). Storefront on King Street, Nuremberg, Germany.

Photo by author

experiences out of the past, either of one's own or of others, which Gadamer called the "fusion of horizons."[18] There certainly are instances in which Austerlitz recalls his own personal direct experience in a piece of architecture.

The fusion of horizons does not stop with the shared experiences between Austerlitz and the narrator or Austerlitz and the reader. In addition, Austerlitz seeks to acquaint himself with his parents, long dead and lost in the past, by way of experiencing their pasts in his imagination in the real buildings. He intentionally places himself in the physical environments in which his parent had experiences: and they are, for example, the camp at Theresienstadt, for his mother, and Nuremberg and the camp at Gurs, for his father. Austerlitz himself has never been to these places, but is re-living (or imagining) the experience that his parent might have had.

Experiencing the Past and the Existential Meaning of Life

For Austerlitz, the search for his lost past is that for his personhood and identity. While Austerlitz, who grew up not knowing his origin, felt acutely in need of his lost past, the past being the personhood applies to everyone, although it is just not so acutely felt. This has been well pointed out by a number of thinkers in philosophy and human geography, including Martin Heidegger, Paul, Ricoeur, David Lowenthal, and David Carr. According to Carr:

> How historicity relates to everyday experience: . . . I gain my identity in opposition to others, but it is also true that one asserts one's identity by joining with others. . . . As a member of a community I become part of a We-subject with an experience of time that extends back before my birth and can continue even after my death. . . . being a member of a community means belonging to a temporally continuous entity whose temporality exceeds that of my own subjectivity. . . . as members of families and other communities, we have a direct and lived relationship to history. . . . It is here that it [the past] functions as part of our identity as individuals and enters into our lives and everyday experience.[19]

The human desire to recall one's own past or to imagine the shared past is so strong that it is as if we look for some sort of solidarity with ourselves of different times. Sebald's *Austerlitz* demonstrates how architecture contributes to the existential meaning of life: it not only brings the past to the present for us, but when it does, it also endows us with the sense of identity and that of solidarity, in the surrounds of both our contemporary and predecessors.

Conclusion: Moving Ahead with His Life

At the end of the story, before Austerlitz leaves Paris for Gurs, he tells the narrator that, after Gurs, he might look for Marie. Austerlitz is resolved to bring to an end his search for his father's past and with it for his self, and to reconnect with Marie, whom he lost once when he had an uneasy experience at Marienbad. When they were there, Austerlitz could not get rid of the feeling that someone else was walking side by side with him. He could not relate himself to the present moment, including Marie. And it was the decisive moment at which their relationship broke with neither of them able to explain what was happening to Austerlitz's state of mind. Of course, Austerlitz now knows that the someone walking along him was himself from the past. That means that he can come to terms with himself, and he can be ready to resume the life, which he had to give a hold while in search for his lost past.

This is a solace that Sebald gives us at the end. Austerlitz no longer needs to dwell in the past. He is ready to take up the present.

Notes

1 Rumiko Handa, *Allure of the Incomplete, Imperfect, and Impermanent: Designing and Appreciating Architecture as Nature* (New York: Routledge, 2015), Chapter 5.
2 Hans-Georg Gadamer, *Truth and Method* (New York: Crossroad, 1989), 152–3.
3 W. G. Sebald, *Austerlitz*, English (New York: Modern Library, 2001), 132.
4 Ibid., 127–8.
5 Ibid., 136.
6 Ibid., 128.
7 Eelco Runia, "Presence," *History and Theory* 45, no. 1 (2006): 1–29; 1 and 10.
8 Ibid., 1.
9 Dan Jacobson, *Heshel's Kingdom, Jewish Lives* (Evanston, Ill: Northwestern University Press, 1998).
10 The time is a continuous flow, without any punctuation. Sebald does not have any paragraph breaks in his writing.
11 W. G. Sebald, Anthea Bell, and James Wood. *Austerlitz* (New York: Modern Library, 2011), 289–90.
12 Ibid., 228.
13 Ibid., 405–6.
14 Ibid., 220.
15 Ibid., 226.
16 James Wood, "Introduction," W. G. Sebald, *Austerlitz*, trans. by Anthea Bell (New York: Modern Library, 2011), xii. Wood links this strategy to another strategy of Sebald's, "extremism," which "cunningly combines the quiet and the loud."
17 Rumiko Handa, *Allure of the Incomplete, Imperfect, and Impermanent*, Chapter 4.
18 Hans-Georg Gadamer, *Truth and Method, A Continuum Book* (New York: Seabury Press, 1975).
19 David Carr, *Experience and History: Phenomenological Perspectives on the Historical World* (New York: Oxford University Press, 2014), 51–4.

8
POETIC IMAGINATION AND THE ARCHITECTURE OF POE

Lisa Landrum

Edgar Allan Poe's best-known stories depict dark and dreary settings. More intriguing for architectural research are two tales featuring protagonists who design dazzling and fantastic settings. These protagonists do not succumb to negative circumstances, as do the hapless tenants in "The Fall of the House of Usher" (1839), but instead strive to overcome adversity by transforming their milieu. A poetic hero in "The Visionary" (1834) and a grieving scholar in "Ligeia" (1838) each fashion a chamber that alters, intensifies, and transcends their involvement with reality. As in all of Poe's fiction, these chambers represent fallible states of mind.[1] But, whereas Usher's house and mind are haunted palaces afflicted by debilitating misery, the persons and places in "The Visionary" and "Ligeia" offer restorative sanctuaries, exceedingly magnificent and magical. These characters and settings embody the resilient fervor of poetic imagination, aspiring to what Poe deemed poetry's ultimate aim: "supernal beauty" via "elevating excitement of the soul."[2] Although the protagonists in "The Visionary" and "Ligeia" ultimately yield—by choice and design—to mortality and madness, the rooms they devise endure as embodiments of poetic desire. As meta-poetic constructs, these settings illuminate Poe's motives and methods as a poet, storyteller, and cultural critic. By interpreting the manifold composition, effect, and agency of these storied chambers, this chapter aims to clarify their value for architectural research. Together with representing modern anxieties, these tales dramatize interactions of psyche and setting, revealing personal imagination and architectural environments to be meaningfully intertwined.

Close Circumscription

In his 1846 essay "Philosophy of Composition," Poe maintained: "a close *circumscription of space* is absolutely necessary to the effect of insulated incident."[3]

True to this tenet, Poe's settings convey both enveloping intimacy and close participation in narrative events. For instance, in "The Fall of the House of Usher" Poe forges fateful links between places, persons, and plots, as the Usher house, siblings, and ancestry mutually suffer physical and moral decline. While choreographing interdependencies of characters and settings, Poe creates all-enveloping atmospheres, establishing what he calls in "Island of the Fay" (1841), "one vast animate and sentient whole."[4] Poe conjures this synthetic whole with immensity of scope and "minuteness of detail" (873), striving, like the narrator before a bewildering landscape in "The Domain of Arnheim" (1847), to circumscribe "combined vastness and definitiveness" (863).[5]

"The Visionary" and "Ligeia" likewise have efficacious settings intricately bound to narrative events. Yet, these tales uniquely emphasize the protagonists' role in designing their own environment. In "The Visionary," the hero boasts of his "originality of conception in architecture and upholstery" (205), and implores a confounded guest to behold the "medley of architectural embellishments" in the private chamber of his Venetian palazzo (211). As this guest lends his ear to the ill-fated hero, his eye wanders curiously over the chamber's magnificent assembly of eclectic artifacts: Greek paintings, Italian sculptures, Egyptian carvings, Arabesque censers, rich draperies, Chinese carpets, Renaissance tragedies, and Etruscan vases—all engulfed in peculiar qualities of light, scent, and sound. In "Ligeia," the grieving scholar is unable to recall the circumstances of meeting his love, but vividly remembers every detail of the chamber he made to alleviate the sorrow of her death: "There is no individual portion of the architecture and decoration [. . .] which is not now visibly before me" (270). Conjuring this pentagonal chamber in a remote English abbey, he recounts its captivating exotica: Egyptian sarcophagi lodged in five corners; a dark Venetian window; billowing gold draperies bearing black Arabesque figures; tufted gold carpets with Bedlam patterns; Indian ottomans; golden candelabras "of Eastern figure"; a vaulted ceiling "elaborately-fretted" with grotesque "specimens of semi-Gothic, semi-Druidical device"; and, suspended from this "excessively lofty" vault by a golden chain, a Saracenic censer casting a faint shadow on the golden carpet, while animating all with "ghastly luster" of "writhing" serpent-like flames (270–1).

Multiform Combinations and Exotic Imaginations

Like the museum interiors of John Soane, Poe's narratively concise but evocatively expansive settings are packed with curios: exotic, antique, and fantastic elements from different times and places. Such fragments were less emblems of loss than means of invention: stimuli to memory, imagination, and synthetic understanding.[6] For Poe, these ornaments purposefully dramatized manifold inspirations at play in creatively conflicted minds. To grasp how eclectic ensembles perform in each tale, it is helpful to recall their role in Poe's compositional philosophy.

Opposing "odious uniformity,"[7] Poe sought poetic fulfillment through "multiform combinations among the things and thoughts of Time."[8] Advocating "unusual combinations," especially "novel arrangements of old forms," he made it the task of Imagination to choose "the most combinable things hitherto uncombined," and the province of Fantasy to join "incongruous or antagonistical elements," in ways engendering pleasurable pain.[9] A paradisical prison in "The Domain of Arnheim" exemplifies Poe's combinatory poetics. The penultimate feature of this landscape is a vast amphitheatre, wherein hundreds of glittering oriels, minarets, and pinnacles soar, all mingled with Arabian perfumes, exotic plants, and foreign dirges. And this synesthetic "mass of semi-Gothic, semi-Saracenic architecture" appears "the phantom handiwork" of not a single mortal architect but a diversity of mythic agencies (Sylphs, Fairies, Genii, and Gnomes) working "conjointly" (870).

Poe's pursuit of variety within unity and composed irregularity developed in relation to aesthetic theories of the picturesque.[10] Yet, Poe concurrently crafted landscapes of the mind.[11] The chambers in "The Visionary" and "Ligeia" harbor ordered chaos of hypersensitive imaginations. Especially striking is their fusion of Eastern and Gothic horizons, mingling strange and familiar, known and unknown. According to one interpreter, this meeting of Orient and Occident "epitomizes artistic excess," while betraying "Poe's rejection of literary provincialism."[12] Like his contemporaries, Poe appropriated Eastern motifs as exotic figures of "sensuality, promise, terror, sublimity, idyllic pleasure [and] intense energy."[13] Yet, he also used them critically and hyperbolically, exposing insufficiencies of Western aesthetics, while symbolizing imagination's striving for universal truth.

Moreover, Poe viewed exotic artifacts with equal fascination and disdain. Spurs to poetic imagination, they were also problematically associated with fetishized spoils of colonialism, false shows of wisdom and empty displays of wealth. In "Philosophy of Furniture" (1840), Poe condemned American practices of parading costly appurtenances. Elsewhere he treated opulence with satire—an effective goad toward social and moral change. For example, in "Bargain Lost" (1832) and "The Duc de L'Omelette" (1832), Poe associated decadent décor with philosophical and aristocratic pretentions prevalent in post-Revolutionary/pre-Civil War America. Although there are elements of social satire in "The Visionary" and "Ligeia," their decadent chambers and indulgent characters epitomize a more poetic conceit: to appropriate and transform worldly materials for transcendental pursuits of supernal beauty.

Bower of Dreams: "The Visionary" (1834)[14]

Throughout "The Visionary" Poe develops close correlations between an unnamed poetic hero, his tragic fate and Venetian milieu. The setting especially dramatizes symbolic tensions between light and dark, levity and solemnity, the transience of life and permanence of art. An anonymous narrator—adrift on a gondola—relays the tale. Through him we first see the conflicted hero near the Bridge of Sighs in the "deep of midnight," stepping out from a "dark, gloomy niche" beneath "solemn cornices" of the Old Republican Prison. Emerging from "shadows—in its architecture," the hero shares characteristics with the "stateliest building in all Venice" (202). From this niche the hero plunges into the canal's abyss to recover a drowning child. He returns the child alive, amid blazing torchlight, to its mother Marchesa Aphrodite, who stands within a threshold of black marble at the canal's edge. As her statuesque figure trembles and blushes, we glean they are secret lovers. She enigmatically promises to meet him an hour after sunrise.

Whereas the hero is introduced in "pitchy darkness" punctuated by torchlight, the next morning we see him at dawn in his palazzo's radiant chamber. Designed to "blind," "dizzy," "dazzle," and "astound," this chamber is burdened by a "fitful stain of melancholy" (210). Gazing about, the narrator beholds Greek paintings, Italian sculptures, and Egyptian carvings. He then describes the exceedingly magnificent light in animate detail: "multitudinous flaring and flickering tongues of emerald and violet fire," together with conflicting perfumes, emanated from "strange convolute censers"; "rays of the newly risen sun poured in upon the whole, through windows . . . of crimson-tinted glass"; and these natural and artificial beams "fitfully" commingled in "a thousand reflections" from shimmering draperies, which "trembled to the vibration of low melancholic music . . . [and] rolled from their cornices like cataracts of molten silver," leaving light to "lay weltering in subdued masses upon a carpet of rich liquid-looking cloth of [Chinese] gold" (205). As in most of Poe's tales, this setting is presented not simply as a physical arrangement of windows, lamps, curtains, and carpets, but as a complexly interactive multisensory ensemble animated with variegated unity of effect.

At one level, this scintillating prism of multi-colored light betrays the hero's "rage for glitter"—a popular rage Poe ridiculed elsewhere as a "gaudy abomination," pleasing only "to children and idiots" (384–5). Even the hero laughs self-mockingly at his "completely ludicrous" chamber (205). Yet, the room's "unparalleled splendor" also demonstrates "brilliancy" of imagination. Poe frequently associated imagination with vigorous light, seeking "poetic fire," and "enkindling of imagination."[15] The first line of "The Visionary" establishes and problematizes this theme: "Ill-fated and mysterious man!—bewildered in the brilliancy of thine own imagination" (200). This opening points to the unbridled imagination of the hero (modeled on Lord Byron), while alluding to the outshining imagination of the storyteller (Poe), who reimagines the poet's death as it "*shouldst be*" (200).[16] This hyperbolic brilliancy also qualifies the chamber, prefiguring its participation in the tale's blissfully tragic end.

Although the chamber blazes with "princely magnificence," this magnificence is indecorous. The narrator is taken aback by the room's lack of "*keeping*" (205); and the poet admits choosing its ornaments with "little deference to the opinions of Virtû" (206). However, these improprieties befit the poet's purpose: "to dream has been the business of my life. I have therefore framed for myself . . . a bower of dreams . . . You behold around you, it is true, a medley of architectural embellishments. The chastity of Ionia is offended by antediluvian devices, and the sphynxes of Egypt are outstretched upon carpets of gold. Yet the effect is incongruous to the timid alone." Overreaching Aristotelian principles, he continues, "Proprieties of place, and especially of time, are the bugbears which terrify mankind from contemplation of the magnificent" (211). The chamber's antagonistic elements and "multiform combinations" are intended to turn the soul toward complex harmonies, seeking, what Poe calls elsewhere, "a wilder beauty than Earth supplies."[17] With parting words, the poet confesses the chamber's ultimate end: "Like these arabesque censers, my spirit is writhing in fire, and the delirium of this scene is fashioning me for the wilder visions of that land of real dreams wither I am now rapidly departing" (211). Then uttering prophetic verses in a final moment of brilliance, and having drunk from a blackened goblet, he succumbs to poison and dies. Thus, he manifests a suicide pact with his lover, fulfilling their promise to meet an hour after dawn in death's "hollow vale" (211).

In the same closing speech, the poet calls himself "decorist," having indulged in a "sublimation of folly" (211). Indeed, his chamber is a somber and sublime folly. Although its dazzling décor failed to secure mortal happiness, the fitting but fatal setting celebrates supernal beauty through meaningfully eclectic artworks. Each piece interpretively expands on key aspects of the story: ancient grotesqueries, embodying chimerical combinations; a Michelangelo marble, reminding that materiality matters; grinning Persepolian masks with vipers writhing out the eyes, honoring tragicomic strife; a luminous painting by Cimabue, recalling filial bonds; a dark Pietà, deifying passion's sacrifice; imperfectly restored statues of Venus and Apollo, projecting quasi-mythic status; two Etruscan vases, funerary urns to reunite victims of impossible love; and a melancholy portrait of Marchesa Aphrodite pointing down to a "curiously fashioned vase"—the source of poison (210). Among these telling artworks, Poe integrates a revealing poem, compactly comparing The Visionary's dilemma to the tragic love of Orpheus and Eurydice—a "dream too bright to last" (208). Although these lovers die, their aspirations to love and to dream persist through the "brilliancy" of shared imagination and poetic artifacts. The chamber's architectural embellishments participate in a transfiguration, attempting permanence through art.[18]

Phantasmagoric Chamber: "Ligeia" (1838)

The story of Ligeia is narrated by her grieving lover. He begins by mournfully recalling her strange beauty: her full raven-black hair and large radiant black eyes. He describes her rare and immense learning: her proficiency in "classical tongues" and "modern dialects"; her passion for "moral, physical and mathematical sciences"; and her prowess in navigating "the chaotic world of metaphysical investigation" and occult wisdom. He also laments her "gigantic volition," which sustained them both (262–6). But, in time, Ligeia grew ill. Her "fierce spirit" waned. After bidding her lover recite her poem on the cruel drama of death, she let out a defiant shriek and died. Crushed with sorrow, the lover abandoned their shared study in a "dim and decaying city by the Rhine," wandered aimlessly, then resettled in an abandoned abbey in England (269). There—in a turreted chamber of his own design—he took a second wife, Rowena, whose fair hair and blue eyes contrasted Ligeia's dark beauty as day to night. Whereas his bond with Ligeia was intensely intellectual, his relationship with Rowena grew mutually apathetic. He came to despise her. Soon Rowena fell ill. Watching Rowena decline, the lover became seized by visions of Ligeia. Appearing to succumb, Rowena's pale body was enshrouded for burial. Then, in the mysterious climax, Rowena's corpse stirred, arose, and advanced to the room's center. The lover rushed to join her. The shroud fell from her head, releasing "huge masses of long and disheveled hair . . . *blacker than the wings of the midnight*" (277). As she opened her eyes, the lover recognized not Rowena but the wild black eyes of Ligeia.

This tale is remarkable for its shocking yet ambiguous climax, which suggests the transmigration of Ligeia's undying soul to Rowena's lifeless body. Ligeia's "fierce spirit" seems to mysteriously quicken then fully possess Rowena, emerging alive from the gossamer death shroud as a dark butterfly from a cocoon. However, Poe rejected the simple reading that Ligeia lived again via Rowena; instead, he implied the lover's acute desire and afflicted consciousness sparked the illusory spectacle.[19] That this climax is not attributable to any single phenomenon is built into the tale. Myriad media and effects cooperatively enable the culminating metamorphosis, including the room's "architecture and decoration" (270), meticulously designed to engender "phantasmagorical influences" (272). Circumscribed as the locus of action, this influential setting performs as memory chamber, bridal chamber, death chamber, and transformative threshold. Its eclectic configuration, activated by prodigious imagination, concentrates and sustains Ligeia's influence.

As transformative threshold, this room is where Ligeia and Rowena meet. Some see these women as distinct incarnations of Romanticism: with dark Ligeia representing metaphysical depths of German Romanticism, and fair Rowena embodying its pale English imitation.[20] Others take them as opposing forms of beauty: Ligeia exemplifying "heavenly beauty which the poet's soul desires; while Rowena stands for that earthly, physical beauty which tempts the poet's passions."[21] These interpretations suggest a stark divide between metaphysical and mundane yearnings. Yet, Poe resisted false dualities, aiming instead to reconcile opposites, including a fusion of materialism and transcendentalism.[22] As he mused in *Eureka* (1848), "the material and the spiritual—accompany each other, in the strictest fellowship, forever" (1306). This suggests that Ligeia and Rowena are less incompatible opposites than inseparable complements. If Ligeia symbolizes poetic aspiration, as many argue,[23] then Rowena offers the prosaic medium through which poetry comes into being. In other words, a meta-poetic allegory animates Rowena's wavering between death and life, relapse and recovery, passivity and transformation. The efforts to restore her "pallid and rigid figure," which the storyteller experiences as a "hideous drama of revivification" (276), may be understood as a poetic struggle to enliven common language.

A meta-poetic allegory also animates the room, similarly enlivened through poetic imagination. The room embodies material interpretations of Ligeia's transcendental agencies. An "elaborately-fretted" and "excessively lofty" vault expresses her manifold and high-minded learning. Her occult wisdom is present through Arabesque ornaments, Celtic latticework, sculpted sarcophagi, and the room's pentagonal architecture—its magical geometry intensifying bodily senses while activating a sixth sense beyond mortal perception. The room's exotic phenomena manifest Ligeia's extra-sensory agencies. The black granite, solid ebony, fretted oak, leaden-hued glass, golden draperies, and perforated gold become vivified by "parti-colored fires" and an "artificial . . . current of wind" (271). This lush configuration of dark substances, reflective metals, vital elements, and scintillating fabrics with black Arabesque patterns creates an animate atmosphere of enveloping phantasmagoria, while generating a unique mirage of Ligeia, "when regarded from a single point of view" (271). Although the tale's mysterious climax seems attributable to metempsychosis and opium-induced delirium, the lover obliquely admits to having designed an anamorphic "contrivance" into this room.[24] The setting, thus, participates in conjuring simultaneously diffuse and concentrated aspects of Ligeia.

Even Ligeia's name exudes enchanting influence, since the Greek word "ligeia" qualified the mythic Sirens' song.[25] This Siren-like agency accounts for her "more than mortal melody," leaving her lover "entranced" (267); and for her beauty, engendering phantasies "more wildly divine than. . . the daughters of Delos," and "more profound than the well of Democritus" (263–4). Indeed, her beauty was "*not* of a classic regularity," rather it had "some *strangeness* in the proportion" (263). Foreign, animal and otherworldly, her eyes resembled those of the Houri (companions of the Muslim afterlife) and majestic Persian antelopes. To her lover, they even embodied the cosmos: "those divine orbs became to me twin stars of Leda, and I to them devoutest of astrologers" (263–4). However, this strangeness was also uncannily common. The "strangest mystery of all," the lover admits, was finding beautiful strangeness in transformational phenomena of the everyday world: "in the contemplation of a moth, a butterfly, a chrysalis, a stream . . . the falling of a meteor . . . sounds from stringed instruments, and . . . passages from books" (265). Intense interest in familiar phenomena was, for Poe, a manifestation of poetic sentiment.[26] All this suggests that Ligeia's influence transcends death by metamorphosing not into Rowena, but into the enlivened memory and imagination of those she's affected. As one interpreter argues, Ligeia lives "because the narrator remembers her."[27] Yet, the lover remembers Ligeia by incorporating her metaphysical agency and supernal beauty into perceptible phenomena of the room. Her influence dwells in his setting as much as his psyche. Like the enigmas of Poe's detective stories, the evidence needed to solve Ligeia's mysterious metamorphosis resides in plain sight: in the tale's narrative architecture.

Recalling the "indecorous" décor of "The Visionary," the restorative chamber in "Ligeia" likewise had "no system, no keeping, in the fantastic display" (270). In contrast to the "perfect keeping" of persons and premises in "The Fall of the House of Usher" (319)—that arguably made its tenants incapable of reimagining their situation—the rooms of these poetic protagonists cultivated harmonic dissonance. Approximating the intentional incoherence of Piranesian space, the eclectic chambers in "Ligeia" and "The Visionary" simultaneously employ and subvert reason to spur poetic imagination toward transcendent truths.

Sanctuaries of Imagination

Popularized as an eccentric dreamer, Poe was in fact entangled with his times. Together with poetry and fiction, Poe wrote nearly a thousand short works of non-fiction for magazines and newspapers, including critical commentaries on "Cabs," "Omnibuses," "Street Paving," and other aspects of his rapidly transforming urban environment. In 1844, Poe wrote a regular newspaper column entitled "Doings of Gotham," which dabbled in architectural criticism. In this series, Poe judged New York's harbor "grievously disfigured" by industry. He expressed contempt for the homogenizing Manhattan street grid. Of the city's picturesque places, he complained: "The spirit of Improvement has withered them with its acrid breath." He ridiculed a public fountain for resembling a "country jail in a thundershower." He derided trivial ornament as "silvered-gingerbread" and "confectionary," and condemned shows of domestic excess: "you see nowhere a cottage—everywhere a temple."[28] In related satires, Poe mocked opportunistic developers (377); lamented misplaced faith in progress (453); rebuked American presumptions of greatness (805–21); and blamed the "Demon of Engine" for parceling rambling riverbanks into commodified building-sites (942–3).

Soon after scrutinizing the "Doings of Gotham," Poe republished "The Visionary" and "Ligeia" in the *Broadway Journal* (1845). Like his cultural criticism, these tales satirized architectural vanities; but they also sanctified powers of imagination capable of overcoming sham progress and conformity. Poe's stories famously play on modern anxieties and universal fears, including his most fundamental fear: a world purged of beauty and wonder. In "The Visionary" and "Ligeia" Poe reveals the potential of literary architecture to revive capacities to wonder, but also to be wary of unlimited imagination.

Notes

1 Richard Wilbur, "The House of Poe," in *The Recognition of Edgar Allan Poe*, ed. Eric W. Carlson (Ann Arbor, MI: University of Michigan Press, 1966), 254–78.
2 "The Poetic Principle," in *Edgar Allan Poe: Essays and Reviews* [hereafter ER], ed. G.R. Thompson (New York: Library of America, 1984), 92–3.
3 *ER*, 21.
4 *Edgar Allan Poe: Poetry and Tales* [hereafter PT], ed. Patrick Quinn (New York: Library of America, 1984), 934. On "atmosphere" in Poe, see David Leatherbarrow, "The Poetics of the Architectural Setting: A Study of the Writings of Edgar Allan Poe," *Via* 8 (1986): 6–15, esp. 9; and Leo Spitzer "A Reinterpretation of 'The Fall of the House of Usher'" (1952), in *The Fall of the House of Usher: A Collection of Critical Essays*, ed. Thomas Woodson (Englewood Cliffs, NJ: Prentice-Hall, 1969), 56–70, esp. 65.
5 Parenthetical page numbers refer to *PT*.
6 I have no firm evidence that Poe knew Soane's collection. However, Poe spent five precocious years in London, from age six to eleven (1815–20), when Soane's house-museum (near the Allan residence) was open for viewing.

7 Poe, "Philosophy of Furniture," *PT*, 385.
8 *ER*, 77. See also, 14, 21, 685–6.
9 *ER*, 277–9.
10 Catherine Rainwater, "Poe's Landscape Tales and the 'Picturesque' Tradition," *Southern Literary Journal* 16.2 (Spring 1984): 30–43.
11 Kent Ljungquist, *The Grand and the Fair: Poe's Landscape Aesthetics and Pictorial Techniques* (Potomac, MD: Scripta Humanistica, 1984), esp. 203–11.
12 Travis Montgomery, "Poe's Oriental Gothic," *Gothic Studies* 12.2 (2010): 16–17, in full 4–28.
13 Edward Said, *Orientalism* [1978] (New York: Vintage-Random House, 1994), 118.
14 "The Visionary" was republished as "The Assignation" (1845). *PT* uses the later title. For scholarly annotations on both tales, see T.O. Mabbott, *The Collected Works of Edgar Allan Poe*, vol. 2 (Cambridge: Belknap Press of Harvard University Press, 1978), 148–69; 305–34.
15 *ER*, 8; and Poe's "Prospectus for '*The Penn*'" (1840), in Stuart Levine and Susan F. Levine, *Edgar Allan Poe. Critical Theory: The Major Documents* (Urbana, IL: University of Illinois Press, 2009), 24.
16 Poe elevates Byron's death to tragic status by altering his real-life circumstance and romance. Thus, Poe honors The Visionary, while outdoing him. See, Dennis Pahl, "Recovering Byron: Poe's 'The Assignation,'" *Criticism* 26.3 (Summer 1984): 211–29.
17 *ER*, 293.
18 Similar arguments are made by Pahl, "Recovering Byron," 216; and González-Rivas Fernández, "'The Assignation': An Aesthetic Encounter of Classical and Gothic," *The Edgar Allan Poe Review*, 10.1 (Spring 2009): 50–62, esp. 54.
19 Letter to Philip Pendleton Cooke (September 21, 1839), LTR-082.
20 Clark Griffith, "Poe's 'Ligeia' and the English Romantics," *University of Toronto Quarterly* 24 (1954): 8–25; and G.R. Thompson, *Poe's Fiction: Romantic Irony in the Gothic Tales* (Madison, WI: University of Wisconsin Press, 1973), 82–3.
21 Wilbur, "House of Poe," 275.
22 Kenneth Alan Hovey, "Poe's Materialist Metaphysics of Man," in *A Companion to Poe Studies*, ed. Eric W. Carlson (Westport, CT: Greenwood Press, 1996), 347–66.
23 Maurice J. Bennett, "'The Madness of Art' Poe's 'Ligeia' as Metafiction," *Poe Studies* 14.1 (June 1981): 1–6, esp. 5; and J. Gerald Kennedy, "Poe, 'Ligeia,' and the Problem of Dying Women," in *New Essays on Poe's Major Tales*, ed. Kenneth Silverman (New York: Cambridge University Press, 1993), 113–27, esp. 120.
24 Barbara Cantalupo, *Poe and the Visual Arts* (University Park, PA: Pennsylvania State University Press, 2014), 103–21.
25 Homer called the Sirens' song *liguros*, meaning "shrill," or "clear" (*Odyssey* 12.44). Later mythographers named a Siren Ligeia. In Poe's "Al Aaraaf" (1829), Ligeia is a goddess of musical harmony working with a goddess of beauty to reveal poetic truths.
26 *PT*, 227, 658; and *ER*, 93–4.
27 Joan Dayan, *Fables of Mind: An Inquiry into Poe's Fiction* (New York: Oxford University Press, 1987): 177.
28 "Doings of Gotham" [Letters 1–6], *Columbia Spy* (May 18–June 15, 1844), www.eapoe.org/works/info/pmdgm.htm, with Jerome McGann and J. Gerald Kennedy, ed., *Poe and the Remapping of Antebellum Print Culture* (Baton Rouge, LA: Louisiana State University Press, 2013), esp. 101–22; and Kevin J. Hayes, ed., *Edgar Allan Poe in Context* (New York: Cambridge University Press, 2013), esp. 372–82.

9
MONTRÉAL MYTHOLOGIES
Narrating the City

Panos Leventis

Introduction

How do architects, historians, or everyday users understand the buildings and cities they study and inhabit? History and historiography, often constructed and presented in objectifying and positivist terms, have provided the primary narrative of engagement with architecture and urbanism. But how do buildings and cities appear to us? How do we experience them? How are, or how might, histories of buildings and cities be told and re-told from different perspectives? Rather than simply recounting traditional histories of cities, how might an added layer of stories of cities further enrich our understanding of the urban experience? After all, in many languages the words "history" and "story" do not exist as separate terms. The engaging and reconciling power of the word, of the text, of the world of literature, can propose alternative readings of the city. Story telling can offer the immediacy and intimacy of experience, and can reserve ample space for multiple readings and interpretations of past and present socio-urban contexts.

This brief narrative of alternating fiction and historiography focuses on the city of Montréal, the unique Euro-American hybrid that ignites the imagination of those who inhabit or visit its shores. Rooted in a Classical understanding of the meaning and purpose of mythology, the text is meant to additionally be read as a humble example and exercise on phenomenological and hermeneutic readings of urban fabrics beyond the case study of Montréal. It is purposefully, and unavoidably, a subjective exercise, and serves as one urban experience that can be added to many others, toward a collective re-imagining and re-construction of the city, in this case of the world of Montréal. This single experience perhaps proves a little harsh on Modernism (or soft on colonialism) but, at its core, the open-ended narrative hopes to insist on the necessity to simultaneously preserve and constantly re-propose Montréal's unique urban and natural sensory experience, character and vision, which were severely (but fortunately not completely) altered during the double advent of, first, a blanket Industrialism and, later, an international Modernism.[1]

---

1 This work is based on a project undertaken while completing doctoral studies at McGill University in Montréal. The text was both originally written and now edited to serve as a methodologically experimental essay of architectural and urban criticism.

Ville-Marie was a unique island-city, I had been told.[2] It was born out of constant struggle. It rose from the waters slowly, with effort, dedication, and hard work.[3] It remained perpetually in motion, overflowing with life and creativity, looking forward, never arresting but to begin anew.[4]

But that was only to be the case until the day I arrived. Since the fateful moment when Bucky left me within no more than two miles from Ville-Marie's central square, everything changed. The city stopped living. It seemed as though something in me, or about me, had exposed all its imperfections—rather, what the city began to think of as its imperfections. During their days and through their nights, the citizens would do nothing but gaze at me. They were awed by what they saw as an unmatched completeness, taken by a harmony until then unknown to them.[5]

Repeating grinds awoke me a few dreams before dawn. An unbearably cold dawn it was going to be, like many others I had known in the short space of time I had spent in still silence, measuring Ville-Marie's skyline. The crushing sounds grew louder, and I felt movement deep in the ground beneath me. I almost rolled out of position. I turned down to face her. She called out in a desperate, broken voice:

> I am in pain! Please, help me!
> I, I believe... I am moving! Please, help me!

---

2 The city of Montréal was founded on May 17, 1642 as Ville-Marie, a small religious mission on the southern shores of Montréal island, by the Frenchman Paul de Chomedey, Sieur de Maisonneuve. The 30-year-old military officer arrived from France, heading a group of 50 missionaries, with the goal of establishing a model Christian town and converting the indigenous tribes to Christianity. Maisonneuve remained governor of the humble settlement for 23 years, aided by the nurse Jeanne Mance, who had arrived with him, and who in 1645 established Montréal's first hospital on Rue Saint-Paul, the Hôtel-Dieu. One hundred years before them, on October 2, 1535, the explorer Jacques Cartier had been the first non-native to visit the island and its impressive Iroquois settlement of Hochelaga, and "in the name of the King of France" gave the name Mont-Royal to the imposing hill at its center.

3 Between Cartier's visit to Hochelaga and Maisonneuve's founding of Ville-Marie, the navigator and cartographer Samuel de Champlain, known as "The Father of New France," founded Québec City in 1608, and in 1611 ordered the clearing of land for the founding of a new settlement on the island of Montréal. His order was to remain unimplemented due to continuous disputes and conflicts with the Mohawk tribe of the Iroquois confederacy over territory and fur trade—the island had been part of Mohawk hunting grounds for centuries.

4 In 1666, when the first census was conducted, fur-trading Ville-Marie could boast a population of 600 French and more than 1000 Iroquois. By the turn of the century, though, the colonists and locally born Francophones vastly outnumbered the indigenous population for a total of almost 5000 inhabitants. While the "island of Montréal" had by then long existed as a toponym, the settlement first appeared in official documents as Montréal, rather than Ville-Marie, in 1705.

5 During the first half of the eighteenth century, the territories of New France experienced a long period of relative peace and prosperity. Historians emphasize that from the very beginning of its existence, Montréal, a newer settlement, was associated with a forward-looking "spirit of independence," with productivity, trade, and industry, while Québec City, its rival settlement down the river and the colonial seat of the French government, would essentially remain an upholder of old traditions and largely rely on government subsidies for its sustenance (see Alan Gowans, *Building Canada: An Architectural History of Canadian Life*, Toronto: Oxford University Press, 1966, pp. 25–26).

FIGURE 9.1 Buckminster [Bucky] Fuller, United States Pavilion for the 1967 World's Fair. Île Sainte-Hélène, Montréal, Canada.

Photo by author

No help arrived. There was nothing to be done. She was completely encircled by his icy hands, which had lost their white rigidity and were transforming into a warm, liquid grayness. He wrapped himself around her. He engulfed, uprooted, and started pushing her toward the west, where the night still held reign. The deafening roar reached the city, echoing from building to building through the empty streets. The citizens awoke startled and surprised. Heads mushroomed out of dark windows. Bodies sprouted on metal stairways. Like a frozen garden of flesh, stone, and concrete, they watched, petrified and stunned, the unbelievable sight that unfolded before them. It wasn't until the second sun arrived, burning brighter and breathing life back into them, that their cries filled the space between the clearing mist and the living waters:

> Laurent is abducting Hélène!

Dark clouds moved in from the north. Thick fog rolled into parks, streets, and squares, filling the entire city. Despite their initial disbelief and confusion, the rulers managed to summon everyone to the Old Port. Some came running down the steps of the central plaza. Groups appeared out of alleys, waving their hands and shouting angry words. Many were carefully helped onto the wet, slippery quays. A few of them didn't even have time to put clothes on—they had to answer the rulers' call immediately.[6]

They turned back to look at the city, as it disappeared into the darkening sky of the morning. No one could remember visibility ever being so low in Ville-Marie. It wasn't possible to distinguish figures among the crowds. Some couldn't even recognize their neighbors, who were standing next to them. How could they hope to keep track of Laurent's moves?

> He is taking Hélène from us!
> The sphere is still within Hélène!
> Where is he heading?
> He will raise them to the heavens!

They were determined not to let that happen. Living alongside Laurent had never been easy. He was extremely temperamental.[7] He had provided the city with water and food in difficult times, but in return, and always without warning, he often took Ville-Marie's children to the heavens where he dwelled. They were never to be seen again.[8]

It became evident to the citizens: Laurent was responsible for creating the ever-thickening fog, in order to proceed, unobstructed, with his scheme. They had to reach high above the fog. They would find him. They would fight him. They did not know how they would fight him, but he would not have his way with Hélène too, especially since I was, however precariously, still resting on her. I had become their necessity. I had become the very essence of their existence. No one remembered

---

6 The Vieux-Port quarter of Montréal includes the sites of both the Cartier and Maisonneuve landings. By the largely peaceful and prosperous first half of the eighteenth century, the area had grown into a bustling port with multiple quays, where not only local trade was loaded and unloaded, but also a lucrative transshipment service flourished.

7 The Lachine Rapids of the Saint Lawrence River, located just south of Montréal island and west of the Old Port, claimed numerous lives during the first decades of Ville-Marie's life, as stubborn sailors and fur traders refused to yield to the geography and power of the river. One of the earliest texts recounting the city's history, *Histoire du Montréal, 1640–1672*, attributed to the Sulpician priest François Dollier de Casson, includes vivid accounts of attempts to cross the Rapids. Casson, who ordered the first survey of the city, was a key figure in the first attempt to dig a canal through the Rapids in 1689.

8 The existence of the dangerous Rapids proved quite beneficial for the city's growth, as, until the Lachine canal was constructed—work would not begin until 1821—it was necessary for boats to call at the port of Montréal for transshipment (it would not be until 1959 when the river would finally be widened at Lachine and opened for navigation, and not until 1979 when the abandoned Lachine canal and its banks would be purchased by Parks Canada).

that since the day of my arrival they had completely forgotten about Laurent, and did not offer their respect and friendship to him as they had always done so before.

No time was lost. They left the quays and formed different groups. They headed, in all directions, toward the city walls.[9] Construction—rather, destruction—began. They removed stone after stone, grouping them in large, tall piles, until the walls were completely demolished. It was necessary for the land to be cleared. They reduced the old markets, the theaters and all the houses to mounds of brick and stone. Adequate quantities of construction material had to become available. Just one hour later, Ville-Marie was a wasteland.[10]

Then, they attempted to reach the heavens. Building after building was hastily assembled, each one higher than its predecessor. The citizens connected the buildings with bridges, and put up shelters and bastions for the imminent confrontation. They carried as weapons whatever they could find: Iron rods, oars, water tanks—Laurent would often transgress from absolute solid to elusive liquid or firing vapor. They stopped only when the entire population was able to ascend and fit onto the heights and the roofs of the new structures. They looked at each other with hope and optimism.

> This is the real Ville-Marie!
> Here we are truly one, united in our effort.[11]

---

9 As early as 1665, when French troops arrived to ensure its safety, Montréal relied on small, fortified towers and other structures for defense. The first wooden fortifications encircling the settlement were realized between 1687 and 1689. Between 1717 and 1741, following Louis XIV's consent, the wooden fortifications were replaced by a stone enclosure more than five meters high and with a perimeter of three kilometers, designed by Gaspard Chaussegros de Léry, the King's chief engineer in New France (see Eds., *The Six Lives of Montréal*, Montréal: Entente sur le Développement Culturel de Montréal, 1997). Léry's orthogonal enclosure of 13 bastions and eight gates remained unutilized when, following Québec City's fall to British troops in 1759, the British were simply given access to Montréal in 1760 after an agreement of surrender.

10 Considered an obstacle to further urban development by the British colonial government, the fortifications of Montréal were gradually dismantled between 1804 and 1817, following the adoption of *The Act to Demolish the Old Walls and Fortifications Surrounding the City of Montreal* of 1801 (see Phyllis Lambert and Alan Stewart, Eds., *Montréal, ville fortifiée au XVIII siècle* [exhibition catalogue], Montréal: Canadian Centre for Architecture, 1992).

11 Henry N. Cobb designed Place Ville-Marie (PVM), a milestone in Montréal's mid-twentieth century development history, shortly after he founded his practice in New York with I. M. Pei in 1955. At the time, the 42-storey cruciform aluminum tower, constructed between 1960 and 1962 over the open trenches and train tracks of Canadian National Railway stations and lines between the Old Port and Mont-Royal, was the third tallest structure in the world outside the United States, and when it was completed, PVM was the world's largest and most complex office development (see www.pcf-p.com/a/p/5503/s.html). Beyond the obvious, if rather simplistic, allusion of the cruciform plan to the Catholic heritage of Montréal, PVM represented the International Style and global Modernism's leveling triumph over local and regional histories, needs, and designs. The "new" city and era that PVC and the numerous skyscrapers that soon filled the Montréal skyline heralded, an era of international commercial success and optimism, all but completely did away with the city's earlier fabric of tree-lined, small and medium scale residential and commercial streets north and west of the Old Port in the name of a vaguely defined "progress." The name "Place Ville-Marie" was personally chosen by the newly elected Montréal mayor Jean Drapeau, whose numerous and grandiose schemes and projects would completely transform the city's urban character during his long and almost continuous 30-year tenure (1954–1986).

They had almost reached the ceiling of fog and clouds, which were stubbornly hovering above the city, keeping the heavens in hiding. The roar was still becoming louder, which assured them that they were close to their goal. They shone lights through the grayness, in order to locate their enraged enemy. Each building beamed blinding white rays into the clouds, madly swirling in search of Laurent.[12]

The sudden appearance of the suns blinded and burnt many. The clouds and fog disappeared, only to reveal a disheartening sight to the citizens, who by now were running down, flying and falling back from that suspended illusion above their city: There was Hélène and I, carried away, not up to the heavens, but toward the west, where Laurent's waters were guiding us.[13]

The obvious decision was taken immediately: The city would sail after us. They left the heart of Ville-Marie in ruin, and headed outwards. The midday heat was intense, but as they reached the east shores of their island-city, thick-leaved trees comforted them. In the middle of the woods they encountered a small clearing, ready as if it was awaiting them. They would be sailing toward the west, and the mast would have had to be located in the east, in order to balance the forces of the wind and the waters. To support a sail strong enough to carry the city down Laurent's turbulent, liquid body, it would have had to be an immense structure, and it would have to be bent, bowing toward the south, for the winds always blew on Ville-Marie from the north.[14]

In order for the structure and the sail to be put in place, the land had to become uniform, with no obstacles such as small mountains, streams, or woods. All was cut, cleared, put away. Construction of the mast finished in less than two hours. Never before had they carried through an action with more dedication. Just as they installed the sail, ready to confront Laurent once more, the winds stopped blowing. The air stood still around them. The air had disappeared. They were suffocating, until someone shouted in relief:

> Behold the wind, see it leave my mouth in force!
> We can make the wind we need with words!

The entire city was now assembled at the foot of the sail, which looked like a giant bird awaiting the air to fill its wings. All they needed to do was shout the

---

12 As if to crown and emphasize the achievements of the city's new era, a rotating beacon was installed on the PVM rooftop and still lights up the night skyline of Montréal, shining numerous beams throughout the region and inviting others to do the same.
13 Already by the 1960s, however, and despite (or perhaps because) of mayor Drapeau's costly visions, and with the gradual rise of rival Toronto further west, there were signs that the prosperity and reign of the city within the Canadian financial, commercial, and architectural narrative could be short lived.
14 Drapeau asked the French architect Roger Taillibert to design a 56,000-seat stadium in the Hochelaga-Maisonneuve district of eastern Montréal for hosting initially a baseball team, and eventually the 1976 Summer Olympic Games. Taillibert additionally designed other structures for the Games, such as the Velodrome and the towers of the Olympic Village that would host the athletes, located within an expanded area that was named Olympic Park. The Olympic stadium's supporting tower for the cables, tensile structure of the retractable roof, sporting a funicular leading to its top, is still the worlds' highest inclined building (see François Rémillard and Brian Merrett, *L'Architecture de Montréal: guide des styles et des batiments*, Montréal: Méridien, 1991).

same words, together, as loudly as they could, into the sail. At that moment, they remembered. They did not all share the same language. How would it be possible to move the city, when different words, spoken in different languages, could not create a wind concurrent, strong and uniform enough to fill their sail?

They left the sail unfulfilled and the eastern lands destroyed. It was already afternoon when they reached the sacred hill in the middle of the city. Their minds and bodies were tired and heavy. The climb was increasingly difficult. Had the hill grown taller in anticipation?

Since Ville-Marie's foundation, the sacred hill had been its refuge and salvation. The thick woods provided building material for the first humble huts, heat for the cold winters, and hideouts during approaching dangers. Plants and animals nourished the hungry. Stones and earth sheltered the weak. The city grew, encircling the hill like a child peacefully nesting under the warm breath of its mother, certain of the love and protection she would infinitely provide.[15]

In their rush and fatigue, they trampled all the plants and destroyed the paths, gardens, and trees that had been dedicated to the hill since the first days of Ville-Marie. For them, all that held no value.[16] From the peaks,[17] they could at least still make out the silhouette of Hélène and me, by now further in the distance, edging toward the shimmering, warm colors of the western light. Their panic and desperation could not become more overwhelming, when the sacred hill awoke under their feet and proclaimed in a thundering tone:

Citizens of Ville-Marie!

You seek to bring back the sphere of universal truth, which you believe you owned since the day it presented itself to you. In your desire to embrace absolute harmony, you are ready to sacrifice everything, even what you once held most dear.

Proceed, then, and offer me myself. You shall then have your sphere. You shall then arrive upon the world of your truth, a world with no mysteries, a world where there is nothing left to understand.

---

15 Mont-Royal (Mount Royal), a geological outcrop of volcanic history, lies in the middle of the island. Since its claiming and naming by Cartier in 1535, the hill has in turn given its name to the city and, eventually, the whole chain of hills that lie between the Laurentian Mountains in the north and the Appalachian Mountains in the south (the Monteregian Hills). From the Iroquois village of Hochelaga to the colonial town of Ville-Marie and the city and metropolis of Montréal, all of the island's settlements have used Mont-Royal as line of defense, area of protection, point of reference, and marker of identity.

16 The park on Mont-Royal was designed in the early 1870s by the American landscape architect Frederick Law Olmstead, who had already designed Central Park in New York City, and was concurrently working on Golden Gate Park in San Francisco. The park opened in 1876 (thought not completed to Olmstead's plans due to the global post-1873 economic crisis), following repeated calls for the protection of the hill, which was being rapidly deforested by firewood companies (see Jean-Claude Marsan, *Sauver Montréal: Chroniques d'Architecture et d'Urbanisme*, Montréal: Editions du Boréal, 1990).

17 At 233 meters, the eastern Colline de la Croix is the taller of Mont-Royal's two peaks, and the highest natural point on the island, while in the western edge of the hill stands the 211-meter tall Colline d'Outremont (Mount Murray).

There was upheaval. No one paused to weigh the words. They gathered all the strength that remained within them, and started. They took the life out of every stone and the color out of every leaf. They crucified tree after tree, until there was nothing but an endless graveyard.[18] They buried the heart of their history, and suspended the soul of the hill high above the hill.[19]

Still, nothing had changed. They were barely able to move. They sat exhausted at the peaks of the sacred hill, as Laurent flowed into the setting suns, with whom Hélène and I were fading into oneness. They wondered how close Laurent brought us to the suns, as I began turning around myself. Flames sprang out of my entire body. They could think of nothing else, but that I was on fire.[20] The structure I was hiding was finally being revealed for Ville-Marie to comprehend.

Look, the sphere is coming back!
Yes, and it is growing!

It was not possible for them to understand that it was not me who was growing. It was Ville-Marie, destroyed by them in a single day, which was becoming smaller.[21] By the time I had encircled the whole island, it was not possible to hear their

---

18 The combined Catholic, Protestant, and Jewish cemeteries on Mont-Royal form the largest necropolis in North America: More than two million people have been buried on the hill. The 31-meter tall steel cross of Mont-Royal, lying on top of the Colline de la Croix since 1924, seems to offer testimony to the hill's inner life, or rather, death.

19 Further emphasizing Mont-Royal's "funerary" character is the imposing Oratoire Saint-Joseph standing on the hill's northwestern edge. Constructed between 1924–56, the Oratoire includes, at a 261-meter peak, the second largest dome in the world, with yet another cross on top of its roof. The Oratoire Saint-Joseph is essentially a large sarcophagus for its conceiver and patron, the lay brother André Bessette (later known as Frére Andrè).

20 The fire of May 20, 1976, accidentally ignited by welding work, destroyed the translucent acrylic skin of 1900 panels of the building now known as the Biosphere, one of Montréal's most iconic landmarks. The Biosphere, the worlds' first complete and constructed geodesic dome, "arrived" in the life of the city as the United States Pavilion for the 1967 World Fair or Expo '67, resting on the Île Sainte-Hélène in the Saint Lawrence river, one of two islands hosting the Expo just south of Montréal's Old Port. Designed by Buckminster "Bucky" Fuller, the building intended to showcase the US's latest structural and technological advances. With its 76-meter diameter steel-frame dome, 35-meter long escalator, monorail, and computer-controlled shading devices, the futuristic building awed the city and the world, and was the most popular pavilion of Expo '67 (see James Ward, ed., *The Artifacts of R. Buckminster Fuller: A Comprehensive Collection of his Designs and Drawings, V. Four: The Geodesic Revolution Part 2: 1960–1983*, New York and London: Garland, 1985).

21 The US pavilion, donated to the city by the US at the end of the Expo, was originally projected by Fuller to measure more than 90 meters in diameter, but structural and budgetary concerns reduced its size by, at the end, almost one-fifth (see Eds., *Montréal Expo 67: Terre des Hommes*, Paris: Banque Nationale de Paris, 1967). Following the 1976 fire, the building remained unused and neglected until it was purchased in 1990 by Environment Canada. Following a few reprogramming iterations, the Biosphere became a Water Museum between 1995 and 2007, focusing on the St. Lawrence and Great Lakes ecosystem, and since 2007 it has housed a unique Environment Museum. Rather than a future-seeing mirror of abstract, ever-developing teleological-technological worlds, the Biosphere has been turning the attention of Montréal's citizens and visitors to preserving their natural surroundings and cultural heritage.

Montréal Mythologies 101

FIGURE 9.2 Buckminster [Bucky] Fuller, United States Pavilion for the 1967 World's Fair. Île Sainte-Hélène, Montréal, Canada.

Photo by author

desperate cries. I can only imagine them looking at me from within, staring at an empty nothingness, an immense prison which was becoming ever more infinite, as Ville-Marie slowly disappeared into fateful perfection.

Tomorrow, Bucky will leave me within view of another city.

SECTION 3
Readings on Architectural Design and Pedagogy

10
THE GESTURE OF DRAWING IN ANTOINE DE SAINT-EXUPÉRY'S *THE LITTLE PRINCE*

Jason Crow

Antoine de Saint-Exupéry's *The Little Prince* offers a sophisticated meditation on being human. Interpreting *The Little Prince* as a moral tale is more precocious than it appears. The book recounts the story of a pilot's crash in the desert where he meets a strange little boy, a prince, who has arrived at the end of a journey to find friendship. The boy asks the pilot to draw a sheep. Desperate to know more about the little prince, the pilot inquires about who he is and from where he has come. As the boy describes his search across several tiny planets, inhabited by dysfunctional adults, the pilot sketches each world to confirm that he understands the boy's story. The book ends with the disappearance of the pilot's new friend and a plea to help find the boy. Central to grasping *The Little Prince's* tropology is an examination of drawing's critical function for the text. In particular, the drawing of an empty box figures the *ex nihilo* limitation that enables a sheep to be imagined. Drawing thus structures the potential for narrative to exist. Storytelling takes place, as a life. Drawing makes, living in, place possible.

Not Illustration

If the relationship between drawing and life is to be gleaned from *The Little Prince*, drawing cannot be confused with illustration. The narrative of the book nests different layers of the text within different types of image—drawing, illustration, and sketch—like a set of Russian dolls. The first layer includes the dedication to Leon Werth, as the little boy that he was, and the postscript explaining Saint-Exupéry's drawing of an empty landscape. The dedication and explanation define the book's audience as those adults who need or wish to regain the imaginative wonder of childhood. The second layer is framed by the illustration of a boa constrictor and the illustration of the little prince in the desert just before he disappears. These images are tools deployed by the narrator to explain how drawing differentiates between adults and children. The penultimate layer is the story of the narrator's crash in the desert and constitutes an explanation of the illustrations of the text. The innermost layer reflects upon the prince's journey as documented in the narrator's sketches, embedded within the crash narrative. The sheep that the prince commands the narrator to create is unique. It is an empty-drawing, which encompasses all of the book's layers by enabling them to take place. To understand the empty-drawing as a special category within the work; it is necessary to demonstrate how the illustrations by Saint-Exupéry, the sketches by the narrator, and the drawings that frame the crash narrative are subordinate to the language of the text.[1]

Saint-Exupéry complains that he abandoned any hope of being an artist as a child, and that the watercolors he painted are only passable illustrations at best. As a result, the illustrations of the text are largely disposable to the author. Illustrations make the world of the text visible for those who have no capacity to imagine the prince's world on their own. Ironically for a children's book, the text explains its images to adults.

The sketches made by the narrator for the prince appear to be similar, but fail when tested against his world. The narrator notes that he purchased paints and pencils to create the images for the book.[2] Although there is an autobiographical element, the narrator is not Saint-Exupéry. The author's watercolor illustrations duplicate the sketches that the narrator describes, but which the reader never sees. The narrator's first set of sketches, the ones that coincide with Saint-Exupéry's illustrations, recreate the originals made by the narrator for the prince at the crash site. Saint-Exupéry's illustrations are thus twice removed from the narrator's sketches, and they suggest the beginning of an infinite regress from the act of drawing in the text.

Even the original sketching by the narrator for the prince is problematic. When the narrator shows the prince his work late in the book, the prince finds it laughable.[3] This reinforces his negative response to the narrator's attempts to fulfill the command to draw a sheep, which fail outside of the drawing of an empty box.[4] For Saint-Exupéry the watercolor illustrations do not evoke the world of the prince and must be explained to the reader who is assumed to be an adult. Otherwise no text would be necessary. The narrator's sketches fail in a similar manner but with respect to the lived experience of the prince.

The unsuccessful attempts at drawing by Saint-Exupéry and by the narrator point toward a general failure with respect to the book's images. The dedication and postscript operate outside of the narrative as tests for the reader between which the story of his journey plays out. They structure the explanation of drawing as the book's conceptual framework for recognizing friendship.

Drawing, the narrator explains in the opening of the story, determines if he is among friends or adults. If he is among friends, he can share true conversation, but if he is among adults, everything will be mixed up and confused.[5] His infamous test deploys the drawing of a boa constrictor swallowing an elephant and an "x-ray" illustration of a boa constrictor swallowing an elephant. A person who only sees the form of a hat is incapable of accessing the invisible and is therefore not someone to engage. Lack of insight into the essential, symbolized by the interior elephant, is perceived as a lack of humanity by Saint-Exupéry. This is the realm of the adult that Saint-Exupéry, outside of his book, inhabits.

A second set of drawing and illustration concludes the book. The first shows the prince in his final moments in the desert, and the second shows the empty desert. The postscript, ostensibly the text of Saint-Exupéry and not the narrator, implicates the author as the narrator and equates the two desert images. The drawing on the final page is "the same landscape as the one on the preceding page, but I've drawn it one more time in order to be sure you see it clearly."[6] Unlike the boa constrictor that opens the narrative, in this case the order of the images is reversed. The explanatory x-ray illustration that shows the prince comes first, and the book ends with a drawing of an empty desert. According to Saint-Exupéry the final drawing should make the prince visible, but the reader only sees the empty place where he could be. Curiously, the narrator encounters the same dubious condition with respect to the only drawing that truly works beyond the text, the drawing of the sheep. The reader knows this drawing as the sketch of the box that hides a sheep within it. The narrator admits that he cannot see sheep through the walls of boxes.[7]

The drawing that fulfills the command of the prince is never seen in the book or within the narrative of the text by the reader. The watercolor illustrations by Saint-Exupéry are second-order historical reflections of the drawings by the narrator. The sketches found in the pocket of the narrator are documentary, and do not include the drawing of the box. At least the narrator does not mention it when he shows his sketches to the prince. The difference between this singular drawing and the text's explanatory images is its success. It accomplishes the narrator's duty by making the invisible visible to the prince. More primary to its uniqueness is the drawing's structural role in delimiting the domain within which the story of the little prince can take place.

Living, a Not-Form of Life

Fifty years before Giorgio Agamben initiated his *homo sacer* project, the prince proposed its resolution. Agamben ends his project on bare life in *The Kingdom and the Glory* where he demonstrates humanity bound to ceaseless administration of life through the confounded economies of theology and politics. The solution to humanity's predicament is anticipated in his work on Franciscan morality—*The Highest Poverty*—where a life can exist outside of command. For the prince living as a not-form of life already exists in the Lamplighter's possible *otium*.

The Lamplighter is unique in Saint-Exupéry's book. His planet so small that it only contains himself and a lightpost. His daily duty is to operate the lamp as the sun sets and rises, but his planet revolves so quickly that he rushes to light and extinguish the lamp to keep up with the movement of day into night and night into day. Unlike the other characters that the prince meets on his journey, the Lamplighter is the only adult that he speculates could become a friend.

In his duty to light up the night, the Lamplighter is a paragon of Saint-Exupéry's belief that all men must act for the greater good.[8] The prince lauds the Lamplighter for his dedication to his task, but despite its benefit to others, the Lamplighter's responsibilities weigh upon him. With no end to his work imaginable, he laments the lack of time to rest. In response the prince imagines a restful mode of existence for the Lamplighter. He observes that the planet is so tiny that the Lamplighter can circumnavigate it in three steps. If the Lamplighter walks at the same pace as the setting sun, he can find respite from his duty by effectively lengthening the day.

The prince finds the imagined restful life especially poignant, as it would allow the Lamplighter to watch the sunset repeatedly. Early in his encounter with the narrator, he explains his love of sunsets and how he moved his chair around his own planet to experience the setting sun over and over again. This "quiet pleasure" of the prince is tinged with melancholy. It represents a love born out of a sadness that he does not elaborate, but the potential rest of the Lamplighter suggests an explanation.

Although the Lamplighter desires a rest that is a lack of action, what the prince proposes is an active leisure closer to the medieval monastic understanding of *otium*, the labor undertaken as respite from the exhausting work of contemplation. The *reductio ad infinitum* of the little prince's solution can be accomplished by walking away from one's "adult" responsibilities, or as the Lamplighter's would say "orders." The result would be the maintenance of the infinite sunset.

The prince's solution does not eliminate the Lamplighter's responsibilities. It defers them to create another mode of existing. The prince implies a similar form of life in response to the Merchant's pill that saves the time of drinking water. He proclaims that he would rather walk at his "leisure toward a spring of freshwater."[9] His journey from home is an even greater expression of a life in *otium*. He abandons his planet and its responsibilities to search for friends that can aid him. Living, for the prince removes one's self from duty through this act of traveling. Traveling suspends the administration of the Lamplighter's house—the economy of his planet—by acting against his being at home in time. The Lamplighter that the prince imagines walks always into exile at the end of day.

Surviving exile is the dominant theme of Saint-Exupéry's *Letter to a Hostage*, published in the same year as *The Little Prince*. Written in 1940, the letter is intended for the adult, Leon Werth, not the adult-as-child to whom *The Little Prince* is dedicated. Both men were strangers in strange lands at the time. Saint-Exupéry was on a ship bound to the United States. Werth was a captive of the Germans whose occupation of France made his home brutally foreign.

Saint-Exupéry's *Letter* cannot propose a return from exile, as his own home is foreign to him. But it is not simply France that has become strange, the world is a foreign place, and the hope of civilization rests on finding a different way to rejoin humanity. It is as if the future is the place from which men such as Saint-Exupéry and Werth are exiled and to which they will eventually return. Echoing medieval thinking about living away from God, Saint-Exupéry wrote, "[Civilization] is founded on the future, not the past . . . We are to each other as pilgrims who, along various paths, strive toward the same meeting-place."[10] Place in Saint-Exupéry's *Letter* is confounded with future. Both are unattainable in midst of totalitarianism that, "refuses creative contradictions, ruins all hope of ascension, and founds for a thousand years, instead of man, the robot of an ant-heap."[11]

Despite the miserable conditions within which Saint-Exupéry and Werth find themselves, exile offers hope in a world that has come unbound. Friendship can transform exile into travel. In the *Letter* Saint-Exupéry explains that it is only by knowing that his friend, Werth, is alive somewhere, "walking afar in the empire of his friendship, which has no frontiers, I may feel that I am not an immigrant but a traveler."[12] Traveling the empire echoed in the prince's journey, and in the Lamplighter's walking. Although flying freed Saint-Exupéry from the world in which he found himself, he eventually became suspect of the transformational escape from the earth that it offered. Years after the publication the *Letter* and *The Little Prince*, he wrote to Werth grieving that the P38 airplane he flew was "nothing more than an instrument for moving from one place to another, and, as in this case, of war."[13]

While the instrumental plane failed to sustain his empire of friendship, two plane crashes provided the future that flying anticipated. These crashes cemented humanity's proper form of life for Saint-Exupéry. In 1930 his best friend, Henri Guillaumet, crashed his plane in the Andes Mountains. Isolated in the middle of a terrible winter storm, Guillaumet walked out of the mountains where Saint-Exupéry found him.[14] The search and rescue of Guillaumet gave Saint-Exupéry a higher sense of purpose, but the downed pilot's struggle proved transformational. Guillaumet almost died walking out of the wilderness. He later told Saint-Exupéry, "I swear that what I went through, no animal would have gone through." Overcoming terrible adversity became the defining characteristic of what it meant to be more than simply animal.

In 1935 Saint-Exupéry crashed his own plane in the Sahara along with his mechanic, André Prevot. Saint-Exupéry had neglected preparations for a record flight attempt from Paris to Saigon. As a result, he flew off course. Despite limited supplies, the two walked out of the desert.[15]

Although the desert held special significance as a place away from the world for Saint-Exupéry prior to the crash, his struggle over the adversity it presented truly changed for him with the experience of the crash. Woven into his book, *Terre des hommes*, the desert begins to stand out in Saint-Exupéry's writing as a symbol of the function of exile. The desert reaches its fruition in *The Little Prince*, where the narrative core is framed by a reimagined version of the 1935 crash. The desert in the book represents the emptiness that is necessary to form a common ground.

Being Empty

Language, in Saint-Exupéry's philosophy, fails to provide a common ground for humanity. The prince grieves, "[L]anguage is the source of misunderstanding."[16]

Saint-Exupéry complains that while language is mechanically sufficient, it fails to "express the essential nature of man." Language splits men from each other. It creates two truths that exist in opposition.[17]

Saint-Exupéry does not address the difference between the two truths that language ends up opposing, but they are demonstrated in his changing attitude toward his beloved airplanes. For Saint-Exupéry, the boy, planes were sources of wonder and joy. For the older Saint-Exupéry, they became instruments of war and torture. The technological problem presented by the machines he loved was bound to the ineffectiveness of words.

> *Car les autres, ils s'imaginent que le mode tient dans les mots et que parole de l'homme exprime l'univers et les étoiles et le bonheur et le soleil couchant et le domaine et l'amour et l'architecture et la douleur et le silence . . . Car de cette affreuse promiscuité des mots dans en vent de paroles ils not tiré l'urgence des tortures. Des mots maladroits, incohérents ou efficaces, des engins de torture efficaces song nés.*[18]

Saint-Exupéry's solution was to exploit language's potential poverty to make it more expressive. He obsessed over the precision of the words he used and over the simplicity of the style of writing he deployed to present his ideas.[19] As much as possible his goal was to render language simpler and simpler.[20] He made the words he used as empty as possible. It was emptiness that allowed words to parallel the desert. Like the desert, empty words offered multiple potential meanings. In the prince's explanation, stars are different for different people. For Saint-Exupéry bare language was a set of empty signs to be filled with meaning, "*remplir le mot.*"[21]

The task of filling language was one of acting not of writing. In *Citadelle*, meaning becomes possible through the exchange of something that will outlast the individual. It is bound to activities such as craft and architecture.[22] The sensual experience of undertaking these activities in common is a symphony,[23] a music for the heart.[24] But the objects only have meaning within the domain, the empire, that has been built by man for man through the gift and sacrifice of time spent. Without this gift, the homeland will be wandered joylessly as if in exile. The domain will seem empty.

Saint-Exupéry stops short of describing the filling of language and desert as a mystical experience. Crafting objects points toward an experience of the divine but only as a positive absence. "I have taken stars, fountains, regrets . . . I have modeled them according to my spirit, and they have served as a pedestal to a divinity which is contained in none of them."[25] He compares the men of occupied France to a pile of stones that are the possibility of a cathedral that exists somewhere in the dream of a man.[26] The cathedral, like language, can only be known to be full when it is imagined as empty.

Fully Empty

The love of a rose fills the heart of prince. How the rose is not empty is the secret that the desert fox teaches. Near the end of his journey, the prince visits the earth where he arrives in the desert. Traveling across it, he discovers a rose garden. Having believed that his rose was unique, he is heartbroken that it is one of many flowers. The fox teaches him that roses that are not tamed—*apprivoisier*—are empty signifiers. They are possessed by no one.[27] Taming in *Citadelle* is founded on possession, but in a curious manner. "To tame is to call, to hold close, to draw to oneself the one who is fleeing through the one whom we possess."[28] The one who flees in that possession is the very one who possesses. To possess the rose, the prince must flee, and thus his journey begins.

Objects such as his rose only become meaningful within a network of relations across the distance constructed by self-exile. This network is the empire of friendship that must be walked.[29] It establishes a condition under which the subject requires the one who is tamed in order to continue to exist. For the fox, this conditioning changes the relationship between himself and the hunters that stalk him. With respect to the prince, fields of wheat become a symbol of the prince's hair and thus make him present to the fox. It is through the transformation of empty object into full object, like the filling of an impoverished word, that an object becomes meaningful.

However, the exchange does not happen without cost. The fox notes that it is the spending of the time needed to tame an object that makes it important. Spending time creates duty, a responsibility to the object. What changes is neither the emptiness of the object nor the condition of the subject that tames. Instead the subject is created through the responsibility for the object's not-being-empty. When the prince returns to the rose garden after having learned the fox's secrets, he realizes that the flowers are "as yet . . . nothing" because they have not been tamed. They are empty as is any other rose. His rose is different only because of the care that he gave it. He watered it. He sheltered it, and he protected it. His rose is the same as every other rose, but because of his duty to it, the prince's rose is full of potential meaning.[30]

Fully Empty Drawing

"Design me a sheep!"[31] In the prince's journey, drawing is the commanded act, the duty, that enacts its own deferment. The drawing of a box for a sheep enacts a form of *otium* in order to bond narrator, author, and reader to the prince and by doing so to create an empire of friendship.

Near the end of the prince's journey, the narrator is dying of thirst. The prince suggests that they walk into the desert in search of a well, an absurd proposition. The prince only responds that a desert is beautiful in that it hides a well.[32] The prince tires. The narrator carries him, and the price falls asleep. He comments to himself, "what I see here [the prince's body] is nothing but a shell. What is important is invisible . . ." The following morning the little prince and the narrator find the well.[33] In the final scene of the book, the little prince is fatally bitten by a snake. The prince comforts the narrator by explaining to him that his body is simply a shell. He will still be present as the laughter of the stars. The story ends with the drawings that function as a test of adulthood. The first depicts the prince in the desert, a shell in an empty landscape. The latter shows only the sterile landscape in which Saint-Exupéry urges us to see the shell that makes the prince visible. Emptiness abounds.

It is difficult to ascertain within the logic of the book if the prince successfully tames the narrator and thus makes him a friend. The narrator's incapacity to see the sheep seems to indicate that the taming has failed. But the relationship is complicated. The prince takes responsibility for the narrator by commanding him to draw, but this implicates the narrator in a reciprocal responsibility. The narrator is given a duty that can only be fulfilled imperfectly in the manner that any gesture remains incomplete. The incomplete gesture, an empty box, is given back to the prince, and thereby entangles him with the narrator in his duty to draw. But just what is the narrator's responsibility?

After the failed attempts at drawing the sheep, the drawing of an empty box creates a special kind of floating signifier. The drawing's emptiness establishes the possibility of sheep-being for the prince if not for the narrator. The empty box thus performs a structural task in that it offers access to the invisible. The narrator takes on the responsibility of providing the vacuity that satisfies the intent of the little prince and allows his story to be. The empty box is another figure of the desert that grounds his existence, one that the narrator can only experience vicariously through the narrative as told to him. Marco Frascari lamented the subordination of drawing in education to illustration.[34] He noted that architecture and embodied experience reciprocally frame each other in a relationship that is very similar to the narrator's experience of box and desert.[35] Drawing creates the frame, the figurative and physical conceptual system, within which architecture and embodied experience are mirrored through the deployment of the story. Narrative arises only within the boundaries of its empty container. The book, the plane, the desert, and the prince fill the bounded vacuum with ever more boxes to be filled. *The Little Prince's* narrator draws empty boxes, and the little prince demonstrates that the emptiness is full.

Notes

1 In this chapter, the illustrations are the images reproduced in the book that were created by Saint-Exupéry for the book, not for the little prince. These are different from the sketches that the narrator of the text, who is and is not Saint-Exupéry, makes during his conversations with the little prince. The only drawings in the text are the empty box that the narrator sketched for the little prince, but which the reader never sees, and the drawing of the empty desert that Saint-Exupéry claims as his work in the postscript.
2 Antoine de Saint-Exupéry, *The Little Prince*, trans. Katherine Woods (New York: Harcourt, Brace & World, 1943), 18–19.
3 Ibid., 79.
4 Ibid., 12.
5 Ibid., 7–9, and ibid., 26–27.
6 Ibid., Postscript, unpaginated.
7 Ibid., 19.

8 Eliot G. Fay, "The Philosophy of Saint Exupéry," *The Modern Language Journal* 31, No. 2 (February, 1947): 94.
9 Saint-Exupéry, *The Little Prince*, 74.
10 Antoine de Saint-Exupéry, *Écrits de Guerre: 1939–1944 avec la Lettre a Otage et des Témoignages et Documents* (Paris: Éditions Gallimard, 1982), 60–61.
11 Ibid.
12 Ibid., 32.
13 Paul Webster, *Antoine de Saint-Exupéry: The Life and Death of the Little Prince* (London: Macmillan London, 1993), 258.
14 Ibid., 119–123.
15 Joy D. Marie Robinson, *Antoine de Saint-Exupéry* (Boston: Twayne Publishers, 1984), 80–84.
16 Saint-Exupéry, *The Little Prince*, 69.
17 E.E. Milligan, "Saint-Exupéry and Language." *The Modern Language Journal* 39, No. 5 (May, 1955): 249–250.
18 Ibid. quoting from Antoine de Saint-Exupéry, *The Wisdom of the Sands (Citadelle)*, trans. Stuart Gilbert (Chicago: The University of Chicago Press, 1950.)
19 Webster, *Antoine de Saint-Exupéry*, 195.
20 Milligan, "Saint-Exupéry and Language," 250.
21 Ibid., 250–221.
22 Saint-Exupéry, *Citadelle*, 44.
23 Ibid., 236.
24 Ibid., 278.
25 Ibid., 72–73.
26 Fay, "The Philosopy of Saint-Exupéry," *Antoine de Saint-Exupéry*, 95.
27 Saint-Exupéry, *The Little Prince*, 64–70.
28 Saint-Exupéry, *Citadelle*, 1098.
29 Robinson, *Antoine de Saint-Exupéry*, 156.
30 Saint-Exupéry, *The Little Prince*, 70.
31 Ibid., 9.
32 Ibid., 74–75.
33 Ibid., 87.
34 Marco Frascari, *Eleven Exercises in the Art of Architectural Drawing: Slow Food for the Architect's Imagination* (New York: Routledge, 2011), 4.
35 Ibid., 5–6.

11
ARCHITECTURE DRAWN OUT OF BRUNO SCHULZ'S POETIC PROSE

Anca Matyiku

When architects design a space, they are imagining a future that does not yet exist. In this sense it can be said that architectural design is an act of fiction; that it explores fictive possibilities that eventually condense into built environments. Could this then mean that fiction has the capacity to facilitate this imaginative process? The argument I pursue here is that not only fiction, but also literary and poetic constructs in general, can be valuable tools in the creative process that leads to architecture.

Typically, architectural design is accomplished through visual or tactile processes such as drawings or models.[1] While these are invaluable tools, they are predisposed toward the visual and measurable qualities of architectural works. However, architectural design is bound up with a complex multiplicity of subtle forces that are not as easy to grasp and manipulate. Among the trickiest and most difficult aspects of the architect's task is to build something tangible that adequately responds to particular cultural undercurrents such as shared values and histories; things that are assumed, implied, or tactfully omitted; the stories and myths that are continuously retold. In other words, the architect engages with this imaginative realm and interpret it in built form. Part of this act of interpretation requires a careful tuning of moods and atmospheric conditions. Atmospheres also contribute to a building's cultural appropriateness, yet they are almost as elusive as "culture."[2] The conjuring of atmospheres is then another precarious aspect of the architect's work.[3] My contention is that literature is a more agile instrument than drawing when it comes to tackling these complex and delicate aspects of architectural design. Thus I propose that literature operate in tandem with drawing, as an instrument for architectural design. More generally, I suggest that literary texts—whether written by the architect or appropriated from another author—be used toward *and* together with drawing in the process of finding the future architecture.

In what follows, I examine how architecture is presented in Bruno Schulz's fiction. The goal is to observe how Schulz's particular linguistic constructions tackle the two difficult aspects of the design process that were identified above: the orchestrating of atmospheres and the operation of interpreting between concrete and subtle aspects of architecture.

Bruno Schulz: An Architecturally Trained Painter and Writer

Bruno Schulz was a Polish author from the interwar period who studied architecture and was also a painter. He lived between 1892 and 1942 in Drohobycz, a small town of the former Austro-Hungarian province of Galicia, now part of Ukraine. Schulz is best known for his short stories, which are semi-autobiographical reminiscences of his childhood.[4] Often discussed alongside writers such as Kafka and Proust, Schulz's work remains distinct and difficult to categorize. His literary style is virtually impossible to paraphrase and it consists of richly layered, playful yet strange depictions that seem to transform mundane events into fantastical occurrences.

A number of the elements that contribute to the idiosyncratic quality of his fiction also make it interesting to this study. For instance, Schulz's fiction concentrates on richly detailed imagery while the plot remains subdued: the stories emerge as tableaus within which very little "happens."[5] His architectural and painterly inclinations are apparent in this insistent imagery, which builds up through a layering of metaphors that often employ architectural language. In other words, when Schulz's literature depicts architecture, the language is affected by his painter's vision, bringing it even closer to image.

Another aspect that contributed to Schulz's unique imagination is the fact that he earned his living teaching arts and crafts—including drafting, carpentry, and painting—at the local high school of his native Drohobycz. This means that unlike most authors who describe architecture, Schulz's imagination was steeped in a daily tactile engagement with materials and craft processes. With this background in mind, my primary focus is to examine how Schulz's manipulations of language conjure architectural representations. I wish to clarify that I do not propose that one should draw new architecture from Schulz's prose. Instead, I look at Schulz's fiction to capture some insights as to how "sketching" might be achieved through literary mock-ups.

On Metaphor and Teasing Out Potential Architectures

The specific interest here is how literary mock-ups can strengthen the *process* of design. I am thus less concerned with how architectural representation explains design intentions to an outside observer. Perhaps we can say that my focus is "drawing" as a tool for discovering or *drawing out* the future architecture.[6] Of interest is how literature and poetic constructs can complement the imaginative process that eventually leads to architectural works.

The conviction that language is crucially productive toward the creative process is supported by the theoretical work of Paul Ricoeur. In his *Rule of Metaphor*, Ricoeur argues that the imagination is primarily linguistic and that the metaphor is its operative principle.[7] This essentially means that the things we see in our imagination are tied to our words for them. Within this process, the metaphor enables us to see things in a new perspective. Ricoeur explains that the basic function of the metaphor is to bring together unexpected combinations of words that challenge pre-existing assumptions about that which those words are expected to designate. This in turn compels our imagination to see new potential realities: to creatively construct imaginative possibilities that do not yet exist. Ricoeur describes that this productive aspect of metaphor is "the function of fiction in shaping reality."[8]

While the metaphor is creatively productive because it creates friction between words and their meaning, Schulz's language goes even further: it explicitly removes aspirations of words having accurate designations to things. His metaphoric constructions are augmented or exaggerated to such an extent that they problematize the assumption that language is referentially transparent. Krzysztof Stala notes that this effect is especially pronounced with Schulz's use of "catachresis" and "periphrasis."

Catachresis: The Improper Metaphor Captures Atmospheric Precision

The "catachresis" is the most prevalent manipulation of metaphor in Schulz's prose. *The Oxford English Dictionary* defines "catachresis" as "the improper use of words; the application of a term to a thing which it does not properly denote; the abuse or perversion of a trope or metaphor."[9] Schulz's language constantly performs acrobatics across and between "proper" categories of representation. He creates dislocations between words and their depictions, which leads to unexpected cross-contaminations and synesthetic interchanges. He often uses words that refer to palpable and visceral experiences—shapes, objects, textures, tastes, temperature—to describe ephemeral and intangible experiences. Consider an example from the story "The Age of Genius." It describes Shloma, the town's petty criminal, stepping from the barber's shop into an empty square, soon after his "usual" spring release from prison. I highlight the instances in which catachresis is most pronounced:

> Having come down the steps, he found himself completely alone on the edge of the large, empty square, which that afternoon seemed shaped like a *gourd*; like a new, *unopened year*. Shloma stood on its threshold, gray and extinguished, *steeped in blueness* and incapable of making a decision that would break the perfect *roundness of an unused day*. Only once a year, on his

discharge from prison, did Shloma feel so clean, unburdened, and new. Then *the day received him* unto itself, washed from sin, renewed, reconciled with the world, and with *a sigh it opened* before him the spotless *orbs of its horizons.* [. . .] He stood *at the edge of the day and did not dare cross it*, or advance with his small, youthful, slightly limping steps into the *gently vaulted conch of the afternoon.* A translucent shadow lay over the city. The silence of that third hour after midday extracted from the walls of houses the pure *whiteness of chalk* and spread it voicelessly, *like a pack of cards.*[10] (author's emphasis)

The architectural setting for this scene is an empty square in the early spring, at Easter time. We are given the words "gourd," "unopened," "edge," "conch," "chalk," and "pack of cards." These words are used within a completely unexpected and inappropriate context. They call upon very concrete objects in order to describe formless things such as silence, a particular afternoon, an "unopened year," "an unused day." Then we are told that silence is capable of extracting "the pure whiteness of chalk" from the walls of houses which echoes the purifying effect of divine forgiveness that is imparted at Easter. This purity is however chalk-like, powdery, and threatens to disintegrate—much like the thief's integrity. The silence then spreads this chalky forgiveness like a pack of cards: it is dealt like fate, or maybe like chance, like fortune-telling or a gambler's game. Schloma *might* dare to make the initial step into the square and tamper with "the perfect roundness of an unused day," which is in fact already more than halfway passed. The chances for another round, for a clean slate, are belated like Schloma, who is forty yet childlike, and we are told spends most of his life in prison. This unlikely collection of words actually construes an image of incredible atmospheric precision: one of hopeful anticipation mixed with hesitation, tainted by the premonition of another judgment that seems to be pre-emptively enacted in the tribunal of market square.

Recall the idea that the orchestration of atmospheric nuances within built spaces is one of the most compelling and yet trickiest aspects of an architect's task. As previously noted, this is due to the fact that the dominant tools of practice and of learning architecture—most typically drawings—favor the visual and have difficulty expressing the wide range of other sensory qualities that permeate built spaces.[11] With this in mind, let us take a moment and imagine a drawing that an architect would make of market square. Such a drawing would very likely focus on the visual and the measurable mass of the constructed elements. It would take a lot of effort for a drawing to be as expressive and atmospheric as the above passage. This brings me to one of my main arguments, which is that language can render intangible atmospheres much quicker than drawing. Furthermore, I suggest that should one endeavor to make such an expressive drawing, the literary passage could focus and anchor its intentions; it could operate as a mock-up for the atmosphere that is intended.

Going back to Schulz's prose, we move on to another example rich in catachresis, the startling misuse of words. The following passage comes from a depiction of the narrator's home during a certain stretch of weeks that are remembered for their ambience of "mournful drowsiness":

> We were beset again from all sides by the mournful grayness of the city which *crept* through the windows with *the dark rash of dawn*, with the *mushroom growth of dusk*, developing into the *shaggy fur of long winter nights*. [. . .] Beds unmade for days on end, piled high with bedding crumpled and disordered from the *weight of dreams*, stood like *deep boats waiting to sail* into the dank and confusing labyrinths of some dark starless Venice.[12] (author's emphasis)

The reader is once again given words for tangible substances that transgress expected categories of representation: "dawn" with "rash," "dusk" with "mushroom growth," "winter nights" with "shaggy fur." Although unlikely, these pairings render the sensation of dread and lethargy incredibly palpable. Krzysztof Stala notes that through the tactic of relieving words from their usual taxonomies, Schulz's words become animated: they "wander freely" and begin to form unexpected connections.[13] This dislocation, Stala argues, can at times render the image more precise. For example, while the simile between beds and boats might seem forced, it relieves the word "bed" from commonly held associations and it actually focuses the image of the bed as a vessel for a journey into the world of dreams.[14]

The Playful Metaphor Proliferates: Tuning Architectural Intentions

Another notable aspect in the passage above is the way the image of the house is built up in a series of metaphors that make repeated attempts to name the same thing: the hostile mournfulness that creeps into the house; the dark rash of dawn; mushroom dusk; winter days growing into shaggy fur. This layering of metaphoric images is another of Schulz's linguistic manipulations—the aforementioned "periphrasis." This is the linguistic tool that most contributes to the textured, painting-like quality of his storytelling. According to *The Oxford English Dictionary*, "periphrasis" refers to "a figure of speech in which a meaning is expressed by several words instead of by few or one; a roundabout way of speaking; circumlocution."[15] Krzysztof Stala describes Schulz's periphrasis as a restless language that has the tendency to proliferate and does not settle on a final representation. This layering produces a playful ambivalence of meaning: it generates an "overgrowth" of imagery, yet not one of these multiple images fully carries the task of representation. The effect is that the images the reader conjures in their imagination mutate and multiply with every reading. An ultimate and unequivocal version cannot be pronounced, and the language sustains an openness of signification. The prose emerges as textured tableaus that are meticulously constructed and appear to immerse the reader in an insistent act of observing. They offer the imagination an inexhaustible capacity for extracting multiple possible images of spatial conditions.

Let us now revisit the connection between language and drawing in architecture. Let us pretend that we are in an architectural drawing workshop and we are given the task of drawing a space. The only direction we are given is that the space take on a somnolent atmosphere appropriate for mourning. For some, this might be sufficient to incite a whirlwind of architectural imagery. For others, the task would seem daunting at first—as happens often enough at the beginning of architectural design. It is quite likely that the task would appear less impenetrable if we were instead invited to draw a space for mourning, that might be reminiscent of a blotchy, itchy light at dawn, and mushroom growth that slowly turns into shaggy fur. If we were in fact to begin this drawing, would most of us think it appropriate to draw mushrooms and shaggy fur? My guess is that if we did, this hypothetical drawing workshop would seem quite uninspired, for reasons that will become clear below.

What these metaphors reveal is that for Schulz, the architectural imaginer, languidness and mourning share something with mushroom-ness, weighty dreams, a furry shagginess that might belong to the winter night, and so on. The actual drawing—and the future architecture for that matter—exist somewhere *between* all these qualities. What the space becomes not only depends on the architect's sensibilities and interpretation but very much solicits them. To restate it another way, it is unavoidable that this imagery *has to be interpreted*, in order to be translated into the architecture. As we might recall, this act of interpreting elements that are slippery to grasp is our primary focus. Once again, while the imaginary possibilities seem countless, the atmosphere sought for by the text is unmistakable.

It is important to remark that this task—expressing the furry shagginess of the winter night into an architectural condition—not only *requires* interpretation but it also *facilitates* it. By itself, the proposition to "design a languid space for mourning" is rather abstract. The further description of this atmosphere as sharing something with "mushroom fur" and the "dark rash of dawn" instills an element of playfulness in the process of achieving this task.

Here I wish to propose that "play" might be an essential element in how one approaches architectural design. I believe that it can actually enable the architect to engage those very slippery complexities of atmospheres and cultural predilections. Because these elements do not benefit from sharp definition, the task solicits an architect's discerning intuition, or a "tacit knowledge" as Michael Polanyi describes it.[16] Polanyi explains that tacit knowledge refers to the things we can grasp pre-reflectively, or the things we know before we can describe with precision. In the case of our example, we "tacitly know" that there is some sense in the coupling between a languid atmosphere and the image of a fuzzy mushroom dusk. Even though it is somewhat tricky to explain why this is so, this pairing seems unproblematic.

Essentially, Polanyi's concept of tacit knowledge brings to the fore that we "know more than we can tell." He suggests that this form of knowledge is particularly useful when we are confronted with something more complex than our conception of it—an aspect we have already ascertained about architectural design. Polanyi explains that we engage with such tasks because we intuitively know that they will lead us to new discoveries. As such, we surrender to the fact that the task before us has the capacity to surprise us. This act of surrender to possibilities that are yet undisclosed echoes H.G. Gadamer's notion of "play."[17] Gadamer explains that in order for a game to exist, there must be something with a capacity to respond, something that appears "to do surprising things of its own accord. [In this way], the player experiences the game as a reality that surpasses him."[18] The play then becomes primary. The result of the game is not pre-determined but it emerges in the act of playing. Gadamer bases his notion of play on Johan Huizinga's *Homo Ludens*, which argues that play is a significant function of culture proper.[19] In fact, Huizinga connects culture-making to both play and poetry: He states that "[poetry], in its original culture-making capacity, is born in and as play [. . .]"[20]

From this we can understand that poetic language is a form of play that draws on an architect's tacit knowledge in order to engage the subtle and complex cultural factors that come to bear on architecture. To go back to our literary example, I propose that if an architect believes that "the furry shagginess of the winter night," is expressive of the appropriate atmosphere, in looking to translate this metaphoric image the architect is in fact postponing design decisions yet focusing her intentions—she is engaging "play" in earnest. In the process, she would be more inclined to discover architectural elements or details that would not have been obvious at first.[21] In this way, "play" contributes a sense of personality and atmospheric character to the future architecture, and can effectively engage the particular qualities that gather under the elusive designation of cultural milieu.

The Metaphors Interlace across Disciplines: A Quasi-Rehearsal for Architectural Practice

Circling back to Schulz's fiction, we noticed that the playfulness of his architectural imagery often involves seemingly misplaced and mildly absurd choices of words, as in the examples of catachresis. In the case of periphrasis, it is manifested in the restless imagery that seems to mutate and multiply with every reading. It is also important to point out that in his depictions of architecture, his choice of architectural words is quite minimal. In fact, his metaphors have the tendency to interlace and cross between disciplines. In the previous example, we noticed the biological, animal-like metaphorical cluster that was layered onto the image of the house. In other instances, the cross-over of disciplines is reversed and architectural language performs metaphorically. In the following example "a new still-empty house" is solicited for its smell and sonority. The passage does not in fact describe an actual house, but a bundle of sensations that signal "The Night of the Great Season":

> The mornings were strangely refreshing and tart. From the quietened and cooler flow of time, from the completely new smell in the air, from the different consistency of the light, one could recognize that one had entered a new series of days [. . .] Voices trembled under these new skies resonantly

and lightly, as in *a new and still-empty house* which smells of varnish and paint, of things begun and not yet used. With a strange emotion one tried out new echoes, one bit into them with curiosity as, on a cool and sober morning on the eve of a journey, one bites into a fresh, still warm currant loaf.[22] (author's emphasis)

The metaphorical leaps presented in this short passage are incredibly rich in catachresis and periphrasis. The synesthetic interchange is especially pronounced: How can skies be new, inside a house, and cause voices to tremble? How does one bite into an echo? How does an echo taste like a still-warm currant loaf that's being eaten precisely "on the eve of a journey"? The fact that Schulz is performing these multiple crossovers and transpositions merits closer examination: his imagination is soliciting those very subtle sensibilities that are necessary to interpret between the elusive and concrete elements of architecture. An interesting parallel to architectural practice can be discerned here: it could be said that Schulz is carrying out this act of interpretation through language. In other words, the metaphoric constructions could be understood to constitute part of an architect's "practice": a quasi-rehearsal for the performance of interpretation and translation across mediums. I venture to suggest that this practice—performed in the medium of language—hones an architect's ability to engage the "tacit knowledge" that was mentioned earlier.

Literary Constructions Engage the Immaterial of Architecture

To conclude, we have observed how Schulz's exaggerated metaphors build up architectural images with remarkable atmospheric precision. This is an important although typically not straightforward task for an architect. We have also observed that Schulz's periphrasis maintains the same atmospherically charged quality, and yet the imagery remains open to manifold possibilities for interpretation. Within this layering of metaphors, words are dislocated from their representational function. Rather than representing the words themselves, a potential architectural space builds up *between* the words and inspires the architect's imagination and interpretive effort. It is essential to note that Schulz's language does not operate as a means to an end; it does not attempt to *describe* architectural spaces as if they were drawings. Put another way, Schulz's language is not subservient to visual representation, but operates as *a medium unto itself*. If one considers the suggestion that language and drawing both operate as tools for architectural design, language does not *serve* the drawing, but functions on its own terms. While drawing is an especially efficacious medium for expressing the material constitution of a future architecture, literary constructions convey the immaterial.

The literary constructions of Schulz's architectural imagery are effective examples because they are amplified and exaggerated. I have also suggested above that in architectural practice, literary constructions might be borrowed from an author or written by the architect. As we have seen, these constructions facilitate the process of extracting architectural design in a way that engages the imaginative landscape and the atmospheric aspects of a particular place. Hand-drawing and literary constructions are thus understood as complementary modes of approaching architectural design.

Notes

1 For the sake of clarity, in what follows I focus on drawing rather than models as the most pervasive tool for working out an architectural design.
2 Alberto Pérez-Gómez provides an elaborate, historically grounded argument that the atmospheric qualities of buildings are crucial to cultural appropriateness. Alberto Pérez-Gómez, *Attunement: Architectural Meaning after the Crisis of Modern Science* (Cambridge: MIT Press, 2016).
3 For additional discussion on the topic of atmosphere in architecture see Peter Zumthor, *Atmospheres: Architectural Environments, Surrounding Objects* (Basel: Birkhäuser, 2006).
4 In the English translation, Schulz's short stories are collected in *The Street of Crocodiles and Other Stories*, trans. Celina Wieniewska (New York: Penguin Books, 2008). All references are to this edition.
5 This has been noted by Krzysztof Stala, to whom we owe one of the most extensive studies on Schulz's fiction. Krzysztof Stala, *On the Margins of Reality: The Paradoxes of Representation in Bruno Schulz's Fiction* (Stockholm: Almqvist & Wiksell International, 1993), 54–67.
6 For a more elaborate discussion on drawing as architectural process see Juhani Pallasmaa, *The Thinking Hand* (Chichester: John Wiley & Sons, 2009).
7 Paul Ricoeur, *The Rule of Metaphor: Multi-Disciplinary Studies of the Creation of Meaning in Language*, trans. Robert Czerny (Toronto: University of Toronto Press, 1977).
8 Paul Ricoeur, "The Function of Fiction in Shaping Reality," *Man and World* 12, no. 2 (1979): 123–141.
9 *Oxford English Dictionary*, s.v. "catachresis," accessed August 5, 2016, www.oed.com/view/Entry/28665?redirectedFrom=catachresis#eid
10 Bruno Schulz, "The Age of Genius" in *The Street of Crocodiles*, 136.
11 An accessible discourse on the dominance of vision in architecture can be found in Juhani Pallasmaa, *The Eyes of the Skin: Architecture and the Senses* (Chichester: Wiley, 2012).
12 Schulz, "Tailors' Dummies," in *The Street of Crocodiles*, 25–26.
13 Stala, *Paradoxes of Representation in Schulz's Fiction*, 31–39.
14 Ibid., 87–88.
15 *Oxford English Dictionary*, s.v. "periphrasis," accessed August 5, 2016, www.oed.com/view/Entry/141026?redirectedFrom=periphrasis#eid
16 Michael Polanyi, *The Tacit Dimension* (Chicago and London: University of Chicago Press, 1966).
17 Hans-Georg Gadamer, *Truth and Method* trans. Garrett Barden and John Cumming (New York: Seabury Press, 1975), 91–111.
18 Gadamer, *Truth and Method*, 98.
19 Johan Huizinga, *Homo Ludens: A Study of the Play-Element in Culture* (Boston: Beacon Press, 1955).
20 Huizinga, *Homo Ludens*, 122.
21 For another discussion on how architectural details might tell a story and contribute to architectural character, see Marco Frascari, "The Tell-The-Tale Detail," in *Via 7: The Building of Architecture* ed. Paula Behrens and Anthony Fisher (Philadelphia: Graduate School of Fine Arts, University of Pennsylvania, 1984), 23–37.
22 Schulz, "The Night of the Great Season," in *The Street of Crocodiles*, 84.

12

WRITING, MODEL MAKING, AND INVENTING IN PAUL SCHEERBART'S *THE PERPETUAL MOTION MACHINE*

Sevil Enginsoy Ekinci

In memory of Christian F. Otto

Reading a Scene

> I have sought for two and a half years to invent a transportable motor that operates perpetually by the action of a weight. I believe that I have succeeded. What's more, I have written a book about it, entitled *The Perpetual Motion Machine*, illustrated with twenty-six drawings, which has been published by the Ernst Rowohlt press in Leipzig, and which may be purchased in bookstores for one-and-a-half marks.[1]

This is how Paul Scheerbart (1863–1915), the German writer known by his visionary literary works, presents his book *The Perpetual Motion Machine*, published in German in 1910 and in English as late as 2011, at its opening pages and within a scene of a laboratory gathering.

This scene sets the tone of Scheerbart's passionate defense of the possibility of the invention of a perpetual motion machine in the rest of the book, and accordingly, his fevered criticism of Robert Mayer's law of conservation (1849), which rejects such possibility categorically. As such, it invites us to read the story that records his innumerous experiments on perhaps the most utopian machine in the history of technology as an incessant process of fantasizing, writing, drawing, and model making.[2]

Reading Futuristic Fantasies

While in the opening scene Scheerbart addresses a scientific/technical audience, in a brief handwritten text accompanying the manuscript of *The Perpetual Motion*

Machine,[3] he reveals his aim to reach not only "engineers and mechanics," but more importantly, common readers who "can skip the scientific and technical details and still find sufficient material of interest." This material corresponds to "the conditions that will ensue should the perpetual motion machine become a reality" or, in other words, to the part that "the author depicts with the most lavish imagination."[4]

Apparently, it is also this part that excites Scheerbart himself mostly while writing the book, and furthermore, which places it within the group of his other fantastic stories. These stories are abundant in visions of colorfully illuminated works of architecture/landscape that move; architectural/sculptural interventions on the landscape in dramatic scales; and theme parks/world expositions/exhibition spaces as playgrounds of such futuristic architectural landscapes.[5]

In the book Scheerbart's "wild imagination" reaches its peak while developing the idea of such a "permanent architectural exhibition." At first he thinks that "any arbitrary chosen tract of land would be suitable for the purpose." Yet he soon realizes that "the future architect must have in view colossal operations over a vast terrain." So he considers "the Spree Forest near Berlin," then "the Black Forest" as a possibility, and finally, decides on "the entire Harz region" for his architectural park displaying models whose scales will be "larger than anything . . . witnessed in architecture up to now."[6]

While creating excitedly these fantasies of the future however, Scheerbart also seems concerned about the potentially harmful consequences of his machine.[7] This concern is actually a manifestation of his skepticism toward "praxis" in general which always carries the risk of destroying "a good many fantasies." Therefore while admitting at the end of the book that "these are naturally only fantasies," Scheerbart also relieves himself from the burden of the "actual reality."[8]

Reading the Diary

In the brief handwritten text Scheerbart also reveals his expectation that, "from a purely literary perspective," his book "should be welcomed by many readers" since it is "written in diary form."[9] Although this particular form is a distinguishing feature of the book, it actually develops within a narrative. This is also a chronological narrative through which Scheerbart presents, summarizes, and discusses his diary notes of his experiments on the machine and of his thoughts about its futuristic results. From time to time, he inserts short fantastic stories into these notes as well.[10] In terms of temporality then, while the diary notes cover a period of 2.5 years between December 27, 1907 and June 16, 1910, the narrative starts and ends at a later time and presumably before the publication of the book in 1910.

So it is on December 27, 1907 when "thinking about composing some brief narratives in which something new—something astonishing or grotesque would happen" that Scheerbart comes up with the idea of an unlimited energy machine. Such a machine, he thinks, can transform "the perpetual force of attraction exerted by the Earth" into perpetual motion "through a system of wheels superimposed on one another." Starting to play with this idea, he designs quickly the earliest version of the machine. It consists of "a large, spokeless double wheel," a "car suspended from double wheels [and] set securely into [another set of] double rails," two "additional wheels provided for safety" and a weight. In great excitement he reaches immediately the conclusion that he can actually produce a perpetual motion. Although he is not very sure whether one of the wheels will work properly or not, he continues with his design and adds two "fixed wheels."[11]

These first versions of his perpetual motion machine are illustrated with three diagrams. In contrast to most of the other illustrations of the later versions of the machine, however, Scheerbart does not refer to them directly in his narration. Apart from this difference, these three and the other twenty-three diagrams in the book are all simple visual representations without any technical details, including scale.[12] Similarly, Scheerbart's narration of these different versions of the machine does not make use of any terminologies of mechanics or formulas of physics. This is actually not surprising at all, since he admits unapologetically: "I had never in my life bothered very much about technical matters. The science of mechanics never interested me in the least."[13]

In the following days, Scheerbart keeps working on the machine without a break by making "drawings of about two hundred wheels—always the same ones in fact." Then consulting a plumber who equips him with "a couple of metal wheels," he produces his first "prototype" of the machine. But this is also his first failure because of the prototype's small size and therefore of the "refusal" of "the wheels to move in tandem," as well as of his "lack of skill" and of inability of "mounting the

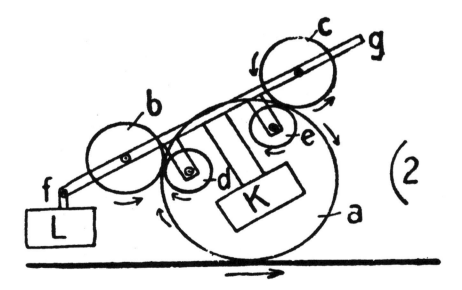

FIGURE 12.1 Paul Scheerbart, *The Perpetual Motion Machine. The Story of an Invention* (Cambridge, MA: Wakefield Press, 2011), figure 2.

Courtesy of Wakefield Press

weights." However these failures do not prevent him from trying again and again and from dreaming about "the broader consequences" of his "great discovery" which, as in the case of many other occasions, he regards "with doubt in the mornings and with conviction in the evenings."[14]

Following this introductory part, his narrative takes mainly the form of diary notes which, he believes, "make clear [his] state of mind at the time." Covering 19 days in total and a period between January 7, 1908 and February 19, 1908 these notes narrate intricately his obsessive pursuits to invent a perpetual motion machine together with his futuristic fantasies as well as with his emotional state oscillating between hope and disappointment, laughter and frustration. After reporting briefly on January 12, that he is "getting nowhere with the prototype," and making similar remarks on January 14, and on January 18, he writes down on January 25: "Yesterday, I tormented myself all day long with the prototype; finally I broke half of my soldered rails in two. I don't know the first thing about the plumber's trade. Such handicraft activity strikes me as quite laughable."[15]

Scheerbart's entry on January 30, which reports that the "contraption" still does not work, ends with a summary informing us that while working on the model of the machine he makes its sketches "in every possible configuration at least fifty times a day."[16] Returning to his diary on February 7, he writes about his futuristic projects and particularly about his architectural park until February 19. Afterwards he resumes his chronological narrative and it is only in the last few pages of the book that his diary notes reappear.

As we learn from this chronological narrative, Scheerbart tries at first to depart from his "original idea" but finding himself in "extreme confusion" he then decides to go back to it. After spending March 1908 by writing "astral novellas" he arrives at an alternative diagram in April 1908. He submits it to the patent office on May 15, 1908, though he does not believe that he has reached the final solution. So without losing any time he develops another one which he takes first to a mechanic who finds "the system unstable," and then, to the patent office again on June 2, 1908.[17]

Despite "doing very badly in terms of finances" and "constantly arguing with [his] wife," the summer months of 1908 seem to be "the most beautiful periods" of his life since he devotes himself to writing "astral epics." But he also admits that "the wheels [begin] to turn once again in [his] mind." So leaving the old prototype aside he starts "working afresh." By making a model of this new version, he observes joyfully on August 14, 1908 that it is "truly in motion." Yet, as we can imagine, he keeps working and after making another model he declares: "With great satisfaction, I bestowed on myself the title of 'master mechanic.'" Unfortunately his optimistic mood does not last long, since it does not work either. Without knowing "how to fix it," he makes another try, and after another visit to the mechanic and another submission to the patent office, the result still does not change. "Seized by a wild fury" and "curs[ing] everything possible and behave[ing] not at all reasonably" upon this result, he fortunately recovers quickly, and not surprisingly, decides to make another attempt. So he starts again in November 1908 by making "more accurate models with little wheels, slats, and screws" and by working "without pause like a craftsman."[18]

In the following months, it seems that he becomes "calmer and calmer," accepts "the nonfunctioning of the prototype with philosophical composure" and feels satisfied about spending "over a year of [his] life" with his "fantasies of 'wheels.'" However he does not cease his experiments and keeps working "perpetually with screws and saws, so that [his] fingers often ache quite a bit, being unused to such activity." Then on December 17, 1908, referring to a few diagrams which represent these models, he remarks that he has finally understood "why all of the prototypes failed to work." After giving up "the whole perpetual motion machine project" for a short period of time, and feeling "not at all unhappy about it," he restarts

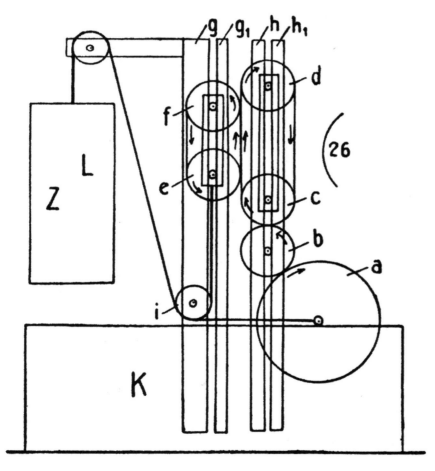

FIGURE 12.2 Paul Scheerbart, *The Perpetual Motion Machine. The Story of an Invention* (Cambridge, MA: Wakefield Press, 2011), figure 26.
Courtesy of Wakefield Press

and finishes another model in January 1909. Although he cannot "succeed in constructing the model accurately enough to allow for the superimposition of weights," he submits it to the patent office in the same month.[19]

Starting on March 4, 1909 and ending on June 16, 1910, Scheerbart goes back to his diary notes by adding to them the names of places, "Zehlendorf (near Berlin)" or "Friedenau (near Berlin)," where he has written them. In this last part of the book, which covers only a few entries, we see his adoption of a different method in his experiments by combining "the rails, shafts, and sprocket chains in constantly different ways." During this process, he discovers "an infinite number of combinations" which enable him to see "many doors and windows," instead of "bare walls" and accordingly which open "new perspectives" for him "onto the most splendid park landscape."[20]

Feeling very excited about this discovery Scheerbart designs "about two hundred combinations –each one different from the others." Finally, on April 5, 1910 he produces his last model, the twenty-sixth diagram, which "no longer works so simply; quite the opposite." He then concludes his book with an enigmatic passage whose interpretation awaits our own imagination: "On 12 July of the year 1910, after introducing a new factor, I succeeded in flawlessly solving the problem. Alas, I can say nothing about it without invalidating its registration at the patent offices of various governments. But I did arrive at a satisfying conclusion."[21]

Reading the Story

Calling his perpetual motion machine sometimes briefly "perpetuum" or "perpetua," and sometimes simply "perpet," Scheerbart refers to it in many sentences and passages remarkably as "story."[22] While making observations about the models of the machine, for example, he notes: "[t]he wheels turned so ponderously that I couldn't see if the story was going or not"[23]; or "[i]ndeed, the whole thing was now a very shaky story."[24] Concerning the particular mechanical components of the machine, he also points out: "wheel c was in fact hindering the entire story"[25]; "I'd said all along that the story could only be accomplished using cogwheels"[26]; "[a]nd now I held g in my hands –and observed that the story was truly in motion"[27]; or "that brings the whole setup into perpetual motion and constitutes in this way the keystone of the whole story, a story with such extraordinary importance 'for humanity.'"[28]

Similarly, while explaining his thought process during his experiments on the machine, he says: "[a]nd here I began, with a vengeance, to examine the entire wheel-story from every angle –day and night"[29]; or "[a]lready in September and October I'd been turning the story over and over in my mind."[30] Furthermore, regarding his emotional reactions during his experiments on the machine or his feelings about this process he reveals: "I will also laugh if nothing comes of this story"[31]; "[s]oon enough, it was clear to me that it couldn't work this way, and I became weary of occupying myself further with the story"[32]; "[t]he story was truly rather toxic"[33]; or "[d]espite this, the story didn't let go of me."[34]

Finally, about the futuristic results of the machine, he declares enthusiastically: "[a]ll the games of potentates are nothing compared to this wheel-story"[35]; "[s]o we will be compelled to concern ourselves with astral affairs. And that, to me, is the most valuable aspect of this whole fantastic wheel-story"[36]; "[n]ow, it cannot be my task to impose my faith in this story on those who do not share it"[37]; "[t]here's no doubt that this wheel-story is going to cause quite a stir"[38]; "[i]f the story works now, it shall be without a doubt the greatest wonder on Earth—an uncanny wonder. If the story doesn't go, we'll surely have before us an even greater wonder of the world."[39]

As a reader of all these "stories," I would suggest that Scheerbart's persistent use of "story" as a synonym for "machine" in such different contexts throughout the book is an issue related to the etymology of the word "machine" itself. It derives from *machina* in Latin, which in turn derives from the *mechane* in Greek, having a double-meaning of military machinery and machinery of the theater. In both cases, it has "the technical meaning of apparatuses, frames, devices" and "the psychosocial meaning of trick, artifice, deception," as Gerald Raunig explains.[40] It shows this double-meaning perhaps most clearly in the word "invention" in English, in the sense that "the machine is an invention, an invented device, and it is an 'invention' as an invented story, as a deception, as a machination."[41] In this regard, as the subtitle *The Story of an Invention* also implies, what Scheerbart tells in his book is the story of his invention of a perpetual motion machine, meaning the story of his invention of a story.

Reading the Book as an Architectural Model

Although the most distingushing characteristic of Scheerbart's book is its literary form of diary, it still seems unsettled among scholars whether the book is an actual record of his actual efforts of inventing a perpetual motion machine, or it is a product of his literary imagination in which he assumes the role of such an inventor. While on the one side there is the claim that they were financially driven real efforts witnessed at the time by Scheerbart's friends and also by Ernest Rowohlt, the publisher of the book,[42] on the other, there is the argument that to read Scheerbart himself as the protagonist of the story is to "confuse mirth with earnestness."[43]

In any case, these seemingly contrasting views should not impede us to see what Scheerbart does in his book and what he is: he tells a story and he is a storyteller. Here, to read and/or to listen to Scheerbart's story together with Walter Benjamin's essay "The Storyteller" can help us to follow him in his storytelling.[44] Deeply interested in Scheerbart's works Benjamin devotes his "Experience and Poverty"[45] and especially "On Scheerbart"[46] to them.[47] Although in these essays Benjamin does not refer to *The Perpetual Motion Machine* his comments on an "idea," with which Scheerbart's works are "imbued," is directly relevant to the book as well. "This idea," says Benjamin, "–or rather, this image- was of a humanity which had deployed the full range of its technology and put it to humane use." Furthermore, Benjamin's addressing Scheerbart as "one of those humorists who . . . seem never to forget that the earth is a heavenly body" makes perfect sense when we approach Scheerbart as a storyteller.[48]

For Benjamin every story "contains, openly or covertly, something useful" and "in every case the storyteller is a man who has counsel for his readers." By "counsel," he means "less an answer to a question than a proposal concerning the continuation of a story which is just unfolding." It is based on "the communicability of experience" in the sense that "the storyteller [who] takes what he tells from experience –his own or that reported by others . . . makes it the experience of those who are listening to his tale."[49]

This is where Scheerbart leaves us, his readers/listeners. It is a place where, in John Berger's words, lies "a story's outcome" and where we feel "like coming out of a house or residence, coming out into the street."[50] Standing there what we have is the book itself in which to write a story/machine is to make a model of this machine/story. The book is a model which records the experience of a design process of making trials and errors, of starting afresh, and of revising earlier experiments by blending different literary forms with drawings and by embracing fantasias, utopias as well as humor. This "craftsmanship," in Benjamin's words,[51] is the "outcome" of Scheerbart's book/model through which we can continue with the story/machine by making it our own experience and communicating this experience with others.

Most importantly, this is also where, I would suggest, the relevancy of *The Perpetual Motion Machine* to today's architectural education lies. Opening into question conventional definitions and categorizations of sketch, study and presentation models, it reminds us that architecture is not always directed toward the realization of building projects. While doing this, it presents us the possibility of making architectural models of fantastic stories which document their own processes of invention through various mediums. As such, it shows us again the communicative power of architectural design as a shared experience of an experimental craft.

More specifically, the relevancy of The Perpetual Motion Machine, I would also suggest, reveals itself in some recent design studio projects, such as the ones in the group of "Architectural Craft and Fiction" at the AA (Architectural Association) school in 2013. In an attempt to "'blur the line between the imaginary and real'," these projects are directed toward "making of narratives about the life and circumstances of the architect and his or her forms of production today" by means of "advanced filmic and digital image-making, animation and hyper-realistic visual simulation" as well as conventional representational techniques.[52]

Furthermore, this is a relevancy that shows us the possibility of covering history and theory in architectural education through some visionary architects and their "models." Here, if Lebbeus Woods is a contemporary case, the Florentine architect Antonio Averlino, better known as Filarete, is an example from the fifteenth century. Woods still communicates with us through his blog as a virtual model of his writings and drawings as well as those of many other architects.[53] Filarete, on the other hand, presents us his *Libro architectonico* as the actual model of his ideal city Sforzinda to read, to look at and to listen to his daily documentation of its construction whose intricate literary form of dialogues in a multi-layered narrative is interwoven with drawings.[54] I believe this is how *The Perpetual Motion Machine*, in Benjamin's words again, "preserves and concentrates its strength and is capable of releasing it even after a long time."[55]

Notes

1 Paul Scheerbart, *The Perpetual Motion Machine. The Story of an Invention*, trans. Andrew Joron (Wakefield Press: Cambridge, MA, 2011), 3. For another English translation by Susan Bernofsky, see Paul Scheerbart, *Perpetual Motion: The Story of an Invention*, in *Glass! Love!! Perpetual Motion!!! A Paul Scheerbart Reader*, ed. Josiah McElheny and Christine Burgin (Chicago: Chicago University Press, 2014), 208–253.
2 See Jonathan Sawday, *Engines of the Imagination. Renaissance Culture and the Rise of the Machine* (London and New York: Routledge, 2007), esp. 116–124.
3 For the original copy of this text and its English translation, see Paul Scheerbart, "Perpetual Motion: A Summary," in McElheny and Burgin, *Glass!*, 254–255.
4 Ibid., 254. When Paul Scheerbart's *Perpetual Motion Machine* was first published, it surprised many who took it as a technical treatise, and therefore, found Sheerbart's transformation from a poet of fantasy to a technical writer rather strange (John A. Stuart, "Introduction," in Paul Scheerbart, *The Gray Cloth*, trans. John A. Stuart (Cambridge, MA: MIT Press, 2001), xliv). But there were also others who believed that the book was "Scheerbart's mockery of an all too practical age" (Rosemarie Haag Bletter, "Paul Scheerbart's Architectural Fantasies," *JSAH* 34/2 (1975): 95, n. 68). Today, the book is interpreted as a "pataphysical" tale with "dry ironies of 'visual proof' in the form of diagrams, schematics, and drawings, subtly blurring the line between oneric reverie and documentary reality" (Gary Indiana, "A Strange Bird: Paul Scheerbart or the Eccentiricities of a Nightingale," in McElheny and Burgin, *Glass!*, 157); or as "a satirical novel" which displays "Scheerbart's ironic attitude toward technology" (Rosemarie Haag Blatter, "Fragments of Utopia: Paul Scheerbart and Bruno Taut," in McElheny and Burgin, *Glass!*, 125).
5 For these other stories translated into English, see *Glass Architecture*, trans. James Palmer (New York: Praeger, 1972); *The Gray Cloth*, trans. John A. Stuart (Cambridge, MA: MIT Press, 2001); *Lesabéndio: An Astroid Novel*, trans. Christina Svendsen (Cambridge, MA: Wakefield Press, 2012); and *Rakkóx the Billionaire and the Great Race*, trans. W. C. Bamberger (Cambridge, MA: Wakefield Press, 2015).
6 All the quotes in the paragraph are from Scheerbart, *Perpetual Motion*, 25–26.
7 Even more than the ecological consequences, what concerns Scheerbart is the militaristic "gross misconduct that the perpetua would make possible." Ibid., 29–30.
8 Ibid., 81.
9 Scheerbart, "A Summary," 254.
10 These stories are "The Barbaric General," "The Millionaire Uncle," "But Now for the Great Crash," "The Obsolence of Labour," "The Great Disruption," "The Solmen Silence," "Wheels and Rings," "The Astral Direction," "The Earthstar," "The Nourishment of Aria," and "The Elixir of Life" (Scheerbart, *Perpetual Motion*, 28–29, 50–60).
11 All the quotes in the paragraph are from ibid., 7–8.
12 In the original edition in German, these diagrams were printed on "a single large sheet folded and tipped into the back cover of the book" (Scheerbart, *Perpetual Motion*, in McElheny and Burgin, *Glass!*, 206).
13 Scheerbart, *Perpetual Motion*, 23.
14 All the quotes in the paragraph are consecutively from ibid., 11, 13.

15 All quotes in the paragraph are consecutively from ibid., 13, 15, 16, 18, 19.
16 Ibid., 22–23.
17 All the quotes in the paragraph are consecutively from ibid., 32, 36.
18 All the quotes in the paragraph are consecutively from ibid., 36, 40, 43, 45.
19 All the quotes in the paragraph are consecutively from ibid., 61, 62, 66.
20 Ibid., 77.
21 All the quotes in the paragraph are consecutively from ibid., 79, 83.
22 This important point is brought to readers' attention by Andrew Joron, the translator of the book ("Translator's Introduction," in ibid., viii).
23 Ibid., 70.
24 Ibid., 36.
25 Ibid., 23.
26 Ibid., 40.
27 Ibid.
28 Ibid., 74.
29 Ibid., 45.
30 Ibid.
31 Ibid., 17
32 Ibid., 32.
33 Ibid., 49.
34 Ibid., 74.
35 Ibid., 13.
36 Ibid., 20.
37 Ibid., 66.
38 Ibid., 69.
39 Ibid., 79, 81.
40 Gerald Raunig, *A Thousand Machines* (Los Angeles: Semiotext(e), 2010), 36–37.
41 Ibid., 37.
42 Haag Bletter, "Paul Scheerbart's Architectural Fantasies," 83; and Andrew Joron, "Translator's Introduction," v.
43 Christopher Turner, "The Crystal Vision of Paul Scheerbart: A Brief Biography," in McElheny and Burgin, *Glass!*, 13. Most probably, this is the "debate" to which W. C. Bamberger, the translator of Scheerbart's *Rakkóx the Billionaire and the Great Race*, refers in his introduction ("Translator's Introduction," in Scheerbart, *Rakkóx the Billionaire*, p. xvi).
44 Walter Benjamin, "The Storyteller. Reflections On the Works of Nikolai Leskov," in *Illuminations. Essays and Reflections*, ed. Hannah Arendt, and trans. Harry Zohn (New York: Schocken Books, 1969), 83–109.
45 Walter Benjamin, "Experience and Poverty," in *Selected Writings*, vol 2, part 2, 1931–1934, ed. Michael W. Jennings, Howard Eiland, and Gary Smith, and trans. Rodney Livingstone (Cambridge, MA/London: The Belknap Press of Harvard University Press, 2005), 731–736.
46 Walter Benjamin, "On Scheerbart," in *Walter Benjamin: Selected Writings*, volume 4, 1938–1940, ed. Howard Eiland and Michael W. Jennings, and trans. Edmund Jephcott (Cambridge, MA/London: The Belknap Press of Harvard University Press, 2003), 386–388.
47 On this topic, see also Hubertus Von Amelunxen, "'... versions of the seemingly imperfect ...' Thoughts on Paul Scheerbart and Walter Benjamin," in McElheny and Burgin, *Glass!*, 275–279.
48 Benjamin, "On Scheerbart," 386, 387.
49 Benjamin, "The Storyteller," 86, 87.
50 John Berger, *Bento's Sketchbook* (London and New York: Verso, 2015), 71.
51 Benjamin, "The Storyteller," 90.

52 Brett Steele, "Architectural Anti-Realism: The AA School in 2013," in *Educating Architects. How Tomorrow's Practitioners Will Learn Today*, ed. Neil Spiller and Nic Clear (London: Thames & Hudson, 2013), 50, 54–55).
53 https://lebbeuswoods.wordpress.com/.
54 See A. Sevil Enginsoy, *The Visuality/Orality/Aurality of Filarerete's Treatise on Architecture*, PhD diss., Cornell University (Ann Harbor: UMI, 2002).
55 Benjamin, "The Storyteller," 90.

13

MELVILLA

An(other) Underline Reading

Marc J. Neveu

Douglas Darden was not necessarily a scholar, but he was a reader of big books. Melville's *Moby-Dick*, Faulkner's *As I Lay Dying*, Shakespeare's *Hamlet*, Hugo's *Notre Dame*, and the poetry of Dante all play important roles in specific projects and appear often in his publication *Condemned Building* (Princeton Architectural Press, 1993). His work, however, did not simply reference great literature. Rather, he used the texts as sites, latent with potential meaning, from which to build architectural worlds. One such example is *Melvilla*, a library, archive, and reading room sited in New York City. Darden believed *Moby-Dick* to be the greatest American novel ever written in that it was the clearest representation of how one struggles between practical production and moral responsibility. The building, first conceived as a factory and a church, was intended to architectural-ize that struggle. Sited at the address in New York City in which Melville finished writing the novel, Darden refigures characters, plot lines, and intentions into architectural form. More than simply setting, one may, in fact, experience the novel as one descends into the building. Darden presented the work in a series of essays, each subtitled as "An Underline Reading," which referenced the act of underlining important passages in the book while making a close reading. This chapter will present a similarly close reading of Darden's building to demonstrate how literature, and specifically the novel *Moby-Dick*, may be understood as a guide for making.

After graduating magna cum laude with degrees in English and Psychology from the University of Denver in 1974, Darden spent 2 years at Parsons in New York, then from 1979 to 1983 at the Harvard University Graduate School of Design (GSD) in Cambridge, MA. Although he graduated from the GSD with distinction, his time there was not particularly rewarding, with the exception of a studio with Stanley Tigerman in his final year. He was inspired by Tigerman's witty critique of architectural agency, evident in *Versus: An American Architect's Alternatives*, written while Darden was his student.[1] Darden dedicated *Condemned Building* to his parents and Tigerman, evidence of the latter's influence. After graduation, he taught at several universities and spent time in Rome as a fellow at the American Academy. He returned to the United States in 1989 and began work at the University of Colorado at Denver, where he taught until his untimely death in 1996.[2]

A decade prior to his death, Darden wrote a review of Thomas Schumacher's recently published *Danteum: A Study in the Architecture of Literature* (Princeton Architectural Press, 1986). In the review, Darden reiterates Schumacher's reading of the Danteum to show that Terragni and Lingeri were "not translating in a representational way the Divine Comedy into architectural form, but by finding an analogic structure based on the numerical system of the Comedy."[3] Darden continued to explain that,

> Terragni's project is not a literal narrative that makes figures of space; instead, it is an architectural poem based on empathy towards the human figure in space. For example, the Danteum contains no form of a truncated conical purgatorial mountain. But through the basic architectural relations of its columns, walls, floors, and ceilings, the project conveys a desire for ascension.[4]

In short, the building does not simply illustrate the book. Darden, in his own building of *Moby-Dick* intended the same.

Darden's fascination with *Moby-Dick* was longstanding. In a recent interview with a friend of Darden's from the 1970s, it is clear that he was obsessed with the book even before architecture school.[5] By 1993 *Melvilla* had been published in at least three versions—in the journals *Site*, *A+U*, and the newsletter for the Melville Society of America (something he was particularly proud of)—prior to the final that exists in *Condemned Building*.[6] From this (somewhat unusual for Darden) extensive literary production, we have a clear sense of his intentions for the work. He explained:

> In 1988, fifty years after the conception of the Danteum, I set about to design a theoretical architectural project which would honor Herman Melville and his great masterpiece, *Moby-Dick*. At the outset, I wished to accomplish two things. Firstly, I sought to design a building, which would be the American equivalent in scope and stature to Terragni's project based on *The Divine Comedy*. This notion of equivalence was not grounded in an estimation of my own work relative to Terragni's, but on my belief that *Moby-Dick* is America's greatest novel. Secondly, I wished to demonstrate that a work of literature could not only be a source of inspiration for an architectural project, but that a novel could more directly in-form architecture; that is, a novel could be the veritable client for a building design.[7]

The earliest drawings date from 1989. The "1988" referenced in the quote may simply be that Darden began thinking about the project while at the American Academy in Rome, or, quite simply that he fancied the calendar connection to the Danteum.

Siting/Setting

The site for the Danteum, along Mussolini's Via dell'Impero and across from the Basilica of Maxentius, was important for a number of reasons. By carving an axis through various fora and adding a monument to one of the great works of Italian literature, Mussolini sought to demonstrate his claim as heir to the Roman Empire. Terragni and Lingeri made use of the geometric organization of the adjacent basilica in their own design. The site was, clearly, fertile ground on which to build. *Melvilla*, somewhat less heroically, also builds upon a loaded site. Darden sited the building in Manhattan at 103 Fourth St., at Eleventh Ave. It was at this address that Melville finished writing *Moby-Dick*. Darden chose not to site the project at Arrowhead in Pittsfield, Massachusetts where Melville spent the majority of time writing *Moby-Dick* because, in the words of Darden,

> In Manhattan the megalomania of Ahab, which propels the novel, turns the sea 90 degrees and builds skyscrapers. Harpoon-piles are thrust downward in a perpetual and perpetuated defiance of the living rock of the Island. This rock is no more and no less than "the snowy hill apparition" of Moby Dick at sea.[8]

Manhatto also happens to be the place from which Ishmael, longing for the sea, leaves from to go to New Bedford.

The site is, however, more than an address. One has the sense that much of Manhattan, and especially mid-town to the lower east side, is flat. It is not but there is the sense of a common datum not unlike the ocean. There is a world above and a distinct world below. The section of *Melvilla* calls out two distinct levels, street level and sea level. It is tempting to make the comparison to being above and below water. I don't think that was Darden's intention. Darden, trained as a ballet dancer for many years, would often state that, "one must go up to go down." This is true for a dancer about to jump as it is for building. Movement along the street level is horizontal. One descends to sea level, loses oneself in the reading of *Moby-Dick*, and then emerges from the depths back to the street. Movement within the building is very much a descension (in opposition to the Danteum's ascension) into the ground. From the grated catwalks at grade from Eleventh Avenue to the "underhang" of the rock that surrounds the project, one is constantly aware of the ground below. Indeed, the building itself is island-like, physically separated from Eleventh Ave. and the adjacent properties.

Program/Characters

The final program of *Melvilla* in *Condemned Building* contains the following spaces described as characters; the Archives, a concrete and steel half-cylinder head, hooded in brushed aluminum slats; the Commons, an over-structured concrete and steel box, punctuated by over-scaled light stacks; Transverse Stairs, multiple runs of varied

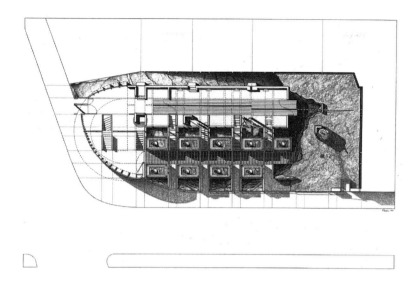

FIGURE 13.1 Grade Level Plan, Douglas Darden, Melvilla, New York, 1989.
Courtesy of Allison Collins, image used by permission from the Douglas Darden Estate

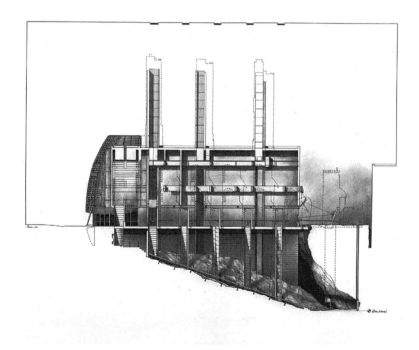

FIGURE 13.2 Longitudinal Section, Douglas Darden, Melvilla, New York, 1989.
Courtesy of Allison Collins, image used by permission from the Douglas Darden Estate

wooden stairs; Nine Reading Vaults made of native cut stone hung on vertical steel trusses with moveable chairs; and a Rock Yard described as the chief substance of Manhattan. The building also houses a first edition *Moby-Dick*. At least two paths, described as "plot-lines," exist in the building. The first path leads the reader (note: not "visitor") from the entry on Fourth Street beneath the monumental hood and archives, through the empty commons, to a dead-end that overlooks the "living-rock" of Manhattan.[9] On the second path, the reader departs from the first path and descends along transverse wooden stairs to gain access to individual reading vaults. Inside the vaults, the reader is able to move up and down the pole while seated. Surrounding the readers are book-lined shelves that act as both structure and library. The second path continues to sea level and leads to a vitrine carved into the rock that contains a first edition *Moby-Dick*. From there, the reader exits back to street level through a hollow column that pierces through the rock above.

All of this is relatively clear to the careful reader of plans and sections. Questions, however, remain; What is the specific relationship to the novel? How is this building more than an illustration of the text?

Building/Thinking

In a letter from March 1991, Darden more fully developed his intentions specifically with respect to his reading of *Moby-Dick* and the form of the project. As stated earlier, *Moby-Dick* was, for Darden, the most important American novel. Critical to Darden's understanding was Melville's depiction of the American mind. From Darden:

> The character of *Melvilla* is circumscribed by my sense of *Moby-Dick* as more than just a compendium of various literary styles and overlapping themes and symbols. Melville shows how the American grain falls apart when it is the product of a standardizing systemic. That systemic (Plato's "honey-head") is oiled by pride and driven by a competitive defiance of nature, and usually, of ourselves too. For Melville all systemic thought is flawed, not tragically, but fundamentally. In Greek drama the blind show the way to the heroes. In America, as Melville see its, there is no Way and to think otherwise is to be blind to reality. Heroes go self-appointed.[10]

In the frontispiece of *Condemned Building*, a further reference to Melville's critique of non-productive philosophizing is written on the edge of a guillotine. "How many, think ye, have fallen into Plato's Honey Head and sweetly perished there?" is from Melville's *Moby-Dick* and it concludes a section in which Tashtego is rescued by Queequeg. Tashtego has been given the honor of bailing the case—cutting an incision into the sperm whale's head and then repeatedly plunging a bucket attached to a 20-foot pole into the hole to retrieve the prized spermaceti. The head of the whale was suspended half over the boat and half over the water. After a sudden movement of the boat, Tashtego falls in the hole he's created and then the head, with Tashtego inside, falls into the water. Queequeg dives in to save him and does so by pulling Tashtego out of the hole by his hair. Melville lauds Tashtego's skill in midwifery—a skill that proves much more useful than philosophizing. The quote references Melville, as well as our own situation. The final "t" in the quote is obscured in shadow and, as such, the "there" also reads as "here."

Darden continued by explaining the two main themes in Melville's work:

> In the broadest sweep, Melville's language is underwritten by two themes which I believe are characteristic of the American mind. The first is an infatuation with instrumental, empirical reasoning. Melville addresses this subject self-critically through a number of linguistic guises; the mock-academician ("Jonah Historically Regarded," Ch. 83; "The Honor and Glory of Whaling," Ch. 82); the quasi physiologist ("Measurement of the Whale's Skeleton," Ch. 103; "The Great Heidelburgh Tun," Ch. 77; 'The Prairie," Ch. 79; "The Nut," Ch. 80); and the New England pragmatist ("Pitch-poling," Ch. 84; "The Lamp," Ch. 92; "Stowing Down and Clearing Up," Ch. 98). The number of probing, self-effacing questions that Melville poses in these chapters even while he presents a barrage of descriptive facts, provoke us to peer into the gaps, irregularities, shortcomings, and failures of modem empirical reason.
>
> The second characteristically American theme that Melville addresses is related to knowing and doing "the right thing." This topic is articulated in the numerous chapters charted through the tale, which contain omens, sermons, biblical allusions, and philosophical musings ("The Chapel," Ch. 7; "The Sermon," Ch. 9; "The Prophet," Ch. 19; "The Mat-Maker," Ch. 47). Through his use of archaic and ecclesiastical language, Melville opens up an ethical arena, which prompts us to examine what is "the right thing" over knowing mere "things." To read *Moby-Dick* is thus to engage in a great volley between American practicum and Cartesian morality, between Yankee know-how and existential doubt. Reading *Moby-Dick* is as if we are holding a Sears catalog in our left hand and the Old Testament in our right. . . . In architectural terms, we can envision a structure that combines aspects of a factory and a church.[11]

Although the project began, literally, as a church, it evolved into the current program of a library. Signs of the intellectual dichotomy presented above, however, remain. One walks into the project and the Sears Catalog and Bible are, literally, on either side.

Plot/Lines

According to Darden there are three main "movers" in *Moby-Dick:* Ahab, Ishmael and the Whale. These three characters inform the morphology of *Melvilla*. Ahab, the hunter, represents a driving line of force, which while being direct, essentially goes nowhere. A quote from *Moby-Dick* expresses Ahab's iron will:

> Swerve me? The path of my fixed purpose is laid with iron rails whereupon my soul is grooved to run. Over unsounded gorges, through the rifled hearts of mountains, under torrents' beds, unerringly I rush! Naught's an obstacle, naught's an angle to the iron way![12]

In *Melvilla* this character is represented by the path at grade level that starts at the entry to the building and pushes through the entire building to a balcony, which is suspended in front of a stone courtyard. The vacant commons hall surrounds the path. Darden related Ahab to America's rail system that traveled east to west, into the unknown but in a very direct way. The corresponding path in *Melvilla* also runs east west and into the unknown.

Ishmael, the witness, exists as an exile on the boundary of things. His path is about the unknowable and this condition is expanded—and created—by his traversing the boundary of the known and unknown over and over again. In the text, Ishmael describes the human will as the shuttle within the loom but not the loom itself. This text is quoted in *Condemned Building* and is etched in a rock set at grade on Eleventh St.[13] This character also infuses the meaning of the reading vaults. The nine vaults are woven into the plans and sections of the building to allow readers to soar and plunge for knowledge and to find the space for learning itself.

The paths run parallel to each other but are related, just as Ahab and Ishmael share the same spiritual crisis. Darden relates the structural grid of each path and, in early sketches, there is even a nod to the golden section also present within the Danteum.

Pre-existing both paths is the whale: Moby Dick. According to Darden, "the whale is a mask and a mystery with a mask; a thin shell over things and the thing from which all shells are made."[14] The front of the building, which is seen as a great monumental hood, represents the role played in the story by the great white whale himself. Moby Dick as whale in the story and form in the building guides the overall structure. Behind the aluminum screen is the archive. That this program is at the beginning of the building should not be seen as unusual. Melville places a list of etymologies and extracts at the beginning of the *Moby-Dick*.

The last space in *Melvilla* is a hollow column with an egress stair leading to the exit. The hollow column connects the deepest bowels of the building to the outside Manhattan. The core starts at sea level, which holds a first edition of *Moby-Dick*. Upon exiting, the reader travels up the hollow column to emerge in a stone courtyard comprised of the bedrock of Manhattan, a material which usually goes unacknowledged in the buildings of New York, but without which no building would stand. The igneous rock of Manhattan marks the site where Herman Melville began writing *Moby-Dick* and it is the last space before exiting, alone. Only Ishmael survives to tell the tale.

Symbol/Metaphor

At the beginning of this chapter, I quoted Darden who praised the Danteum for not being a literal narrative. Does Darden live up to his own expectations? In some ways yes, in some ways, no.

In various drawings, Darden refers to the lower portion of the entry canopy as the "teeth of the whale." There are thirty "I" beams—the same number as the crew on the Pequod. One walks into the project and the Sears Catalog and Bible are, literally, on either side as one enters. The stone on the west end of the project is often referred to as "Greylock" in the project sketches. This is a direct reference to Mount Greylock, the tallest mountain in Massachusetts and one whose snow-covered profile Melville has described as a sperm whale emerging from the ocean.

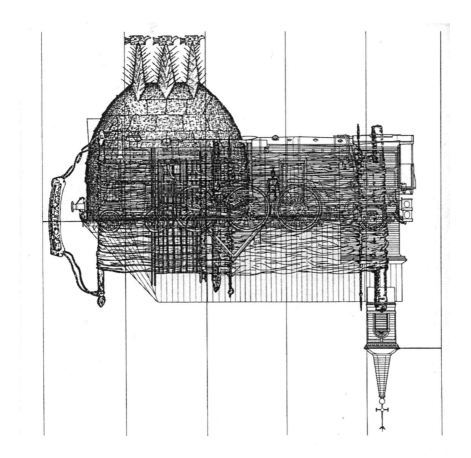

FIGURE 13.3 Dis/continuous Genealogy, Douglas Darden, Melvilla, New York, 1989.

Courtesy of Allison Collins, image used by permission from the Douglas Darden Estate

It was Melville's inspiration for *Moby-Dick*. Melville even dedicated his next book to Mount Greylock. The Composite Ideogram is composed of four literal references (Iroquois Meeting Hut, New England Meeting House, Iroquois Hand Loom, and a Locomotive) that, when combined into a Composite Ideogram, closely resembles the section of the project.

With such obvious references it would seem that, in architectural terms, Darden is proposing a duck—a building whose meaning is clearly revealed in its form.[15] One might argue that a duck is a literal narrative, something that Darden clearly did not intend. Darden was aware of this potential reading and offered a different take. Rather than simply accepting a building as a duck or decorated shed, he asked, what sort of duck? From Darden:

> If "a building is a duck," and as I said, I am perfectly willing for a building to be a duck, it is very important to ask the next question of what else could the building be, and what else should it be? In the very least, we must become more particular as designers and ask, "What kind of duck? Is it a duck under glass? Or is it a duck in a pond?" Architectural iconography—and all iconography, for that matter—gathers its meaning through the mileau [sic] which is created through and around it.[16]

When discussing Venturi's characterization of a building as a duck, Darden referenced Herman Hesse's *Steppenwolf*. The main character of the story, Harry Haller, questions his identity relative to bourgeois society. He does not fit in and imagines himself to be a lone steppenwolf. He is both man and wolf. But, as Hesse describes, we are in fact many more than two: "Man is an onion made up of a hundred integuments, a texture made up of many threads."[17] Our identities, as the main character of the novel, and the reading of architectural form are multifaceted. It is not possible to simply be a duck. To extend the analogy, this whale may be a duck, but it is also a wolf.

Darden differentiated between the symbolic and metaphoric understandings of building. The symbolic offers a one-to-one correspondence between things; in the metaphoric, new meaning emerges. Darden clearly saw his work as allegorical. He explains:

> Allegories do not create a singular one-to-one correspondence between things. That type of correspondence is found in parables. Parables create stories in which the fox stands for one thing and the tortoise for another. Instead, allegories suggest that metaphors, or more precisely, the whole operation of a metaphor, has a chance to *aerate the soil* of telling a story by accentuating qualities that are shared between fictional and real things. Why is this so important? Firstly, our whole lives gather meanings through stories. Secondly, the separation between fictional and real things is not so neat as most adults would have us believe: we learn about ourselves and our history through the commerce that is described between the fictional and the real.[18]

FIGURE 13.4 West Elevation, detail, Douglas Darden, Melvilla, New York, 1989.
Courtesy of Allison Collins, image used by permission from the Douglas Darden Estate

The title page of *Condemned Building* presents ten "allegorical" works of architecture. *Melvilla* was certainly intended as such. Darden's understanding of metaphor is very similar to the philosopher Paul Ricoeur, who Darden had been reading. For Ricoeur, building upon the writings of Aristotle, a metaphor demonstrates a fusion of horizons, from which new meaning emerges.[19] This new meaning allows for the re-description of reality that is at the root of fiction and is crucial to the understanding of our identity.

The other point made by Darden concerning the Danteum related to the physicality of the building. One, literally, ascended through space. The same happens here; one must go down to go up. There are constant indications of the body in space; entering under the screen; walking over grated catwalks; the vertiginous gap between the street and the building; the descension into the reading stacks; the up and down movement within the stacks; movement to the vitrine; and, finally emerging, alone, back to the street. An early elevation for *Melvilla* contains one of the only depictions of a person Darden's archive of drawings. He rarely, if ever, drew perspectives, and people are almost non-existent. That said, the body, and usually the body in motion, is constantly present in his descriptions of how the building is performed.

It is for these two reasons—the surplus of meaning found in form and the kinesthetic understanding of space—that I would propose that the work is not a direct translation per se. I would propose, however, that Darden does indeed "architecturalize" the between practical production and moral responsibility by rewriting the book in architectural terms based upon a very close (underline) reading.

Notes

1 Stanley Tigerman, *Versus: An American Architect's Alternatives* (New York, Rizzoli: 1982).
2 I am indebted to Allison Collins (Darden's widow) and Ben Ledbetter (one of Darden's life-long friends) for access to Darden's personal and professional affects left in his office at his death. All of the material—drawings, photocopies, photos, hand written notes, recordings, correspondence, etc.—have been donated to the Avery Library to join the drawings that were donated in 1997. Both donations were by Collins; the latter was organized by Ledbetter. Prior to the donation, I was able to catalog the entire archive.
3 Douglas Darden review of *The Danteum: A Study in the Architecture of Literature* by Thomas L. Schumacher. *Sites* 16–17 (1986).
4 Ibid.
5 Phone conversation with Pamela Goodrich-Yohe on April 15, 2015. Pamela knew Darden before he left Denver for New York and then Boston. At that time, he had read and greatly admired *Moby-Dick*.
6 See Douglas Darden, "Melvilla: an underline reading." *Sites* 24 (1992): 66–71, "Melvilla: an architect's reading of Moby-Dick." *A+U: Architecture & Urbanism* 272 (1993): 54–71, and "Melvilla" *Melville Society EXTRACTS* No. 91 (Nov 1992): 1–10. The text in *A+U* and *Melville Society EXTRACTS* are essentially the same text, much of which is also copied in various correspondence. The essay in *Sites* is a majority images and is similar to what is presented in *Condemned Building*. In addition to Darden's own writing, Michele Bazan Giordano has also written on *Melvilla* and while Darden was alive. See Michele Bazan Giordano, "Melvilla: a theoretical project." *Arca* 72 (1993): 12–17.
7 Darden, "Melvilla: an architect's reading of Moby-Dick," 55.
8 Ibid., 56.
9 "Plot lines" . . . are used by Darden in various sketches of the project
10 The quote is from a letter dated March 16, 1991 from Darden to Pelle' [Pellegrino] D'Acierno, a professor of comparative literature and languages at Hofstra University.
11 Darden, "Melvilla," 3.
12 Herman Melville, *Moby-Dick or, the Whale* (New York: Harper Brothers, 1851): 186.
13 In another project, Temple Forgetful, sited in the Roman Forum, Darden engraves a similar stone with the well-known phrase from Victor Hugo's *Notre Dame*—ceci tuera cela—that forever link building and writing.
14 The quote is from a letter dated March 16, 1991 from Darden to Pelle' [Pellegrino] D'Acierno, a professor of comparative literature and languages at Hofstra University.
15 In contradiction to a decorated shed, a duck, according to Robert Venturi, the "duck is a special building that *is* a symbol; the decorated shed is the conventional shelter that *applies* symbols." See Robert Venturi, Denise Scott Brown, and Steven Izenour, *Learning From Las Vegas* (Cambridge, MA: MIT Press, 1977): 87. Melville is quoted on the same page.
16 Darden, "In/n conversation," 2.
17 Herman Hesse, *Steppenwolf* (New York: Henry Holt and Company, 2002 [1927]): 61.
18 Darden, "In/n conversation," 6–7.
19 The idea of metaphor is explored throughout much of Ricoeur's writing. His most clear statement can be found in *La métaphore vive* (Paris: Èditions du Seuil, 1975). See also *Time and Narrative* vol. 1–3 and *Hermeneutics and the Human Sciences*. Darden's writing at this time seems heavily influenced by the work of Paul Ricoeur. It was at this same time that Darden met with Alberto Pérez-Gómez, who suggested he read the French philosopher's work.

14
DREAMING THE CITY THROUGH UNICORN SKULLS

Reading Murakami with Agamben

Paul Holmquist

If the self-reflective task of theory within the discipline of architecture is, as David Leatherbarrow writes, "to witness and comprehend the emergence of both ideas and buildings from the cultural context that endows them with vital significance,"[1] the challenge in teaching architectural theory is to enable students to apprehend these ideas as architectural concerns, in relation to architectural experience. Yet how to do so remains an open question. In this chapter, I suggest that literature may offer an approach. Reading literature together with philosophy, while asking architectural questions of both, potentially allows these questions to find their proper footing with respect to contemporary cultural conditions. I took this approach in teaching a recent graduate-level theory seminar for students in the professional design program at the McGill University School of Architecture.[2] The course explored how architecture and the city have figured as the paradigmatic sites in which the human, in the Western tradition, has been imagined theologically, philosophically, politically, and artistically through an ambivalent engagement with animality. Coursework was structured around the reading of a work of literature, Haruki Murakami's *Hard-Boiled Wonderland and the End of the World*, together with a work of philosophy, Giorgio Agamben's *The Open: Man and Animal*.[3] In Murakami's magical realist fiction, animals often serve as the occasion and means to pose questions of human nature, identity, and the self by eliding the boundaries between them.[4] In Agamben's theory, the very impetus to distinguish the human from the animal is rendered problematic. Reading Murakami with Agamben promised to enable the students to negotiate the political and philosophical complexity of the human–animal relation both imaginatively and conceptually, and prepared them to explore in their own research how the human is traversed through the animal, and the implications of this process for architecture and the city. I will discuss this promise of reading literature and philosophy together by first describing how, in Murakami's novel, animals metaphorically take central roles in two cities, or worlds, that are the settings for the struggle to realize a fully human sense of self, which through narrative allows the reader to inhabit the human–animal relation as a qualitative, spatial, and temporal condition. I will then examine how Agamben's critique of what he calls the "anthropological machine"—the fatal externalization of man's own animal nature in order to "produce" the human—can illuminate the philosophical relationships between human, animal, and the city in the novel. In conclusion, I will discuss how, by reading Murakami with Agamben, students were able to explore the diverse ways that the human–animal relation becomes a concern for architecture and the city through research into architectural projects, artifacts, theories, and practices as well as technologies, art, literature, and other cultural forms.

Inhabiting Worlds

In Murakami's novel, two distinct worlds unfold in parallel narratives in which the unnamed protagonist struggles to grasp his sense of self. The first is a futuristic Tokyo appearing as the Hard-Boiled Wonderland of the novel's title, evoking the manic, consumer-driven Japanese society of the late 1980s' so-called "bubble economy." The second world is that of an enigmatic walled town called the End of the World or simply the Town, where people have no desires or memories and history seems to have stopped. The protagonist of the story is a Calcutec—a neuro-encrypter of data—who works for the System, the ruling techno-governmental organization. In the parallel narrative, he finds himself having inexplicably arrived in the Town with no memory of who he is or where he came from. He is designated the Dreamreader and assigned to read the "old dreams" within the unicorn skulls kept in the Town's Library. Over the course of the novel, we come to learn that the Town is a simulated image of the protagonist's own core consciousness lodged deep within his subconscious mind—a neuro-technical experiment gone awry— to which his living consciousness, in the manner of a time-bomb, will shift over in a matter of time. The novel tells the story of the protagonist's dawning self-awareness as he falls out of the world of desire, action, memory, and death into an eternal inner world of mere existence.

In both worlds, the protagonist's self comes to be at stake through particular relationships with animality and animals: in Hard-Boiled Wonderland, through a mortal struggle in opposition to animality, and in the End of the World, through the sacrifice of animality. Each relation is experienced through the narrative as an inhabitable condition in which the reader experiences distinct qualities of animality and humanity. In the first world, the protagonist's dawning awareness of his own life and self, in response to the effective time-bomb planted in his brain, plays out in opposition to the inhuman INKlings, or "Infra-Nocturnal Kappa," a species of repulsive, terrifying amphibious beings whose subterranean realm underlies the city of Tokyo.[5] Ostensibly running for his life from enemies of the System, the protagonist's visceral confrontation with the INKlings and their world throws his own animality in high relief against his presumed human self. Above ground, we share his sensual experience of the corpulence of bodies, the vividness of colors, and the variety, richness, and tactility of things and places. We share as well the pleasures of his appetites, and his particular tastes in sex, Italian food, Bourbon whiskey, fashion, music, and literature. Below ground, however, his mind and senses are overwhelmed by watery darkness, filth, and the perpetual assault of unseen INKlings. He suffers intense pain from a gaping, bloody abdominal wound as he struggles to run, swim, and climb through increasingly perilous situations. His bodily functions go absurdly awry; all the while, artificial memories are triggered by the impending rift in his consciousness and threaten to sever him from his authentic self. Counting down to the changeover to the End of the World, the historical dimension of his life appears through his confrontation with animality. Along with the reader, he begins to realize who he is, or has become—along with his own tentative stake in himself—just as he is about to lose this sense of self forever.

In the parallel narrative of the End of the World, the self comes to be at stake through a sacrificial relation to animality in the Beasts, the unicorns that wander throughout the Town. The switch from the outer to inner world initiates the loss of the protagonist's desiring and remembering self—his mind—which is figured by his shadow that the Gatekeeper has cut away from him to slowly die. His impending loss of desire and memory is experienced in the places of the Town, which lack color, memorable character, and any identifiable atmosphere except for a pervading silence, mystery, and "vague sense of loss."[6] Instead, there is only the peace born of giving up the burden of self-realization, and the cessation of all striving, conflict, and suffering. It is the docile Beasts who take on this burden of self for the townspeople by soaking up "discharges of mind" into their bodies, and eventually dying from the "weight of self" the Town has forced upon them.[7] The Gatekeeper burns their bodies to destroy the accumulations of "mind," and their skulls, boiled clean and buried to leach out additional vestiges of mind, are placed in the Library, where the final traces are released as light through the discerning touch of the Dreamreader.

In the End of the World, through the protagonist's recognition of his implicit complicity in the cruel injustice imposed upon the Beasts, a third relation to animality appears: the promise of a yet-to-be-discovered self independent from animality, in harmony with man's given nature. After resolving to join his dying shadow to escape the Town and reclaim his capacity to desire, remember, suffer, and die, the protagonist decides to stay in the world he has created deep in his consciousness and "see out the consequences of my own doings."[8] He embraces the fragmentary memories and remaining emanations of his partial mind to "find the key to [his] own creation, and to its undoing."[9] He submits to banishment to the Woods east of the Town, which constitute a third inhabitable condition: a "mysteriously peaceful world" evoking the pristine order and beauty of primeval nature.[10] No Beasts enter this arboreal domain, which is "infused with the life breath one senses in the wild" that gives the protagonist "release."[11] In the Woods, the "trees and plants and tiny living things partake of a seamless living fabric; in every stone, in every clod of earth, one senses an immutable order."[12] The people who live in the Woods lead simple lives digging coal, cutting wood, gathering edible and useful plants and producing simple goods to trade with the people of the Town. Yet they can sense the beauty of the Woods, and of things. It is into the wondrously new world of the Woods that Murakami's protagonist ventures in order to discover himself anew.

Illuminating Worlds

The struggle to constitute a self in conflict with, or at the expense of, animality in Murakami's novel can be illuminated by Agamben's critique of how the human has been conceived in Western theology, philosophy, and politics in terms of the historical overcoming man's animal nature. In *The Open*, Agamben sets aside the traditional "mystery" of man's conjoined animal and human natures to ask instead how these two natures have come to be articulated from man's given, undivided being. In his analysis, the human has always been produced by separating out so-called animal attributes and characteristics from within man and distinguishing them from what is properly human: man's own muteness from his capacity for language, or the merely biological existence in common with animals from the fullness of man's relational being.[13] This animality, as defined and externalized in non-human animals, is then what must be overcome and redeemed in the historical process of becoming fully human. Agamben calls the conceptual operation to define and produce the human the "anthropological machine."[14] While this machine operates politically throughout the sphere of culture, Agamben argues that the city, as the *polis*, has historically functioned as the paradigmatic site of human realization, spatially and temporally transacted in opposition to animality.[15]

Yet Agamben shows how remnants of man's animality persist beyond what is thought to be the final achievement of the human in Jewish and Christian theology, ancient and modern philosophy, and science, in man's corporeality and natural life. In doing so, he takes up Alexandre Kojève's reading of Hegel's political philosophy in which man, having concluded the historical task of self-realization as human, is paradoxically left only to manage his natural, or animal, life.[16] Agamben argues that in the post-historical condition, the natural life of man has become "bare life," or life reduced to sheer biological existence, which is properly neither animal nor human.[17] This singular conception of a merely living life has been produced, along with the human, as man's own animality through the anthropological machine, and is what remains in the failure to conclusively establish the human. For Agamben, this bare life has been delivered over completely to power in late modernity through a biopolitics of administration and risk, in which the concentration camp has supplanted the *polis* as the paradigmatic site of deciding upon the human.[18] The anthropological machine has done its work, according to Agamben, but continues to idle.[19] He sees but two possible choices in response: taking up the care of man's natural life and turning away from the question of the human, or embracing the animality of man's given being to reclaim the question of his nature and potentiality outside of the fatal dynamic of the anthropological machine.[20]

In light of Agamben's critique, we can discern the question of the animal and human at issue in Murakami's novel and its political significance. Furthermore, we can see how the novel then lets us inhabit the oppositional condition of Hard-Boiled Wonderland and the sacrificial condition of the End of the World as two modes of the post-historical idling of Agamben's anthropological machine, in which human qualities beyond bare life come to be at stake through a relation to animality. In Hard-Boiled Wonderland, the perpetual struggle between the System and its enemies for control of information, variously allied with and against the animal INKlings, can be seen as analogous to that of the anthropological machine to maintain the human through a futile "history" of consumer-driven technological progress. In the protagonist's fateful entanglement in this struggle, and the risk to his natural life, he comes to see the heretofore unremarkable qualities of his life as stemming from impulses that are precious for their own sake. Although these qualities and impulses take their shape in the tastes and preferences that, in post-historical consumerism, comprise the care of man's bare life in terms of his emotional and physical well-being, they are not born of them. The protagonist becomes aware of how desiring and remembering intimately comprise his sense of self above and beyond his given, natural life, and even more so in knowing that he will soon lose it.

The End of the World, on the other hand, can be seen to starkly embody a grim vision of the post-historical condition Agamben refers to as "concluded humanity": merely living, without desire or memory, or future or past, and without tastes, feelings, or identity. In this world, actions are purposeless and have "no special meaning," and people have "nothing to achieve . . . and nowhere to get to."[21] The standstill of history is achieved through the sacrifice of the Beasts, who take on not the burden of man's animality, but of his humanity in the form of excess mind—the impulses to desire, feel, and remember. Rendered corporeal in the Beasts, man's ever nascent being as human is subjected to a continuous biological death. Learning of his own complicity in the death of the Beasts, the protagonist resolves to take back upon himself the burden of his mind within the Woods, where unicorns do not go. There, possessed of a partial, yet still emanating mind, he can begin to discover anew the potentiality of his self outside of the oppositional and sacrificial dynamics of the anthropological machine.

The protagonist's decision to go into the Woods can be interpreted in light of Agamben's second possible response to the idling of the anthropological machine: embracing the animality of man's undivided nature. Murakami's description of the Woods resonates with Agamben's citation of Walter Benjamin's notion of the "saved night," wherein the world is relieved of the burden of transacting man's redemption—and of being redeemed for his sake—and set free to remain within its own nature. For Benjamin, the saved night recalls a "nature that await[s] no day, and thus no Judgement Day . . . of a nature that is neither the theater of history nor the dwelling place of man."[22] For Agamben, it suggests the anthropological machine itself at a standstill in which human and animal are held suspended, opening new possibilities for dwelling in the play between them.[23] Into that space, he writes, "something for which perhaps we have no name, and which is neither animal nor man settles in between nature and humanity and holds itself in . . . the saved night."[24] In the saved night of the Woods, the protagonist delivers himself over to the "blessedness" of given nature and human nature relieved of the burden of overcoming, and in effect embraces the animality of his being by not seeking to redeem it.

FIGURE 14.1 Great Flight Cage, Richard Dimon and Daniel, Mann, Johnson & Mendenhall (DMJM), National Zoological Park, Washington D.C., USA, 1964. Image from the seminar "Belonging to the Emperor: Animals, Architecture and the Imagination of the Human," ARCH 541—Special Topics in Architecture, McGill University School of Architecture, 2014.

Photo by author

Exploring Worlds

In Murakami's novel, the human–animal relation illuminated by Agamben's theory can be inhabited as narrative conditions comprising distinct worlds, in which students recognized it as a properly architectural concern, and a constituent of architectural experience. They then went on to explore in their own research how this relation could be discerned in particular architectural projects, artifacts, theories, and practices, as well as in technology, art, literature, and other cultural forms. The students were asked to consider how the animal appeared within various spatial, social, imaginative, and technological conditions, and could be revealed as intrinsic to the order and qualities of the experience of architecture and the city. Their topics reflected how, in reality, the oppositional, sacrificial, and non-dependent relations to animality foregrounded in Murakami's novel ambiguously coexist and comingle.

The research undertaken by the students was diverse and provocative.[25] For instance, one student analyzed how Damien Hirst's artwork *A Thousand Years* (1990) evoked the sheer dichotomy between animal and human life by contrasting their respective kinds of temporality, corporeality, and consciousness. Another took up the leash as a dialogical architectural device, allowing dogs to share the socio-political space of city with people, while yet articulating their exclusion as moral agents. On a similar theme, another student showed how the intimate relationship with guide dogs helped people to realize their fullest dignity and moral capacities as persons by more fully and freely inhabiting the space of city. The theme of sacrifice came forward strikingly in a paper on the 1916 trial and execution of Mary the Elephant for the "murder" of her handler. The public spectacle of hanging the massive animal—a uniquely human punishment—from a railroad crane was seen as making visible the triumph of the human as a technological animal, transacted historically over and through non-human animals. Another student analyzed how the Japanese film monster Godzilla evolved since the 1950s from the destructor of human cities to their savior. He argued that the creature embodied natural animality as the victim of human technological self-realization, as well as the redemptive agent of this realization that must suffer to restore humanity to the natural order.

A number of students investigated the interdependence and ambiguity between human and animal as mediated in landscapes, ways of life, cultural forms, and technologies. One student examined the role of the Apis bull cult in the mythical founding and development of the ancient Egyptian city of Memphis. Another looked at how the beluga whale was intrinsic to the traditional ethos of Quebecers on the island of Isle-Aux-Coudres, in the Charlevoix region on the Saint Lawrence River, until the early twentieth century. This student described how in 1962, a documentary film team organized a hunt in order to reawaken the consciousness of this ethos among the community. They kept the whale alive throughout and ultimately transported it to an aquarium in New York. The pervasiveness of animals in media and other cultural forms led one student to survey how animals as corporate "trade characters" saturate the virtual, imaginary space of the city through advertising, and another to re-read Lewis Carroll's *Alice's Adventures in Wonderland* to show how space and time change when animals use human language. Students also explored how media and technology subsume both animal and human natures. One student showed how the classic Warner Brothers Studios' Wile E. Coyote and the Roadrunner cartoons (1949–94) rendered natural landscapes inhabitable to the post-World War II generation by anthropomorphizing animals and technology together in the popular imagination. Another examined how the idealization of human mastery over the animal became virtually realizable in the computer game Zoo Tycoon, which obliterates the distinctions between the human, animal, and technological within instrumental simulations based on the same computational models underlying the digital design tools used in architecture.

By reading Murakami with Agamben and exploring the human–animal relation as an architectural concern in their own research, the students were able to go a long way toward fulfilling the self-reflective task of architectural theory "to witness and comprehend the emergence of both ideas and buildings from the cultural context that endows them with vital significance."[26] Murakami does not allow us to inhabit the Woods, but leaves us to imagine what such a world outside of Agamben's anthropological machine might be like, how it would feel, and how we too might find our natures and sense of self anew as human no longer dependent upon an excluded animality, nor reduced to bare life. Likewise, we must imagine the nature and role of architecture and the city in such a world set apart from both Hard-Boiled Wonderland and the End of the World, and only intimated by the Woods. Reading literature with philosophy thus not only allows us to comprehend key cultural questions of human nature and identity as architectural concerns, but to recognize the capacity of architecture as a discipline to join literature and philosophy in posing these questions.

Notes

1 David Leatherbarrow, "Architecture Is Its Own Discipline," in *The Discipline of Architecture*, ed. Andrzej Piotrowski and Julia W. Robinson (Minneapolis, MN: University of Minnesota Press, 2001), 95.
2 "Belonging to the Emperor: Animals, Architecture and the Imagination of the Human," *ARCH 541—Special Topics in Architecture*, Summer 2014. I greatly appreciate the support I received in teaching this course from Director Annmarie Adams and Professor Alberto Pérez-Gómez. I also thank Angeliki Sioli and Yoonchun Jung for their interest in the course, and for the opportunity to reflect upon it in this chapter with the benefit of their insightful comments and suggestions.
3 Haruki Murakami, *Hard-Boiled Wonderland and the End of the World*, trans. Alfred Birnbaum (New York: Vintage Books, 1993); Giorgio Agamben, *The Open: Man and Animal*, trans. Kevin Attell (Stanford, CA: Stanford University Press, 2004).
4 Works by Murakami featuring animals in this way include *Dance, Dance, Dance*, trans. Alfred Birnbaum (New York: Vintage, 1995); *The Wind-Up Bird Chronicle*, trans. Jay Rubin (New York: Vintage Books, 2011); *A Wild Sheep Chase*, trans. Alfred Birnbaum (New York: Vintage, 2002); and *Kafka on the Shore*, trans. Philip Gabriel (New York: Vintage, 2006). For a particular discussion of the role of animals in Murakami's fiction relative to questions of the self and the human see Amy Ty Lai, "Memory, Hybridity and Creative Alliance in Haruki Murakami's Fiction," *Mosaic: a Journal for the Interdisciplinary Study of Literature* 40, 1 (March 2007): 163–79.

5 *Kappa* are mythological, aquatic sprites from Japanese folklore said to prey on those who came upon the ponds and rivers they inhabited, reputedly by tearing out their vital organs. See Ria Koopmans-de Bruijn, "Fabled Liaisons: Serpentine Spouses in Japanese Folktales," in *JAPANimals: History and Culture in Japan's Animal Life*, ed. Gregory M. Pflugfelder and Brett L. Walker (Ann Arbor, MI: Center for Japanese Studies, The University of Michigan, 2005), 70.
6 Murakami, *Hard-Boiled Wonderland*, 37.
7 Ibid., 334–5.
8 Ibid., 398–9.
9 Ibid., 399.
10 Ibid., 147.
11 Ibid.
12 Ibid.
13 Agamben, *The Open*, 35–8; 13–16.
14 Ibid., 26–7, 29, 35, 37–8, 79–80.
15 Ibid., 72–3, 75–7. While citing Martin Heidegger in particular, Agamben implicitly invokes the entire Western tradition of political philosophy following from Plato and Aristotle.
16 Ibid., 5–12; 76.
17 Ibid., 38.
18 Ibid., 15; 22; Giorgio Agamben, *Homo Sacer: Sovereign Power and Bare Life*, trans. Daniel Heller-Roazen (Stanford, CA: Stanford University Press, 1998), 181. In *Homo Sacer*, Agamben analyzes the notion of "bare life" in relation to sovereignty, and to his own theory of biopolitics following from Michel Foucault's concept of biopower.
19 Agamben, *The Open*, 80.
20 Ibid.
21 Murakami, *Hard-Boiled Wonderland*, 317.
22 Walter Benjamin to Florens Christian Rang, December 9, 1923, trans. Rodney Livingstone, in Walter Benjamin, *Selected Writings*, vol. I, *1913–1926*, ed. Marcus Bullock and Michael W. Jennings (Cambridge: Harvard University Press, Belknap Press, 1996), 389. Cited by Agamben, *The Open*, 81.
23 Agamben, *The Open*, 83.
24 Ibid.
25 I refer to the work of the following students, in order of mention: Andrew Lockhart, Léon Dussault-Gagné, Daniel Nedecki, Robert Hartry, Fouzi Ouadhi, David Cameron, Pierre-Charles Gauthier, Carlo Tadeo, Andrea Vickers, Nina Mihaylova, and Julia Chang.
26 Leatherbarrow, "Architecture Is Its Own Discipline," 95.

SECTION 4

Readings on Contemporary Architectural Reality and Practice

15

WE BUILD SPACES WITH WORDS

Spatial Agency, Recognition, and Narrative

Caroline Dionne

The question of our spatial agency, of how we can produce certain spatial conditions through our actions and words, is increasingly brought to the forefront in today's architectural, urban, and educational contexts. That the deeds of designers and planners may impact on spatial production is pretty obvious. But how are we to account for the role of "users" in the production of space?[1] Can users—understood here as dwellers, inhabitants and, most importantly, as social actors and citizens—claim active participation in "making" space, in shaping our cities, in the act of building? In this chapter, I propose to investigate spatial agency from the point of view of the relationship of words to actions with focus on Paul Ricœur's concept of *recognition*. Through a synthetic reading of *The Course of Recognition*, I will emphasize how agency is co-dependent with narrative processes, thus underlining the potential of literary imagination for action. I will do so from a strictly theoretical perspective, because I believe that terms such as *agency*, *action*, and *participation* merit to be critically re-appropriated and carefully defined rather than become banner slogans for what could be seen as yet another fleeting trend. A series of images runs in parallel to the text with projects by Patrick Bouchain and Loïc Julienne (Construire). Meant as a bridge between theory and practice, these photographs show some of the ideas discussed here in action.[2]

Agency and the Conditions of Collective Design Practices

Speaking in terms of spatial agency—of our capacity to actively "make" space—brings to front the idea of a potential that needs activating, of a dynamic where processes hold sway over a stabilized, observable state of things. When it comes to designing and transforming our built environment, such processes are understood to be first and foremost interdisciplinary—bringing together actors form a wide array of fields—and, at times, participatory—involving end-users in design processes. Several of today's design practices are thus essentially collective, partaking to what has been referred to as the "participatory movement." For such exercises to work, two aspects are generally advocated. First, a heightened level of *care* for others and openness to their point of view is wanted: through collective action federated around a common project, we can build more ethical, humane environments where individuals and societies can thrive. Second, there is an understanding of agency enactment as tied to the possibility to voice out our own interests. Simply put, the idea is as follows: if we get together and talk (express our needs, emit an opinion), problems can be better understood and, eventually, solved. The question of *what is to be said* and *how it should be said*—of the type of linguistic interaction we should engage in—remains essentially open. A keener understanding of agency will reveal that it does indeed rely on processes of language and, most importantly, on an acknowledgement of the non-objective means of communication usually associated to the realm of literary fiction. As we shall see, agency begins with our capacity to narrate, to tell stories, to *fictionalize* our experiences.

Saying and Doing in Paul Ricœur's Polysemy of Action

Ricœur's *The Course of Recognition* offers one of the farthest-reaching philosophical investigations and careful examination of agency as a concept inextricable from language-based processes. In this late work, he proposes to follow the historical and philosophical course taken by the term "recognition" through its various lexicographic accounts. Focus is on subtle semantic shifts, twists, and derivative processes by which the word acquires, through usage, unexpected proprieties. This specific course chosen by Ricœur therefore yields to producing what he has called "a ruled-governed polysemy," understood as an operative response to the impossibility of aggregating a comprehensive theory of action. The richness found in lexical accounts of the term recognition, in variations and derivations, contributes to a well-founded, yet plural conceptual framework for human action.[3]

Ricœur's exploration begins with re-examining the origins of the concept. The Aristotelian take on action was established in matters of ethics, and governed by the idea of one's actions being driven by rational—reasonable—desires: the exercise of one's practical wisdom or *phronësis* led to the pursuit, through one's deeds, of a wholesome life, understood as the utmost fundamental task. From Aristotle's conceptualization of action, we can gather that its principle resides in the subject's own will and power of decision: the cause of action begins *with the agent*, and action is to be understood as a means rather than an end. Hannah Arendt has pointed out how in the world of the ancient Greeks spoken and written accounts of the deeds of heroes served to orient mimetic processes through which one's quest for fame and posthumous recognition could unfold. In this regard, Ricœur writes:

> There exists a strong thematic continuity from Homer to the tragic writers and Aristotle (. . .). The philosopher, like the epic poet and the tragic poet,

but also like the orator using rhetoric in public speech, speaks of characters who, in [Bernard] Williams's terms, are "centres of agency" and beings capable of "recognizing responsibility."[4]

Simply put, the narrated deeds of heroes provide a scale upon which to weigh one's actions.

However—and this is where Ricœur's conceptual effort begins,—despite the possibility to acknowledge a continuity—a kinship—between our current understanding of action and that of the first philosophical moments of our tradition, Ricœur recognizes that a gap has set itself between Greek thought and our modern condition. The age-old question of self-knowledge therefore needs to be re-opened in light our modern self-reflexivity, where man occupies the central position both as enquirer and object of knowledge.

Recognition as a Source of Knowledge

Ricœur's *The Course of Recognition* opens with carefully observing and thematically ordering the plurality of meanings and possible usages of the term recognition. This is motivated by two impulses. First, although the history of philosophy proposes a plethora of stances for a theory of knowledge, only rare instances address the concept of re-cognition (literally, to "know anew"), which is, in Ricœur's view, a key mode of knowledge formation. Second, when recognition is discussed as a concept in various philosophical occurrences, the potentially conflicting significations of the term are rarely discerned. Identifying the implicit or unsaid meanings that lay in the folds of language and emerge at the intersections of lexical accounts, Ricœur can trace the philosophical—phenomenological—path of recognition as a concept. He does so through carefully examining the grammatical shifts inherent to how we use the word as a verb. In a first instance, recognition is used in the active voice "to recognize": I recognize something for what it is (recognition by identification); I recognize myself as unique (selfhood) and in terms of sameness in relation to another (alterity); I recognize what I have done (confession). Ricœur then goes on to examine the passive voice, "to be recognized": I am recognized as guilty, as worthy (judgment); I strive to be recognized by others in my capacity to act (processes of mutual recognition). Following this semantic course allows Ricœur to propose an understanding of man as a capable actor. Understanding action in the modern context therefore begins with a reflection on our capacities, on the different mode of saying "I can": I have the power to speak (*pouvoir dire*); I have the power to do, or make (*pouvoir faire*); I have the power to tell stories and to narrate myself (*pouvoir raconter et se raconter*).

With *The Course of Recognition*, Ricœur connects the production of meaning and knowledge to our capacity to act, understood as an outcome of the possibility we have to speak for ourselves.[5] It is by voicing out a perpetually unstable and fragile understanding of *who I am* to others that I can manage to take a measure of myself, if only temporarily. Self-knowledge begins in self-narration. Grounded in the semantic slips and looming misunderstandings that condition language processes, the production of meaning—the course of making sense of things—is always partial: it emerges through a constantly reiterated process by which we recognize ourselves (and are recognized as such by others) within a given social context. As we shall see, the term recognition in its plural semantic weight involves *fictionalization*—a creative recounting and retelling of events and experiences. In sum, our capacity to act rests, in Ricœur's terms, upon a possibility for recognition that begins with narrative processes (*mise en récit*): the stories we tell (how we narrate ourselves as another) convey a different type of truth, one that goes beyond the principles of truth by correspondence (*adequatio*).

Our condition of being immersed in the world implies that we find ourselves in a liminal condition between the possibility to abstract—to identify and represent an underlying order—and the possibility to act—to transform a given reality, to build a world according to our will. Back and forth movements between those two spheres are never direct: a detour, an unexpected turn of events always interferes in the course that goes from idea to action, and back. Moreover, our understanding of any given "thing" relies on an acknowledgement of its opposite: knowledge is co-dependent with "not knowing." The "real," Ricœur emphasizes, is incongruous. Similarly, the formation of social space follows a dynamic that, far from even, involves disorderly conducts, disagreement, and conflict.

Action through Narration

It is through our capacity to narrate ourselves, to cast our day-to-day experience via fictional practices, that we can generate meaning and concurrently transform space into place. However, the production of a more or less stable form of knowledge—from knowing something, to self-knowledge, and ultimately, to identifying the means available to us in social interaction—remains, for Ricœur, an open-ended, fallible, and ultimately unresolved process, but one that should be sought. The course of recognition is therefore subject to error, burdened by the threat of mistaking oneself and of being mistaken. He writes:

> The power to speak, which we deliberately placed at the head of the modalities of the "I can," is burdened by a difficulty in putting things into words, even an inability to speak. This inability shows that we can always mistake the underlying motivations that hinder our need to say something. (. . .) The kinship among secret, inhibition, resistance, disguise, lie, and hypocrisy is as close as it is hidden.[6]

In other words, the means by which we gain our sense of selfhood through our engagement with others is also the place for misunderstanding. "We do not mistake ourselves without also being mistaken about others and our relations with them."[7] Overcoming what hinders our capacity to engage with others through action implies, Ricœur insists, "an acceptance of a kind of companionship with misunderstanding, which goes with the ambiguities of an incomplete, open-ended life world."[8] This acceptance must, Ricœur insists, replace the fear of error.

The process of understanding who I am, where I stand in relation to others, and what I can do is thus always caught, from Ricœur's phenomenological standpoint, in a temporal unfolding that both ensues and impairs this understanding.[9] The back and forth movement between past and future (appearance/concealment) that conditions the phenomenological encounter with (or within) the "things" of the world, is addressed by Ricœur through two intimately related themes: *memory* and the *promise*. Acts of remembrance allow us to re-invite into the present an event that took place in the past. We do so in ways that are never literal: memories are forged by means of a creative process of imagery and narration.[10] Likewise, to promise implies bringing into the present the possibility of a yet unrealized future. The promise is also a statement: I voice out an imagined, potential reality that rests on my own acknowledgement of what *I can do* (or believe so). Ricœur's coupling of memory with the promise suggests that the latter—the act of promising—similarly partakes in the kind of knowledge formation rendered possible by processes of recognition. Once again, these are processes that take place on thin ice: the act of remembering is connected with the danger of forgetting (*l'oubli*), much like the possibility of breaching one's promise hovers above any act of promising (*la trahison*). The strength of Ricœur's analysis of action resides precisely in this indepth acknowledgement of the limitations that mark the course of active life. An awareness of these limitations is what allows us to grasp the phenomenon of knowledge in its precariousness. Paradoxically, it is this same awareness that engages us in a *longing for* knowledge, and for self-knowledge through our interactions with others.

This capacity that is ours to give meaning to experience by means of imagination, and to re-tell our experience with recourse to fiction—this capacity to speak, to *narrate* ourselves and our relationship to others—grounds, as we have seen, our capacity to act. There is however a distance between what I imagine myself doing, and the reality in which my actions take place: a potential need to be actualized, a step taken between the recognition of one's capacities and the enactment of one's capabilities. Man becomes truly *capable* as he (re)claims the right to see his capacities recognized. This can only take place, Ricœur insists, through rare, yet crucial instances of mutual recognition.[11] Between my own awareness of *what I can do* and the process of actualizing this potential through action, a risk needs to be taken. Action implies the likelihood of failure, the possibility for intentions to be mistaken and for deeds to go unrecognized: to act is to take risks. Our agency therefore often remains latent; we tend to delegate it to other agents.

The Space of the Gift and Mutual Recognition

Ricœur's third study on mutual recognition begins with an account of such processes in condition of social and political struggle: 1) mutual recognition through love but grounded in the struggle for intimacy with another (eros);

2) through the notion of rights in judicial conflicts and procedures; and 3) through social esteem and the struggle to be socially acknowledged. As a counterpoint to these conflict-based instances of mutual recognition and the complex questions of social justice they usually raise, Ricœur proposes to address the modalities of a similar process in less conflictual contexts, that is, in "times of peace." This allows him to examine mutual recognition in relation to the somewhat more disinterested form of love found in the Greek concept of agape (unconditional love, charity) as it is made manifest in the non-monetary exchange of gifts (*don*). For Ricœur, agape is the rarest yet utmost symmetrical mode of mutual recognition. It operates at a level where disputes are suspended, where a sense of selfless gratitude emerges. The fragility and scarcity of this most precious form of mutual recognition finds its anchoring in the festive, ritualized, and celebratory character associated with acts of giving. The modalities and limits of mutual recognition are, once more, tied the necessity to dare, to take risks:

> The experience of the gift, apart from its symbolic, indirect, rare, even exceptional character, is inseparable from its burden of potential conflicts, tied to the creative tension between generosity and obligation. These are the paradoxes and aporias arising from the analysis of the gift as an ideal type, which the experience of the gift carries in its pairing with the struggle for recognition. The struggle for recognition perhaps remains endless. At the very least, the experiences of actual recognition in the exchange of gifts, principally in their festive aspect, confer on this struggle for recognition the assurance that the motivation, which distinguishes it from the lust for power and shelters it from the fascination of violence, is not illusory nor vain.[12]

Mutual recognition achieved through the exchange of gifts is therefore not only rare, but extremely fragile. The generosity of the gift is inextricably tied with the expectations of receiving something back, a gift-in-return (*contre-don*).

In our societies, the necessary rules that preside over forms of exchange are usually framed in terms of *justice*. We are assigned roles, tasks, rights, and duties, advantages and disadvantages, prerogatives and burdens. Set in a dialectic relationship with the prescriptive and normative character of justice, we find *love*, and more especially agape as a pure generosity expressed in the act of giving. The tension between these two modes of exchange becomes, once again, perceptible in the way we use language: while "agape declares itself, proclaims itself, justice makes arguments." If justice implies a somewhat "logical" form of reciprocity, the reciprocity found in agape can be described as a "mutuality," a form of exchange that Ricœur insists is best interpreted not logically, but symbolically."[13] In line with Luc Boltanski's take on love and justice understood as competencies within the framework of a sociology of action, Ricœur then asks:

> Can we build a bridge between the poetics of agape and the prose of justice, between the hymn and the formal rule? It is a bridge that must be built, for

these two realms of life, that based on agape and that based on justice, both refer to one and the same world of action, in which they seek to manifest themselves as "competencies."[14]

Literary Imagination for Collective Design Practices

I would now like to return to the question of agency in relation of user-centered, participatory architectural approaches and attempt to bring to the forefront some assumptions that have oriented the writing of this chapter: the idea that literature plays a crucial role in our understanding of action, and that narrative processes learned by means of exercising our skills as speakers and writers ground architectural making in *praxis*.

As *The Course of Recognition* pointedly identifies, our propensity for narrative processes and, most especially, for self-narration, is at the heart of our capacity to act, to deploy our agency. Knowledge and understanding are inextricable from our capacity to imagine a reality that does not yet exist: to project. Simply put, I forge my understanding of a thing, a person, or a situation on the backdrop of what may have been *and* what could be. The act of making that founds architectural and urban practices therefore emerges from our aptitude, as speakers (*locuteurs*), to *metaphorize*, that is, to establish connections between distant, apparently unrelated things, between ideas and perceived objects, between what is real and what is possible: collective place making begins with a story, composed and shared by means of our literary imagination. In Ricœur's words: "literature is both a means of amplification and one for analyzing the resources of meaning available in the use of everyday language."[15] The development of the modern novel, which took place precisely at the margins of scientific inquiry and philosophical investigation in the space left open by the claim for transparency proper to modern scientificity, represents a catalyst of situations of life. Literary fiction accounts for quotidian events with the kind of realism that maintains a strong tension between our own life-knowledge and the representations we forge of what a society is and could be. Like all forms of art, the truth of literature cannot be paraphrased, demonstrated, or stabilized: it engages our lives in a quest for knowledge that requires, as Ricœur pointedly states, a certain kind of faithfulness.

The question of our spatial agency, of this capacity we have to speak for ourselves, and to engage, as architects, makers, and inhabitants, in self-aware, critical, and ethical building *praxis* indeed merits to be investigated if we are to redefine the potential for architectural and urban practices to partake in creating the necessary condition for, to speak with Lefebvre, *new ways of life* to take shape, for meaningful places of social cohabitation to emerge. What motivates action in its most generous and mutual sense is the simple, yet crucial possibility of being recognized as capable. If we follow Ricœur's argument, this would mean that, as architects and social actors, we actively engage with the modalities of narrative processes. A new set of skills would need to be developed if we are to value the architect's competencies in the social perspective of the conduct of one's life with others, and through action.

In order to imagine and build places to live and share, and cities where we can act, we most likely need to re-appropriate the know-how of the orator, of the storyteller, and of the writer, bringing literary imagination to play a key role in the acquisition of our trades. This brings to front the question of how modern literature in general, and the modern novel in particular, might be seen as a source of knowledge—a form of theory in its own right—that offers insight for developing such tools and skills. What this means for us, as practitioners, as teachers and students, and as users, indeed merits to be further investigated.

FIGURE 15.1 Metavilla is the intervention by Patrick Bouchain and EXYZT for the 10th International Venice Biennale. The title of the intervention jests with the discursive meta category as it offers a playful critique of middle-class living ideals through a participatory installation and communal living experiment. Understood phonetically, Metavilla also means "put your life here" (*mets ta vie là*). This play on word guided the intervention, which consisted in collectively creating living conditions within the pre-existing space of the French pavilion. Visitors would directly partake in producing the space of the intervention as they engaged in the simple activities of everyday life: cooking, eating, doing dishes, sleeping, cleaning, making art, and having conversations. Engaging in a rather informal dynamic, people were invited to "pitch in" according to what they could do best: explain, organize, negotiate, mediate, design, build, repair, prepare meals, talk, etc.

Courtesy of Cyrille Weiner, 2006

FIGURE 15.2 The series of bedrooms available for the visitors/designers/inhabitants of the French Pavilion over the course of the 10th International Venice Biennale. Turning the pavilion into a living space required extensive negotiations with the organizers, as visitors were usually expected to leave the site at a given hour. In order to grant them security access overnight, they had to be labeled performers and the experiment framed within the language of contemporary art. Patrick Bouchain and EXYZT, Metavilla.

Courtesy of Cyrille Weiner, 2006

FIGURE 15.3 In the context of the extensive rehabilitation of Le Channel, Scène Nationale in Calais, France, Patrick Bouchain, Loïc Julienne, François Delarozière and their team experimented with a series of participatory tactics. In order to launch what was imagined as a rather unconventional design/building/artistic programming/performative building operation, workers from all the different building trades were asked to collectively design and build the "construction-site hut" (*cabane de chantier*). This commonly shared space was assembled using discarded, left-over materials from the most recent construction site they had been working at (resources that usually end up in trash bins) and the construction workers' know-how and savviness. Set at the hearth of a 2-year "open to the public" construction site, the "hut" was used as the workers' cantina, as a public bar and restaurant, a conference and meeting room for building discussions and public events and as the headquarters and office for the artistic programming of the Channel activities.

Courtesy of Construire, 2007

FIGURE 15.4 Over the course of the rehabilitation and building operation, Le Channel remained open to the public not only as a construction site but as an active performing arts venue. The competencies of a power-shovel operator meet the skills of a contemporary dancer in the context of one of the numerous interdisciplinary collaborations.

Courtesy of Construire, 2007

FIGURE 15.5 In Tourcoing, Patrick Bouchain, Loïc Julienne and their team joined forces with a citizen-driven initiative to rehabilitate a former industrial, low-income neighborhood threatened by demolition by a commercial housing development operation. They experimented with a new device: the "architectural basic service dispensary," or, if you wish, something like a walk-in architectural clinic (*Permanence architecturale*). From the onset, an abandoned shop was transformed and made available to the public and architects: it became the headquarters of the projects strategic development. There, inhabitants of this neighborhood could claim rights on their houses and apartments, and get the tools to negotiate with the city administration on terms to maintain and renovate their homes. A long process of discussion took place on site, around collectively designed large scale models of the individual houses. Users and workers found a tribune to present themselves, and to share their everyday experience and knowledge of the place.

Courtesy of Sebastien Jarry, 2013

FIGURES 15.6 This social housing rehabilitation and transformation project conducted in Boulogne-sur-Mer questioned the distinction between designer and users in the most profound of ways. A young architect working with the firm, Sophie Ricard packed her suitcase and went to live with the inhabitants of an extremely poor and segregated community. There, she was confronted with issues that we usually tend to dissociate from purely architectural problems: extremely high levels of unemployment, violence, malnutrition, illiteracy, etc. The project demanded a heightened level of care as the architect settled into one of the abandoned units and progressively got to know her neighbors. Only then could the building process begin, little by little, and in ways that would bring to front the somewhat latent or forgotten skills of each inhabitant. She worked closely with members of a given household, adults and children alike, to fine-tune design decisions, choosing colors, materials and finishes that would make sense with their specific idea of what their house should look and feel like. A series of artists and architects also took residency at Sophie's place to lend a hand and contribute to the process. Together, they organized and engaged in everyday activities geared toward sharing knowledge, from building a park and public square to gardening, cooking, knitting, sewing, music and reading workshops, to name a few.

Courtesy of Construire, 2013

Notes

1 I use the word "users" for lack of a better term and in its widest sense, as it relates to usage understood as a customary practice in a specific, socio-spatial configuration and tied to how we *make use of* things, networks, places (in French, *usagers*).
2 I have pursued a similar, more condensed exploration of Ricœur's argument in relation to Construire's collective approach to architectural practice in Caroline Dionne, "A leap of faith in the realm of the possible," *OASE*, no 96—Social poetics: The architecture of use and appropriation (2016): 73–78.
3 See Paul Ricœur, *The Course of Recognition*. Translated by David Pellauer (Cambridge, MA: Harvard University Press, 2005), introduction.
4 Ricœur, *The Course of Recognition*, 80. Ricœur follows here Bernard Williams' notion that there exists some unacknowledged similarities intrinsic to "the concepts that we use in interpreting our own and other people's feelings and actions." See Bernard Williams, *Shame and Necessity*. Berkeley: University of California Press, 1993.
5 See in this regard, Paul Ricœur, *Lectures on Ideology and Utopia* (New York: Columbia University Press, 1986); *Soi-même comme un autre* (Paris: Seuil, 1990); *Memory, History, Forgetting*. Translated by Kathleen Blamey and David Pellauer (Chicago: University of Chicago Press, 2004).
6 Ricœur, *The Course of Recognition*, 257.
7 Ibid.
8 Ibid.
9 For Ricœur, the play of appearing, disappearing, and reappearing is the occasion for cruel disappointments that also can include "self-deception." "The test of misunderstanding shakes our confidence in the capacity of things and persons to make themselves recognized." Ricœur, *The Course of Recognition*, 256.
10 Already in *Memory, History, Forgetting*, Ricœur begs the question of the reliability and truthfulness of memory. He posits that a search for truth determines memory as a cognitive issue. See Ricœur, *Memory, History, Forgetting*, 55.
11 In line with an analysis governed by derivative polysemy, the different categories of recognition treated in the series of studies that form Ricœur's book are not mutually exclusive or simply successive. Rather, each type of recognition partakes to the two others.
12 Ricœur, *The Course of Recognition*, 246.
13 Ibid., 219.
14 *The Course of Recognition*, p. 224. See also Luc Boltanski. and Laurent Thevenot, *De la justification: Les economies de la grandeur* (Paris: Gallimard, 1991) and Luc Boltanski, "Agape: Une introduction aux états de paix," in *L'amour et la justice comme compétences* (Paris: Metaille, 1990).
15 Ricœur, *The Course of Recognition*, 5.

16
THE ARCHITECTURAL TURN IN CONTEMPORARY LITERATURE

David Spurr

In the remarks that follow I would like to trace a shift that has taken place in the last 100 years in the relation between literature and architecture in Europe and North America. I shall treat the history of this relation in two stages. The first concerns the avant-garde in both cultural forms in the decades before World War II: high modernism in literature and modernist architecture. Although neither of these two movements took much account of one another, both can be understood as original and innovative responses to the conditions of modern existence. The second stage of this relation concerns the period of the last 50 years, in which literary works have increasingly demonstrated a consciousness of the built environment created by the newly globalized economy. I call this newly critical awareness of the built environment the architectural turn in contemporary literature.

Formal innovation in modernist architecture, whether that of Le Corbusier, Frank Lloyd Wright, or Mies van der Rohe, generally took place as the concrete realization of an aesthetic program, with its own reflection on the nature of dwelling, work, and the relation to a natural environment. In both architecture and literature such innovation was largely motivated by the desire for emancipation from forms no longer adequate to modern life, a movement which led to *vers libre* in poetry and to *plan libre* in architecture. Modernist literature from Baudelaire to Eliot registers the fragmentation and discontinuity of the urban environment, while opposing to this fragmentation a certain continuity of subjectivity and literary form: Baudelaire's classicism, Proust's *recherche*, Woolf's moments of being, Joyce's stream of consciousness and his mythic parallels. Formal experimentation in modernist literature was part of the project of redeeming the destructive character of modern life manifested in the modern urban environment, as is documented in essays such as Georg Simmel's "Die Grossstädte und das Geistesleben" (The Metropolis and Mental Life, 1903).[1] Both literature and architecture broadly conceived of art as a model of action, even as a utopian project: modernism meant emancipation from an established order, and even an ideal vision. This is clear in the discourse of every modernist architect from Adolf Loos to Louis Kahn, and of modernist writers like Pound, Eliot, Joyce, and Woolf. Modernism in its various manifestations had a fundamentally utopian character even if, in the analysis of a historian like Manfredo Tafuri, such utopianism may have functioned as a distraction from the real forces of capitalism driving the broader phenomena of modernity.[2]

We now live in an era where, globally speaking, architecture no longer has any serious ideology. As early as 1975, Philip Johnson celebrated this absence by saying, "The day of ideology is thankfully over [. . .] There are no rules, only facts. There is no order, only preference. There are no imperatives, only choice."[3] But choice as a function of what? What Johnson failed to acknowledge is that in the absence of any values to justify its autonomy, architecture as a practice hands itself over to the forces of the market. Form no longer follows function, but fulfills the demand for visibility in competition with other images. In the twenty-first century, the most spectacular formal innovation often appears motivated by the same considerations that go into commercial product design: the need to establish brand identity and market position. In this process, the emphasis has shifted from architecture as the design of space to architecture as image. We live in an economy dominated by the image, where the image itself is a form of capital. The most visible architectural works are created as images, and are widely disseminated as such by the global media.

The circulation of images is part of what Manuel Castells has called "the space of flows" in the postmodern economy: the flow of capital, information, technology, organizational interaction, and sounds and symbols as well as images. Architecture has become a material support for this space, which supersedes the more historical production of architectural meaning in history and *place*, that is, where form, function, and meaning once were generated within the boundaries of physical contiguity.[4] Postmodernism in architecture, like modernism, derived its energy from the breakdown of traditional codes. But the great modernists did so from within a historically rooted culture in the name of progress and rationality. The recent architecture of the global economy, by contrast, implicitly declares the end of history and, by extension, the end of architectural meaning, except insofar as this architecture can be understood as symptomatic of the conditions of its production in the global network of power and finance. The openness, transparency, and freedom implied in the modernist *plan libre* have been superseded by systems of security, concealment, and controlled access. The classical principles of proportion and harmony present in the work of architects such as Mies van der Rohe have literally lost ground to the big, the tall, and the flashy.

On the level of actual construction, what Rem Koolhaas calls "junkspace" refers to the total adaptation of architectural construction to the demands of globalization and the consumer society.[5] This is a truly global phenomenon. Its formal logic is that of addition, proliferation, successive transformations, and a spatial continuity that maximizes flow: the movement of persons and goods from one point to another. Junkspace is the opposite of the architectural tradition of grammar, composition, permanence, and definition. For Koolhaas, it is not really architecture at all; it is what fills the absence of architecture in our historical moment.

Faced with this character of the built environment, many works of contemporary literature have taken a critical stance toward architecture, one that simply never occurred to modernist writers of the first half of the twentieth century. Junkspace figures prominently in much of these more recent works. In novels like *La carte et le territoire* (2010), Michel Houellebecq evokes a contemporary world where the absence of metaphysical value gives way to a kind of ontological drift: "a monstrous and global lack" in contemporary existence, as he puts it.[6] The built environment is both the scene of that drift and the concretization of that absence. His vision of the contemporary built environment has much in common with that of J.G. Ballard, whose great theme, from *Crash* (1973) to *Kingdom Come* (2006) is that of the effects of modern infrastructure on human psychology and social relations.

The architect Louise Pelletier has written a novel called *Downfall: The Architecture of Excess* (2014), where she marks the contrast between the idealism of modern architecture in the days of Le Corbusier and what it has become today. "Although modern architecture emerged as a result of a political movement aimed at democratizing architecture, it soon became more of a style that succeeded in reconciling innovative forms with capitalist ambitions."[7] Her novel is part of a new literary movement that confronts this manifestation of capitalist ambitions in architectural form. The form of capitalism at issue here is that of its latest stage that, as David Harvey describes it, involves "the de-linking of the financial system from active production and from any material monetary base."[8] As an example of the architecture that is symptomatic of late capitalism, Harvey cites Philip Johnson's AT&T building in New York (now the Sony Tower). With its kitsch "Chippendale" roofline and pink granite façade, the building is postmodern not just in style but also in its capitalization: "debt-financed, built on the basis of fictitious capital, and architecturally conceived [. . .] more in the spirit of fiction than of function."[9]

But it is precisely literary fiction designed to reflect the *Zeitgeist* that has taken up the critique of the architecture of finance capital. A lively illustration is to be found in the recent fiction of Joseph O'Neill. In *The Dog* (2014), the narrator works in Dubai as attorney for the family office of a clan with worldwide financial holdings. He lives alone in a building called the Situation, one of the gleaming high-rises overlooking the Persian Gulf, which resembles in every respect an actual building designed in imitation Art Deco called the Address.

He works at the Dubai International Finance Centre, an actual place of beautiful office buildings, broad plazas, and calm pools, all of them gray, blue, or white. These harmonies of form and color, he feels, are signs of a feeling shared by those who participate in this economy that

> ours is a zone of the win-win-win flow of money and ideas and humans, and that somewhere in our processes and practices, [. . .] are the omens of that future community of cooperative productivity, that financial nationhood, of which all of us here more or less unconsciously dream.[10]

FIGURE 16.1 Emaar Properties Group and Atkins, The Address Downtown Dubai, Dubai, United Arab Emirates, 2008.

Photo by David Waddington

If there were a manifesto of global finance capital, that would be it. Places like Dubai, with its inequalities and corruption hidden behind serene façades, are merely its concentrated essence.

Dubai seems nonetheless to occupy a certain place in the contemporary literary imagination as the nexus of global capital, aggressive architecture, political repression, and the scandalous treatment of the migrant workers who actually build its shining towers. Arnon Grunberg's novel *De man zonder ziekte* (The Man without Illness, 2012) follows a Swiss architect to Dubai, where he has been commissioned to design a library with an underground annex to serve as a bunker for the Emir.[11] He is guided by a book called *Architecture in the Era of Faust*, and his design must compete in the Dubai skyline with a building constructed in the shape of a champagne bottle, complete with a penthouse in the cork. Falsely accused as a spy, he finishes his days in the depths of a Dubai prison.

In Zia Haider Rahman's acclaimed debut novel, *In the Light of What We Know* (2014), the principal character, Zafar, is an investment banker turned human-rights lawyer who finds himself in Dubai with a view of what is described as the world's most luxurious hotel, the Burj Al Arab, or Tower of the Arabs, a fleet of Rolls Royces drawn up in front. The roof has a helipad, from which he has seen, in a magazine, the photograph of a solitary man hitting a golf ball "into the blue abandon of the Arabian Gulf."[12] This resplendent vision leads to another, more earthly, of "thousands of men, most of them South Asian [...], working with their hands, pulling heavy loads, a dozen dying in the assembly of each new skyscraper, crushed by concrete or sliced by high-tension wire."[13] Zafar's thoughts finally turn philosophical. He reflects that in a 100 or 200 years every human being in Dubai, every captain of industry and every hotel cleaner will be no more, but that these buildings of concrete, glass, and steel will stand: not all of them, but "enough will persevere without *them*. It is a thought that stills me, that brings a moment of calm."[14] In the mode of *vanitas vanitatum*, he imagines the high-rises of Dubai standing at the edge of the desert, mutely testifying to a vainglorious past, like the ruins of Shelley's "Ozymandias."

In *The Art-Architecture Complex* (2011) Hal Foster has documented the recent movement in architecture, as in art, toward an aesthetic of the mediated image.[15] Buildings like Frank Gehry's Guggenheim Museum in Bilbao (1997) and Koolhaas' own CCTV headquarters (2012) in Beijing are more important to contemporary culture as striking and original images rendered on television and the internet than as buildings having a properly architectural function. As images, they create a visual identity for the cities where they are located and the institutions they house, despite the fact that nothing in their form or materials is authentically local to the regions where they are built. Gehry's museum stands for Bilbao not because it is of Bilbao but because it happens to be there; it could have been built anywhere. It is an arbitrary signifier that both represents Bilbao and cancels out Bilbao as a necessary signified. In semiotic terms, we would say that it is underdetermined as a sign of any intended referent. What it really stands for is a kind of absence: the absence of place in the globalized space of a contemporary built environment increasingly experienced as a virtual rather than a concrete reality.

To what Foster calls the art-architecture complex, we need to add a third term, one suggested by the literary works I have discussed up to this point. That term is capital. What I shall call the art-architecture-capital complex, then, creates the built environment by means of finance capital in order to generate consumer spending. The ephemeral form of the shopping mall is a conventional example, but more recently the talents of star architects like Gehry and Koolhaas have been devoted to creating the proper environment for the sale of luxury goods. Luxury goods, such as handmade designer shoes and Swiss watches, occupy an intermediate position, economically and aesthetically, between basic consumer items and works of art. In this respect they correspond perfectly to works of architecture that aspire to the status of art while remaining functional.

In evoking the art-architecture-capital complex I am thinking of Koolhaas' Office for Metropolitan Architecture (OMA) and its designs for Prada stores, including the Prada Epicenter in New York. The firm's website tells us that this is "an exclusive boutique, a public space, a gallery, a performance space, a laboratory," all "part of OMA's ongoing research into shopping, arguably the last remaining form of public activity, and a strategy to counteract and destabilize any received notion of what Prada is, does, or will become."[16] In other words, don't think of Prada as a designer and retailer of luxury goods whose directors were investigated for tax evasion; that would be a hopelessly received notion. Think of it rather as an incredibly sophisticated research project on one of the last surviving remnants of public space. In this case, as in the publicity materials for Dubai luxury apartments cited by O'Neill, marketing slogans serve as a substitute for any real architectural philosophy. If such architectural projects are bound to the economy of a high-end market, they are also liberated from the historically modernist imperative in which architecture assumed the task of preserving the capitalist economy from revolution by taking on a measure of social responsibility. Le Corbusier pointed out in 1922 that both the working class and the class of intellectuals, historically the fomenters of revolution, were poorly housed. "C'est une question de bâtiment qui est à la clé de l'équilibre rompu aujourd'hui: architecture ou révolution";[17] building is the key to alleviating the current social inequality: it's architecture or revolution. What is different today is that architecture no longer has to function as a stay against revolution. The kind of alliance between workers and intellectuals that once created the conditions for revolution is simply no longer possible. Architects and their wealthy clients are free to do what they like. This may be good for architecture's aesthetic autonomy, but not for architecture as a project in social responsibility.

The most recent manifestation of the heady mixture of spectacular architecture, luxury goods, and capital is Gehry's Fondation Louis Vuitton in Paris, a profusion of glassy wings rising from a cubist core in the Bois de Boulogne.

The building as a whole is a good example of Gehry's architecture of exploded fragments. He compares the core of the building to an iceberg, and its extended

FIGURE 16.2 Frank Gehry, Louis Vuitton Foundation, Paris, France, 2014.
Photo by Yvette Doria

wings to the sails of a ship billowing at full breeze. The glass wings lack any function beyond that of creating a striking image. The building is designed to house the Louis Vuitton Foundation for Contemporary Art, which consists mostly of the personal art collection of Bernard Arnault, who financed the project. The project thus draws on the increasingly related markets of contemporary art and luxury goods, while creating a literal example of what has been called "logotecture": architecture designed to promote brand identities. In keeping with this function, the familiar LV is affixed, in letters 8 ft (2.4 m) high, over the entrance to the building: here is where consumer society and the society of the spectacle find their point of intersection. The LV logo appears, in this case, in the crushed-metal form that is Gehry's signature, in such a way as to superimpose his own signature on that of Louis Vuitton. If in this case the LV logo is merely affixed to the building's façade, there are other cases in which the architectonic form itself is designed after the corporate logo. This is the case with London's National Westminster Tower (now Tower 42), designed by Richard Seifert in 1980. The 183 m tower is made of a concrete core surrounded by three "leaves" of cantilevered floors. When seen from above, this assemblage forms the three hexagonal chevrons of the NatWest logo. This observation is made, not without irony, in Rahman's *In the Light of What We Know*, much of which takes place in the heady world of high-wire investment banking and the selling of risky derivative products such as collateral debt obligations (CDOs).

Returning to the Louis Vuitton Foundation in Paris, let us acknowledge that there is nothing new in an original work of architecture being commissioned by a wealthy patron. What does seem new in the first decades of the twenty-first century is the intensification and the power of the alliance between star architecture, consumerism, and media buzz. In the process, architecture as object gives way to architecture as consumer product image, whose creation is driven by the demands of a capitalist economy for ceaseless formal innovation. As if to drive home this point, a recent campaign by the luxury group LVMH (Louis Vuitton Moët Hennessy) acknowledged the perfect identity between architecture and its own consumer products by building, in Moscow's Red Square, a two-storey pavilion in the form of one of its traveling trunks.

It would nonetheless be reductive to regard the Louis Vuitton Foundation from the perspective either of an austere Marxism or of a classical modernism requiring that form follow function. In fact, Gehry's building—with its Piranesan ramparts, labyrinthine passages, sudden clearings of space and light; its waterfalls and reflecting pools; its wild plungings and soaring elevations—represents a total release of the architectural impulse, a prodigality that spends without counting, like a wealthy customer in a Louis Vuitton shop. This is the architecture of excess in its entire gaudy splendor, and the effect on the visitor can be one of exhilaration and *vertige*. There exists an aesthetic tradition of ecstatic excess both in the architecture of baroque and rococo, and in the writings of Coleridge, Whitman, Hart Crane, and Bataille, to which Gehry's building could be compared. In order to bring it back to the economic context, however, I want to suggest that Gehry gives way to what Robert Shiller called the "irrational exuberance" that led to the bubble in technology stocks before the crash of 2000, and the bubble in housing prices before the crash of 2007.[18] In economic terms, irrational exuberance describes a kind of delirium in the financial markets as they detach themselves from real asset value, and this delirium can be extended to an architectural form dedicated to the *jouissance* of its own *fuite en avant*, the ecstatic headlong rush into the void of its own meaning.

Earlier I noted that in the face of the fragmentation of the modern environment, modernist literature proposed a certain continuity of subjectivity and literary form. But in the literature of the last 30 years, the situation is reversed. Rather than opposing subjective continuity in literature to objective discontinuity in the built environment, writers today register the discontinuity and disorientation of subjective consciousness faced with the oppressive continuity embodied in the seamless connections between architecture, media, capital, and consumer products. At the same time, contemporary literature manifests a heightened architectural awareness. Its writers have taken up positions of resistance against the newly globalized forms of the built environment. One way to account for this resistance is to note that literature with serious artistic pretensions has been relegated to a marginal status in the cultural landscape, and so remains relatively independent of the market forces driving other media such as film. Literature's position on the margins of contemporary popular culture grants it a certain critical distance.

This critical distance is expressed in two ways. The first consists of a fairly straightforward analysis of the human costs of the contemporary built environment, such as Ballard's *High-Rise* (1975), which recounts the total deterioration of human relationships in a high-rise apartment building.[19] William Gibson's *Virtual Light* (1993) foresees the deepening social inequality of the near future in the confrontation between international real estate developers and the local residents of San Francisco who, after a massive earthquake, have fashioned makeshift dwellings on what remains of the Bay Bridge.[20] More recently, Dave Eggers' *The Circle* (2014) tells a harrowing story of Google-style surveillance conducted from the sky, on street corners, and in the bedrooms of domestic dwellings.[21]

The second mode of resistance in literature consists of what we might call critical mimesis, by which I mean writing designed to show the effects of the built environment in its own form. Here I would include works like Ballard's *Crash* (1973)[22] and, more recently, David Cronenberg's *Consumed* (2014),[23] novels about people whose subjectivities are wholly saturated by the logic of consumerism, where the effects of the product-environment are entirely naturalized. In Cronenberg's novel, the infinite reproducibility of every object in the form of images ultimately destroys the distinction between image and object, and between image and body, so that bodies are dismembered and consumed as images in a manner that makes it impossible to say whether this process is literal or figurative, real or simulated. The critical position occupied by such works has something in common with what Adorno has written about lyric poetry in modern society: that it is a sundial telling the time of history. Just as on a sundial the time of day is told by the shadow cast by the sun, so literary works register our own moment in history by following the shadows cast by the bright lights of shiny surfaces, video screens, and LED displays.

Like other star architects, Tadao Ando does work for powerful commercial concerns. In 2001 he submitted a project for Pinault's Vuitton Foundation when it was originally planned for the Ile Séguin in the Seine. More recently, in Milan, he has converted a former Nestlé chocolate factory into a headquarters and theatre for Giorgio Armani. But such projects have not prevented him from being critical of a certain tendency in postmodern architecture. In 2002, on the occasion of the opening of his Modern Art Museum in Fort Worth, Texas, Ando told an interviewer,

> A great problem arose when the postmodern sensibility entered into contact with market consumerism. It ceased being a mode of expression, and became a product. Everything became a superficial image, a world of interchangeable surfaces which only reflected the fashion of the moment.[24]

Elsewhere, Ando has insisted on the spiritual dimension of human dwelling: "The place for the spiritual and that for the physical should not be considered two separate things. They can be integrated into one single space of dwelling."[25] With Martin Heidegger, Ando believes in an architecture that evokes the essential elements of human dwelling in an existential sense, but in the twenty-first century he is conscious of the radical uncertainty in dwelling, and of human existence in general. At the Fort Worth museum, the classical forms of the interior are interrupted by elliptical spaces. "We have to reflect on the possibilities inherent in uncertainty, to awaken to its new possibilities. I want these ellipses to reflect this dynamic instability. I think the ellipse symbolizes very well the movement into the next millennium."[26]

If the traditional stability of human dwelling must be abandoned, then in order to avoid the mere nostalgia for a world that no longer exists, architecture must come to terms with human existence as it obtains in the present historical moment. Castells proposes two alternatives for a future architecture of resistance to the market forces outlined above. One is that new architecture build the palaces of global capital in such a way as to expose "the deformity hidden behind the abstraction of the space of flows."[27] The problem here, it seems to me, is one of the ambiguity of the gesture. When Gehry builds a new business school in Sydney that looks like a brown paper bag, is he consciously exposing the deformity of the system or, what is more likely given his public persona, thumbing his nose at those who would question it? Castell's other alternative is that architecture "root itself" into places, people, and culture in order to preserve some measure of meaning and to reconcile culture with technology.[28] Something like this may already be happening with the renewed interest in local materials and indigenous architectural forms. Whatever happens, we may be confident that the best literature will continue to testify to the new forms of the built environment and will attempt to assign a meaning to them that resonates with the real nature of experience.

Notes

1 Georg Simmel, "Die Grossstädte und das Geistesleben," in *Jahrbuch der Gehe-Stiftung Dresden* 9, ed. Thomas Petermann (Dresden: Zahn und Jaensch, 1903), 185–206.
2 Manfredo Tafuri, *Architecture and Utopia: Design and Capitalist Development*, trans. Barbara Luigia La Penta (Cambridge, Mass.: MIT Press, 1976).
3 Philip Johnson, *Writings* (New York: Oxford University Press, 1979), 260.
4 Manuel Castells, *The Rise of the Network Society* (London: Blackwell, 1996), 423.
5 Rem Koolhaas, "Junkspace." *October* 100 (2002): 175–190.
6 Michel Houellebecq, *Interventions* 2, (Paris: Flammarion, 2009): 156.
7 Louise Pelletier, *Downfall: The Architecture of Excess* (Montreal: RightAngle International, 2014), 216.
8 David Harvey, *The Condition of Postmodernity* (London: Blackwell, 1990), 297.
9 Ibid., 292.
10 Joseph O'Neill, *The Dog* (New York: Pantheon, 2014), 106.
11 Arnon Grunberg, *De man sonder ziekte*, (Amsterdam: Nijgh & Van Ditmar, 2012). French translation: Arnon Grunberg, *L'homme sans maladie*, trans. Olivier Vanwersch-Cot (Paris: Editions Héloïse d'Ormesson, 2014).
12 Zia Haider Rahman, *In the Light of What We Know* (London: Picador, 2014), 492.
13 Ibid.
14 Ibid.
15 Hal Foster, *The Art-Architecture Complex* (New York: Verso, 2013).
16 "Prada Epicenter New York," Office of Metropolitan Architecture, accessed February 13, 2015, www.oma.eu/projects/2001/prada-new-york.

17 Le Corbusier, *Vers une architecture* (Paris: Flammarion, 1995), 227.
18 Robert Shiller, *Irrational Exuberance* (Princeton: Princeton University Press, 2000).
19 J.G. Ballard, *High-Rise* (London: Jonathan Cape, 1975).
20 William Gibson, *Virtual Light* (New York: Bantam Spectra, 1993).
21 Dave Eggers, *The Circle* (San Francisco: McSweeney's, 2013).
22 J.G. Ballard, *Crash* (London: Jonathan Cape, 1973).
23 David Cronenberg, *Consumed* (New York: Scribner's, 2014).
24 Tadao Ando, *Du béton et d'autres secrets de l'architecture* (Paris: L'Arche, 2007), 115. My translation.
25 Jin Baek, *Nothingness: Tadao Ando's Christian Sacred Space* (London: Routledge, 2009), 191.
26 Ando, *Du béton*, 69.
27 Castells, *The Rise of the Network Society*, 423.
28 Ibid.

17
"LIKE THIS AND ALSO LIKE THAT"

Tactics from the Tales of Nguyen Huy Thiep

Lily Chi

The short stories of Nguyen Huy Thiep generated heated debate when they first appeared in the early decades of post-war Vietnam. Even with the easing of censorship under Renovation (*Doi Moi*) policy, Thiep's writings were provocative. Translations abroad garnered equally intense international interest. Written in simple, spare language, but blending historical, mythical, and fictional figures in sometimes complex, nested temporal structures, Thiep's richly diverse stories have been variously compared to those of Jorge Luis Borges, Gabriel Garcia Marquez, Milan Kundera, Salmon Rushdie, among others. Translations appeared in English, French, German, Russian, Chinese, and Japanese, and accolades followed, including, in 2007, France's *Chevalier des Ordres des Arts et des Lettres*.

This chapter will look not so much at the situations *in* Thiep's stories as the situation in which he wrote and his manner of address therein. In reviewing both, I will suggest that Thiep's tactical craft of storytelling offers intriguing insights for architectural work in contemporary cities.

Two Stories

Nguyen Huy Thiep was born in Hanoi in 1950 when, he was told, "the skies were full of French planes."[1] The Viet Minh's armed struggle against French colonization blossomed that year into a war of global proportions. As did most urban residents of North Vietnam, Thiep spent the most of the next 25 years in rural exile: a period of material deprivation but rich in other sustenance. Thiep attended village schools, but grew up at the side of a learned grandfather and his small circle of intellectual friends: Catholic priests and Confucian scholars who read widely in both Vietnamese and Chinese language, and who spent their time debating literature, reciting poetry, and composing verse. In this transplanted universe, Thiep went to university, studied history, and became a teacher in the remote northern highlands. As the war intensified, the school was driven deep into the jungle, and life became exceedingly difficult. But even in this circumstance of isolation, shortage, and constant hunger, Thiep found fortune in the form of a library, evacuated into the jungle from Son La province. Thiep estimates that he read several thousand books there during that 10-year period, starting with literature, then

FIGURE 17.1 Nguyen Dinh Dang, Illustration for "The General Retires," pen on paper, 1990.

Courtesy of the artist

moving onto politics, economics, and philosophy. He also began to write, throwing much of it away. His earliest published stories only came later, 10 years after the war ended, when he returned to Hanoi.

In "The General Retires" (*Tuong Ve Huu*, 1987), a son narrates the return of an elderly war hero. In the comings and goings around an extended family in the suburbs of Hanoi, a panorama of the city's post-war society unfolds: modern urbanites and country folk, nouveau-riches and simpletons, old timers and naifs. Their words and deeds render a Breugelesque portrait of human frailty: self-interest, heartlessness, greed, ignorance... They also reveal by degrees the General's pitiful disorientation and increasing alienation in this crowd—and not only his, but also that of the characters from each other. The story's simple, restrained narration, shorn of complex internal dialogues or allusions, but keen in its insight into the effect of words and actions, heightens the pathos of their predicament. In this as in Thiep's other stories, there are no heroes or antiheroes. Despite their faults, the characters are ambivalent: noble but naive, good intentioned but weak, heartlessness out of practicality. Even the General had enlisted not out of love for country, but to escape a cruel step-mother.

If stories like "The General Retires" piqued state critics for their frank portrait of post-war conditions and their subtle prodding of a sacred war, Thiep's historical fictions pushed the limits of tolerance. "Fired Gold" (*Vang Lua*, 1987) is the second of three ambiguously overlapping tales involving some of Vietnam's most iconic historical figures—in this case, Gia Long and Nguyen Du. Gia Long was a brilliant warrior who unified Vietnam under his rule in 1802, but who is reviled by the current social state for putting down a peasant rebellion, and for his use of French assistance, opening the country to later colonization. Nguyen Du was a poet and official under Gia Long's rule. His epic poem, *The Tale of Kieu* [*Truyen Kieu*] written in Vietnamese rather than traditional Chinese, is revered as a founding work of Vietnamese literature.

Thiep's story is a series of nested narratives, beginning with the voice of the author, but proceeding through citations from "found" historic documents. We meet Gia Long through the diary of his French advisor, whom he calls Phang. In Phang's descriptions, the King emerges as a complex, tragic figure, fully aware and burdened both by the cost and obligations of absolute power, and by the weakness and vulnerability of his realm. Even Phang's characterizations of Gia Long seesaw between might and impotence.

Phang's view of Nguyen Du is more damning: "A slight, young man... creased with misery... drowning in the soft muck of life."[2] In Phang's musings, the scholar/poet is the counterpoint to Gia Long the warrior/politician, but both are stymied by an "impoverished life and stagnant nation." Phang's ruminations on both men constitute some of the most striking—and controversial—statements on leadership, scholarly pursuits, politics, and contemporary society in Thiep's fiction.

Following these excerpts from Phang's diary, the narrator returns to report that gold is discovered in the north and Phang leads an expedition to search for it. Phang leaves no account of the expedition, so the story follows the memoir of an

FIGURE 17.2 Nguyen Dinh Dang, Illustration for "Fired Gold," pen on paper, 1990. Courtesy of the artist

anonymous Portuguese, who describes Phang as "a cruel man . . . dazzled by gold" and "blind to reason." His aggression and poor judgment aggravates a disastrous encounter with hostile natives. The Portuguese memoir ends without telling what happened to the expedition.

In the absence of further information, the narrator offers three conclusions, inviting the reader to select "the most suitable" for him or herself.

Conclusion 1. All survive with the gold, and Phang is richly rewarded for his work, but dies violently after consuming the gift of a meal sent to him by the King.

Conclusion 2. Only Phang survives with the gold, and is rewarded by the king. Phang moves back to France, where he "conjures" stories of Vietnam's beginnings as a nation, when it acquired borders, a Latinized writing system, release from China's power, and joins in "the community of humanity." Europe achieves maturity in understanding that "the beauty and glory of a people are based neither on revolution or war, nor on ideologists or emperors."

Conclusion 3. Everyone is killed by the king's troops disguised as natives. Gia Long appoints his own kin to develop the mine, and spends the rest of his life in melancholic retreat.

The story closes with a moral: "The Nguyen Dynasty of King Gia Long was a great depraved dynasty. Please pay attention dear readers, for this was the dynasty which left many *lang* [royal tombs, mausoleums]."

"Fired Gold" thrilled its readers, but alarmed officials for its heretical reading of history, the crafting of which indicted not only Gia Long's Vietnam, but also contemporary, *post-war* Vietnam. In addition to the overt critical statements noted above, instances of double-meaning or anachronistic diction and phrasing wrest the story's temporal frame into twentieth-century Vietnam. Thiep's readers would hear in the closing word *lang*, for example, a warning not only about the Nguyens, but also the mausoleum builders of Lenin, Mao, and Ho Chi Minh.[3]

At the same time, the story's diverse narrative voices displace each other to such an extent that they effectively bracket one another. The most inflammatory statements, for instance, come from Phang, a foreigner whose character is discredited by the Portuguese's memoir, by the hollowness of the conclusion, and by the final moral castigating Gia Long as a model of depravity. That moral's blunt dismissal of Gia Long, however, appears cartoonish after Phang's more nuanced observations, making it seem more *pro forma* than reliable. The entire tale is itself bracketed by the narrator's own opening disclaimer. Having been shown the ancient documents cited in the tale, the narrator writes that he "freely amended and reorganized extraneous details and edited the documents so as to make them consistent with the telling of [the] story." As state censors came to see, Thiep's own voice—earnest or ironic—is not easily pinned down.

Writing Post-war Vietnam

The General Retires and *Fired Gold* exemplify both the diversity of Thiep's short stories and their common traits. Neither offers clear-cut protagonists. In the first, poignantly human foibles are set in the context of material temptation, social pressure, and the dynamics of a changing world. The latter examines the same in the magnified lens of history, moral models, and cultural principles, using narrative structure to both assert and suspend what it probes. In both, strikingly clear, simple narrative prose and gripping stories that attest to Thiep's aspiration to be "first and foremost . . . a storyteller."[4]

International and expat critics have eagerly placed stories like "Fired Gold" in twentieth-century literary currents beyond Vietnam such as surrealism and magic realism. Some see in their shifting points of view and deferred resolutions a link with the postmodernity of J.-F Lyotard, Umberto Eco, and others.[5] Thiep has, however, expressed greater affinity to ancient Chinese literature, Vietnamese classical writing and poetry,[6] and, in particular, the "idioms, folk-poetry, fairy-tales, folk stories and anonymous verse" learned from his grandfather, all of which have a strong oral dimension.[7] Thiep has also repeatedly rejected the reduction of literature—and his work in particular—to a "political or social project."[8]

How does this tally with the biting indictments in "Fired Gold" and other stories that so flustered state critics? Or with his belief that "a writer has a duty to write the truth, even if it's painful"?[9] Or his assertion, citing the eighteenth-century scholar Nguyen Thi Nham, that "writers must encourage a certain humanity; fight the bad, support the good?"[10] Finally, the vernacular forms of storytelling that Thiep cites have a strong didactic component in practice. What, in short, is the character of critical utterance in Thiep's fictions?

One answer might be found in the particularities of Vietnam's literary history, including the context in which Thiep began publishing. Thiep himself noted about this context:

> Lê Quí Don once said, "The literature of the earth is the grass, the trees, and the flowers. The literature of human beings is ritual, music, law, and education." Literature, in other words, is venerated like a universal truth, or something very grand. Later, because of the influence of various political ideologies, officials placed too heavy a burden on writers: they were supposed to educate the people and to direct popular tastes. But it's not right to give writers such responsibility.[11]

If an eighteenth-century philosopher could assume a parallel between natural and human order and thus entrust literature with moral guidance, this was no longer possible for Thiep and other writers in late twentieth-century Vietnam. What was universal is now ideological, and what might have had the force of nature, is now an unreasonable burden—or power—conferred upon fallible individuals.

In 1948, as the Viet Minh sought to prepare North Vietnam for the escalating global war, the Communist Party adopted a program enlisting cultural work for defensive and national purposes. Literature and art was to guide society toward new collective principles, set out the goals of revolution against feudalism and colonialism, and cultivate resolve for the struggles of nation building. This was the literary tradition in place until the adoption of Renovation policies in 1986.

The war period produced striking, poignant examples of writing, but by the mid-1980s, the situation had changed. Nguyen Ngoc, the renowned editor who first published Thiep's writings, offers a most illuminating assessment of the postwar context.

> War is violent but simple. In war all relationships between people and society are gathered and reduced to one: life and death. People have to live in an abnormal way. Abnormal can mean noble. At the same time . . . it involves the suppression of many ordinary—but also rich and complicated—human relationships. The abnormality of war pushes these relationships aside. In war once you have determined the problem of life and death then you can live easily. In war, strangely, society is also purer. . . . The fire of war burns away the narrow-mindedness and complications of everyday life.
>
>   Peace is completely different. In peace one confronts again the ordinariness of everyday life. Ordinary but eternal. All the complications that were hidden during the war now arise and surround one every minute of the day. . . . If during the war there was only one question, live or die, now innumerable questions of all kinds and shapes rise up from the depths of society. . . . But when people search after literature hoping to find in it some

> comfort, some shared confidences, they hear, just as before, the same loud heroic song, a song that now has become lost and strange.[12]

In this new world, "writers have to find a new way to write." Writers and artists have "to become not just tellers of stories or drawers of pictures but also intellectuals . . . to reflect on the problems of society and of the country and to ponder the fate of people." While Vietnamese literature has had a long tradition of engagement in social affairs—a tradition emblemized in the saying, *literature carries doctrine*—this is no less true in modern times, Ngoc argued. However, this engagement must be different today. Where previous literature sought "to encourage and mobilize people to follow the path of orthodoxy," it must now "criticize and condemn," and "look at problems from different angles, from the level of details and parts up to the entire system."

Ngoc inaugurated his editorship of *Van Nghe* on the theme of "Facing up to Life," and for its first story, published Thiep's "The General Retires."

> After many long and endless periods of opposing invaders this is really the first time the Vietnamese people have had to confront not enemies from outside but ourselves, to ask who we really are, what our history really is. (Certainly it is not by chance that among Nguyen Huy Thiep's extremely multifaceted short stories there is a group referred to as "the history stories." Actually these are stories that *liberate* history from the myths that have been woven around it for many lifetimes). . . . One can say that this is the first time in literature that the Vietnamese people have become so decisively engaged in self-revelation.[13]

For post-war Vietnam, situated between twentieth-century socialism, the remnants of feudalism and colonialism, and emergent global economics, the challenge was how to move from a brutal present-past to a better future. In the sense that fiction can give life to the indeterminacies and unresolvable quandaries that politics—or even philosophy—cannot tolerate, it is possible to see how Thiep could both argue for literature *as* literature, refuting its traditional reduction to doctrine, *and* aspire to an equally traditional Vietnamese literary aspiration to "fight the bad and support the good."

"Both Like This and Also Like That"

> There are many different ways of looking at something . . ., no way is more powerful than any other, no way represents the unique and absolute truth. Something can be both like this and also like that. The world, in its basic nature, is *da nghia* [multidimensional, polysemantic].[14]

Nguyen Ngoc wrote the above in reference to the novelist Bao Ninh's devastating account of the horrors of the war and its traumatic after-effect on one returning

North Vietnamese soldier. An internationally acclaimed work, *The Sorrow of War* was banned for revealing the ugly side of a still "sacred" war, and Ninh, himself a veteran, stopped writing thereafter. Ngoc's statement could well describe Thiep's stories, wherein the world is literally "both like this and also like that"—where alternative possibilities remain in open argument. From the crafting of descriptions to the construction of plot resolutions: competing ideas, opinions, even destinies are left in place, unresolved, not even hierarchically weighted.

Thiep's stories exemplify what Nguyen Ngoc and the editors of this volume have already noted: the potential of fiction as a medium for probing the polyvalent complexities of human situations. Thiep's readers are invited not only to consider hitherto unexamined conditions, but also to deliberate between alternative possibilities and destinies.

"Both like this and also like that" applies to Thiep in another interesting way. For his heretic reading of history, and his damning statements on post-war Vietnam, Thiep was put under surveillance and generally harassed—but his work was never banned. As Thiep's defenders and one American critic has pointed out, the contentious statements in these stories are made by debatable characters, whose opinions and even credibility are countered by other characters or by events in the stories themselves. "Both like this and also like that" thus describes not only the world unpacked in Thiep's stories, but also a tactical utterance, a form of dissident writing, to quote the critic Peter Zinoman. A tactic, as we all know in reading Michel de Certeau, is the creative cunning practiced by the weak against the strong. Tactics do not confront or displace a system, but weaken its monological authority in producing unintended, counter-productive, excessive meanings.

Thiep speaks often of the deliberative craft demanded by the short story form, and his own preoccupation with this constructive dimension: from the careful choice of words, to the crafting of time frames, narrative genres, even "formlessness and apparent aimlessness" in plot construction.[15] He is also explicit about writing being a *tactical* craft:

> Writing requires cunning. Similar to life, you have to be wise to survive, as in the folk saying "stupidity leads to death." A most important experience in life is that of knowing when to appear and act, when to show your face and when not to. That is the skill of a lifetime for all Vietnamese intellectuals from ancient times to present. Sometimes you have to stir up the East, other times the West, try doing this and doing that. . . . It is important to know the appropriate time to appear and to act."[16]

I find this idea of "both like this and also like that" compelling to consider in the context of architecture in the contemporary city. Can architectural work learn something from this craft of tactical dissidence? Reading Nguyen Huy Thiep and also Nguyen Ngoc, I was struck by a parallel between the "doctrine" of political regimes from which they sought to liberate literature, and the coercion of global capital on the architecture of "world cities." In recent decades, architecture has seen remarkable favor by city and nation builders in the global competition for investment and prestige.[17] Even the smallest boutique firms in the United States have seen opportunities to carry out cherished creative and critical experiments across the globe. But is design invention in the narrow space of political, urban, or corporate branding truly inventive, let alone critical? Globalism has many faces beyond the iconic towers, museums, and entertainment venues that call for architectural design. Equally prominent, but less often seen are mass movements of workers across the globe, tenuous self-built settlements on the margins of the iconic city, heterotopic urban realms. . . . Such conditions challenge traditional ideals about civic architecture offering space and coherence to the public realm. (It is debatable whether cities should still be seen through the prism of nation-states). They also seldom figure in the programs and intentions of architecture's state and corporate clients. Given these realities, is the discipline consigned to a choice of two irrelevancies? Or can we see in Thiep's dissident craft a model for a different kind of critical operation—one that works from *within*, biding its time to find opportunities for "doing this and doing that"?

Such spatial and architectonic operations can in fact already be found in many cities of the world. Indeed, on first reading "Fired Gold," I was struck by how much the story's tactical craft brought to mind urban practices on the streets of Hanoi in the early decades of the market economy. Here, in Hanoi's oldest quarters, the physical city is but a substrate that is continually layered, unmade, and remade by entrepreneurial occupants.

These covert operations of adaptation, accommodation, or appropriation make room for lives and livelihoods that are intricately intertwined with the city's formal economy, but often have no legal or literal space in that economy. Quasi- or extra-legal, they are literally *excessive* creations that layer the host fabric with alternative, temporal architectures. Hanoi is certainly not unique. Through the cunning of urbanites elsewhere, we have seen how a quotidian apartment building can *also* be

FIGURE 17.3 Left: 6am, 69 Hang Trong Street. Right: 11am, 69 Hang Trong Street, Hanoi, 2013.

Photos by author

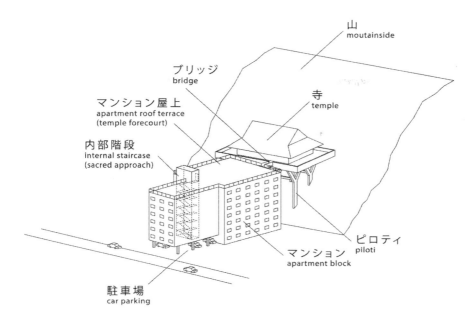

FIGURE 17.4 Atelier Bow-Wow, Apartment Mountain Temple, Tokyo, documented by Atelier Bow-Wow for *Made in Tokyo* (Tokyo: Kajima Institute Publishing Co., Ltd, 2001).

Courtesy of Yoshiharu Tsukamoto

FIGURE 17.5 Gathering place of Filipino domestic workers on Sunday mornings, Foster and Partners, HSBC headquarter building, Hong Kong.

Courtesy of Winston Yeo

a temple ascent and ritual forecourt; how a monument of international banking can *also* be a gathering place for expatriate domestic workers [. . .]

Such examples make it possible to imagine how architects might "write" urban architecture in the vein of Nguyen Huy Thiep's tactical fictions. This writing would make opportunistic play with the rules of capital—its protocols of development and its orthodoxies of high design and iconic singularity—to engage unscripted urban actors and dynamics *even as* it ostensibly fulfills obligations and pleases its patrons. Following Thiep's lead on the potential of literary vernaculars, designers might re-examine the most prosaic elements of the architect's craft. Need *program*, *site*, and *form*, for example, remain bound in one-dimensional, monological relation to one another? Might *site* be sought in temporal, situational, and scalar terms *as well as* physical extent, as the urban examples cited above suggest? In this layering of simultaneous or alternative *sites*—in the marvelous capacity of time and scale to mask and reveal—might *program* and *form* be similarly released from mutual monogamy for extracurricular formations in the city?

In seeking opportunities to create *da nghia* architectures that are "both like this and also like that," the designer may heart in the fact that Nguyen Huy Thiep, on his return to Hanoi, worked as an illustrator, a laborer, a salesman, and *a black market trader* as he honed his dissident craft.

Notes

1 Nguyen Huy Thiep, "Interview," *Journal of Vietnamese Studies* 1.1–2 (2006), 485–498.
2 All citations of this story are from Nguyen Huy Thiep, "Fired Gold (Vang Lua)," trans. Peter Zinoman, *Viet Nam Generation Journal & Newsletter* 4.1–2 (Jan. 1992), accessed October 15, 2005, www2.iath.virginia.edu/sixties/HTML_docs/Texts/Narrative/Thiep_Fired_Gold.html.
3 Peter Zinoman, "Nguyen Huy Thiep's 'Vang Lua' and the Nature of Intellectual Dissent in Contemporary Vietnam," *Viet Nam Generation Journal & Newsletter* 3.4 (Jan. 1992).
4 See, for example, Mai Ngu, "Cai tam va cai Tai cua nguoi viet," *Bao Quan Doi Nhan Dan* (August 27, 1988).
5 Greg Lockhart, "Nguyen Huy Thiep's Writing: Post-Confucian, Post-Modern?" *Journal of Vietnamese Studies* 6 (Jan. 1993); Hue Tam Ho Tai, "A Postmodern Critique of History and Literature in Vietnam: The Fiction of Nguyen Huy Thiep," *Viet Nam Forum* 14 (1993); Dao Trung Dao, "Mot Vai Ve De he Binh Van Chuong Tu Nhung Tranh Luan Ve Nguyen Huy Thiep," *Hop Luu* 4 (1992); Le Xuan Giang, "Nha Van Doi Thoai-Phong Phung Du," *Tap Chi Van Hoc* 2 (1989); Peter Zinoman "Declassifying Nguyen Huy Thiep," *Positions* 2.2 (1994), and "Nguyen Huy Thiep's 'Vang Lua and the Nature of Intellectual Dissent in Contemporary Vietnam'," *Viet Nam Generation Journal* 3.4 (1992).
6 Thiep lists, for example: Sima Qian's *Historical Records* (109BC), whose dry writing style has been likened to his own; Cao Xueqin's *The Dream of the Red Chamber*, a microcosmic social universe in itself (18c); Wu Cheng'en's *Journey to the West* (16c); Luo Guanzhong's *Three Kingdoms* (220–280), and Nguyen Du's *The Tale of Kieu* (early 19c).
7 Thiep often remarks on the importance of this oral logic:

> I tried to make my writing as concise and spare as possible, in keeping with the older tradition I had absorbed from my grandfather. To write well, one must know how to employ a certain spareness and truthfulness [*chan thuc*]. . . . A writer must first and foremost be a storyteller. . . . The story needs a plot that its readers can retell easily afterward.

As he often does, Thiep illustrates this point with a story, a practice common to oral teaching:

> My grandfather once told me a story about a literary examination in Vietnam, during the seventeenth century. The king ordered that essays be written in praise of the prosperity of the imperial court. Many examinees wrote flowery verse, comparing the king to the sun, or likening life in the realm to life in heaven. But the king was dissatisfied. Finally, an unknown student produced a poem that contained the following line . . . "Your servant," he wrote referring to himself, "is very happy these days. Thanks to your Majesty, I've been able to marry a third wife." The student, who had two wives already, explained that because he lived in such a prosperous time under the reign of such a benevolent king, he could marry wife number three. People were surprised and thought that the student must be joking. But eventually, they came to appreciate his honesty. Subsequently, he passed the exam."
>
> Thiep, "Interview," 491.

8   Thiep, "Interview," 492.
9   Mon statut est étrange. Je suis un écrivain toléré, pas interdit. Pourquoi mes livres sont-ils publiés ou refusés? Impossible de savoir. "A nos vingt ans" a été refusé par tous les éditeurs qui n'ont pas voulu prendre le risque de le publier. Sans doute parce que je décris les problèe cruciaux de la jeunesse. Mais un écrivain se doit d'écrire la vérité, surtout si elle est douloureuse.
Interview in "Nguyen Huy Thiep ne sortira pas du Vietnam," *L'Obs* (May 22, 2012).

10 Thiep, "Interview," 498.
11 Ibid., 497.
12 Nguyen Ngoc, "An Exciting Period for Vietnamese Prose," trans. Cao Thi Nhu-Quynh and John C. Schafer, *Journal of Vietnamese Studies* 3.1 (Winter 2008), 197–198.
13 Ngoc, "An Exciting Period," 204.
14 Ibid., 205. Note: the translators use "polysemantic" for *da nghia*.
15 I'm not one of those who writes a lot . . . [but my short stories] are all different, each one has its own characteristic. My objective is to write in different formats/styles [*kieu*]. Some stories just a piece of life. . . . Others move chronologically . . . Others take place within a century. . . . Other stories are subtle and may seem aimless but actually they are meaningful renditions of human destiny and general morals. . . . Some stories are interconnected such as "Con Gái Thuy Than", "Nhung Ngon Gio Hua Tat".
Thiep interview in "Nha van Nguyen Huy Thiep muon lai duoc lam . . . vien chuc, *Thu Tuc* (September 9, 2007).

Thiep notes that in "The General Retires," even "the empty spaces separating each section are fashioned in such a way to suggest a multitude of images and ideas to the reader;" (Thiep, "Interview," 496).

16 Thiep interview, "Nha van Nguyen Huy Thiep muon lai duoc lam . . ."
17 See, for instance, Richard Florida's ground-breaking and hugely influential *The Rise of the Creative Class* (New York: Basic Books, 2002).

18

LOST AND LONGING

The Sense of Space in E.M. Forster's "The Machine Stops"

Susana Oliveira

> Space is real, for it seems to affect my senses long before my reason.
> Bernard Tschumi, *Architecture and Disjunction*, 1994

"Only connect": this is the wistful command from E.M. Forster's novel *Howards End* (1910), which expresses the desire to escape an alienated society, to recover a lost sense of the "real." Just one year before, in the short story "The Machine Stops,"[1] Forster had already showed the horrors that he imagined would result if humanity renounced all physical contact in favor of machine-mediated connections. While working on "The Machine Stops," his only piece of science fiction, or at the very least while contemplating the story, Forster wrote in a diary entry:

> Jan, 27 (1908): Science, instead of freeing man—the Greeks nearly freed him by right feeling—is enslaving him to machines. (. . .) The little houses that I am used to will be swept away, the fields will stink of petrol, and the airships will shatter the stars. Man may get a new and perhaps a greater soul for the new conditions. But such a soul as mine will be crushed out.[2]

Forster dreaded the loss of natural space and the disappearance of the traditional house and environment. Hence he made an interpretation of the rapidly developing modern world in "The Machine Stops," in the form of a dystopia, or an anti-utopia. He was thus introducing, for the twentieth century fiction, a theme that novels such as *We*, *Brave New World*, and *1984* popularized.[3]

As to the twenty-first century reader, "The Machine Stops" will seem strikingly resonant of our present world. Yet, and in spite of its actuality, there has hardly been any in-depth discussion about "The Machine Stops." As far as I know, those specifically devoted to its architectural content are even scarcer.[4] This is rather surprising because the story depicts and explores the built environment, and a peculiar concept of home and society that can be extrapolated in manifold ways into the contemporary world. Issues such as techno-mediated habitats, underground structures, surveillance technologies, and globalization, were already present in "The Machine Stops." In the context of the history and theory of architecture, this story also provides an exciting pretext to talk about home as the *machine d'habiter*, the archetypal Man as Measure, as well as allowing reflections on space and mechanization, just to name a few topics.

In the following, I explore selective instances from this narrative where the concept of space is thematized and, in a way, re-discovered or re-defined. I analyze and compare them in parallel with contemporary examples from architecture and philosophy. Forster's precocious spatial concerns seem uncannily pertinent today and his vision relevant to discussions about the future of our cities and to the general discourse of architecture, while asserting an original vantage point. I examine the context of "The Machine Stops" as a space in which Modernity, and Modernism, projects into our undetermined, yet ominous, future.

"The Machine Stops" portrays a futuristic technological world-state where the Machine, a gigantic and complex underground network, caters for all its inhabitants' needs. As readers, we are left untold on what happened earlier and above this huge underground Machine. But we can guess, considering what is happening nowadays on the surface of the Earth, as megacities worldwide are running out of room to grow and experts are planning to expand underground facilities for a range of purposes including business, residential, retail, and transportation.[5] For example, Matsys, a design studio engaged both in speculative and built projects with architecture, engineering, biology, and computation, established in 2004 by Andrew Kudless, has been exploring several ideas for collective and individual underground habitats. Their Sietch Nevada project, inspired by Frank Herbert's 1965 novel *Dune* as the "first planetary ecology novel," proposes a future urban infrastructure for the American Southwest. The Sietch would be a dense, underground community in which the caverns, being cellular in form, would "brim with dense, urban life: an underground Venice,"[6] in the architects' words. Drawing on the example from the existential conditions inside the Machine, however, one may doubt about the cheerfulness of such prospect.

The people in Forster's tale live alone in small pod-like rooms in a honeycomb of vast, multi-layered cities spread across the globe, without contact with its surface and with nature. Ultra-fast trains, and airships for longer distances, physically connect each single unit to others. The comforts of food, clothing, and shelter are all taken care of by the inclusive and revered Machine, along with numerous opportunities for one-to-one and one-to-many electronic communication in real time with voice and image.

Every habitation unit is a perfect replica of every other, creating a sealed homogenous network. While the rooms keep people largely isolated from experience, the world outside the rooms is also shielded. Few are allowed to visit the "outer world" on the surface and, if they do, they'll be punished with euthanasia or ostracism. The undetermined narrator of "The Machine Stops" thus comments on how the system was updated to immobilize, isolate, and entrench people within the confines of their minimum satisfaction. Inside the Machine, individuals live a fictional mediated experience, further and further removed from direct contact. According to Literature Professor Silvana Caporaletti, ". . . *The Machine Stops* depicts a fictional world that possesses an uncanny quality: fiction has replaced experience and reality."[7]

The reader is asked to empathize and relate, as the story opens with a direct exhortation: to imagine this small, windowless hexagonal cell "like the cell of a bee."[8] The cell is empty except for a desk, an armchair, and the "swaddled lump of flesh" that is Vashti, a woman. There is light, fresh air, and music, but these are emphatically unnatural, "lighted neither by window nor by lamp." The colors are neutral and Vashti is "white as a fungus."

The narrative then focuses on Kuno, who calls his estranged mother Vashti via a screen. The young man describes how he disobeyed the Machine and ventured outside his cell to go above the ground. In reply to Vashti's worries, Kuno explains how he realized that the relationship with space is central to the problems of their society: "[We] have lost the sense of space. We say 'space is annihilated', but we have annihilated not space but the sense thereof. We have lost a part of ourselves."

This passage is remarkable. It claims that our embodied experience is an essential component of our apprehension of reality, hence it anticipates the philosophical work of Maurice Merleau-Ponty and other cognition studies, which have revealed the degree to which our thinking and experience of reality depends on our embodied

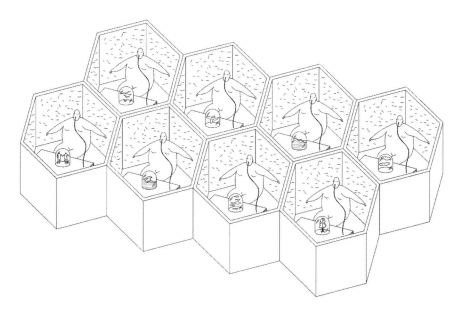

FIGURE 18.1 Carolina Moscoso, *Untitled*. Original AutoCAD drawing, 2016.
Courtesy of the artist

interactions with the world and with others. In Forster's imagined underground world—here graphically interpreted by architect Carolina Moscoso—ideas and abstractions or, to be exact, information and hyper-mediated connections, reign.

The further removed from direct experience and the more abstract an idea, the better.[9] The body is starved while the mind was indulged. The body is the victim in Forster's tale. At one point the narrator comments "by these days it was a demerit to be muscular." Indeed, in one of the more striking exchanges in the story, Kuno tells Vashti of his first experience with genuine physical activity:

> I determined to recover it [the sense of space], and I began by walking up and down the platform of the railway outside my room. Up and down, until I was tired, and so did recapture the meaning of "Near" and "Far". "Near" is a place to which I can get quickly on my feet, not a place to which the train or the air-ship will take me quickly. "Far" is a place to which I cannot get quickly on my feet; [. . .] Man is the measure. That was my first lesson. Man's feet are the measure for distance, his hands are the measure for ownership, his body is the measure for all that is lovable and desirable and strong.

Kuno is describing the process of recovering his "sense of space." From his curiosity for the world outside—echoing Forster's longing for a pre-Machine world—he discovers the increased possibilities of his own body. So, the body/machine connection is desirably to be replaced by a body/nature relation. As Christine Van Boheeme puts it, in regard to Forster's time, the body in Modernism was "virtually lost hence always talked about."[10] Nevertheless, the choice inside the Machine is no longer between body and nature. In fact, there is no choice at all, and the annihilation of the sense of space implies the annihilation of both body and space—which, in this story, are depicted as two characteristics of the natural outside world. For the feeling or experience of space is given through the feeling of being able to move and have bodily experiences freely. To retrieve one's sense of space is thus equivalent to finding one's sense of body. Being deprived of this possibility is to lose a part of oneself; to become incomplete, less and less human.

Bruno Latour's contemporary considerations on the on-going globalization seem to address similar concerns:

> The real choice is between two utterly different distributions of spatial conditions: one in which there is a vast outside and infinite space but where every organism is cramped and unable to deploy its life forms; the other in which there are only tiny insides, networks and spheres, but where the artificial conditions for the deployment of life forms are fully provided and paid for.[11]

"Tiny insides, networks and spheres . . ." evoke precisely the conditions inside Foster's Machine. Life on the vast outside of a globalized scenario seems to be equally non-deployable. Since most human needs are fulfilled, in the first instance it seems as an ideal society. However, this utopia fails, both because of its inability to accommodate difference and change and because of its imposed constraints to the body.

"The Machine Stops" cautions us about these and, surprisingly, debunks some contemporary discourse and idealization of cyber culture, which fantasizes with a kind of liberation from movement, exempting the body from its perceptual and material limits through action-at-a-distance. Elisabeth Grosz has extensively thought about the implications of technology on the body. In her study *Architecture from the Outside* she concludes that such "supersession and transcendence of the body is impossible. The body's limits [. . .] are the limits of technological invention."[12]

But the point in Forster's story is that the effects of the Machine on the body do not derive from technology, neither from prosthesis nor immersion, but from imposed immobility and the consequent perception deficits. As Kuno pointed out, it is not space that has been annihilated "but the sense thereof." So the sense of space is part of his identity, yet not of the place or space-as-built. It is part of the identity of the subject as a spatial living entity.

In Forster's time, "space" was mostly a philosophical concept. It had entered the architectural vocabulary around the 1890s, only two decades before. The incorporation of the ideas about space in relation with the body appear more frequently after 1900 to culminate, according to Adrian Forty, in the existential with Moholy-Nagy: "Space, formed by the biological sensibility of man, became a continuous force field, activated by man's movement and desire for life."[13] Such is the desire and impulse that sets Kuno in motion, a desire for life and nature. But, if not space itself, what could be "the sense of space thereof" he's talking about?

When considering the cell architecture projects developed since the 1960s, from Archigram's *Living Pod* to Walter Pichler's *Sitzgruben*,[14] one may observe that somehow they embodied the spatial and existential conditions Forster imagined and described in "The Machine Stops." Those conditions were not only incorporated but also desired in Israeli-born artist Absalon's project *Cellules d'Habitation* (1993). It consisted of six living pods, each for a single person, designed to achieve an ascetic and secluded existence, already counting on its implied physical limitations. The geometry of each cell was made to express the tension between inner and outside realities. As Absalon wrote:

> The Cell is a mechanism that conditions my movements. With time and habit, this mechanism will become my comfort . . . The project's necessity springs from the constraints imposed . . . I would like to make these Cells my homes, where I define my sensations, cultivate my behaviours.[15]

The individual sense of protection and isolation from an outside world was highly desirable and body constraints seem to be but a minor loss in this case.

In developed Western and Westernized societies, emotional and physical seclusion, distant connectivity, hyper mediation, automation and remote control, increasing sophistication and prosthetic uses of electronic devices, that become body extensions, permeate contemporary life. We live in small flats, work in small offices, travel in fast trains and airships, exchange ideas, texts, pictures, and sounds with people across the globe that we have never met, increasingly constrained in matters of time and space. It seems that cell architecture dreams of introversion, autonomy, self-sufficiency, and disconnection, have been somehow fulfilled—if not as built at least as lived metaphors. So maybe Forster's hypothetical world is now more real than fictional, as the cautionary turned prophetic.

This idea is reinforced by users' accounts of actual experiences of real confined spaces. A characteristic one is a 2011 description by the at-that-point architectural student Michail Vlasopoulos regarding one of the capsules in the famous Nakagin Capsule Tower, built in 1972 in Tokyo by the Japanese architect Kisho Kurokawa. Vlasopoulos' manifesto echoes Vashti and Kuno's experiences inside the Machine cell, while emphasizing the optical dominance over the kinaesthetic: ". . . I definitely live inside a retina. We all do in Nakagin tower: homunculi in a compound eye of a fly, only with no cohesive nervous system to collect the external stimuli."[16] Likewise, the Machine inhabitants relate to the world mainly through their visual system, each cell being equipped with a central audio-visual monitor. It is not visual perception that has been impaired by the Machine but the whole body and its potential activity.

In *The Production of Space* (1974), Henri Lefebvre develops a radical critique of "space," dealing with almost all its possible meanings (even if it had little impact on architectural practice). Lefebvre's analysis of "social space"—a totally foreign notion in Forster's time, of course—is a critique of the entire tradition of architectural space, erroneously understood as free and neutral. One of the reasons is that the whole practice keeps privileging vision above the other senses and sustains a tendency for the image, the spectacle. More recent discussions by Juhani Pallasmaa, and Neil Leach, among others, recall Lefebvre's core idea that space is experienced through all the senses thus architectural practice should evidently reflect this.

Lefebvre also identified an early symptom of the transitional loss "from nature to abstraction in the evolution of the systems of measurement, which proceeded from measuring space with parts of the body to universal, quantitative, and homogeneous systems."[17] So, when Kuno learns his "first lesson," that his "feet are the measure for distance, his hands are the measure for ownership, his body is the measure for all that is lovable and desirable and strong," he is somehow reverting the process, from the Machine's disembodied world of ideas toward the much desired embodied experience of nature.

Space is to be understood not as abstract, but as the space of lived experience. This may be a part of Kuno's lessons and Forster's moral: the sense of space depends on direct, sensorial experience. With his visual sense intact, Kuno was able to perceive space visually, just as he used to do with the screens in his cell, perspective devices after all. The Machine's built space, Kuno's pre-condition when we first met him, might be "real" insofar as he is able to see it and conceptualize it as something external. His body and the existing space were two distinct entities. But even if he acknowledged its existence, he could not fully sense it (as argued, visual perception is not enough). Hence the significance of Kuno's timid yet brave incursion outside his cell as it tacks several concerns that are at stake in these discussions on space, and discloses a fundamental dichotomy between "experienced" and "real" space.

However, recent experiments in cell habitation units seem to move in the direction to overcome such confines and dichotomies. Unlike the 1960s to 1990s projects, and the Machine's cells, both conceived as if against all external reality, new individual minimal units are extroverted and aspire to establish a strong relation with the natural environment while keeping the core aspects of cell habitation units. Such is the case of the *TreeHotel*, produced for the Lisbon Experimenta Design 2009 and located in several gardens across Portugal since then. Designed by Dass, a studio based in Lisbon since 2008 and founded by architect David Seabra and designer Susan Röseler, it is a mobile minimal habitation unit with reduced visual impact on the landscape that aims at its contemplation and integration, made mostly of recycled materials.[18] The ecological and sustainability concerns are also significant developments in recent proposals, as well as the interest on the natural world and its events—mostly ignored, negated, or despised by the Machine and the previously mentioned cell architecture projects alike.

Another interesting example of this trend is the *Self Sustained Modules* developed by Cannatà and Fernandes in 2003. These prototypes consist on a typology of modules, functionally flexible, that can give answer to the problems of temporary

FIGURE 18.2 Fátima Fernandes and Michele Cannatà, *Self Sustainable Modules*. Photomontage, 2003.

Courtesy of the artists

housing, serve as environmental observatories or to other uses. The basic unit is completely autonomous from any infrastructure. According to its authors, "it is destined to areas where deep modifications are not possible or profitable" like natural parks or city squares where the unit would stand almost as a transparent object. "Each module or container, besides giving answer to a new form of space appropriation, pretends to be open to the use of new materials and technologies . . ."[19]

In spite of these advancements and implied *promesses de bonheur*,—and even if customization, flexibility of spatial configuration, and more sustainable construction materials are foreseen in most cases—these architectural examples prioritize above all the visual experience of nature. That is, the natural environment is still mostly understood and passively incorporated as visual landscape and the body/space dichotomy endures.

Bernard Tschumi's epigraph at the beginning of my chapter was not only a poetic choice, as he's been discussing the ambivalences of the definitions of space since the 1970s. We can safely say that Kuno lived in a *deprived space*, an expression that Tschumi borrows from the Italian art historian Germano Celant: here, in opposition to the remote exterior space, ". . . the subjects only 'experience their own experience.' "[20] Of course, "the concept of space is not in space."[21] Thus it may be inferred that the visual perception of space is not space either. So, when Kuno ventured himself into space by exercising his body and movement, by both experiencing and thinking that he experienced, he overcomes the edge of such dichotomy or, in Tschumi's terms, he overcomes the *paradox*. The experienced space, rather than a perception or a concept, is a *process*, a way of *practicing space*.

As readers, we are taken to participate, through Kuno, in such a process: his quest is ontological. Due to the contemporary ubiquity of virtual spaces, Kuno's cautionary tale is now acutely pertinent as it compels us to question taken-for-granted notions and to seek different ways of experiencing and "practicing" space; and consequently of designing and building it.

The Machine's living unit reduces architecture to its sheltering function while, at the same time, imposes an extremely contrived social mediated interaction and the loss of an individual sense of space. As the timeliness of such anxieties shows, "The Machine Stops" proves to be highly significant and rich for questioning the relationship between corporeality, representation and nature in our hyper-mediated present world. Yet Forster did more than just reprise the nostalgia for a pre-industrial world; he also wished and foresaw a future after the Machine, where home does not mean the removal from nature, nor privacy the loss of human relationships and touch.

Notes

1 "The Machine Stops" by E.M. Forster was first published in *The Oxford and Cambridge Review* in November 1909. It was later included in the collection *The Eternal Moment and Other Stories* in 1928. Here I use the PDF e-book edition.

2 Michelle K. Yost, April 19, 2013, "Fear the Machine: E.M. Forster's 'The Machine Stops'," *A Study of the Hollow Earth* (blog), accessed May 6, 2015, https://thesymzonian.wordpress.com/2013/04/19/fear-the-machine-em-forsters-the-machine-stops/.
3 Respectively, *We* (1921) by Russian author Yevgeny Zamyatin, *Brave New World* (1931) by Aldous Huxley, and *1984* (1949) by George Orwell.
4 This short story is also studied in two very recent researches, namely in Olivia Bina et al., *The Future Imagined*, and Nick Dunn et al. *A Visual History of the Future*. See: Bina, Olivia, Sandra Mateus, Lavinia Pereira, and Annalisa Caffa. "The future imagined: exploring utopia and dystopia in popular art as a means of understanding today's challenges and tomorrow's options" (paper presented at the *5th International Conference on Future-Oriented Technology Analysis (FTA) – Engage today to shape tomorrow*, Brussels, 27–28 November 2014). Dunn, Nick, Paul Cureton and Serena Pollastri, S 2014, *A Visual History of The Future*. Future of Cities: Working Paper, no. WP14, Government Office for Science, London. http://uhra.herts.ac.uk/handle/2299/14481
5 Durmisevic, Sanja. "The future of the underground space." *Cities* 16, no. 4 (1999): 233–4.
6 "Sietch Nevada" (2009), *Matsys Studio*, accessed June 7, 2015, http://matsysdesign.com/category/projects/sietch-nevada/.
7 Caporaletti, Silvana. "Science as Nightmare: 'The Machine Stops' by E. M. Forster." *Utopian Studies* 8, no 2 (1997): 2.
8 All quotes inside single quotation marks refer to the mentioned edition of "The Machine Stops."
9 Sacasas, L.M. " 'The Machine Stops,' Life Begins," *The Frailest Thing*, (2011), (blog), accessed May 6, 2015, http://thefrailestthing.com/2011/04/01/the-machine-stops/
10 Quoted in Seegert, Alf. "Technology and the Fleshly Interface in Forster's 'The Machine Stops': An Ecocritical Appraisal of a One-Hundred Year Old Future." *The Journal of Ecocriticism* 2, no. 1 (2010): 33–54, accessed May 10, 2015. www.academia.edu/1180205/Technology_and_the_Fleshly_Interface_in_Foster_s_The_Machine_Stops_An_Eccocritical_Appraisal_od_a_One_Hundred_Year_Old_Future
11 Latour, Bruno. "Spheres and Networks: Two Ways To Reinterpret Globalization." *Harvard Design Magazine* 30 (2009): 143.
12 Grosz, Elizabeth. *Architecture from the Outside: Essays on Virtual and Real Space* (Cambridge, MA: The MIT Press, 2001), 52.
13 Moholy-Nagy, *The New Vision* (1928) as quoted in Forty, Adrian. "Space," *Words and Buildings: A Vocabulary of Modern Architecture* (London: Thames & Hudson, 2000), 256.
14 The *Living Pod* was conceived in 1966 by Archigram member David Greene as an object that could work both as habitat and as vehicle, able to resist a hostile environment yet to simulate an earthly atmosphere in a confined space. Austrian artist Walter Pichler designed the *Sitzgruben* (The Seating Pits) in 1971, where subterranean concrete cells could totally isolate a person from the world, a concern expressed by Pichler throughout his life, and more famously through his 1960s *Prototypes*.
15 Lucarelli, Fosco. "How to Isolate Yourself and Inhabit Everywhere: Absalon's Living Cells (1991-1993)," *Socks* (February 3, 2014), accessed June 7, 2015, http://socks-studio.com/2014/02/03/how-to-isolate-yourself-and-inhabit-everywhere-absalons-living-cells-1991-1993/
16 Vlosoupoulos, Michail. "Nakagin Capsule Tower: A Manifesto." *Abitare* (February 28, 2011), accessed June 2, 2015, http://www.abitare.it/it/ricerca/pubblicazioni/2011/02/28/nakagin-capsule-tower-a-manifesto/
17 Henri Lefebvre, *The Production of Space*, trans. Donald Nicholson – Smith (Oxford, UK; Cambridge, MA: Blackwell, 1991), 338–9.
18 After serving as hotel during the Lisbon Experimenta 2009, the TreeHotel toured Portugal before finally landing at the Jardim de Estrela in Lisbon where it stands today. The project has received numerous prizes including the Larus Architecture Award in 2010, accessed February 2, 2015, www.dass.pt/portfolio-item/treehotel-2/.

19 "Self Sustained Modules," Cannatà & Fernandes Arquitectos, accessed April 10, 2016, http://cannatafernandes.com/pt/built/self-sustained-modules/.
20 Bernard, Tschumi, "The Architectural Paradox," in *Architecture Theory since 1968*, ed. M. K. Hays, (Cambridge, MA; London: The MIT Press, 1998), 224.
21 Tschumi, "The Architectural Paradox," 226.

IMAGE CREDITS

Figure 1.1: Courtesy of Henri Lavina
Figure 1.2: Courtesy of Musée de l'Histoire vivante
Figure 3.1: Courtesy of Norwegian National Library
Figure 3.2: Courtesy of Oslo Museum
Figure 4.1: Courtesy of National Archives of Korea
Figure 4.2: By author
Figure 5.1: By author
Figure 6.1: By author
Figure 6.2: By author
Figure 6.3: By author
Figure 6.4: By author
Figure 6.5: By author
Figure 6.6: By author
Figure 6.7: By author
Figure 7.1: By author
Figure 7.2: By author
Figure 7.3: By author
Figure 9.1: By author
Figure 9.2: By author
Figure 12.1: Courtesy of Wakefield Press
Figure 12.2: Courtesy of Wakefield Press
Figure 13.1: Courtesy of Allison Collins
Figure 13.2: Courtesy of Allison Collins
Figure 13.3: Courtesy of Allison Collins
Figure 13.4: Courtesy of Allison Collins
Figure 14.1: By author
Figure 15.1: Courtesy of Cyrille Weiner

Figure 15.2: Courtesy of Cyrille Weiner
Figure 15.3: Courtesy of Construire
Figure 15.4: Courtesy of Construire
Figure 15.5: Courtesy of Sebastien Jarry
Figure 15.6: Courtesy of Construire
Figure 16.1: Courtesy of David Waddington
Figure 16.2: Courtesy of Yvette Doria
Figure 17.1: Courtesy of Nguyen Dinh Dang
Figure 17.2: Courtesy of Nguyen Dinh Dang
Figure 17.3: By author
Figure 17.4: Courtesy of Yoshiharu Tsukamoto
Figure 17.5: Courtesy of Winston Yeo
Figure 18.1: Courtesy of Carolina Moscoso
Figure 18.2: Courtesy of Fátima Fernandes and Michele Cannatà

INDEX

Locators in *italics* refer to figures. US spelling is used throughout.

Absalon's living cells 198
Agamben, Giorgio 107, 145–152
agency, spatial 157–168
Algeria *see* Oran
Alice's Adventures in Wonderland (Carroll) 152
allegories *see* metaphors
Ando, Tadao 179–180
animality, Murakami and Agamben 146–152, *150*
Another Man's Room (Choe) 39–45
apartments, Seoul 38–45
architectural design, influence from novels (Part III) 3–4, 103
  The Little Prince (Saint-Exupéry) 105–112
  Melvilla (Darden) 134–143
  Murakami and Agamben 145–152
  The Perpetual Motion Machine (Scheerbart) 123–131
  Schulz, Bruno 114–122
architectural experience 1, 2
  Another Man's Room 41
  Murakami and Agamben 145, 151
  poetic receptivity 61, 62
architectural practices 4
  spatial agency 157–168
  Thiep, Nguyen Huy 182–192
architectural turn 171–180
Aristotle, definition of metaphors 25

Austerlitz (Sebald) 72–83, *82*
authorship, *Seiobo There Below* (Krasznahorkai) 52, 54–55, *55*

Bachelard, Gaston 62, 64
Ballard, J. G. 173
Benjamin, Walter 129–130, 131
Bilbao 175
Blomstedt, Aulis 1–2
boredom
  Labyrinthine boredom 10–17
  Oran 9–17
Both like this and also like that (Thiep) 188–190
Bouchain, Patrick 157, *164–168*

Camus, Albert 9–17
Canada *see* Montréal mythologies
Cannatà, Michele *200*, 200–201
capital 176–178
Carroll, Lewis 152
Castells, Manuel 172, 180
catachresis 116, 121
Chinese New Year 73–74
Choe, Inho 39–45
Christ, *Seiobo There Below* (Krasznahorkai) 50, *55*, 55–57
circumscription of space 84–85
collectives, participatory movement 158, 163–164, *164–169*

critical distance 178–179
critical mimesis 179
Crossley, Nick 20–21
cultural context, Schulz's poetry 114–115

Darden, Douglas 134–143
desire
    Hunger 31–34
    Last Nights of Paris 20–22
drawing
    The Little Prince (Saint-Exupéry) 105–112
    Schulz's poetry 116
Dubai 173–175, *174*

economic context of architecture 172, 176–178
emotions
    desire 20–22, 31–34
    Hunger 27–29, 31–34
    Last Nights of Paris 20–21
ethics
    Hard-Boiled Wonderland and the End of the World (Murakami) 146–152
    Moby-Dick (Melville) 139
exotics in Edgar Allen Poe 86

fabrics of reality 3, 49–59
The Fall of the House of Usher (Poe) 84, 85
Fernandes, Fátima *200*, 200–201
fictionalization 160
fiction/nonfiction crossover, *Seiobo There Below* (Krasznahorkai) 57–59
Filarete 130–131
Finland *see* Hvitträsk
Fired Gold (Thiep) *185*, 186–188, 190
Forster, E. M. 194–201
Foster, Hal 175, 176
France *see* Paris
futures
    architectural practices 180
    Hard-Boiled Wonderland and the End of the World (Murakami) 146
    The Machine Stops (Forster) 195
    The Perpetual Motion Machine 123–124

Gadamer, H. G. 120
Galindo, Pierre 17
Gehry, Frank 175, 176–178, *177*, 180
The General Retires (Thiep) 183–185, *184*, 186–188
globalization 172–173, 175–178, 197–198
Grunberg, Aaron 175

Hammerborg 30–31
Hamsun, Knut 27–35
Hard-Boiled Wonderland and the End of the World (Murakami) 145–152
Harvey, David 173
Hirst, Damien 151
historical context
    Austerlitz (Sebald) 72–83, 82
    Montréal mythologies 93–101
Houellebecq, Michel 173
Howards End (Forster) 194
humanity, Murakami and Agamben 146–152
Hunger 27–35
Hvitträsk 62–66, *66–71*

ideology of architecture 172
imaginary, *Austerlitz* (Sebald) 75–79
imagination *see* literary imagination; poetic imagination

Johnson, Philip 172, 173
Julienne, Loïc 157, *166*, *168*
Jung, Yoonchun 1–2
junkspace 172–173

knowledge
    recognition 159–160
    tacit 119–120, 121
Koolhaas, Rem 172–173, 176
Kopland, Rutger 61, 62, 63–65
Krasznahorkai, László 49–59
Kristiania, Hamsun's *Hunger* 27–35, *28*, *34*

language
    The Little Prince (Saint-Exupéry) 109–110
    recognition 158–159
    Schulz's poetry 116, 118–119, 121–122
    Last Nights of Paris (Soupault) 20–25
Latour, Bruno 197
Lefebvre, Henri 199
Letter to a Hostage (Saint-Exupéry) 108–109
Ligeia (Poe) 84, 85, 88–91
literary imagination 1–2, 4, 163–164, *164–169*
literature in architecture (Part II) 1, 3–4
    Austerlitz (Sebald) 72–83
    Montréal mythologies 93–101
    poetic imagination 84–91
    poetic receptivity 61–66, *66–71*
    Seiobo There Below (Krasznahorkai) 49–59
    see also architectural design, influence from novels

The Little Prince (Saint-Exupéry) 105–112
Liverpool Street station, *Austerlitz* (Sebald) 74–75, *76*, 79
Louis Vuitton Foundation 177, 178

The Machine Stops (Forster) 194–201
markets in architecture 172
Melvilla (Darden) 134–143, *137*, *141*, *143*
Melville, Herman 134, 135–141
metaphors
   Austerlitz (Sebald) 77
   Last Nights of Paris 25
   Melvilla (Darden) 141–143
   Murakami and Agamben 146
   Schulz's poetry 115–121
The Minotaur (Camus) 10–17
Moby-Dick (Melville) 134, 135–141
modernism in literature and architecture 171–180
Montréal mythologies 93–101, *95*, *101*
Morgenbladet 30–31
Moscoso, Carolina *196*, 197
Murakami, Haruki 145–152
mutual recognition 161–163

Ninh, Bob 188–189
nonfiction/fiction crossover, *Seiobo There Below* (Krasznahorkai) 57–59
Norway *see* Kristiania

O'Neill, Joseph 173, 176
The Open: Man and Animal (Agamben) 145–152
Oran *12*
   awaiting Oran 17
   boredom 9–10
   Labyrinthine boredom 10–17

Paris
   Austerlitz (Sebald) 72–83
   Last Nights of Paris 20–25
   Louis Vuitton Foundation 177, 178
parks, *Last Nights of Paris* 23–24
participatory movement 158, 163–164, *164–169*
past events, *Austerlitz* (Sebald) 72–83
Pelletier, Louise 173
periphrasis 118, 120–121
The Perpetual Motion Machine (Scheerbart) 123–131, *125*, *127*
Pessoa, Fernando 61, 62
place
   Hunger 30
   Last Nights of Paris 22–23
   poetic receptivity 61–66, *66–71*

play, Schulz's poetry 120
Please Look after Mom (Kyug-Sook) 38–39, 44
Poe, Edgar Allen 84–91
poetic imagination 84–91
poetic receptivity 61–66, *66–71*
Polanyi, Michael 119–120
postmodernism 172
Prada 176
prostitution
   Hunger 29, 33–34, 35
   Last Nights of Paris (Soupault) 20, 22, 24

Rahman, Zia Haider 175, 177–178
readings *see* literature in architecture
reality
   of architecture 4
   Austerlitz (Sebald) 75–79
   poetic receptivity 64
   see also fabrics of reality
recognition 157, 158–168
rejuvenation 51–53
resistance, modernism 178–179
Ricoeur, Paul
   Melvilla (Darden) 143
   metaphors 25, 116
   spatial agency 157, 158–167

Saint-Exupéry, Antoine de 105–112
Scheerbart, Paul 123–131
Schulz, Bruno 114–122
Sebald, W. G. 72–83
Seiobo There Below (Krasznahorkai) 49–59, *55*
semantic innovation 4
Seoul *39*, *45*
   Another Man's Room 39–45
   apartments in narratives 38–45
   Please Look after Mom 38–39, 44
Shin, Kyug-Sook 38–39, 44
Sioli, Angeliki 1–2
situations of life 1–2
social justice 162–163
social space 199
The Sorrow of War (Ninh) 188–189
Soupault, Philippe 20–25
South Korea *see* Seoul
space
   circumscription 84–85
   The Machine Stops (Forster) 196–197, 198, 199–201
   modernism 172
   social 199
   see also place
spatial agency 157–168

spatial proximity, *Hunger* 30
stone monuments, Oran 12–15, *14*
storytelling
   The Perpetual Motion Machine 128–130
   spatial agency 157, 160–161
   Thiep, Nguyen Huy 182–192
   see also architectural design, influence from novels
straight horizontal 24
surrealism, *Last Nights of Paris* 24

tacit knowledge 119–120, 121
Tafuri, Manfredo 172
Thiep, Nguyen Huy 182–192, *190–191*

topography, *Hunger* 27–35
Tschumi, Bernard 201

unfamiliar places (Part I) 3
   Kristiania, Hamsun's *Hunger* 27–35
   Last Nights of Paris 20–25
   Oran and boredom 9–17
   Seoul's apartments 38–45

Vietnam, Thiep, Nguyen Huy 182–192
The Visionary (Poe) 84, 85, 86–88, 90–91
Vlasopoulos, Michaeil 199

Woods, Lebbeus 130–131

Taylor & Francis eBooks

Helping you to choose the right eBooks for your Library

Add Routledge titles to your library's digital collection today. Taylor and Francis ebooks contains over 50,000 titles in the Humanities, Social Sciences, Behavioural Sciences, Built Environment and Law.

Choose from a range of subject packages or create your own!

Benefits for you
- Free MARC records
- COUNTER-compliant usage statistics
- Flexible purchase and pricing options
- All titles DRM-free.

Benefits for your user
- Off-site, anytime access via Athens or referring URL
- Print or copy pages or chapters
- Full content search
- Bookmark, highlight and annotate text
- Access to thousands of pages of quality research at the click of a button.

Free Trials Available
We offer free trials to qualifying academic, corporate and government customers.

eCollections – Choose from over 30 subject eCollections, including:

Archaeology	Language Learning
Architecture	Law
Asian Studies	Literature
Business & Management	Media & Communication
Classical Studies	Middle East Studies
Construction	Music
Creative & Media Arts	Philosophy
Criminology & Criminal Justice	Planning
Economics	Politics
Education	Psychology & Mental Health
Energy	Religion
Engineering	Security
English Language & Linguistics	Social Work
Environment & Sustainability	Sociology
Geography	Sport
Health Studies	Theatre & Performance
History	Tourism, Hospitality & Events

For more information, pricing enquiries or to order a free trial, please contact your local sales team:
www.tandfebooks.com/page/sales

Routledge
Taylor & Francis Group

The home of Routledge books

www.tandfebooks.com